COUNCIL
OF
SOULS

FATED ETERNALS

JEN PRINTY

Council of Souls
Fated Eternals: Book Two
A Red Adept Publishing Book

Red Adept Publishing, LLC
104 Bugenfield Court
Garner, NC 27529
http://RedAdeptPublishing.com/

ISBN 13: 978-1-948051-00-2
ISBN 10: 1-948051-00-1

First Print Edition: October 2017

Cover and Formatting: Streetlight Graphics

For my daughters,
two of the strongest and bravest young women I know.

Now I am become Death, the destroyer of worlds.

J. Robert Oppenheimer

PROLOGUE

ARTAGAN

I WAIT IN THE SHADOWS, WATCHING the door of San Jose Mission. From the dilapidated buildings and barred windows, it's clear the charity isn't in the safest part of town—a fact I've used to my advantage. My next assignment has volunteered here for the last ten years, handing out meals to the homeless and encouraging the down-on-their-luck patrons. The thought of what lies ahead sends a familiar prickle up my spine to the base of my neck, more robust than any drop of Scotch. I rub my hand over the gooseflesh that ripples up my forearms. Retrieving a pack of cigarettes from my blazer pocket, I tap a slender roll from the box and light it. I take a long drag, the cigarette's tip burning brightly in the darkness, and try to dislodge the dread constricting my chest. The kindhearted and the martyrs are always the hardest.

Close to an hour passes before a small, frail woman I know to be Trisha Lambert steps from the mission and locks the door behind her. She slows in a pool of light cast by a streetlamp, her hand fumbling in a purse slung over her arm.

I glance to my left. One of the neighborhood junkies

skulks out of a nearby alleyway. From the lad's crazed, bloodshot eyes and pasty, sweat-soaked skin, I can see he's jonesing for a fix. Just as I planned.

Upon hearing the junkie's approach, Trisha looks up, startled, but the alarmed expression fades as a concerned smile spreads across her lips. "Charlie, there you are. I was wondering where you were tonight. You're too late for a hot meal, but I could get you a sandwich or maybe a cup—"

The sight of a pistol Charlie has slipped from his pocket cuts off the woman's words. Although his hands shake, he's able to aim the barrel in Trisha's direction.

"Y-Your money," Charlie stammers out.

"You don't want to do this," Trisha says. "You're sick. Father Matthew offered to get you help. Remember? Let us help you."

Charlie glances around, uneasy, avoiding Trisha's pleading gaze. Then with a hesitating nod, his posture slackens, and he drops the gun to his side. His body language tells me the lad is reconsidering my plan, thinking of backing out.

I grumble under my breath, although I can't say it's unexpected. This possibility is the reason I'm here and not cozied up with a curly-haired brunette in a pub somewhere. I push closer to the shadow's edge and coax Charlie forward, planting the memory of the high he so desperately craves deep in the gray folds of his brain, reminding him of the ecstasy that could soon be his if he completes this simple act. The lie makes my stomach churn. No murder is ever simple.

Charlie's tongue darts out, wetting his lips. He strides forward and raises the gun. As his grip tightens on the handle, a pop of gunfire echoes through the night.

Trisha's eyes go wide with surprise. She clutches her chest, falling backward onto the uneven pavement.

Charlie drops the gun and rushes in to snatch the

purse, but stops. He stands, staring, his gaze glued to Trisha's unmoving body sprawled on the ground. A brief sound of agony comes from him, and the lad begins to pace, striking his temples with his fists. Then, slumping to his knees, he buries his face in his hands.

I take a long drag on the cigarette and toss it to the ground, squelching the burning ember with the heel of my shoe. Stepping out of the shadows, I bend and pick up the gun. At the young junkie's side, I hold out the weapon, whispering thoughts into his frazzled mind, inviting him to save himself from a life full of regrets. Almost in a trance, Charlie takes the gun from my outstretched hand. He presses the barrel to the spot just under his chin, and with a sudden bang, my task is complete.

The lad's dead before his head hits the asphalt. My gaze returns to Trisha, her heart's blood creeping its way around her like a crimson aura. I crouch by her side as I remove a pewter flask from my pocket—a memento I picked up from a merchant in Rome over five hundred years earlier. I dab a bit of alcohol on my thumb.

Trisha turns her head in my direction, struggling to open her eyes. Her lips move, but I hear only gurgling gasps.

"Shhh, it will be better soon," I say, my voice weary.

After reciting the last rites in Latin, I draw the sign of the cross first on her forehead and then on the palms of her hands. Trisha gasps for air, her body fighting against the inevitable. A prolonged, sickening rattle follows, her eyes roll back into her head, and she lies still.

I swig what's left of the Scotch to calm my nerves and steady my trembling hands, ignoring the rush of euphoria sinking into the marrow of my bones. I stand, turning my back on the scene, and leave through the shadows to reemerge in a dark alleyway behind The Maiden's Head Tavern—a seedy little hole-in-the-wall on the back streets of Edinburgh.

I sit at the counter, resting my elbows on a cracked vinyl bumper, and wait for the bartender to take notice of me. At the end of the bar, the bartender laughs and carries on with a boisterous group of patrons. After nearly ten minutes, he still hasn't acknowledged my presence. I let my gaze glide over the littered shelves of bottled delights and then back to the empty spot in front of me.

I grimace, shaking my head.

Once the group settles down, the bartender glances in my direction, and I raise my hand. He flicks a sharp gaze over me and, tossing a dishrag over his shoulder, walks my way. He stops in front of me, grabs the rag from his shoulder, and wipes the countertop. "You all right, mate?"

"Fine," I snap. "Scotch. Neat. Macallan eighteen-year if you have it. If not, twelve will do."

"I only ask because I have a sixth sense about these kinds of things. Probably comes from seeing all types, from the brokenhearted to the down-on-their-luck sort. I'm a good listener if you need to talk." His voice dips upward with a coaxing tone.

I know bartenders are the poor man's therapist, but this bloke is taking his role too seriously.

"Just the Macallan," I say.

When the bartender returns with my drink—on the rocks, I note, not neat—he offers a listening ear once again. I refuse, mumbling my thanks. Finally, the bartender goes back to jabbering with his cronies. I close my eyes and savor the Scotch fumes before indulging in its rich, woody taste. I'm about to take a sip when Death slips onto the stool next to mine.

"How did you find me?" I grumble into my glass.

"This is your hometown. You were born, what, a block from here? Besides, you always come to this particular pub when you're trying to make a decision. Do you think I don't notice these things?" Death turns to look at me. The light from the overhead lamp shadows his deep-set garnet eyes and illuminates his forehead and the ridgelines of his hollowed cheeks, making his face look remarkably skeletal.

An involuntary shiver quakes through me, and I raise my glass in a toast, the amber liquid sloshing against the side, almost spilling over the rim. "To a life of servitude and the humdrum of time. Oh, and let's not forget, here's to destroying a young girl's life." I down my drink, taking pleasure in its fire trailing down my throat, washing away the cold truth of my words.

"Always so dramatic," he says, running his fingers through his dark, collar-length hair. He takes in a deep lungful of air before he goes on, undeterred. "Vita's scheme, Serevo's betrayal. If not your plan, they were your aspirations. You're a smart man. You had to see Leah Winters's immortality came with a price."

I had suspected. Of course I had.

I was once just a soul immortal. When my mortal body died, my soul returned in a new body, though I didn't retain any memories of past lives. But now, my body wasn't mortal, and I would never age or die naturally—luxuries denied me when my ancestor, Brennus, a son of Death who was driven mad by his cunning twin sisters, Vita and Domitilla, took his own immortal life. With his dying words, he thrust his council seat upon me along with true immortality, changing me forever.

Being the only one to go through that metamorphosis, I wasn't sure if the two—immortality and the council seat—were inexorably linked. However, that didn't stop me from pursuing reprisal against Vita and Domitilla for Brennus's death and my new status. Then again, what choice did I have? The twins had taken their revenge on my family and the entire Brennus line, including me, so I've been out for blood, either for revenge or self-defense, ever since. So when an opportunity presented itself to rid the world of one of the twins and give Jack and Leah their forever, I took it.

With the connection between the council seat and immortality unclear, I hedged my bets, going as far as creating false evidence to make the other candidates in line for Vita's position appear ineligible. What I hadn't expected was for Death to discover my lies before I intended. He took my smears as truths, but he kept his discoveries to himself. So when Vita picked Serevo with her last breath and the craving for Leah's death vanished, I assumed I'd won, that Leah was immortal without the burden of her ancestor's council seat. I was wrong.

"Are you listening, Artagan?"

I peer sidelong in Death's direction.

"I said I would not allow my children to do what they wish without consequences any longer. And I meant it. If I did, what kind of father would I be? This imprudent feuding must stop if we're ever to be a happy family."

I burst into laughter. I can't help myself. "Happy? Ha! I can see it now—Domitilla and me sitting around a campfire, toasting marshmallows, and singing 'Kumbaya.'" Another round of laughter rolls through me.

He ignores this. "I'm giving you one week before I induct Leah Winters into the council. You've had ample time to prepare her. That you've squandered it is not my fault. I understand these events aren't easy for you, but you will do your job. I'd rather not lose another child, but don't confuse my fondness for you as weakness."

"Fondness, is it?" I snort and look back to my Scotch.

He slams his fist on the counter. A growl reverberates deep within him, rattling the glasses and vibrating the floorboards. A flash of red-hot agony bolts through me, and I attempt to stifle a cry. The bartender and customers look our way. Death's gaze flashes in their direction. They all quickly turn their attention away as if they've seen a glimpse of the monster he is.

"This is not a game. Remember, Artagan, our choices seal our fate—and the fate of others. I'd hate to see anything happen to Jack. I am quite aware of your partiality for your family." He pats me on the back, sending a cold shiver to my core, and he slides from the bar. His words linger in my head as he strolls toward the door and vanishes.

One week.

I roll my neck to relieve the tension. Bones pop and crack. Death aimed his not-so-veiled threat not only at me, but at the chink in my armor as well. I'd do just about anything to protect my family, and he knows that.

Right on cue, my phone buzzes. I fish the cell out of my pocket. Jack's name flashes on the screen. I ignore the call. It will be better for Jack if this is a surprise. No time to plan something heroic.

Reckless, over-the-top, combative—all perfect descriptions of Jack's reaction when he finds out his beloved is to become a card-holding member of the Concilium Animarum. If I give him time to scheme, I know he'll toss all caution to the wind. Since I'm a betting man, I'd put all my money on him fleeing with Leah. Of course, he'd get himself killed in the process. Yes, surprising Jack is best.

A heaviness drops into my gut, a pang of remorse I'm confident a hundred tumblers of Scotch won't lessen.

As if transported from heaven for my personal deliverance, a shapely brunette ambles up to the bar. She glances in my direction, and I grin. A crimson smile overtakes her full lips, and she slides into Death's vacant spot by my side. Wafts of her perfume dance around me, its exotic scent tantalizing my senses. I raise my hand to the bartender while still ogling her skintight dress. I'll buy her a drink to start. Knowing what troubles lie ahead, I need to lose myself for a while and, at least for a moment, forget it all.

CHAPTER ONE

JACK

A CHILL ROUSES ME FROM SLEEP, and I delve deeper under the covers to flee the cold. Fingers outstretched, I run my hand over the soft woven fibers of the sheets, searching for Leah. The other side of the bed is empty. Not even a remnant of her warmth remains. I hoist myself onto one elbow and look into the flood of moonlight streaming in through the slightly open window. A crisp breeze ruffles the dingy curtains and skims across my bare shoulder, causing me to shiver. Despite the mid-autumn nip in the air, I shove the blankets off and sit up to scan my bedroom. Among the stark walls and bargain-basement furniture, I find myself alone.

Studying again. I sigh, forcing my fingers through my matted hair. *Or worse, another nightmare.*

We returned to Portland, Maine, after our bout with the children of Death. To my delight, if not my surprise, Leah took to her newfound immortality as if it were her destiny all along. In full Leah fashion, she leaped in feet first, making lists upon lists of things she wants to do and places she wants to visit.

Immortality through Leah's eyes has granted me a

new perspective. I see now eternity doesn't have to be the fiendish burden I've always thought it to be, but instead, time used to experience one's deepest aspirations and most frivolous whims. But as life has so relentlessly taught me, happiness is seldom enduring. To prove its point, life over the past week has brought drastic changes.

Dreams that were at first only scattered—a natural reaction to everything Leah had been through, I told myself—now plague her, growing in intensity. She claims my presence subdues their effects, and she spends most nights at my apartment. But when I find myself abandoned in these cold wee hours, I fear, despite her reassurance, I'm a distraction at best.

I constantly remind myself dreams are nothing new for Leah. Nighttime reveries have been part of Leah's life since before we met, ever since she almost died of cancer six years ago at the tender age of thirteen. Back then, her dreams were of an era she had never lived, about the past that belonged to Lydia Ashford—my decades-lost love whose soul now resides in Leah—and me. According to Leah, these new dreams have nothing to do with our history, but to my dismay, she shares little else.

The light of the hall peeks into the darkness of my room around the gap of the door. I swing my legs off the bed and grab a shirt from the clean pile strewn alongside the dirty pile on the floor, sniffing it to be sure it's wearable. Fighting to tug my arm through the evasive sleeve, I hustle down the hallway toward the living room.

Leah sits cross-legged in the far corner of my lumpy, brown-and-golden-plaid sofa with a blanket draped over her shoulders. Her Renaissance history notes lie forgotten by her side as she hunches over a tattered drawing pad. Crumpled balls of paper litter the floor and couch cushions. Pencils of every color clutter the coffee table. She sketches with the fervor of a madwoman, the pencil point darting in a zigzag pattern across the white paper.

Her sloppy blond ponytail bounces and sways with each jerky movement. Suddenly, she rips the drawing from the pad, crumples it, and throws it across the room before returning to the next blank sheet. She's so frustrated that she doesn't notice her movement has caused the blanket to fall off her shoulders.

I lean against the doorframe and consider what to say, concentrating on the small, delicate curls that fringe her hairline while attempting to ignore the unease mounting in my chest. My eyes trace the arch of her back to the only visible souvenir from the accident—a thin, almost indistinguishable pink scar across her upper shoulder blade. It's a solemn reminder of how close I came to losing her to death. The wound was only a scratch compared to her other injuries and had healed even before I left to bargain my life to save hers. Because of the surprising success of Artagan's scheming, this mortal keepsake will be her last. Now her vessel will heal as fast as mine—a side effect of immortality.

I still wonder if I would have been so eager to follow Artagan and his scheme into the shadows of Death if I'd known he was the one who *gathered* Lydia. I thank my stars I didn't. Without his plan, Leah would be dead or living a long life without me. And me? Well, who knows where I'd be. With my past offenses, probably not heaven. Either way, one of us wouldn't have lived through our ordeal. Now, because of Artagan, Leah and I will have our forever—a debt I can never repay.

I take another deep breath and move from the door. "Can't sleep?"

Leah startles. Her emerald eyes snap to me. A remote look—the same expression I've encountered for days—has replaced her habitual smile. "Jack. You scared me."

"Sorry. Didn't mean to." I step toward the sofa. "Did you have another dream?"

She nods. Her gaze retreats to her drawing, her heart-shaped face shadowed so most of her features are hidden.

I swipe the spurned paper balls out of my way and take a seat on the sofa next to her. "What about?"

For a fleeting second, uncertainty flits across Leah's face. She tilts her tattered sketchbook in my direction. "Him. Every dream has been about him."

A thin-faced man looks out from the pure-white vellum, a humorous expression drawn on his lips. The color of his hair matches his eyes—both a sooty brown. His shoulder-length hair and full beard make it difficult to pinpoint the decade in which he was born. He could be from today, the '70s, or the 1870s.

"So you haven't been dreaming about the accident," I say, my voice low and hoarse. "I guess I assumed."

"That would be too normal." Leah laughs a little unsteadily. She shakes her head, staring at the drawing for a moment before her attention returns to mine. "No, just him."

Neither of us speaks, and an awkward silence falls between us, both of us staring at the man in her drawing.

"And who is he?" I ask, not looking at Leah when I do.

"I wish I knew." She pauses, as if selecting her words carefully. "I think he might be someone from a past life. One other than Lydia's. My first dreams of you started after I almost died. This second brush with death seems to have stirred up a whole new batch. I guess there's no telling how long my soul's been kicking around." She lets out another nervous laugh.

It feels as though something large has lodged in my throat, and I take a couple of swallows to clear it. I'd assumed there'd just been one past life. That assumption was naïve on my part.

"After the dream, I wake freezing, no matter how many blankets I have piled on, and my throat burns. Well, not burns, but it's the best description I can come up with.

Maybe I died of hypothermia or drowned. Or he did." She flicks through her sketchpad, past a dozen portrayals of the same long-haired man.

"I've been up sketching, hoping I might remember something about him. Lydia's memories always came to me so easily, even if I didn't understand their meaning. But nada. This time, nothing helps. He's still as much of a stranger as he ever was. It's very frustrating." She lets out a quick huff through clamped teeth.

I study her. Beneath her eyes, the dark half moons are more pronounced, and the ever-rosy bloom of her cheeks has faded. "My mum always said everything becomes clearer with a good night's sleep. You look tired." I run a thumb over the soft skin under her eye.

Leah's mouth curves upward, but it's a ghost of one of her captivating smiles. "Mine says something like that, too. It must be a mom thing." She sets her drawing pad next to the pencils on the coffee table. Her gaze lingers on the sketch before she takes my hand. I interlock our fingers and lead her back to my room.

Clouds have overtaken the moon, leaving the room pitch black. We curl together on the bed, her back pressed against my chest. With time, Leah dozes off into a semblance of peace, and my thoughts sink into conjecture. Providing these dreams are memories, it's logical someone would become prominent like I had before. It's clear this man was important to Leah. If not a lover—the knot in my stomach tightens, and I shrink from the thought—then a father or a sibling. I know I'm being foolish, but logic doesn't seem to have a place here. Leah loves me, despite all my flaws. Still, the thought of her being with someone else bothers me. Now I understand the jealousy she felt about Lydia.

In the company of Leah's gentle breathing, I slip into sleep. My dreams are not kind. Again and again, Leah forsakes me for the man in her drawing. Every time I wake, I reach for Leah's hand. The haunting emptiness left behind by the nightmares retreats with her touch.

I suck in a deep breath and open my eyes. Leah is sitting next to me dressed in jeans and a baggy sweatshirt. A sliver of sunlight pierces through the window, casting a shimmery luster across her fair hair.

"What time is it?" I shove up onto my elbow, smothering a yawn.

"Almost six," she says, assembling her flowing locks into a sleek ponytail and securing it with a tortoiseshell clip. As she watches me, a hint of laughter touches her full lips.

I groan and close my eyes, flopping my head back onto the pillow.

She places a quick kiss on my mouth and then laughs. "You can go back to sleep, but—ta-da—I got a name."

My eyes pop open.

Leah laughs, and I relish it. I didn't realize how much I missed that clear, bell-like sound. "Come on. I got up early and made muffins and coffee. I'll tell you all about it. Oh my gosh, listen to me. I sound like you now." She laughs then hops from the bed and vanishes out the door.

I toss the covers off me and scramble after her.

The kitchen smells of baked pumpkin and cinnamon. Leah stands at the counter, pouring the remains of a pot of coffee into a mug. I glance at the drawings of the hairy man strewn across the table. Twelve pairs of sooty-brown eyes glare up at me.

The muscles of my shoulders tense beneath the soft cotton of my T-shirt. I steel my nerves as I slide into a swivel chair at the dinette and then lift a sketch to study it closer. *He could use a shave, that's for damn sure. Not to mention, his nose is too pointed, and his eyes too... Shit, I'm jealous of a bloody drawing.*

"So who is he?" I ask, tossing the paper back onto the table.

"His name came to me this morning. Just popped into my head. Meet Mr. Daniel Harris. I Googled him. Do you know how many Daniel Harrises there are in the world? Tons. And those are only the living ones. Then again, he's probably been dead a long time. I mean, what's the likelihood I have two immortal men in my life? Or lives, I should say." Leah smirks, but the humor doesn't light her eyes. She's holding something back. I can tell.

"There's more. Please tell me everything."

After placing a steaming mug and a muffin in front of me, she plops into a chair. "Like before, I know details."

"Thank you. What do you mean details?" I take a bite of muffin and try to appear relaxed.

"He works, I mean used to work, for a company called Lowe, Smithe & Simon. I looked them up. They've been around since the 1870s. Anyway, Daniel worked construction. An ironworker, I think."

On first-name basis, are we? I clench my jaw, and my gaze shifts to the table as Leah continues. My bitterness toward Mr. Harris is childish and unreasonable. Leah loves me. I know this with the utmost certainty in spite of last night's dreams. So I strive to hide my jealousy. I pick chunks from the crumbled top of my muffin, and my thoughts wander to the past, remembering my sister Ruth's words.

In the summer of 1865, after I killed Richard Hake, I'd fled to Ruth, who by that time was married and living in York. She had nursed my crippled spirit and helped me free myself from an opiate addiction. During the wee hours of the morning, when my withdrawals were at their strongest, Ruth read aloud. Scripture mostly, Proverbs being her go-to book in times of trouble. I'd lie there, shaking among the sweat-soaked sheets, and focus on the assurance in her voice. *A sound heart is the life of the flesh: but envy the rottenness of the bones.* The verse branded itself onto my soul because, even in the withdrawal-induced fog, the truth of those words rang true. On the dark streets of London, I'd felt what envy does if left to fester. It changed me into an obsessive, vengeful fiend who yearned for the happiness others took for granted.

And jealousy is just another head of the same monster, I remind myself.

I try to keep up with the conversation, but I'm so preoccupied with my thoughts it takes me a moment to realize the room has fallen silent. I feel Leah's gaze burning into the side of my head.

"So what's up?" she asks, setting her mug on the table.

"Nothing. Everything's fine," I say, but I answer too quickly.

"Oh my God! You're jealous, aren't you? Of him?" She points at the drawings, the man's eyes still staring at me. "He's nothing. He's just a man—"

"Who lives in your dreams." My face flashes hot. "Sounds familiar, doesn't it?"

Leah pushes up from the table and slides into my lap. She catches my chin between her forefinger and thumb and guides my face upward. "I love you, Jack Hammond. No past life can change that. I'm spending my forever with *you* and no one else."

"You are only nineteen, Leah. That's quite a promise."

"And what were you doing at my age?"

"That was a different time. We were expected to mature much quicker."

"Whatever. I wouldn't be wearing your ring if I weren't one hundred fifty percent sure. You know that. So why the jealousy?"

I sputter, at a momentary loss, and then give a quick shrug. My eyes glance at Leah's hand now resting on my chest, its warmth seeping through the light layer between us. I let out a long, labored sigh. "I don't know. Stupidity?"

"I kinda like that you're jealous." A tempting gleam dances across her shadowed face. She leans in, and when our mouths meet, my lips tingle and a warmth spreads through me. The sensation of her body touching mine reminds me of how alive Leah makes me, no longer the hollow shell I was before her arrival. My arms wrap around her waist, drawing her closer. All I can hear are the rapid beats of my heart. Then, chuckling, I begin to pull away.

Leah refuses to allow any space between us, molding herself to me. "Not yet," she murmurs. Her mouth recaptures mine, and her tongue slips between my lips. I kiss her as long as I dare before drawing back.

She grins at me, unrepentant, and then leans in again to kiss me along the neck.

After our engagement was official, Leah made it clear that she expected us to consummate our love. Although I have to admit loving her has made my principles harder to adhere to, her virtue remains intact. In my day, some affairs waited until after marriage whether the yearnings agreed or not. Or maybe they just weren't talked about.

"We've spoken about this," I say, grasping hold of her wrists and pushing her gently away.

Perturbed, Leah frowns. "I know, but your ways are ancient and old-fashioned."

"Perhaps." I glance down for a moment. Right or wrong, I still like that she desires me in such a way. "Just remember, in my day—"

She bites her lip, fighting a giggle.

My eyes narrow. "What?"

"I'm sorry. It's just whenever you say that, you sound like my grandmother." Her voice shifts into a tone befitting an elderly headmaster, shaky and condescending. "In my day, we walked to school, uphill, both ways, in the dead of winter—shoeless."

I glare. "I suppose I do. Then again, I am over twice your grandmother's age."

"I may have to rethink our relationship," she teases.

"Really?" A smile tugs at the corner of my mouth.

"Uh-huh. Maybe I shouldn't be engaged to such a decrepit old man." She brushes her lips along my cheek, her breath hot against my skin. Warmth floods through me again, playing havoc with my resolve.

"I-I think we should talk about something else, love. How's school?" I ask, conflicted. Half of me hopes the question will derail her advances. I'm trying to ignore the other half.

She leans away and stares at me with a pinched expression. "Now?"

"I think it would be best."

"Maybe I should finish telling you about Daniel, then," she says.

I give a half shrug. "All right."

Leah slides from my lap and into the neighboring chair. She adjusts a few strands of hair that have loosened from her ponytail and then meets my gaze, an air of resignation on her face. "Daniel was married twice," she says, annoyance evident in her tone. "His first wife was a real nutjob. She threatened Daniel more than once, saying she was going to kill herself and take him with her." She cringes. "She even stopped by his house from time to time under the guise of seeing the children, despite a restraining order, but it was just an excuse to see Daniel. And he's allergic to shellfish. Besides his occupation, that's all I got so far, but at least it's something."

A wintry chill lifts the hair on the back of my neck. I ignore the sensation and focus on the new question that springs to my mind. "Did you know such personal tidbits about me?"

"Yes, but they weren't so morbid." She smiles, and her eyes twinkle. "You preferred your brown wool frock coat to your gray one. The lilacs in your mother's garden were your favorite flower for not only their scent, but also their color, although you told no one except Lydia. You thought William would have made fun of you because he considered purple 'a lady's color.' You were right. He would have teased you relentlessly. Oh, and you hated Mrs. Mills's eggnog. You thought she added too much nutmeg." She pauses. "And before you freak, I know these kinds of details about all the members of Lydia's life—her parents, her brother William, and her sisters, not just the man I love. So don't worry about it. These details only mean I knew Daniel Harris and nothing more."

"So they are nothing outside your norm."

Her mouth opens as if to say something but then snaps shut.

"All right, out with it. Don't worry about sparing me. I'd rather know everything up front. If you know all of those details, you also know I hate surprises."

Leah nods a tad reluctantly. "The information about Daniel didn't come with dreams as it did with my life as Lydia. I just know it. Like I know the sky is blue. The dreams are different as well. There's no scenery, no storyline, just his face." Her gaze falls away, and she fiddles with her emerald-and-pearl engagement ring, twisting the golden band around her finger. "Instead, I feel his emotions— sorrow, fear, regret, sometimes relief. I know the feelings aren't mine. When they come, it's like they're pushing in on me, constricting me from the outside."

"And that hasn't happened before?"

"No. Never. It's like my brain got rewired after the accident."

My mouth goes dry.

"I don't want to talk about it anymore. Not now, at least. Besides, I need to get ready."

"All right, if that's what you need. Maybe we should take off for the day. We could take a ride up the coast. Get a bite to eat." I peer at the window. A glistening frost trims each pane along the bottom, proclaiming the upcoming winter. "It might be too chilly for a motorcycle ride, but we could take your car."

She lets out a little snort. "We'd be lucky if that hunk of junk makes it out of the city. It's been making an awful squeaking noise. I'm pretty sure it needs a new fan belt, but with everything, I haven't had a minute to look at it." She sighs. "Besides, I can't. Work, remember? I can't leave Rachel in the lurch."

"You should have told me. I can take a look at your car. I know my way around an old Bug. And I'm sure Rachel would understand," I say. Leah rolls her eyes, but the exasperation vanishes. Not finding the resistance I'd expected, I continue. "We'll keep our excursion close to home. You know what they say—'all work and no play makes Jack a dull boy.'" I waggle my eyebrows.

"I thought I was the tempter around here?"

"I have my moments."

One brow arched, she allows a hint of a smile to return to her lips. "We've talked about this," she says, parroting my words from earlier. She's right, we have. My shoulders droop with the acknowledgment. "I won't abandon Rachel on such short notice, even if it's just for a day. I'm lucky she held my job in the first place," Leah goes on. "Other bosses wouldn't have. She's a good friend."

"Exactly, and because she is your friend, she'd agree with me."

"Possibly, but you'd both be wrong. And you had better not say anything to Rachel, either. I don't need her feeling guilty. Even though I'm perfectly fine, she won't let me do any heavy lifting, and she's keeping my shifts to five hours max. She's turned into a real mother hen. It's sweet, I guess, but it's getting on my nerves.

"Then there's school." Leah stands, grabbing her knapsack from the floor. She tucks in her laptop then the notebooks and sketchpads. "The dean of students took pity on me by letting me make up my work instead of missing the whole semester. I'm grateful, but as it is, I'll have to cram like crazy to maintain my GPA. I can't repay the dean's generosity by ditching, now can I?"

I blow out a puff of air. "No fair, playing on my proprieties like that."

"Hey, a girl's gotta use her fiancé's archaic manners when it's to her advantage." She smiles. "So…"

I stand and reach out to brush an escaping strand of hair away from her eyes. "I get it. School first, fun later."

Leah pecks me on the cheek, swings the bag over her shoulder, and then stops short. "Since I can't go out today, how about you go to a Halloween party with me? They're throwing one at the dorm tonight. I thought I could dress up as Cleopatra. I still have the costume from last year."

"I haven't been to a real party in over a century. Do they still dance?"

Leah grimaces. "Well, yeah, but it's different from what you're thinking." A pink flush creeps across her cheeks. "I have a confession. I can't dance. Unless you count the revolving sway we did in high school."

"Revolving sway?" I smirk.

With a sigh, Leah steps away and drops her backpack to the floor. She raises her arms in a circular position as if they're wrapped around a bloke's neck and shuffles from side to side, spinning in place like a slow-moving top.

"Impressive," I say, trying to stifle a smirk. Leah scowls. She bats at my head, and laughing, I duck, successfully dodging her flailing hand. "One of these days, I'll teach you how to dance properly. I had quite the moves." I wink.

A big smile breaks out across Leah's face. "You know what they say about a man who can dance?" she teases. The way her eyes regard me sends warmth to my face.

"No, and I don't think I want to."

"Remember, it will be a late one," she says. "After class,

I have that art history test to study for with a couple of friends before the party. How about meeting me at the dorm around nine?"

"Nine?" I hunch my shoulders and slide my hands into my pockets. Then, fearing I look like an overindulged child told he has to have porridge for dinner, I straighten to my full six feet.

"Yes, nine. That will give me enough time to get Cleopatra-fied. I'll meet you in the lobby." Leah leans in for a kiss, hiding a grin. "We'll make sure you don't turn into the dreaded dull boy, 'kay?" Her lips brush mine, and as she pulls away, I smile back.

"Give me a minute to dress, and I'll walk you to work. Oh, and don't forget to leave your keys on the table. I'll take a look at your car this afternoon after job hunting. I didn't count on jobs being so scarce in Portland during the off-season. Not many businesses are hiring new employees now that the tourists are gone. But no worries. Something's bound to pop up."

Leah opens her mouth as if to make a comment but presses her lips into a white slash for the second time this morning.

"What?" I ask, restraining my annoyance with some difficulty.

She lets out a sigh. "I've been debating whether to tell you, but you'll find out one way or another. Someone dropped these off at the coffee shop." She retrieves a folded piece of paper from the front pocket of her backpack and hands it to me.

As I unfold the paper, I see "Rare Books' Grand Reopening Saturday, October 29th" printed in block lettering along the top of the flier.

"The twenty-ninth. That's today," I say. Since we returned to Portland, the thought of Ed's little shop closed and abandoned has left a hollowness in my gut. Enough so that I've avoided Rare Books, actually shunning Exchange Street altogether. "Do you know who dropped them off?"

"Not for sure. I wasn't there. But Rachel described the woman as 'very grandma-ish.'"

Despite the old yet familiar hollow feeling settling in the pit of my stomach, a small smile tugs at the corner of my mouth. "Sally."

CHAPTER TWO

I SHIFT MY WEIGHT FROM ONE foot to the other, staring at the herringbone design of the brick sidewalk. Rare Books's yellow storefront looms in front of me. The shop has changed in my absence—I have to admit, for the better. A newly painted sign hangs above the door. The once- grimy windows have no streaks. Not even a smudge of a stray fingerprint dirties the now-sparkling panes.

The sign says Closed, but I try the door, anyway. It opens. Even though I know what memories lurk only a few short paces away, I take courage by the bollocks and step through the door into a moment I've been dreading.

A familiar buzzer whines. The sound sends a sharp shiver straight through me. In my mind's eye, Ed sits perched behind the now-vacant counter with that silly, crooked grin on his face. His horn-rimmed glasses slide down the bridge of his nose, and he nudges them back into place before they reach the tip. The hollowness grows, settling behind my ribs—a mixture of nostalgia and ache. I draw in another quick breath as the once-pacifying, musty smell of aged paper overpowers my emotions, sending moisture to my eyes. I linger close to the door, not daring to venture farther.

Past the row of towering bookshelves, Sally hustles to

the front, talking to herself. I notice she's still wearing the engagement ring Ed gave her the night before he died. Her pace slows as she fumbles with the precarious stack of books piled like cordwood in her arms. I step forward to help, and Sally's gaze lands on me. The delicate latticework of creases fans out around her eyes as her mouth turns upward in a smile.

I bow my head in greeting, ever the Victorian gentleman.

"Well, it's about time you showed up," she says, sliding the stack of hardcovers onto the counter. She tucks back a loose wisp of salt-and-pepper hair, pinning it away from her face. "If you hadn't come today, I figured I'd have to hunt you down."

My eyes narrow in confusion.

"I heard you were back," she clarifies. "You need a job. That's why you're here, right?"

"No. Er, well, I do. But that's not why I came."

Sally props her elbow on the counter. "Are you sure?"

I stare blank faced at her. "Leah picked up this flier." I pat myself down until I find the folded handout I stuffed into my pocket. After jerking it out, I unfold the paper. "I wasn't certain if I'd come, but well..." I shrug, not knowing what else to say.

Sally purses her lips, a touch of amusement tugging at the corners. "As Tolkien would say," she muses, holding up a battered copy of *The Fellowship of the Ring*, "'not all who wander are lost.'"

I glance around and try to ignore the nagging suspicion that Sally knows more about my motivations than I do. "Old place looks good," I say in a placating tone. "Cleaner. It's nice to see the shop still open. A relief, honestly. I pictured some businessman turning the place into one of those chain bookstores."

"Ed would have hated that. He'd probably haunt the place until he scared them out." Sally chuckles, and then her expression falls somber. "In all truthfulness, I deliberated long and hard about reopening. When I found out Ed left the shop in my hands, I thought about closing it permanently. But I didn't have the heart.

"The funny thing is, when Ed was alive, I had a list of chores a mile long. Now the leaky faucet in the bathroom, the squeaky hinges, and that infernal dying-cat door buzzer all seem to lend to this place's charm. Like Ed. He had his quirks, and they drove me crazy, God knows. But in the end, those oddities are what I loved most about him."

She retrieves a lace-trimmed handkerchief from the pocket of an apron tied around her waist and dabs her eyes. "Enough of that. There's plenty of time for reminiscing later. When can you start?"

I hang my head, finding my shoe fascinating. "I'm not sure I can. It's just—"

"I know," she says, a restrained sadness remaining in her voice. "But dealing with one's grief is healthier than letting the sorrow fester."

I look up, but I don't meet her gaze. *Brilliant motto, but unfortunately not the way I do things.*

"Avoidance just leads to heartache later. Besides, you know this place inside and out. I could use your help. The adage is true. Good help *is* hard to find." She divides the pile of books into two stacks and shoves one into my arms then takes the other for herself. "I understand, with everything going on with Leah, the timing might be tricky. Then again, a man still has to eat."

I stare as Sally turns and walks toward the back shelves. Shifting my stack to a more comfortable position, I follow. "Everything going on with Leah?" I ask.

"The accident in York. Will she be all right?" Sally glances over her shoulder.

My mouth hangs agape. Unsure of what to say, I settle for a nod.

"Thank goodness. Oh—" She stops short, so quickly I

almost plow into the back of her. As I rock back on my heels, she faces me. "Congratulations are in order."

I cock my head to the side.

"Your engagement."

"A bookstore owner might not be your calling. Have you considered a job as a fortune-teller? Where did you hear all this?"

"From the girl at the coffee shop. Rachel."

I snort. *Of course.*

"Talkative one, isn't she? I swear I know her whole life story." Sally laughs. "I couldn't be happier for you. If you need any help at all, you know where to come. Just like if I needed anything, I know I could ask you," she says, heading toward the aisle in the far corner.

Dammit. Spreading it on a little thick, don't you think, Sally? My nineteenth-century sense of chivalry rears its ugly head. I heave an inward groan and follow. "Who else would I ask but my new boss?" I say through stiff lips.

She spins around to face me. "So that's a yes?"

I sigh. "It's a yes."

"How does eight to five, and every other weekend sound?"

I answer with a bob of my head.

"We'll expand our hours for the holidays, but we'll talk about that later. And remember, if you need any time off to help Leah with her recovery or the wedding plans, ask. Have you set a date yet?" she asks, setting her stack of books on a cart waiting at the head of an aisle marked Early Modern Britain.

I slide my stack next to hers. "No, not yet. Between her work schedule and school, we haven't had time to discuss it."

"Well, no hurry. You two are young. All the time in the world." Sally covers her mouth and stares at the two piles, frustration on her face. Then she glances toward the back room before her gaze returns to me. "I'd planned to have the place in tip-top shape before today's grand opening, but the book dealer sent the blasted shipment to Portland, Oregon, by mistake, and it didn't arrive until this morning. Talk about giving an old lady a heart attack." She pauses, glancing around. "Look, the shop is opening in a little over an hour. Maybe it's too much to ask, but that's never stopped me. Is there any way you can start today?"

I release a long exhalation. "Yes, ma'am. Why not?"

Sally presses her palm to her heart. "Thank you. You're a lifesaver. But never call me ma'am."

I spend the morning sorting and shelving a mountain of boxed books—a chore I revel in. It's like being reunited with dozens and dozens of old friends. Sally lends a hand in between the steady stream of customers. The shop has never been so busy. I can't help wondering how many people are here only to get a peek at a crime scene. Murder being such a rarity in Portland, every single one of them makes the news. The thought tightens my throat.

Kneeling on the hard wooden floor, I make headway on a large stack of Dickens and then move on to poetry by Keats and Byron. However, I find the busywork cannot barricade my thoughts from the past. As the day rolls by, more and more memories stream in, the most brutal being the sight of Ed's crumpled body, lying in a pool of his own blood. Others are less gruesome but just as painful—Ed attempting to waltz, his unexplainable fondness for Lou's Lobster Trap, all his failed crossword attempts and the questions that would ensue. Each memory causes the same deep ache in my chest, not as harsh as the ache of Lydia's memory, by any means, but still relentless.

At five past five, the last patron leaves, and Sally flips the Open sign to Closed. I grab the broom from the back room and begin to sweep the day's grime into neat, small heaps, looking forward to escaping this den of memories. Healthier or not, I've had enough of dealing with grief for one day.

"Even with a few hiccups, it's been quite a successful day. I knew things would work out," she says from behind the counter, thumbing through a pile of receipts.

I huff then chuckle, leaning on the broomstick. "You sound like Leah."

Sally looks up from the receipts. "How so?"

"She believes things will work out for the best, too."

"Some would call that faith. Powerful stuff. Just a tad can move mountains." She points at the mound of emptied boxes, broken down and stacked by the back door, waiting for me to haul them to the dumpster.

"Yeah, maybe." I shrug and return to sweeping. "But I might argue it was sweat and muscle that moved that particular mountain."

Sally chuckles and then chatters on about the triumph of the reopening while I brush the last of the dust piles into the trash.

With the floor swept and the bundle of boxes tossed in the dumpster, I leave work and walk to the five-and-dime. I sort through a heap of masks jumbled together in an aisle bin. Despite the mass, choices are slim. A couple of washed-up superheroes mixed in with the usual suspects: vampire, mummy, Frankenstein, and of course, the legendary werewolf. I reach for the Frankenstein, then remembering Leah's going to be Cleopatra, I grab a mummy mask and head to the register.

After, I swing by Leah's place to look at her car, and I quickly agree with her assessment. The belt is fraying, with a bit of glazing. I'm irked after calling a dozen auto parts stores only to find out the needed belt is out of stock, and each clerk says he must order the part. Three weeks is the quickest turnaround I can find.

With hours to kill before the party, I head back to my

apartment and poke around in the kitchen only to find my choices are few here as well. Over a bowl of Cap'n Crunch cereal, I lounge on the sofa. Emotionally exhausted, I lean my head back against the cushion and click on the television.

A man dressed in an ill-fitting gray suit attempts to sell me a set of Ginsu knives. "Forever sharp," he says over and over again. His monotone voice lulls me closer to sleep. I fight against my drooping lids, but exhaustion soon wins.

When I open my eyes, the world is distorted and vibrantly colored. I'm pulled through a current of images like a rudderless boat, at the mercy of the outgoing tide. I see Vita hovering over Ed's lifeless body, his eyes staring into space; Vita hunting, drifting from room to room in Leah's dormitory, searching for her; and then the Shadow Creature, red eyes flaming as it waits to judge. Although somewhere in the back of my mind I'm sure Vita is dead, panic still takes root.

The flow of pictures slows, dumping me in the middle of a desolate moor. Above me, the moon glows over the vast landscape, bleaching the surroundings into a bleak palette of grays. A raven's call warns, making me jump. I turn to find the winged omen sitting on the head of a statue, scraping its beak along the white stone. The marble figure dressed in a long robe looms over me, its carved face hidden by the hood. Bone fingers grip the long-handled blade of a scythe.

I step back as the statue moves, its head looking up from its once-frozen position. From beneath the brim of the hood, Vita glares down at me, the pale moonlight robbing her face of color. Her eyes burn with an aqua-blue light. She sneers, showing off her pearly teeth, and raises a scythe. With a swing, the blade sails toward me, flashing silver.

I wake with a start, heart hammering beneath my ribs.

Staring at the ceiling, I attempt to calm my breathing. *Just a dream,* I tell myself over and over again. *It's only a nightmare.* Vita isn't going to rise from the burrows of Shadow Death—the immortal's equivalent to hell—and hunt us. Those days are behind us. But what of Vita's twin, Domitilla? With her alive and well, I have a hard time believing she's not planning to exact payback for her sister's death. Whether Domitilla will aim her revenge only at Artagan, or at Leah and me as well, remains to be seen.

Night has overtaken my small living room. Light flickering from the TV distorts shadows into oblong shapes along my wall. I check the time, and I'm surprised to find it's close to nine. Before heading to Leah's, I splash water on my face and run a comb through my hair. I hurry out the door, almost forgetting my mask.

Outside, the street gleams with an icy sheen. Sleet clings to my hair. I hunch my shoulders, flipping up the collar of my leather jacket to guard against the chill. Icy pellets sting my unprotected cheeks. I hug close to the building and quicken my steps.

The redbrick, Queen Anne-style home that houses Leah's dormitory is alive, the party in full swing. The pulsating beat of the music rolls out into the street, rumbling under the soles of my feet. I follow a girl in an orange raincoat up the granite steps. She holds the door open for me. I catch the door just above the girl's head and invite her to go first.

The girl glances up to thank me, and awareness lights her eyes. "You're Jack, right? Leah's fiancé?" she shouts over the music.

I nod. "Have we met?"

"No, I've just seen pictures Leah has in her dorm room. I'm Michelle, one of her study partners. Tell Leah I missed her tonight at the study group, and I hope she feels better. She has the flu, right?" she goes on, probably seeing the surprise in my eyes.

Sick? Not bloody likely. Immortals don't get sick. No stuffy noses or spiking fevers. One benefit I've never tired of possessing.

"Thank you. Will do." I then add "Nice to meet you" for good measure.

Michelle waves and disappears into a menagerie of dancing ghouls and monsters.

The first floor of the dormitory, generally deserted and drab, has been transformed into a discotheque. I press through the packed bodies, searching for my Cleopatra. But I cannot find Leah, so I head for the stairs.

At Leah's door, I knock. No one answers. I wipe my sweaty palms on my jeans before trying the knob. The door creaks open. The room sits in darkness except for a dim glow of candlelight. Within, I hear the sound of rustling fabric.

"Leah?" I say.

"Come in," she replies, but her voice sounds nervous.

CHAPTER THREE

FLICKERING CANDLES LINE THE TOP of the bookshelf and clutter the bedside table, their flames wavering amid the thick shadows. A trace scent of jasmine drifts toward the door. I try the light switch. Nothing. I stay close to the entry and shut the door. I squint as my eyes adjust to the lack of light. My gaze roves the room and settles on a solitary figure sitting on one of the twin beds—a silhouette I recognize at once.

"I met your friend Michelle downstairs. She claimed you were sick. I knew that wasn't true, but is everything okay?"

Leah pushes from the bed and walks toward me. My eyes trace the gentle curves of her body emphasized by the cling of a spaghetti-strap nightdress, lingering for a moment on the swell of her hips before moving to the hem trimmed in lace, touching her mid-thigh. The ivory satin glimmers in the warm glow of the diffused candlelight.

I try not to stare, but how can I not? Leah looks like she stepped out of one of Klimt's Golden Phase paintings, and it's hard to believe this beautiful woman is mine. Leah's far more than I deserve.

I take a large gulp of air, puffing out my cheeks. *Be the gentleman,* I remind myself. *Eyes up, dammit.*

"Sorry if I woke you," I say. "I thought we were meeting in the lobby at nine."

"You didn't. And we were," Leah says, her voice uneven, low-pitched. "I decided we could use alone time instead. I texted you," she adds, moving closer.

"Oh." I reach for my phone but stop as I glance around the room, taking in the scene once more—the mood lighting, the apparel, or lack thereof. My eyes find their way back to her face, attempting to avoid her figure, but I'm achingly aware of her proximity. I rake my fingers through my rain-soaked hair, my perpetual habit whenever I'm nervous or flustered as I am right now. I find myself staring at the satin nightdress again.

"It's new. Do you like it?" Leah asks, running her hands down the silky fabric.

I let out a tense chuckle. "Very much. Probably too much. Leah, what are you up to?" I ask, although it doesn't take a rocket scientist to decipher her intent. Leah Winters is attempting to seduce me. And from my racing heart rate and body stirring with need, she's doing a bang-up job.

Her answer doesn't come in words. She inclines against me and rolls to her tiptoes to claim my mouth with hers. It's as if someone doused my body in kerosene and lit me ablaze. No flames, only heat. Although I want nothing more than to continue, I force myself to step back.

"Don't your horror flicks warn against this kind of behavior?" I tease then let out another edgy chuckle. "Especially with All Hallows' Eve right around the corner."

"Good thing we're immortal, huh?"

"I'm trying to be honorable here, but please don't push it. I'm no priest."

"Could have fooled me." Leah runs her fingertips down my chest, playing with the buttons of my shirt. "I realized today in the middle of Renaissance history that we've technically been a couple since 1862. I think that counts as a long-term relationship, don't you?"

She stares at me, her mouth parting. My eyes focus on her lips, and my resolve wavers.

"You want to kiss me," she says with complete confidence.

"I always want to kiss you."

"But this time you want more. I can see it in your eyes." She edges closer so her body is less than an inch from mine. I can feel the warmth radiating off her, and she whispers, "I want you."

"A-And I you, with every fiber of my being. But, ah—" is all I'm able to stammer out before she presses two fingers to my mouth.

"That's all I needed to hear."

Her lips crush mine, and for a split second, it's nearly painful. The kiss—long and inviting—swallows my words and muddles any argument. I feel Leah's beating heart through the thin layers of fabric between us, its quickening rhythm echoing my own. I may be a gentleman, but I'm still a hot-blooded man at my core. When I don't push away, her kisses soften. She yanks my shirt loose at the waist and, with trembling fingers, tugs at the buttons.

Instead of pushing her away, I pull her to me, holding her tight against my bare chest. My tongue runs along the curve of her lower lip and invades her mouth. She tastes of peppermint. All the while, my noble side argues in the background, but right now, desire has a much stronger voice.

Three quick raps on the door interrupt our intimate moment and stop me dead in my tracks. *Respectability saved by a knock.* "I should—" I start, my voice husky.

"Ignore it." Her lips brush along my jaw, and for the second time this evening, a jumbling fog overtakes my thoughts.

Another knock follows.

Leah groans. "You gotta be kidding me. If that's Nathan or Max, I'm going to kill 'em," she mutters, glaring at the door, and then glances at her negligee. "You should get it. I don't need those two seeing me like this. I think Nathan has finally got the hint that it's not going to happen."

"Agreed."

"But be quick." Her lips press hard to mine once more, robbing me of what breath I've managed to catch.

"I was right," I mutter when her mouth releases mine.

She looks up with a quizzical eye.

"You are here to torment me." I smile and pry myself from her.

I walk toward the door as another knock pounds, this one more persistent than the others. As the door swings open, the weary eyes of Artagan meet mine. Reeking of stale ale and cheap perfume, he sports a five-o'clock shadow. His hair doesn't have the usual well-groomed look, either. Instead, it's ruffled and unkempt, and his clothes are wrinkled as if he has been sleeping in them for days. There's something fierce and almost unhinged in his expression.

"You look like hell," I say as I step out of the room and close the door partway to hide the scene behind me from any prying eyes.

Artagan looks me up and down. He lifts one eyebrow and grins. "Sorry. The timing couldn't be helped."

"No worries. In all honesty, I should thank you. Where have you been? It's like you fell off the edge of the earth."

Artagan gives a half shrug, his gaze inspecting the span of the deserted hallway. The only noise, a steady thrum of music, floats up from downstairs.

I huff, irked by his evasiveness. But then again, what else should I expect? "So you're here. That must mean you got my message. Have you found any reason for Leah's soul memories?" A spark of excitement pushes past the annoyance.

His gaze returns. "No. Dead end after dead end." He pauses, looking over his shoulder again.

I glance down the hall. "Anything wrong? You don't seem yourself."

"We should talk."

"All right. Give us a minute, okay?" Not waiting for a response, I turn toward the door. Movement in my peripheral vision catches my eye. A silhouette glides out of a shadow at the end of the hall. A moment passes before I recognize him, and my breath freezes in my throat. The newcomer is Death. Two other figures, whom I remember from my time in the catacombs as Thanatos and a man Artagan called Soulless, join him.

Artagan sighs. "I am sorry about this."

"What the hell?" A singular conclusion rushes into my mind. Artagan was wrong. The Concilium Animarum are here to collect their pound of flesh. In their eyes, I'm sure the bargain I made with them back in the catacombs had failed, saving Leah but still leaving me alive. My heart rate speeds to a gallop as panic rushes in, so crushing and suffocating I can barely breathe. I clench my jaw and click the door shut. Then, swinging around into a defensive position, I hurl Artagan one heated glance of reproach.

He cannot meet my eyes.

Death walks forward, his long trench coat swishing with his movements. His dark hair, slicked back, emphasizes his narrow face and hollow cheeks. Sunglasses hide his distinctive eyes.

"Hello, Jack." Death's voice is gentle and polite, refined even. Even so, his tone sends an icy tingle flaring along my spine.

I press my back to the door and keep my hand on the doorknob.

Death offers his hand but drops it when he realizes I have no intention of accepting the gesture. "We're here to see Leah," he says. "I'm looking forward to meeting her."

"Not bloody likely. We can keep whatever this is between us."

Soulless whispers something to Thanatos and chuckles, then in two strides, he moves to Death's flank.

Soulless folds his thick tattooed arms across his barrel chest. "Move aside," he says. His face relaxes into a calm, almost agreeable expression, but his eyes, dark as shards of night, cut through me, leaving me chilled to my depths. Still, I stand my ground.

Feelings of desolation and fear press into my mind. Muscles strain and rebel. My fingers twitch on the cold metal knob. I find I'm of two minds. Most of me demands I stay where I am—a barricade between Death and Leah—but in the dark recesses of my brain, an impulse urges me to welcome them. I clamp my teeth together and fight the battle of wills rising within me.

Just as I feel I'm winning, the pain hits, threatening to bring up my meager supper. Beads of sweat bloom along my forehead and trickle down my face in salty paths as the waves of pain grow stronger.

I lift my eyes just enough to find Artagan, looking for his help. He stands on the sidelines next to Thanatos, a picture of perfect ease, except that his hands are balled into fists and hanging at his sides. His eyes are fixed on something at the end of the corridor, avoiding my gaze.

Thanatos's glaring, thin-lipped face appears to say, *This throttling is my doing.* It's only then I notice Thanatos's hand clasped on Artagan's shoulder, holding him in place.

As another wave of pain overtakes me, my knees buckle, and I lose my grip on the doorknob. I coil in on myself. The floor, seeming to rise up, slams into me. I lie in the fetal position at Soulless's feet. Choking and coughing, I roll to my back.

"Jack? Everything okay?" Leah's muffled voice calls from behind the closed door. The sound of footfalls moves within the room.

Shit! I push through the pain and will myself to my

feet, but an unseen power forces me back to the floor. The door creaks open, followed by a sharp intake of breath.

"Jack!" Leah says.

"Go," is all I manage to push out.

Now dressed in a flimsy T-shirt and sweatpants, Leah places her small frame in front of me as a shield. I attempt to grab her leg to hold her back, but the pain restrains any useful movements.

"I don't care who you are, but you better get out of here, or I'll call the police!" she says, brandishing a round-tipped knife.

"I fear the authorities wouldn't be much good here, Leah." Death removes his sunglasses, showing off his eyes. His smile broadens, and his eyes flash orange-red as if emitting their own light, like the eyeshine of an animal in the dark.

In a burst of panic, I push myself to my knees. Fire rips through my limbs. My wrists and ankles feel chained to hundred-pound weights. "Back. Inside," I say through gritted teeth. My face contorts with another round of pain.

Leah looks at me. Fear traces her features for half a second before her expression shifts, her face turning fierce as her glare returns to our guests. "Stop it!" she hisses, pointing the small knife at the council members as if she's wielding a saber. "You're hurting him!"

The sensation of domination dissipates, recoiling and folding in on itself until all that's left is a pinpoint of fire in my gut. I haul myself to my feet and resume my defending stance, maneuvering myself between Leah and the others. Every muscle in my body aches.

"Are you okay?" Leah says, stepping back to my side.

I nod, not peeling my stare from Death. I grip Leah's hand with mine in a show of solidarity.

Death looks past me as though I don't exist, the fearsome gaze replaced with a gentle air. "Things got a little heated. It was not *my* intent. My apologies."

"If this is about my bargain with the council," I say, "it's not Leah's fault. I take full responsibility for the debt and its payment." The bargain had been simple—my immortal life for Leah's mortal one. The council thought the bargain was lopsided, but despite this, my request was voted upon and granted.

"Do you?" A smirk lurks at the corners of Death's mouth, and he glances at Artagan. "Well, it's nothing as morbid as that. We're just here to talk, an introduction of sorts. But one best done in private."

Let him in. No harm will come to Leah. I promise on Olluna's grave. Artagan's voice comes as a breath into my mind, calming and soothing. I exchange a fleeting glance with him. I've never heard him invoke his late wife's name in such a way before. His expression is smooth, unreadable. Then he gives me an encouraging nod.

With a deep breath, I squeeze Leah's hand before my gaze returns to Death. "Fine. Come in." Leah's posture stiffens. I feel the tension rolling off her. "It will be okay," I say, an edge in my soft voice.

I step aside, pulling Leah with me. With a sense of queasiness, I watch as Death and his children parade past.

Artagan stops before Leah and dips his head. "After you, lassie," he says.

Leah glances at Artagan then at me. She must see something that satisfies her because she releases my hand and walks in ahead of him.

Before I can take a step, Artagan pushes by, a faint attaboy smile tugging at his lips. "Button your shirt," he whispers, batting me across the stomach, "and for God's sake and mine, be polite. No matter what."

I grimace and button my shirt. Then, tucking the shirttail into the confines of my waistband, I walk into the room and close the door behind me, shutting us in the lion's den.

Although the candles still flicker, Leah has turned on the lamp by her bed, changing the room's mood from one of romance to business as usual. She lingers by the door, keeping as much distance from our guests as she can in this small, confined space. Arms folded across her chest, her steady gaze locks on Death. Despite her guarded exterior, her fear is plain from her ashen face. After Death's little game in the hallway, she's aware of what horrors hide beneath their casual exteriors.

I step to Leah's side and give her a look of reassurance, although it doesn't make me feel any better. Artagan leans against the wall, placing himself just to my right.

Death stands in the middle of the room, his eyes roving over her collection of books—classics mixed with a few modern treasures—and the stark white walls littered with reproductions of Gauguin, Van Gogh, and Chagall. Thanatos and Soulless position themselves on either side of Death. Relaxed but at the ready, just in case I need another beating, I surmise. From the smirk on Soulless's face, he's hoping for another round.

"Well, you have superior taste." Death flashes a smile. "I have a fondness for Gauguin myself. The emboldened way he used color has always attracted my eye. And his *Vision after the Sermon* is my favorite as well." He gestures to the picture on the opposite wall.

Leah doesn't respond.

"It truly is a pleasure to meet you," Death continues. "I wish all my children could be here, but you'll meet them all soon enough."

Leah stares at him, a touch of skepticism in her expression.

"Where are my manners?" Death steps closer, holding out his bony hand. After a moment's hesitation, Leah places her hand in his. He smiles. "I'm Death, my dear. But you can call me Dīs or Hades, if that makes you more comfortable."

Leah's eyes widen, and I watch the color drain from her cheeks, but her chin stays pointed upward. Death's proximity only adds to my mounting anxiety. I feel the muscles in my shoulders tense, and the back of my neck prickles with a surge of icy needles. I consider stepping between them to break his hold, but as I stride forward, he says, "She's fine." Then, resting his hand on my shoulder, he holds me in place.

"These are some of the members of my council: Thanatos, Muan," he says, gesturing at Soulless. The two men nod. "And this is Artagan."

Leah draws her hand away in disgust. "Jack mentioned your council. He told me about what they do and what happened at that monastery."

"Then I fear you've heard a slanted view," Death says.

"I've heard the truth. Jack and I have no secrets. Your children are no more than glorified murderers."

"Secrets between lovers are as numerous as the stars."

"That's a cynical view," Leah says.

"Everyone has secrets." Death smiles, amused, then he steps away, moving back to the center of the room. "It is true that people die by our devices." He pauses, taking that moment to study me. "Your father was a vicar, was he not?"

I nod, and Death's gaze looks to the ceiling.

"To everything there is a season, and a time for every purpose under the heavens. A time to be born and a time to die," Death recites, emphasizing the last word.

"I know the passage," I snap.

"Some might say we're ordained by God." Death's attention returns to me for a moment, and he smiles before his eyes flick to Leah. "It's true that we reap mortal souls, but I like to think that we serve a higher purpose. I like to think we're the ones who teach mortals life is worth living. Jack and my council didn't meet under the best of circumstances, and that has tainted how he sees us."

I snort, but Death's gaze stays on Leah.

"I hope you don't hold a grudge. What happened in York was nothing personal," Death adds.

Leah's expression grows fierce. "Call me silly, but it was personal to me. And to Jack. So thank you for coming and welcoming me to the immortal family, but I'm afraid you're making my fiancé uncomfortable, so I must ask you to leave."

My posture tense, I worry Leah might be pushing Death too far. Beside me, Artagan chuckles under his breath. *I see what you like in her.*

"Right to the point." The crispness in Death's tone is unmistakable. "I'll admit I like your spirit. Once trained, you'll give Domitilla a run for her money. The others doubted. Even Artagan thought I was a fool, but I knew you were the right choice."

Choice? I stand, stunned, frozen by the currents of horror as the final puzzle piece clicks into place with an audible *snap*. The reason for their unexpected visit. Why Artagan looks like hell. A lump forms at the back of my throat as my brain scrambles to find any other logical excuse for what I heard.

When Death speaks again, his voice sounds some distance away, like he's talking from the next room. "Since Jack seems to have told you everything else, I'm sure he's told you whose descendant you are. My deceased daughter Vita."

Leah nods. "I can't say I'm proud of the lineage since she tried to kill us both." She gestures from herself to me.

"Vita was always a tenacious child. The transitions may be rocky at first, but I will help you adjust, as any good father would. You are my daughter now. I'm here to welcome you to the Concilium Animarum, the Council of Souls. I'm bestowing Vita's seat on you. It's a great honor."

Rage rises like a flaming phoenix out of the cold ashes in my chest. The intensity thaws me from my solid state.

My hands tremble at my side. "You son of a bitch!" I'm not positive if my words are coherent or only ring clear in my head. I raise my fist.

"Jack, no!" Artagan yells.

CHAPTER FOUR

MY FIST FINDS ITS TARGET and lands with an audible *smack* against Death's bony jaw. His face a mask of surprise, Death stumbles backward into the bedside table, sending it tipping and crashing to the floor. The crystal candlesticks shatter into hundreds of tiny pieces, and he falls into the wreckage. Muan steps forward, his black eyes glinting with expectancy, but stops when Death waves him off.

Gaze locked with mine, Death grinds his hands into the shards of glass. His eyes remain cold and speculative, but amusement plays on his lips. After shoving himself to his feet, he extends his arms to show me his palms. The skin is clear and smooth, not like he heals quicker than the rest of us, but as if he had incurred no damage at all. He steps closer so only inches separate us. His frosty breath wafts into my face, and his bright eyes drill into mine. "My children advised me you might be difficult. You don't disappoint."

Muan chuckles, his arm now draped around Leah's shoulder. Leah stares at me, her expression frantic.

"Keep your filthy hands off her!" I shout, forcing out each syllable. Unable to escape the cloud of anger, I thrust forward.

"Idiot," Artagan murmurs. A snakelike arm shoots around my neck, enclosing my throat with a stifling hold, and he hauls me backward. I struggle, but Artagan constricts his grip. He retreats, dragging me with him. His words hiss in my ear. "You're done. Do you hear me? Done! Or you'll end up maimed or worse."

As his grasp threatens me with unconsciousness, a clacking, like a train on its tracks, rattles in my ears, and my vision recedes into a long, blackened tunnel. I stop battling. He loosens his arm, allowing my vision to return to normal.

Death's voice flows like a disjointed melody. "I assured my children no man who went to such measures to save the woman he loves would put her in jeopardy." He glances at Leah before his attention revisits me. "Am I wrong?" he asks, his tone composed as if he couldn't care less which path I choose.

I shake my head, still trying to catch my breath.

Death studies my face, and then his gaze fixes on Artagan. "Release him."

Artagan's arm uncoils, and I take in several calming breaths.

Death outstretches his hands to Leah. "Welcome, my daughter."

Leah stares at him, her eyes cold and expressionless. Then, in the face of whatever fear churns inside her, Leah walks straight into Death's embrace. An intense hollowness springs into my chest. I shove my hands in my pockets to hide the shaking.

"With that settled, you and I need to talk, my dear." Death offers Leah his arm. She glances over her shoulder and gives me a reassuring nod before reluctantly slipping her hand into the crook of Death's elbow. He leads her to the wall, and they melt into the shadows, followed by Thanatos. Muan lingers behind, surveying me before stepping into the veil of shadows. Only his arrogant laugh remains, echoing in my head.

In a burst of panic, I rush to the wall. My fingers run over the unmoving space where Leah vanished. My breath becomes ragged, and the beat of my heart roars like a freight train in my ears. I'm acting like a madman. I can see it, feel it, but I cannot control it.

"Of all the childish, shortsighted things you could have done..." Artagan's words mumble off into garbled ramblings.

My focus snaps to him. "Where the hell did they take her?"

Artagan stands on the other side of the room, pinching the bridge of his nose. "There are not enough rewards in Heaven for this type of shit."

"Where, dammit?" I step toward him, my entire body trembling now.

Artagan looks up. His face is hard as if carved from stone. "For a father-daughter chat. Leah will be back soon enough." After a long pause, he continues. "Do you realize Death could exterminate you with a blink of an eye? And if that happened, what good would you be to Leah? She'll need you more than ever."

"Don't you lecture me. How long did you know Leah was Vita's replacement?"

Artagan glances away.

"Answer me! How long?"

He walks to the window and stares out at the city lights. "I suspected from the beginning, but for certain, since the night I dropped you off in York."

I grind my teeth. "In all that time, you didn't feel the need to mention it? You should have warned me of this possibility from the start."

Watch what you say. At delicate times such as these, the shadows sometimes have ears. Artagan's voice warns in my head, and he faces me. "What would you have done?

Tell me. Would you have had the fortitude to give Leah up when there was the slightest chance of keeping her forever?"

I exhale, my glare falling to the floor.

"Didn't think so."

"You're wrong. I would have, but you never gave me the chance. If you knew from the beginning that this was a possibility, why didn't you?" I remember Artagan's story of how he requited Olluna's death. "Revenge. Of course. I fooled myself into thinking your plan was all about saving Leah and my happiness. But it was never about that, was it? For you, it's always been about revenge, no matter the cost. Whether it's a town of harmless villagers or a nineteen-year-old girl with her future in front of her."

"You might be right. In all honesty, I don't care if you forgive me or not." A tightening of the muscle in his jaw tells me he's lying. I keep the observation to myself and let him continue. "I understand that absolution might be more than you can give. But if we are as alike as we seem, you would have given anything for this future, and I bet so would she." He smiles.

"It wasn't your choice."

"Perhaps not," he says, then his words invade my mind. *That doesn't change the fact that that plan was the only foreseeable way to stop Vita. She thought she could come after those I love without consequence. She was wrong.* His eyes spark with hatred as he glances at the spot where Leah disappeared. "We all have our demons to bear. For now, you're safe, and so is your Leah, if you allow it."

"Safe? She's with Death. How is that safe?" I yell. Artagan doesn't respond. I grab his shoulder to get his attention and shove him toward the door. "I'll find my own way to keep her safe."

In a rush, my back hits the wall. Artagan's forearm presses into my throat. "Accept this situation as reality. If you don't, you'll only make matters worse and risk her life and yours. Being Death's descendant may grant you immortality, but like I said, Death has the power to revoke it. Remember who gave me this." With his free hand, he points to the crooked scar across his right cheek. I remember the story. There had been a misunderstanding with Kemisi, Death's eldest daughter, and in anger, Death had retaliated, giving Artagan the scar. "These circumstances are unfortunate, I agree, but they aren't a death sentence as long as you mind yourself and don't turn them into one."

Artagan releases me. "Can you think of nothing so valuable to Leah that she would sacrifice anything to protect it, including herself? If my gut is right, she's as self-sacrificing as you are. Besides, what would you do? Run?"

I break eye contact.

Artagan snorts. "That's the precise stupidity I'm talking about. Death is not Vita. They're not even in the same ballpark."

"I realize that," I say.

"Do you? Death would know what you were up to from a mile away. Who wouldn't? Look at you, all crazy eyed. Veins pulsing in your neck. You always wear your emotions on your sleeve. It's your worst trait." He grumbles something under his breath in Gaelic, maybe. I believe I catch a bit of Scottish brogue seeping into his voice with the foreign tongue. From his tone, it's a colorful expression, whatever the language.

There's a long, tense silence before he speaks again. "Listen carefully. Death may not *see* us. He surrendered that ability when he gave up his reign over our mortality and made us immortal. However, he will have no qualms about using Leah's loved ones to control her. If she defies him in any way, she will put her family in danger. We both know death is far harder on those left behind."

The muscles in my throat constrict in a convulsive swallow. I know he's right.

Artagan leans closer, eyes intent on me. "To be honest, I'm not worried about Leah. My real concern is you, because if you challenge him on Leah's behalf again, losing your life would be the best outcome. He has an arsenal of pain at his disposal that will leave you wishing for an end. Therefore, for Leah's sake and mine, be on your best behavior. Yes, sir. No, sir. That's it."

He closes his eyes, and a palpable silence falls over the room. When he opens them, the rage has receded, leaving his expression drained. "Some things just are, no matter how much we wish the contrary."

"What? No master plan this time?" I ask, matching his tone. "No way to bargain—?"

Careful. Artagan's voice flows into my head, cutting off my train of thought, and he taps his finger along his lips. "You can't bargain your way out of the council. As you can imagine, if there were an avenue besides death, I would have taken it a long time ago. I'll be back tomorrow evening for her first lesson. Nine sharp. We'll meet at your place. I assume it's larger than this shoebox." Artagan steps to the wall, departing into the shadows.

I slump onto the bed and let my head sink into my hands. My stomach rolls, forcing a sour taste into my mouth. Fate had a plan. I laughed in its face and told it to go to hell. And where is Leah at this moment? With Death. I risked everything to prevent this, and yet she's with him just the same.

My attention drifts to a handful of framed pictures arranged in a cluster on the bookshelf. Leah's mum, sitting at her potter's wheel, smiles at the camera. Leah, Grady, and me in York. Leah and her brother, Grady, standing arm in arm in front of Redding Boarding School for Boys. He was so excited that day, prattling incessantly as he showed us around the school where he works as a history teacher. Leah's family has shown me nothing but kindness, and over the brief time I've known them, accepted me as one of their own. And now, they're at risk because of something I've done.

As the minutes tick by, paranoia grows. I pace the room, my eyes glued to the exact spot where Leah and Death disappeared.

Close to midnight, Leah returns. She has a difficult time meeting my gaze. When I wrap my arms around her, she's cold as ice. I bring her closer, rubbing her back.

"Do you want to talk about it?" I ask.

"I don't think I'm allowed." Leah's voice falters on the last word. She shrugs away and, with a pained expression, looks toward the shadow stretched across the adjacent wall.

Remembering Artagan's firm warning about eavesdroppers, I grab a notebook off the floor and push it in her direction. She stares a moment, then comprehension flashes in her eyes. She takes the notebook and a pen from the table, and she sits on the bed. Turning to the first blank page, she begins to write. Her scribbles are far less legible than normal, probably because of stress. Then she hands me the notebook.

Death threatened you, Grady, and my mother. It was all very polite, but I understood his meaning as clear as day. Obey or else.

I glare at the letters on the page. My face burns. On this account, at least, Artagan was telling the truth. I sit next to her and write in my florid script.

Artagan warned me of that possibility too. I'm sorry bargaining with the council put you in this position. How are you doing with all this?

Reluctantly, I offer the pad back. Leah reads and snorts. "Good question. There's a lot to digest. It's still soaking in."

I suck in a deep breath and take her hands in mine. "Know I'm here for you, and I'll do anything you need."

"The first thing you can do for me is stop feeling guilty. I can see it in your eyes. You're blaming yourself. When you went before the council, you weren't thinking about your well-being. Your focus was saving me. That's what you do for someone you love. So no more, Jack. No more blame, no more looking backward. Keep your eyes on me and our future together. Know I love you, and let that be enough," she says, her voice softening. "And I'll do the same."

Her words release the tension building in my shoulders and neck, but nothing can rid me of the sickness in my stomach. She tightens her grip. The metal of her engagement ring pushes into the flesh of my palm. A reminder of a promised future we're to share. I lift her hand and press it to my heart.

"Fierce, aren't you?" I attempt a smile.

She raises her chin, tilting her head to the side. "When I need to be. Yes."

"Tell me one thing," I say, lifting her round-tipped knife off the bedside table and holding it up. "What were you planning to do with this? It looks a bit too dull to be of any real use." I swish the triangular knife through the air and then lunge.

"It's not supposed to be sharp. It's a palette knife. For mixing paint," Leah adds. "You're good, by the way. Nice flourish. It looked like a move from one of the old swashbuckling movies my dad used to watch on Sunday afternoons."

"Fencing training, but I'm years out of practice. I won't say I'm good, although I used to be."

"Back then, wasn't that reserved for the rich and famous?"

I snort. "I guess. Mostly the educated. The poor were more preoccupied with sensible things, like putting food on their tables. I didn't learn by choice, I can tell you that. Lady Ashford caught William and me poking a townie with a stick." I smile at the memory. "The boy had pulled Lydia's hair and made her cry, so her brother and I rushed in to protect her honor. When Lydia's mother—your mother—found out, she wasn't impressed by our heroic use of the materials at hand, and so made us learn fencing, although I'm not sure Lady Ashford's plan to have two prepubescent boys trained in the use of pointy metal objects was her best one. But I suppose the sword practice kept us out of trouble most of the time."

"Always my protector."

"I try. You haven't answered my question, you know." I wiggle the knife back and forth.

"I wasn't thinking. I knew I had to protect you."

I frown.

"If anyone should understand, it's you. In England, you were willing to sacrifice everything to keep me safe. Think how it looked. You were on the ground. Four guys—one of them freakishly huge, by the way—were standing around you. What did you expect me to do?"

"Run," I grumble. "Or go back to your room and lock the door."

Leah gives me a dry stare. "Lot of good that would have done."

I lower my head and shrug. "Still, it would be reassuring if self-preservation was in the forefront of your mind."

"Your sexism is showing," she teases. "Besides, you're one to talk. I overheard what Artagan said. Maimed or killed."

"He lies." I keep my tone as lackadaisical as I can.

"A family trait," Leah mutters.

"Fine. Let's make a deal. You do whatever you need to keep yourself safe, and I'll do the same."

"Deal," she says. "I'm holding you to it."

I grin. "I'd expect nothing else." I fold her into my chest and kiss her on the top of the head, savoring the sweet fragrance of her hair. Now I have two promises to uphold. The other being the vow I made months ago to keep Leah safe, whatever the cost. Hopefully, the two won't collide.

"It'll be all right, you know. In the end, I mean," Leah says. "We just have to be brave enough to live the life thrown in front of us."

Her unwavering reassurance has no influence over my fear and concerns. I wish I had her brand of faith. So steadfast in her beliefs, it's as if she can peek into the future and see a happy ending waiting there for us.

CHAPTER FIVE

THE NEXT NIGHT, AT NINE sharp, as promised, there are three quick knocks on the door. The sound reverberates through the apartment, causing every muscle in my body to stiffen. Leah sits next to me on the sofa, frozen, her hands clasped in her lap.

"I'll get it," I say, giving her knee a squeeze of encouragement. I stand and walk to the door because I have no other choice. If it were up to me, I'd stay in my seat for the rest of time rather than walk these ten short paces to the door. I run my sweaty palms along my jeans.

This morning, Leah insisted we ignore the darkness looming on the horizon, maintaining that we should carry on with our regular schedules of work and school. I elected not to push the matter. If Leah wanted to forget what was to come for a few hours, who was I to argue? The whole scene last night was horrific, and my little stunt did nothing to make the event any easier. Following her wishes was the least I could do.

I take a deep, cleansing breath and open the door.

Pausing at the threshold, Artagan gawks at my humble accommodations. He looks more like himself—black hair groomed and slicked back from his clean-shaven, angular face. His pressed, tailored blazer is well fitted to his lean frame. A small leather knapsack hangs over his shoulder. His gaze darts around my apartment, from my old sofa to the seen-better-days dinette. He stares for a moment longer before his mouth twists into a smirk. "This place is a dump."

Regardless of the storm of emotions seething inside me, I cannot let Artagan get under my skin, not tonight. No matter what happens, Leah needs me calm. I roll my shoulders. The tension recedes a little.

"It's home," I say flatly.

"I suppose." His incredulous gaze lands on Leah, and he bows at the waist. "Good evening, lassie. I half expected to show up to find Jack had stuffed you in a trunk and shipped you off to Timbuktu." He eyes me again. When he gets no reaction, he grins. "Better. Maybe there's hope for that temper of yours yet."

"Maybe if you didn't provoke him, you wouldn't see that side of him," Leah interjects.

Artagan raises his eyebrows. "You are a cheeky one. We'll get along fine."

He plops his knapsack onto the coffee table and unbuckles the flap. After removing a small bunch of dried twigs tied with a string, he slips a lighter out of his blazer pocket and ignites the twigs. When the spark has grown into a steady flame, he douses it. Ribbons of smoke curl and spiral in the air. Smelling of stale cigarettes and weed, the odor clings in my nostrils and makes me cough. Artagan fans the smoke, dispersing it first to the east and then to the north and so on, all the time muttering incoherent words under his breath.

"What are you doing?" I ask, wrinkling my nose.

"Smudging. It's a little trick I learned from the Native Americans. They believe it wards off evil spirits. It also prevents shadow walking. But once done, we can talk without the fear of someone listening in. Everyone will have to use the door for the next week or so, but it's worth the sacrifice." He carries the smoldering bundle around the apartment, waving the smoke back and forth and paying careful attention to every corner, behind every door.

When the ritual is complete, Artagan sets the slow-burning bundle in the center of a forgotten plate on the coffee table. "There, now let's get down to business." He reclines in a chair, folding his arms behind his head. I move to the sofa and sit next to Leah.

"Before we start, I have a few questions," Leah says.

"I'm sure you do." Artagan smiles.

"So you're training me. What will that include?"

"Many things, but I think it would be best if we take one step at a time."

"And if I can't do this? What happens then?" She purses her lips, and worry lines etch her face. I reach for her hand. My touch seems to relax her.

"You can do this. And you will." Artagan speaks with conviction. "But let's not get ahead of ourselves. First you need to know how the council formed. 'Dust you are, and to dust you will return.' I trust you recognize the scripture."

Leah gnaws on her lower lip.

"Genesis. The curse of mankind," I answer in a monotone voice. It was the favorite sermon topic of my father's successor. The old vicar preached variations of this topic, banging his fist on the pulpit and screaming at the parishioners to repent.

Artagan nods. "Or if you think about it, the creation of Death."

"So he's right. God created him," Leah says.

"That remains to be seen. The quandary we find ourselves in now began in ancient times, back when the earth was new. Some legends say Death had three daughters—triplets named Clotho, Lachesis, and Atropos—with an immortal. When the girls were old enough, Death trained them in secret, teaching them his skills. Like many fathers, he claims his greatest wish was to have children and pass his trade on to them, creating a dynasty. It's said when their mother found out what Death was doing, she was horror-stricken. She ran away with her daughters and hid them. You might have heard of the triplets. They call themselves the Moirai."

"The governors of fate," I say.

"One and the same. But unfortunately, that is not the end of the tale. When Death could not find his young daughters, alone and brokenhearted"—Artagan rolls his eyes in sarcasm—"he devised a plan."

"You don't believe Death missed his children?" Leah asks.

"Love often desires devotion whether present or not," Artagan says. "In my experience, Death loves no one but himself, no matter how much he hopes you'll think otherwise. And I bet you'll agree with me by the end of my tale.

"Death's plan was simple. Have children with mortal mothers, and after the child's birth, *gather*, essentially kill, the women so no one could ever steal his children from him again. His first attempt went horribly wrong. Like the Moirai's mother, the woman attempted to hide the child. Enraged and far too eager to teach his new offspring his trade, when he found them, Death made the girl gather her mother. It was a cruel act that destroyed her."

"How old was she?" I ask.

"Almost seventeen. I'm still not sure how the mother hid her for so long. The story doesn't say."

I stare at nothing, my eyes narrowing. If this is how he shows his affection to his child, imagine what he'd do to a mere descendant like Leah.

"Wait. I thought Jack said Thanatos was the oldest of the Endless," Leah interrupts.

"That is what you told me," I say, glancing at Artagan.

"I did, didn't I? Well, in my defense," he says, raising his hands, "there isn't much human left in the girl. All that remains is savage. Because of this, Death can't allow Morrighan on the council. She's far too wild for such pomp and circumstance.

"Thanatos claims her mother was a druid witch from the area of the Black Sea. Whether that's true, I don't know. From all the firsthand accounts, Morrighan holds great magical powers, including the ability to shapeshift. Some say she can turn into a raven, and God knows what else.

"After his mistake with Morrighan," Artagan continues, "Death learned, and after that, he chose the mothers much more carefully, picking women easily manipulated. Under his strict guidance, he let the children live with their mothers until they were old enough to care for their own personal needs, and then he raised them himself. However, my ancestor, Brennus, was only two when he went to live with his father after his mother hanged herself."

"And other mothers? What happened to them?" Leah asks. "Easily manipulated or not, I can't imagine they let Death take their children willingly."

"Done away with in private," Artagan says, voicing my conclusion, "well out of the child's sight."

Leah shifts uncomfortably at my side.

Artagan grasps her reaction at once. Grimness darkens his eyes, and his mouth lifts into a grudging smile. "Death's strategy worked, though, to the extent that none of the other children are feral lunatics."

I snort. "What was Vita?"

"Savage, yes, but Vita was far too cunning to be insane," he says. "Believe it or not, in the beginning, Vita and her twin were said to be sweet, even sanguine."

My eyes narrow. "That's a far cry from the beast I met."

"Yes, and therein lies the rub." His eyes focus on Leah again as if he's trying to see into her soul. "Were Vita's malicious qualities buried, waiting to emerge, or were they tendencies cultivated by Death? Nature or nurture—the age-old debate. And like it or not, Vita's infernal blood courses through your veins, possibly along with some of her family traits."

My posture goes rigid. I can feel my blood pressure rising. "Leah's nothing like Vita," I say. "Besides, how do you know it's true that Vita and her sister were sweet, cheerful children? All of this happened, what, a thousand years before your birth?" Leah places her hand on my leg. I purse my lips and look away. "I'm just saying you trust this legend to be accurate, but you said yourself that's seldom the case. I bet Vita was always cold-hearted, even as a child."

"I hope that's true. However, if that were the case, Vita's evil tendencies were well hidden. My source is reliable. It's a firsthand account. Along with a council seat and immortality, Brennus left me a journal of sorts." He tugs a small, worn leather book out of his inner breast pocket then hands it to me. "It's a personal account. He had no reason to lie."

Leah leans against my shoulder. I tilt the book in her direction as I thumb through the brittle pages cluttered with chicken scratches in a language I don't recognize. "What language is this?" I run my fingertips over the script.

"Proto-Germanic. It's mostly history, with his thoughts peppered among the assorted facts. Brennus was a dark and brooding soul, plagued by his own personal demons. A trait I wage war against every day, a trait shared through his lineage." He nods in my direction, daring me to disagree. "Nature or nurture."

"She's nothing like Vita," I reiterate, handing the book back.

His attention wanders to Leah. "The point of my little history lesson isn't to scare you, but to warn you. Whatever the case may be, nature or nurture or both, Death would like nothing more than to turn you into a carbon copy of his recently departed daughter. He must see something in you that makes him believe that transformation is possible, something he didn't see in the other descendants, or else he wouldn't have chosen you. Be wary. He's good at camouflaging himself to become what you need. If you need a friend, he will be loyal. If it's a lover, he'll be devoted. If a father..." Artagan raises one thick eyebrow. "He's cunning. Therefore, you must question everything you feel and whatever the voices in your head tell you. You must make sure those thoughts and feelings are your own and not what he wants you to think and feel. I cannot stress how important this is. Understand?"

Leah nods.

"Let's begin. If I'm right, and I usually am, our mark should be leaving work right about now."

Leah gives him a hard stare. "Wait. Now?"

A pang ripples through my chest, but I keep the pain from my expression.

"No rest for the wicked." Artagan grins, but his eyes lack excitement. "Besides, orders are orders. I've set everything in motion, so tonight you are only accompanying me. Tonight we are sending a man named Daniel Harris to meet his maker."

Leah sucks in a long breath, wavering a little. "I've been dreaming about him. I thought the accident stirred up past-life memories as my cancer did with memories of Jack. But Daniel Harris has nothing to do with a past life, does he?"

"No, he does not," Artagan says. "I'll warn you, the first will stick with you. The particulars may fade, but his name, his face, that will always remain. However, with each gathering, more of the instincts Death has bestowed upon you will awaken until, eventually, all of this will become much easier."

The pang in my chest grows into an ache of guilt. I glance at Leah. Her face tenses, the small lines around her eyes visible. She plays with her hair, wrapping a strand in loops around her finger.

"Always remember, there are ways to show kindness even when taking a life," Artagan continues. "A death with as little suffering as possible is the kindest gift we can give them."

"So you remember your first?" Leah asks. She doesn't look up but keeps her gaze aimed at the floor.

"That I do. But it was neither quick nor kind." Artagan takes in a long breath. "I'll never be as cruel a teacher as Thanatos was. I promise you." He sucks in another breath, his expression hardening. "His name was Andre Labonte. He lived in France near Bourges. The area has changed since 1393, but it's still a beautiful city, despite any unpleasant memories I may have of it. Labonte was a lieutenant under Charles the Mad. He fought in the Hundred Years' War. He didn't have the privilege of dying in battle. My fault. Instead, he met his maker on the hard floor of Bourges Cathedral, bleeding out among the pews." Artagan's voice falters. He removes a pack of cigarettes and lighter from his pocket, his hand quivering. "Mind?"

"No, have at." I don't have the heart to say no. In all honesty, I've only seen Artagan in such a state once, when he told me the story of Olluna's death.

He smiles back then takes a long drag and lets trails of smoke ascend from his nostrils. More relaxed, he continues. "Labonte had suffered a near-fatal injury during battle—a failed attempt on my part. Healed and scheduled to return to the front the next morning, he went to the cathedral to pray. At the foot of a statue of Mary, under the virgin's watchful eye, Thanatos furnished me with a knife and told me that, because of my failure, the lieutenant would have to die by my hand. I remember thinking the blade was far too small for the job. I was a crude deliverer of death. We'll leave it at that. He asked for a priest to perform last rites, begged for one, but I stayed silent, too high on the euphoria to care about the final resting place of the man's soul." He drops his chin to his chest and rubs the back of his neck. "Thanatos made the task as personal as possible to either indoctrinate me or break me. I don't think he cared which. No one on the council was fond of having a former soul immortal around back then. They've grown used to me over the years."

Artagan glances up, his eyes meeting Leah's straight on. "It won't be that way for you, I promise. I'll make this first gathering as easy as I can, but you have to follow my instructions to the letter."

Leah nods, swatting at a tear.

"Whether we like it or not, death is a part of life, a part of us, and we must do our jobs. I want you to focus on a point inside, a place that makes you feel safe and makes you feel like you. Whether a memory, a feeling, or a person, hold on to it and don't let go. All right?"

Leah nods again.

Artagan takes another quick pull on his cigarette. "Time for a little quiz. What do you know about this bloke? Many details flowed in when you received the name for the gathering—hobbies, favorite foods, etc. It's our job to decipher which are important and which are just filler."

Leah lists the details one by one. Some she has told me, but many she has not. With everything we now know, the connection is obvious. The psychotic ex-wife and her death wish, an allergy to shellfish, even his job are all ways Leah could kill Daniel Harris. Bile rises, leaving a bitter taste in my mouth.

"Good. Very good. I'm sure you can see how we could use this information," Artagan says, pleased. However, I know the man well enough to hear the performance in his tone. "Normally, this kind of gathering would take a couple well-laid thoughts, but tonight we will do it the old-fashioned way, so to speak. Do you know where Mr. Harris will be this evening?"

Leah opens her mouth to say something but then closes her lips tight and shakes her head.

Artagan narrows his eyes and tilts his head in her direction. After a moment, he speaks. "I'm your instructor. I already know the answer."

She looks at him as if she suspects he's lying.

"He's meeting colleagues for a late dinner at Harris's favorite restaurant, Bartolini's." He smirks.

"Oh." Leah's shoulder slump. "Then why do you need me?"

Artagan ignores this. "We'll have to use the sous-chef. I fear he'll be looking for work tomorrow. Tonight, he will make a fatal error. You will distract the sous-chef, causing him to contaminate Harris's dinner with shellfish."

Leah's face turns ashen. "But why can't this be done without hurting someone else? This sous-chef has a family to support. It seems wrong—"

"I know this will be difficult, but this is the simplest, most direct path to our goal. I will be there holding your hand the whole way. As I said, this will become easier. Are you ready?"

"No." Defiance snaps like sparks in Leah's eyes.

Artagan stands and holds his hand out to her. "Sorry. No choice, lassie."

Without his help, Leah hoists herself to her feet.

At the door, I retrieve my jacket from the coat hook.

"No, Jack. You're staying here." Artagan's tone is commanding, but it doesn't stop me from slipping my leather on.

"I'm coming. Debate over," I say, looking him square in the eye.

"I don't want you there," Leah says from behind me.

I spin around.

"Please, don't argue," she says. Her expression is a poor attempt at serenity. Her eyes tell the real story, eerily vacant.

"Don't you think—?"

Leah shakes her head.

I look at my feet, not wanting Leah to see how much her words sting. "If that's what you want, love."

"With that settled, it's time." Artagan opens the door.

My jacket left behind, thrown on the couch, I trail them out of the apartment and to the far end of the deserted hall.

"This should be far enough out of the reach of the smudging." Artagan's gaze returns to Leah, his face holding a rare excitement. "You, my dear, have oodles of faith, so this should be a piece of cake for you. No matter what happens, keep Daniel Harris planted in your mind. Have you seen the movie *The Matrix*? Remember when Spoon Boy tells Neo there is no spoon?"

Leah nods.

"There is no wall." Without pause, Artagan walks into the shadow, passing from sight into what can best be described as a mist, although the vapors are thicker and far less transparent.

Leah steps to the darkened corner, studying it as if trying to find the secret to a magician's trick. She jumps backward in surprise when Artagan's hand materializes palm up from the shadow. Leah places her hand in his, and taking an uneasy step, she disappears.

I sit alone in my room as the night wears on, and the darkness has no intention of relinquishing control without a fight. With nothing to divert my attention, the minutes tick by, and anxiety has its way with me. Too filled with nervous energy to remain still, I pace the confines of my apartment like a caged animal. I act as judge and jury to myself, second-guessing every decision, all the while condemning my own actions. I cannot deny that Leah would not be in this predicament if not for me. At 1:05, I cannot take the silence any longer. I swing off the bed and stumble out into the living room, groping through the dark, not bothering with the light. I need fresh air, a drink, anything besides this dark quiet.

A whimper startles me.

I fumble for the lamp and flick the switch, blinking to adjust to the changing light.

Huddled on the sofa, Leah looks at me with puffy, red eyes, her cheeks shining with tears.

"How long have you been here? You should have woken me." I sit down next to her and pull her against me. She buries her face into my chest. Her body trembles, and her breaths become harsh with the sound of sobs. I hug her while she cries.

When Leah speaks, her voice is shallow and hoarse. "I'm a monster."

"No, you're not!" Our eyes meet, and I fight to keep my voice steady. "None of this is your fault, love. It's mine and Artagan's. Never yours."

She shakes her head but says nothing. Her eyes remain on mine a moment longer, then she looks away. "Tell that to Daniel's kids. He was a father of four. I took a father away from his children tonight. Oh God!" Her words dissolve into another round of weeping.

Feeling helpless and ill equipped, I say, "Tell me what to do, and I'll do it."

"Hold me."

I tighten my embrace.

"Make me forget his face." She pauses. "Tell me a story from our past, a happy memory."

I lift her into my lap and wait for her tears to wane before I start. "Lady Ashford threw the most elaborate balls. Do you remember?"

She sniffles and nods against my chest.

"I hadn't been home for two years," I say, stroking

71

her hair. "Away at school, I'd worked odd jobs on the holidays, determined to pay back Sir Robert's generosity. My mother begged me to come home for Christmas. That time I couldn't deny her. I rode the train to Lidcombe with William. He told me about the ball his mother was throwing and insisted I come. I didn't make any promises and planned not to go. I'm so glad I changed my mind." I kiss the top of her head.

"Lady Ashford spared no expense for a party. Every festivity began with a five-course meal. Pheasant was always on the menu since it was Sir Robert's favorite. That night, she even brought in the grand orchestra from London, said to have performed for Queen Victoria herself. I remember making my way through the crowd, looking for a familiar face when I found—"

"Me," Leah interjects.

Since her near-death, Leah has become more comfortable with the fact she and Lydia share the same soul, often talking about Lydia in the first person, almost like, in her mind at least, the two lives have melded.

I nod. "That was the moment I realized that the little girl who used to trail William and me around like a shadow was gone, and she had been replaced with the most beautiful and captivating woman."

She glances up and smiles. It's weak but still a smile.

"I still remember what you were wearing. The most ornate deep-lavender gown, its neckline adorned with ribbons. Your hair was swept back in a bun, which showed off that beautiful swanlike neck. I didn't leave your side for the rest of the night, causing us to become the tittle-tattle of Lidcombe, as my mum put it."

"Mother—Lady Ashford," she corrects herself, "was furious because everyone was staring, and I'd opened myself up to gossip."

"Lady Ashford was wrong, you know. None of the partygoers were staring because they saw a scandal. On the contrary, your beauty amazed everyone. You captivated them all. Just like you do every day."

Leah laughs.

"Too cheesy, huh?"

"Maybe just a little," she says, and then taking a deep breath, she relaxes and curls herself into my chest.

I chuckle. "Better?"

She bobs her head.

"Try to sleep," I whisper, and then I start to hum a lullaby my mum sang when I was a child. By the end of the second verse, Leah's asleep in my arms. I look down into her now-tranquil face, but hints of tear trails still stain her cheeks. It's clear being apart through this ordeal did neither of us any good. I turn my attention to the window. Shades of pink, orange, and yellow paint the sky. I slip out from under Leah's weight and grab my cell. At the window, looking out at the waking city, I dial Artagan's number. The call goes straight to voicemail.

"Next time, I'm going. Leah needs me there," I say. With the easy part handled, I snap the phone shut. Now all I have to do is convince Leah.

CHAPTER SIX

"**H**AS ANYONE TOLD YOU WHAT an arrogant son of a—?" I groan. Pain pulsates through me like thousands of tiny electric shocks. My muscles contract and expand, demanding actions my mind has not ordered. I grit my teeth, shoving the commands away, and I glower at Artagan.

"Frequently. Now stop resisting. It only makes it hurt more. Besides, you're the one who said you wanted to be part of this. Mind control is a very useful skill, but it takes a lot of practice. Welcome to the party." Artagan's lips thin, producing an unsympathetic smile.

When Artagan showed up on my doorstep spouting the promise of staying in tonight, the news was a relief. Although being Artagan's personal marionette has been humiliating, if shedding my dignity is what it takes to keep Leah away from a night like last, even for a few hours, pain and humiliation are small prices to pay.

Concealing the pain the best I can, I shift my eyes from his, and my attention centers on Leah. She sits curled on the sofa at the opposite end of the room, her knees tucked under her chin. She stares at me, her face pale. From her contorted expression, you'd think I was being drawn and quartered.

"I'm fine. No harm—" My vision blurs with a new throbbing wave much stronger than the last. My hands tremble at my side. An impulse to step forward floods my mind. Despite my objections, my feet oblige.

"See?" Artagan says, eyeing Leah. "With the right amount of force upon the will, you picture an action, and presto, it happens. Watch, now he'll kneel."

With a moan, my knees buckle, and I hit the floor.

"Artagan, enough!" Leah snaps. "Mind control. Useful stuff. I get it."

Artagan folds his arms behind his back and rocks back on his heels, pivoting away from me. The pain evaporates, leaving my body sore and fatigued but no worse for wear. I push myself to my feet. Preparing for the next round, I take in a gulp of air.

"Up and at 'em. It's your turn, lassie." Artagan gestures for Leah to stand, and she does as she's asked. Rubbing her arm, Leah shifts her weight, being careful not to make eye contact with either one of us.

"Do your best," Artagan encourages. "After a time, this ability will take a single thought. For now, it will require an immense amount of concentration. Now, just as I told you. Place your full focus on your subject, and then imagine an action, breaking it down step by step." He points in my direction. "This skill, used correctly, will keep your life as normal as possible."

"What if I suck at this? What then?"

"You'll do fine. An assignment's free will may get in the way from time to time, even with the best-laid plans. But as long as you know the disposition of your target and your instrument's nature, that won't happen as often as you might think."

"Instrument?" Leah asks.

Artagan purses his lips. "A mortal used to carry out a task for a gathering, such as Bartolini's sous-chef. Now, focus. Make Jack do something. Remember, nothing against his nature, like strangling you." He smirks, eyeing me. "Or me, hopefully. Those kinds of acts will take a higher skill level than you have at this moment. Just keep it simple."

Leah looks my way, apprehension flickering across her face. "But I don't—"

"Stalling again, I see," Artagan says. "I suppose you could just forfeit, and I'll be the winner."

"Come on, Leah," I coax. "It's just a game. You can do this. You can't let the old windbag win."

Leah's expression lightens. "Lady's choice?"

Artagan nods once.

A mischievous gleam dances across her face. I close my eyes and brace myself. Then I let Leah permeate my thoughts, giving her every advantage in this little competition. At first, there's nothing but blurry depictions. However, as time passes, the vague, sporadic pictures congeal, strengthening into a solid image. In my mind's eye, my hands rise to cradle her face. I let them obey. Instead of the throbbing pain, a faint, warm tingle surges through every muscle. It's almost pleasurable. To the naïve, it would seem like nothing more than a swell of adrenaline or a change of emotions. I open my eyes. Barely conscious of Artagan's presence, I bend my head toward hers. By Leah's command, I begin the kiss, but in a burst of heat and without prompting, I prolong it.

"Okay, okay. Break it up." Artagan's voice cuts in. "Cheaters, both of you. Not a good enough test to hone your skills."

I pull back but keep one arm around Leah's waist. "I like her way better."

"I'm sure you do. Who wouldn't?" Artagan chuckles. Raising his eyebrows, he looks to Leah. "Commanding him to kiss you is like telling a lemming to jump off a cliff. No sport. If that's the best you got, I suppose it'll have to do. I win."

Leah's expression stiffens. She twists out of my grasp and stares me down, a spark of determination in her eyes. Concentrating, she bites her lower lip.

Still riding the high of the kiss, I outstretch my arms. "Hit me with your best shot, love."

A new vision spills into my mind. Before the image takes full possession of my thoughts, my hand curls into a ball, and my arm jolts upward. My fist strikes me square in the face. I stumble back, eyes stinging, jaw throbbing. A hiss escapes between my teeth as my ass hits the floor.

Artagan's rich baritone laugh fills the apartment.

Leah's hands fly to her mouth. "I meant for you to hit *him*," she says, pointing at Artagan. "I'm so sorry. Let me get you a cold washcloth."

"Oh, he's all right. The bleeding's already stopped." Artagan heaves a sigh as Leah runs from the room. "This is something you will practice even when I'm not around," he calls down the hallway but receives no response except the sound of running water. His eyes fix on me. "Mind control is good for more than the art of gathering. It's a needed skill in a family such as ours."

My brow furrows as I push myself off the floor. "Protection?"

Artagan nods. "You don't want her to become anyone's puppet."

"Let's do it again," I say to Leah as she hustles back into the room, dripping washcloth in hand.

"No," Leah says, her focus on my nose.

"I assure you, I'm fine." Using the washcloth, I swipe at the drying blood. "See?"

"I don't like hurting you," she counters. "Can't you understand that?"

Drawing a deep breath, I hold it for a moment before releasing it. "If this skill will keep you safe, you have to practice. If that means I have to go through a little discomfort, so be it."

"You're not fooling anyone. What you've been going through is more than *a little discomfort*. How about if the situation was reversed? Are you saying you'd have no hesitation in hurting me?"

I stay silent, but I don't break eye contact. True, the mere thought of causing Leah pain sends a stab of revulsion straight through me. Despite her misgivings, this is how it has to be. The likelihood that this skill could ensure Leah's life is as normal as possible, coupled with the potential of keeping her safe, is too big a prize to pass up. Pain be damned.

With another deep breath, I begin my argument. "Listen—"

Leah juts out her jaw, and she folds her arms across her chest. I know this stance all too well. My face flushes.

"For all that's holy, child, you're more stubborn than he is," Artagan says. "All right, I'll be your guinea pig so you can get a handle on it. But just this once, mind you. After that, you will practice on lover boy whether you like it or not. Got me?"

Leah nods, but I don't put stock in the sincerity of her response.

Artagan proves to be a more challenging opponent. Her first attempt does nothing. The cocky bastard stands in the middle of the room, a smug grin plastered across his face, telling Leah to work harder. After over two hours of attempts, hope appears on the horizon when Artagan winces. Soon, the pompousness disappears from his lips. He grits his teeth.

I lounge back on the sofa, propping my feet on the coffee table. "I see why you found this so amusing."

Artagan's penetrating eyes lift to meet mine. "Piss off."

"Watch your language. There's a lady present," I say.

He glares, and I smirk back.

"Remember, resisting makes it hurt more," Leah adds.

I chuckle.

Artagan's eyebrows furrow, and he glances to the floor. His body contorts ever so slightly, evidence of the battle of wills raging inside. His left arm raises a fraction as his right hand inches toward his hip. He groans, shoving his arms back to his sides. "I'm not singing that."

"What? Not your style?" Leah asks. "I'm sure I can come up with something. Hmm... what do you think, Jack? Maybe 'Wrecking Ball' by Miley Cyrus? Or better yet, Madonna. My mom listened to her *Like a Virgin* album endlessly. I know all the songs by heart. Let's see, there's 'Material Girl' or 'Dress You Up.'"

The pain vanishes from Artagan's face. He scowls and raises one arm, placing the other on his hip. When he speaks, it's all but a growl. "I'm a little teapot. Now, knock it off."

A bell-like laugh bursts from Leah. The sound startles me. I haven't heard that pure, brilliant sound in weeks. I look to her. Her lips erupt into one of her breathtaking smiles. "Score!" she says, throwing her hand over her head and collapsing next to me on the sofa.

Artagan chuckles and then clears his throat. "Good job. You're strong, stronger than you think. With practice, your skills could rival Thanatos."

"Is that good?" she asks.

"Very. His talent with thought manipulation is second only to Death himself. We may have found your saving grace." Artagan pauses. "Another time, we must work on resisting. Although painful, it is necessary."

Of course. The other side of the coin. Something used as protection could also be a weapon. I keep my expression placid, although I'm sure I'm not fooling anyone. Leah knows me too well to fall for my little charade. Her gaze drifts in my direction. I look to the ground, avoiding her prying eyes.

Leah's the one to break the quiet. "Whatever it takes. Like Jack said, if this keeps me safe, I gotta practice."

"It might be best for all involved, including my jaw, for Jack to take that night off," Artagan says then smirks.

I don't respond.

"It's a skill she needs," he adds in my direction.

With a huff, I shake my head. "No, I'm no hypocrite. I'll be here."

The shrill ring of a phone wails from Leah's sweatshirt hung over the dinette chair, driving her from the couch and me to my feet in an involuntary response. Rising when a lady rises is a habit I've carried with me through the years, ingrained into my very soul by repetition and my mother's persistent reminders when I was young. Leah digs the screeching mobile out of her pocket. Glancing at the screen, she moans. "It's my mom. I need to take this." She presses the phone to her ear. "Hey, Mom. What's up? ... No, I'm at Jack's. It's really not a good—"

Leah listens, drumming her fingers on her thigh.

"Yup, I know," she says.

Again, she listens.

"Yes. That's what I said, Mom." Leah rolls her eyes and signals she's heading to my room.

After she disappears down the hall, Artagan reclines on the sofa, lighting a cigarette.

Clearing my throat, I lean forward, propping my elbows on my knees. "You're what, six hundred years old, give or take a few years? You've had centuries to master this skill, and Leah disarmed you in a couple of short hours. Peculiar, wouldn't you say?"

"Stranger things have happened," he objects.

"You let her win."

"Don't tell her. After everything, Leah deserves some fun, even if it was at my expense."

"You're a softy. Who knew?"

"Shhh. I wouldn't want to ruin my reputation."

I glance at my closed bedroom door. "Well, thank you. I haven't heard Leah laugh like that in a while. Good call."

"Praise? I bet that hurt." He takes another puff on his cigarette.

"More than Artagan's Puppet Theater."

"Now, about you tagging along." He raises a hand to cut off my protest before I can even start. "Let me finish. I'm fine with it on two conditions. No interference. No commentary. Those are my rules. One misstep, you're out."

I twist two pinched fingers over my lips and toss the imaginary key over my shoulder. "Now, if I can just get Leah to agree. I brought up the idea this morning. It didn't go so well. She's afraid I'm going to see her as a monster. I told her I never could, but..." I sigh.

"Good luck with that." Artagan laughs and then grows serious. "Well, if you ever convince her, understand that when it's time for the other council members to train her, you won't be allowed to go. Rules and such. The only reason I can let you accompany us is that you're my descendant."

I keep my voice as even as possible. "The others will be involved in Leah's training?"

"Oh, yes. Death's orders. I assumed Leah told you. Death would have filled her in on all these details the first night."

"No, she didn't say a word." My eyes wander to the closed door again. "All of them, huh? Even Vita's twin? And Muan?"

"From what I understand, Domitilla has received a pass. But yes to Muan. Only because he insisted upon it. He hates being left out. To be honest, I'm not sure what Muan and his brothers can teach Leah besides brutality. Unfortunately, it's not my call."

"Brothers? How many are there?"

"Thanatos claims there were nine at the beginning, but now there are six. Muan, then there's Izel, Pacal, Acan, Tepeu—now, he's a strange one." Artagan chuckles. "He hasn't been able to look me straight in the eye since I stumbled in on him a few years back. He was stark naked, his whole body painted blue, mumbling some incoherent chant. Trying to relive the good old days, I guess."

"That, or preparing for an audition with the Blue Man Group," I say, trying to look serious.

"Or that." He chuckles. "Whatever the reason, there are images a man can never burn from his memory no matter how hard he tries. And that is one of them." Still smiling, he shudders. "The last brother is Hachäk'yum. I call him Yum for short. As you can imagine, he hates that."

"And you keep right on calling him it."

"You know me too well." He takes a quick haul on his cigarette. "Kemisi believes the Soulless are the sons of Ammit, an ancient female demon from the Egyptian religion known as the Eater of Hearts. A few of the council members think they're soul eaters."

"But you're not sure."

"Slapping a label on them doesn't change what they are. Nothing can kill them. That's for damn certain. Not poison, nor blade. You name it, they're immune, like mutant cockroaches. And they're a secretive bunch."

"So I take it you've tried to kill them?"

"Not myself, no, but some of the council have. Otmar said in the beginning even Death gave it a go, to no avail. The Soulless are a pestilence. It's the one thing we all agree upon." Artagan grins. "If Thanatos's stories are true, a Mayan king created them in secret to cheat Death."

"But now they work for him?"

"Just Muan, really. The others aren't official council members. It was a deal Death made with them. Power for loyalty. I think it scares Death to have something wandering this earth that he can't control. But this all happened well before my time. If you want all the gory details, you must ask Thanatos. What I know for sure is the Soulless are impulsive, lack empathy and shame, and have a grandiose sense of self. And those are their best traits. The only talent any of us are sure Death gifted them was shadow walking. Allegedly, they burn paper dipped in their victims' blood, sometimes even removing their hearts. Besides bloodlust, I'm not sure why they would do this. The world would be a much better place if none of them existed."

"So the missing brothers, what happened to them?"

"No one knows." Artagan's forehead wrinkles for an instant, and he sinks into his thoughts, puffing on his cigarette.

Quiet moments pass until Leah's return.

"Sorry, that took longer than expected," she says. "My mom was just being my mom."

"It's getting late. I should be going." Artagan stands. "Jack." He nods in my direction. "Leah, it was a distinct pleasure." He takes Leah's hand and, with a dramatic bow, kisses the back of it. "We will resume our training tomorrow night. Eight sharp," he says over his shoulder, walking toward the door. Then he leaves.

The remnants of a blush still staining her cheeks, Leah glances at me. "Remind me to keep him away from Rachel."

In the weeks that follow, life develops a new rhythm. Wake, work, training. Wake, work, training. I make Leah practice mind control every spare moment in accordance with Artagan's instructions. Now that I've found a way to help keep her safe—in some sense of the word—I'm obsessed. Artagan spends most evenings at my apartment, teaching Leah the finer points of mind control, and makes no mention of another gathering. Leah's abilities grow by the day, accompanied by her confidence. In this I find solace. Although it's not the future we wished or planned for, we both have fallen into its tempo.

Until one morning I wake, and Leah is gone.

CHAPTER SEVEN

GONE TO THINK. *LOVE, L.*

    I stare at the neon-orange Post-it stuck on the refrigerator and run my fingertips over the curved indents of her rushed handwriting.

Over the last few nights, Leah's dreams have returned, haunting her sleep. She hasn't confided in me yet. From her restless nights, I know the dreams aren't happy ones. So before I found the note, I assumed Artagan fetched her for a gathering. Without me, of course. Seems Leah has yet to agree to let me accompany them.

I know I should leave her alone about the subject. No means no. But something deep inside of me, a fear I don't even understand, won't let me drop it. Although I've broached the topic several times, all attempts went as well as the first, none earning me the reply I'd hoped for. Leah's response has been that she'll think about it. Desperate, I came close to telling her about my involvement with Hake and his murder, hoping she'd see she isn't the monster in this duo, but I lost my nerve at the last moment when I couldn't find the words. Too many regrets revolve around my time spent with that man, most of my darkest sins committed that year. Although the majority of the details from that year are fuzzy or forgotten, every moment of the night I killed Hake is burned into my memory.

Richard Hake had figured out my secret and threatened to tell all. To silence him, I beat him and left him bloodied and unrecognizable, and very dead. Similar to Artagan's story of Lieutenant Labonte, I'd shown Hake no mercy, even when he begged. However, no one had ordered me to do it. Nausea rolls through me with the memory of Hake's life withering in my grasp, and the euphoria that whirled in afterward. And Leah thinks she's a monster. *Ha!*

It's easy to see my lapses in judgment now—being pummeled nightly at the fight house, only to return the next day healed and ready for more, was a dead giveaway that I was different. But I fell too deep in sorrow and flew too high on drugs to consider the ramifications. Back then, my only happiness came from a small brown bottle labeled laudanum.

The other obstacle to telling Leah is that the admission is bound to lead to questions about guilt and shame. Even now, confessing the remorse that shadows my actions would do her no good. I suppose I could tell her that after Hake's murder I never thought of him again and that his pale, bloodied face never haunted my dreams. But that would be a lie. Instead, I chose a different truth. I told her I could never see her as anything besides a strong, compassionate woman, beautiful inside and out.

I dress and get as far as the staircase before changing my mind. Charging out after her will only make Leah more adamant. No one likes being strong-armed into doing something they don't want to do.

After I return to my apartment, I make a pot of coffee and try to keep my mind occupied. Then, slumping into a chair at the cramped dinette table, I drum my fingers on the Formica tabletop while I wait for the coffee to brew. The silence, once my norm, feels stifling. I've grown accustomed to Leah's morning routine, and without her cheerful chatter, it's too quiet.

A neighbor's footfalls thud from the outer hallway,

resonating through the paper-thin walls. They're far too heavy for Leah, but the noise still draws my eyes to the door. Her blue parka with a fur-lined hood hangs abandoned on a coat hook. I glance at the window. Dense clouds suffocate the sun, threatening an impending storm. As if a sign, icy pellets make a soft pinging sound against the windowpane. My eyes return to her parka.

No questions. No sales job. The coat. That's all, I convince myself.

Out on the sidewalk, her jacket in hand, sleet stings my cheeks like icy pins and needles. The wind off the sea chills me to the bone. I tug the leather collar around my neck, a weak defense against the cold, and head toward the waterfront on a hunch. Leah once mentioned that the sound of the waves helped her think.

I take a shortcut down a damp, crooked alley leading to the bay in the distance. The sheltered space provides a reprieve from the weather. By the time I emerge onto the adjacent street, the sleet has stopped. I veer down Custom House Wharf—a working dock lined with warehouses on one side and lopsided wooden buildings on the other, which offer some protection from the relentless wind. If she went to the waterfront as I suspect, this is as good a place to begin my search as any other.

Luck is on my side this morning. I find Leah at the edge of the pier, sitting on a row of stacked crates, her knees pulled up under her chin, her arms wrapped around her slender frame. Strands of hair yanked and pulled by the gusts of briny sea air whirl out from under the hood of her sweatshirt. My pace slows as I approach. Lacking an invitation, I suddenly feel like an intruder. I debate whether I should just go.

Leah sniffles, wiping her nose on her sleeve.

Wrestling the awkwardness, I walk to her side and lean on the crate next to hers. Not looking in her direction, I set her parka atop the weatherworn box and then retrieve my handkerchief, yellowed by age and a little frayed around the edges, from the pocket of my jacket and lay it on the coat. I tuck my hands under my armpits to escape the frigid chill and stare out at the bay. In spite of the wail of the wind and the sloshing of the waves, an unmistakable silence hangs between us. With a sidelong glance, I attempt to read Leah's thoughts through her facial expressions, but years of hiding her thoughts and dreams, first from her mother then her brother, has taught her how to conceal her real emotions well. The only hint of what she's feeling comes from the set of her jaw. She's determined. Of that, I'm sure.

Leah picks up the handkerchief. After ironing out the piece of linen between her hands, she runs her pointer finger over the hand-embroidered JFH.

"F? I don't even know your middle name."

When I give no response, Leah smiles. "That bad, huh?"

I shrug.

"How did you know where to find me?"

"You once mentioned walking down by the wharfs helped you think."

"And you, being you, remembered that." The corner of her mouth curls upward.

"Here." I hold out her parka by the collar. "You must be freezing."

Leah uncoils her legs and slides her arms into the sleeves. I pull the coat over her shoulders, tugging it around her.

"Thank you," she says, and then her gaze slips away back to the choppy waves.

"You okay? More dreams?"

Leah lifts her shoulders and lets them drop.

"I should go back," I say, pushing off the crates. "I just thought you might need your coat."

"No, stay. I was coming back soon, anyway." Her

hushed words come out with a solemn inflection. She glances away. "We need to talk."

My stomach gives an uneasy flip. In my experience, nothing happy ever follows those four simple words.

She looks at me and smiles. It's a melancholy, but still breathtaking, expression. "I've never told you about my cancer, have I? Not the details."

I shake my head.

"It was a miracle I survived. I had Ewing sarcoma, stage four, to be exact. By the time they found it, it was already in my lymph nodes. So yeah, not a hopeful diagnosis. Life seemed grim back then." Her expression turns solemn as she speaks.

I slide closer, wrapping my arm around her shoulders.

"At first, I felt guilty about being sick. My family had just started recovering from my dad's death, and then my body had the audacity to come down with some rare form of cancer. I know, stupid, right? But it was the way I felt. The battle ensued. Surgery, chemo, radiation, the whole enchilada. It worked at first, then not so much. By that point, I should've been pissed or scared. I mean, when you're thirteen, the biggest worry you should have is what to wear to the middle-school dance. That night I almost died, I felt peaceful. I had come to grips with the fact I would die—almost looking forward to it. I guess I was tired of fighting. And just as I thought I was slipping away, you happened, or at least the dream of you did. After that, something inside me changed, and I knew I'd live, that everything would be okay. Familiar, huh?"

I give her a half-hearted smirk.

"Everything around me screamed my belief was wrong, from my disease-riddled body to the solemn expression on everyone's faces when they thought I wasn't looking. Nurses whispered the word *denial* a lot. If you haven't noticed, I can be just a teensy-weensy bit headstrong."

"You don't say?"

"You can't say anything. I don't care what Artagan says. You're just as stubborn as I am."

"Nonsense. I'm as flexible as a contortionist," I tease.

"More like a lead pipe." Leah laughs, bumping me with her elbow. "You pretty much know the rest. A handful of tests and a couple MRIs later, the doctors discovered the tumor was shrinking, and after a few weeks, they declared me cancer free. They called it a miracle. But I've told you what I felt that night."

She breaks eye contact. "In the countless support groups my mom forced me to go to, they talked about acknowledging your illness and how that would lead to peace. I call it peace, but what I felt that night was far different from anything described in those meetings. It felt hot like someone had lit hundreds of sparklers inside me. The feeling then exploded and spread throughout my whole body, consuming me. I never linked it to my healing. At the time, I credited it to one of the experimental drugs they pumped into my system by the truckload. Since then, I've felt a similar feeling, except the sensation's much tamer and not painful. More like a warm, enduring peace. Whenever that feeling comes, I know I'm on the right path, like I have a compass inside me, pointing me where to go."

"Have you ever felt the first feeling again? The internal sparklers?"

"It's the only thing I remember from the coma. Then I woke up," she says.

"What can that mean?" I ask, more to myself.

"I don't know. But I mentioned it to Artagan. He had no idea. Whatever it is, I know I need to listen to it and follow my gut, even when it flies in the face of what others think I should do." Leah presses her lips together so hard their color changes to white.

"There's more."

Leah stares and then nods her head. "I'm quitting school."

My eyes narrow in disbelief. This is the very thing Artagan warned us about. Has she forgotten? "No, you can't. Please be logical."

"When we ran to England, before I knew why, I felt that same warm, enduring peace again. It's why I went with you so easily, even though your lie was lame." Leah shakes her head. "It seemed crazy, but it was the right thing to do. If I had refused to go, you would have stayed, and Vita would have killed you. I know that now, but back then it was just a feeling."

"You cannot base every decision on a feeling, especially when you don't even know what it means yet."

"I'll call my mom this afternoon and let her know," she says as if I haven't said a word.

"Leah, please listen!"

"Grady will have a conniption and say I'm crazy." She rolls her eyes. "Thank goodness he's planning on spending Christmas break with Charlotte and her family. I don't think I could take him and Mom ganging up on me. Mom by herself will be hard enough."

"And I thought you were out here deciding whether you'd let me escort you on gatherings. But this? Your brother will be right!" The instant the words leave my mouth, I regret them.

A look of betrayal flashes in her eyes. "I've heard it all before, Jack Hammond. Certifiable, delusional, unreasonable—those words don't faze me anymore. I have to follow what I know is right, no matter what people think. And that includes you." She pulls away.

"I apologize. I didn't mean it the way it sounded."

"It's not Grady's decision. Or yours. It's mine, and I've made it. Like it or not, being a member of the Concilium Animarum is my life now. To keep you, Grady, and my mom safe, it needs to be my focus. Quitting school is the right decision. I know it in here." She points at her chest, right above her heart.

My mind spins in a thousand directions like a hummingbird in flight, never settling in one spot. "Of course, you have to do this job, and do it well. I get that. However, you cannot give up everything you've always wanted because of it. None of us would want you to do that. No matter the price. You are an artist, an ability ingrained in your heart and soul. It's part of who you are. You couldn't paint as you do if it weren't. And what about Artagan's warning? Who benefits if you forget who you are? I can only think of one."

Leah cuts me off. "No one has persuaded me to do anything. Quitting school is my idea. Like you said, I need to become good at this. Until I realized I was good at the hocus-pocus mind-control crap, I wasn't sure that was a possibility. I have hope now, and don't you dare try to take it from me." Her gaze falls away. "Besides, I will keep painting. I never said I wouldn't."

Frustration swells inside me, but I stamp it down. "All right. If this is what you believe you need to do, so be it. I'll support you in your decision."

"But you don't agree."

"No," I say with a shake of my head.

"Your support's enough for now." Leah gives me a little smirk. "At least Artagan agrees with me. He said I have all the time in the world to pursue art school later if I want to. And for the foreseeable future, my focus needs to be on my new job."

Her words take me by surprise. "Artagan agrees?"

Leah runs her hands along her jeans as I do on mine when I'm nervous. "Artagan found me here. He claimed it was a coincidence." She shrugs, looking skeptical. "I told him about the feelings and my decision to quit school. He didn't think I was crazy. He listened and agreed it would be best for now. He even suggested he might be able to pull a few strings and get me into École des Beaux-Arts in

Paris. Down the road, of course, but can you imagine? Art school in Paris!"

My jaw tenses. "Did he now?"

Leah nods and draws in a quick breath.

"There's more, isn't there?" My throat constricts in anticipation of her answer.

"Yes." A faint redness blooms across her cheeks.

"Give it to me. I'm sure my imagination can conjure far worse things than reality. Then again, maybe not, since not in a million years would I have dreamed up the possibility of you quitting school."

She scowls at me. "He's renting a house in the West End. And since I can't live in the dorms any longer, he suggested I move in there."

Inhaling, I push from the crates and move to the pier's handrail. Resting my hands on the splintering wood, I glower at the dark water. "I was going to suggest you move in with me. You're there most of the time, anyway. I know it's not much, but whatever I have is yours."

"Mr. Traditional wants me to shack up at his place?"

"Well, I..." I feel the tips of my ears growing hot. I turn to face her, leaning back against the rail.

Leah stares at me, lips puckered into a teasing smirk.

"You said all the kids are doing it nowadays," I say and then chuckle, feeling uncomfortable in my own skin. When I continue, my voice is formal and stiff. "I figured I could sleep on the sofa if need be. But it appears you and Artagan have it all figured out."

"You need to learn to let people finish before you get all pissy. I told him I couldn't move in unless you came, too." Leah slips off the crates and walks to my side. "I should have talked to you first. I get that. And if you're not comfortable with the living arrangement, we won't go. Moving in with you sounds like heaven, even with you sleeping on the sofa. I just never thought you'd think officially living together was a good idea. With appearances and all," she adds, grinning, but the smile doesn't touch her eyes.

Cupping her cheek in my palm, I run my thumb over the soft curve of her lower lip, eyeing her mouth. She bends her head into my touch. I kiss her on the forehead then between her eyebrows.

"When you move in, we can set up a studio in the living room. By the windows so you have natural light. I know my apartment's small, but we'll make it work." I pause. "I'd suggest checking with your mum first, but I get the distinct impression that matters little these days. And whatever will Grady think?" My expression twists into teasing horror. "Maybe it's best we don't tell him."

"We're engaged. He'll expect it," Leah says. My brows dart upward. "*Everyone* expects it, Jack."

"Well, I realize your friends won't care, but I'm sure your mother will."

She laughs. "My parents lived together for three years before they got married. She was pregnant with Grady."

"Oh... I see." I swallow hard. My sense of propriety was losing against everyone, including my growing libido, not to mention Leah's sex appeal. Maybe suggesting she move in wasn't the best strategy for my abstinence-until-marriage plan.

Leah stifles a laugh, probably prompted by my horror-struck expression. She rolls up on her tiptoes and brushes her lips along my cheek, igniting a fire deep inside me. I breathe in her perfume, causing my heart rate to speed up. *Yup, definitely a bad idea.*

"If it makes you feel better," she says, saving me from improper thoughts, "I'm holding on to the job at the coffee shop as long as I can. I owe it to Rachel."

"At least that's something." I rest my chin on top of her head. "Just promise me you'll remember who you are. We can make it through anything as long as you do that."

"I promise. And you promise never to let me forget."

"Never." I smile.

A little past one, Artagan strolls into the bookstore, all smiles as if he just won the lottery. I grimace and turn, pushing the heaping book cart toward the back of the shop, its squeaky wheels only adding to my annoyance.

"I can tell by the look on your face, Leah filled you in on her decision," Artagan says, following me.

"She did." I turn to face him. "École des Beaux-Arts?"

"What?" Artagan raises his hands in surrender. "An old friend of mine is the dean of students."

"Right." I roll my eyes and resume my course toward the back.

Rare Books is an awkward place for the conversation I've been rehashing in my head all morning. No matter his reasoning, some faux pas have carried through the centuries, and one of them is asking another's betrothed to move in, whether he extended the invitation to me or not. Artagan is older than I am. He shouldn't need an explanation in proper etiquette. However, our man-to-man chat is a conversation best saved for private. Despite the quiet corners, with Sally in the back room and the occasional customer, the shop holds no privacy.

"Call it a preemptive strike," he persists. "Leah believes the decision to quit school was her own. Maybe it was. But in case it wasn't... ever played chess?"

"Ages ago," I say, walking into the darkened aisle with rows of classics stacked to the ceiling.

"Then you know sometimes you have to sacrifice a pawn or two to capture the king. If this isn't Leah's own decision but Death manipulating her, the promise of École des Beaux-Arts will keep her dream alive in her heart."

"So you're lying to her. Don't promise things you can't deliver."

Artagan looks offended, an annoyed frown wrinkling

his stern brow. "Who says I can't deliver? Antoinette would do just about anything for me." He winks and lifts a leather-bound copy of *Wuthering Heights* from the book cart. Flipping through the yellowed pages, he smiles. "Hmm, the Brontë sisters. Such a delightful pair."

If the comment is a distraction tactic, the ploy works. One of my eyebrows rises in speculation. "You're suggesting you knew Charlotte and Emily Brontë? No. You know what?" I say, snatching the book out of his grip. "Call it a hunch, but I have a feeling I don't want to know. And you wonder why moving in with the likes of you is bothersome. Your bedroom probably has a revolving door." I shove the timeworn book onto the shelf with the others, using more force than needed.

"Revolving door. It's not a bad idea, you know." Grabbing another book off my cart, Artagan hums an old pub favorite—a song about long nights and women with loose morals—while perusing its antiquated pages.

"It's a good thing you're the way you are," I say, interrupting his melody. "Immortal, I mean. With your kind of behavior, I'm sure you've been at the wrong end of a blade defending your dishonor and the ruined reputation of some lady too many times to count."

Artagan chuckles as if laughing at his own private joke and leans against the shelf. "Aren't we high and mighty today?" His tone is condescending. "I see my little proposal of moving in has rubbed you the wrong way."

"What do you think?"

"I *think* you're overreacting. Not to mention being a bit childish."

I mutter an unrepeatable suggestion of what he can do with his opinions, not bothering to look at him.

He laughs again. "Just so you know, I fully expected you to join Leah. *Mi casa es su casa.* I'm surprised you haven't scurried home to that rathole of yours and started packing as we speak, since you're not the type who's comfortable with his *betrothed* living with an unattached man as dashing as myself." He pauses. "In my house of depravity."

I glare at him but say nothing.

His attention wanders back to the book. "Before you make any rash decisions, though, you may want to hear my news. The council is arriving within the week. Including Domitilla, I might add."

"I didn't expect them to come so soon," I say.

He shrugs, seeming not to notice my reaction. "There's no formal meeting set as yet, though Thanatos has acquired our new temporary headquarters—an abandoned church on High Street. So we can expect them all very soon."

Nothing unexpected, I reassure myself, ignoring the lump lodged in my throat.

There's no trace of any grave concern in Artagan's expression, but I can tell he's carefully monitoring it. "Having Leah move in is a precaution. That's all."

"Jack," Sally says, appearing at the entrance of the aisle. "I need you to—" She glances up from her papers and stops dead. Her gaze narrows, crinkling the fine lines around her eyes and across her weathered cheeks. Her thin lips twist from a smile into a grimace. Just as abruptly as she appeared, Sally turns and walks away, disappearing behind the tall shelves.

Artagan cocks his head. "Well, that was interesting."

"Yeah." I step forward and then spin around. "Please tell me you don't know her? Tell me she is not one of your many conquests. I think I'd have to scrub my brain with lye."

"Both you and your brain will be happy to know I've never seen your boss before in my life. And if her virtue isn't intact, it has nothing to do with me."

"You sure?"

"Why would I lie about that? Fear of you?"

My eyes roam back in the direction Sally disappeared.

"She's a good judge of people. She probably can tell you're a philandering asshole from a mile away."

Artagan tosses the book onto the pile. "And she'd be right. Looking forward to being roomies." He is still grinning from ear to ear when he vanishes into the shadows.

The remainder of the day is quiet—categorizing books, packing shipments, and waiting on customers. All conversation between Sally and me is casual. Although I catch her staring at me now and again—her eyebrows drawn together, expression tightened—she doesn't mention Artagan. I am more than happy to let the topic drop. I have much heavier matters on my mind. Besides, if Artagan's lying and they have shared some tawdry romance, I have no desire to know even a smidgeon about the details.

However, to my dismay, as soon as the open sign swings to Closed, Sally turns to me. "Who was that man with you earlier?" she asks, her voice devoid of emotion.

"He's my uncle," I improvise. If she's aware he's family, that may keep her questions to a minimum. I hope.

Her stare is unmoving. "I thought you said all your family had passed?"

"Yes, he and my mother had a falling out long ago. She told me he was dead. Apparently, she lied." *Not bad for on the fly.* Although I hate diminishing my mother's good character, desperate times sometimes demand casualties.

"Take care, Jack. There's something about him I don't trust. Maybe it's what your mother saw in him as well. The reason she lied."

"He's okay. But thanks for worrying about me."

Sally pats my arm. "You're a good boy. I've always had a good vibe about you. I'd hate to see you fall in with the wrong sort." With that, she wanders off toward the back room.

I shrug off Sally's warning. With her keen awareness of people, it's only natural she'd notice Artagan's dark nature. Artagan's revelation, however, sticks with me.

The Concilium Animarum is coming, descending upon Portland like the last plague of Egypt.

Later that night, as I lie in bed with Leah nestled to my side, my stomach churns. Wide awake, I stare at the ceiling throughout the night. Although not a shock, the predictability of this event doesn't prevent the dread burrowing its way into every cell of my body.

CHAPTER EIGHT

"**S**UBTLE. UNDERSTATED,**"** I SAY, MY tone landing somewhere between sarcastic and amused. I walk up the wide granite steps of the Georgian Revival, with my black duffel slung over my shoulder and a couple of boxes that belong to Leah in my arms. Portland's West End is the affluent side of town, stocked with elegant mansions and stately brick townhouses. Artagan's new home is what I expected. With its towering white granite columns and ornate honey-colored facade—a hue bearing a striking resemblance to the buildings of Lidcombe—the house is lavish and completely over the top.

Part of me believes this little arrangement is more about keeping tabs on me than a watchful eye on Leah. Although I've stifled my instinctive reactions, it's possible Artagan doubts my recent turnabout will last under the added pressure of the Concilium Animarum's arrival. After the behavior I displayed the last time I encountered the council, ending with me socking Death in the jaw, I suppose any prudence on his part is justified. If I'm right and this is Artagan's motive, game, set, and match to him because his little ruse worked. I'm here, bags in hand. While I cannot fault Artagan for any unease, I'm determined to prove him wrong. Leah's well-being demands it.

I turn.

Leah stands frozen on the sidewalk, a carton of books clasped in her hands. Her eyes squint into the Sunday midmorning sun, and her mouth hangs open. I cannot help laughing at her expression.

"I kept the lease on the old apartment if you've changed your mind," I tease.

"I'm coming." She climbs the stairs, hesitating after each footfall to gawk and study the old manor further. "Are you sure this is the address he gave you?"

I nod.

"Of all the places Artagan could have chosen, he picked Westward Mansion. I mean, when he mentioned the place was on the Western Promenade, I knew it would be roomy, but holy crap."

I huff. "Why am I not surprised? Of course it has a name. The monstrosity is big enough to have its own zip code."

"And it's haunted. A group of ghost hunters did a show on the mansion a year ago. They caught a bunch of evidence, some noises, and even a few orbs."

"The house is old. It's bound to make some groans and squeaks."

She flicks her hand, waving away my interruption. "Captain Abram Andrews, the man who had the house commissioned, killed his wife and one of their servants in an upstairs bedroom after discovering they were hooking up."

I grimace up at the upper-floor windows.

"According to the show, the captain went on to murder everyone else in the house—his kids, the rest of the servants, even his mother. Thirty-four in all. There's a poem, too." Leah smiles and recites the poem.

"When Captain Andrews found his wife,
He grabbed his blade and took her life,
But when the captain killed her lover,

He slaughtered them all, including Mother."

"Well, that's cheery."

Leah grins. "The stories also say no man between the ages of nineteen and twenty-two has survived living in the house since. They all died mysteriously."

"By the captain's ghostly hand, no doubt."

"That's what they say. And you don't look a day over twenty." She cringes in mock horror.

I laugh. "Under the circumstances, I believe the old captain has met his match," I say with a wink.

On the porch, still chuckling, I juggle the boxes and shift most of the weight onto one arm to ring the doorbell. A muffled sound of chimes tolls from inside, and the massive oak door swings open. Artagan's beaming face greets us, a cigarette dangling from his lips.

"Captain Andrews, I presume," I say, bowing my head.

Leah snorts.

"Hitting the sauce a little early, huh, Jack?"

"That would explain my lack of judgment. I am moving in here of my own volition, remember?" I say.

"True." Artagan's grin widens. "Welcome home."

The grand foyer is dusky for an entrance hall as imposing as this one. Constructed of dark tiger oak, the trim and wainscoting diminish any brightness cast by the sconces. The only furniture, a grandfather clock, ticks from the far side of the sweeping staircase.

Despite the beauty, an unmistakable heaviness weighs on me. Although I've never been what you'd call a believer, I can't shake the feeling I'm being watched by unseen eyes. Hairs rise on the nape of my neck and the back of my arms. The only haunting I've ever experienced came from memories, not ghostly apparitions. Nevertheless, I'm beginning to wonder if Leah's stories might hold truth in them after all.

From the brightness in Leah's eyes, I can tell she's a

staunch believer. She studies the room, her expression teetering between wonder and trepidation.

"Lovely, isn't it? The place cost me plenty, but it's worth every last cent," Artagan says, mistaking her sentiment as one of awe and not eerie curiosity. "All this, not to mention a carriage house around back. There's room to park both your vehicles in there, if you like."

I bend my head in thanks.

With my duffel and knapsack, and Leah's six boxes, two matching cherry-colored suitcases, and three totes—why a wisp of a girl needs so much luggage, I'll never understand—stacked by the stairs, Artagan offers to show us around before we settle in.

Every room is as extravagantly decorated as the last, with intricate woodwork and lavish furnishings throughout. The dining room is the most Victorian. A long claw-foot table takes center stage, skirted by mahogany Queen Anne armchairs. Overhead hangs a gilt-bronze crystal chandelier, sending speckles of light dancing to and fro across the mustard-colored walls. I feel my posture straighten by the second. Slouched shoulders were frowned upon in the nineteenth century, especially by my mother.

"And through that passageway"—Artagan points toward the back of the dining room to a darkened doorway—"there's a handful of bedrooms, the domestics' quarters back in the day. At the very end of the hall, I've set up my office, but we can save that for later. Come, I'll show you upstairs."

The upper floors are just as formal. Leah's room is furnished much like mine—a four-poster bed covered with a quilted coverlet, a fireplace with an intricate mantel, and a winged settee sitting beside it—with one exception. At the far end, by the northern window, stand an easel and a table filled with art supplies.

"So you don't forget who you are," Artagan says.

Leah looks at me, eyebrows raised.

"Don't blame me." I toss my hands up in surrender. "I didn't say a word."

"You can have the rest of the day to settle in," he says with a quick bob of his head. "Oh, and by the way, if you see a flaxen-bearded Viking wandering the halls, it's only Otmar. He'll be staying with us."

I keep my expression steady. "Otmar?"

"Yes. Kemisi, too. I trust them. Well, as much as I trust anyone," he says. "Besides, having them here provides us with extra sets of eyes and ears, just in case."

His words halt my thoughts. A cold prickle blooms at the base of my neck, and I push it away. My forehead furrows. "Because of Domitilla? And our involvement in Vita's death?"

"Revenge would be in no one's best interest. Death has made that clear. Unlike her sister, Domitilla is a self-preservationist. However, they do say not to put all your eggs in one basket, which is why Otmar and Kemisi will stay here. Only as a precaution, nothing more," he adds.

"Let them know we appreciate their help," Leah says.

Artagan bows then walks toward the door. "Meet me in my office tomorrow morning at ten o'clock."

"Tomorrow? But it's Thanksgiving," she says.

He stops. "Is it?"

Leah nods.

"Well, I'm sorry, lassie, but our time is seldom our own. Make sure you bring your jacket. We'll be going on a field trip of sorts." With that, he slips out of the room, closing the door behind him.

My heart sinks. I wonder if "field trip" is code for much bigger things, like another gathering. With the question of me tagging along still not answered, my heart descends farther into the pit of my stomach. I peer at Leah, who has conveniently directed her focus to her new art supplies.

I suck in a deep breath. "Sorry about your holiday. You said nothing about it. Was your mum expecting you?"

"Us. Mom was expecting us." Leah lifts a paintbrush and sweeps her finger back and forth along its bristles. "I didn't tell you because I hadn't decided if I wanted to go yet. She's not thrilled with me for quitting school, and well... I'm tired of lying to her. I knew if I told you, you'd try to talk me into it. But I guess none of that matters now."

I want to come up with a declaration so brilliant it will sweep all her misgivings away. Falling short, I settle for kissing the top of her head.

"I'll text her. Tell her I have to work. At least that's not a lie." She laughs, but the tone falls flat.

"About that. I was wondering if you've decided if I, er—" I suck in a quick breath of air. "May I accompany you and Artagan on your jaunt?"

"Jaunt?" Leah snorts.

"I know you're afraid I'll see you in a different light, but that couldn't be further from the truth. I'm no altar boy, despite what you think." Again, the confession of Hake's premature death slips to the tip of my tongue, sending a flurry of regrets through me.

Leah stares. She must see something in my eyes because her brow wrinkles.

I glance at the floor, preparing for the questions sure to follow. But none come.

Accompanied by a long exhalation, she answers, "You can come."

I step closer and kiss her forehead on the small space between her eyebrows. "Thank you," I whisper.

After we finish unpacking, we spend the rest of the afternoon in my room in much-needed normalcy—me sprawled out on the bed, reading my tattered copy of Gaskell's *North and South* for the umpteenth time, and

Leah sitting cross-legged, back pressed against my side, laptop open.

"Is it Francis?"

I look up. "Is who Francis?"

"Your middle name," Leah says. "From your reaction, I'm betting the name's embarrassing, and because nowadays, Francis is more of a girl's name. I mean, it can't be Fred or Frank. Nothing's embarrassing there." She gives me a sideward glance. Her face twists into a pouting expression she saves for those moments when she's annoyed or concentrating.

With a sigh, I turn my eyes back to my book.

"I will figure this out, you know."

"I have no doubt."

"Then why don't you just tell me?" she says, exasperated.

"Where would be the fun in that?" I grin.

"Francisco?"

I snort a laugh. "*Olé.*"

Gradually, our conversation dwindles until we're only talking now and again as Leah slips deeper and deeper into her research.

The next morning, coats in hand, Leah and I hurry through the dining room to a cramped doorway tucked at the back corner. A lack of windows leaves the hall shadowed. Although the rest of the house smells of sage from smudging, in the hallway, any trace of the sickly-sweet scent has vanished. Odd. I'd have expected Artagan to lock up his office tighter than Fort Knox.

I knock on the door at the end of the corridor and earn a quick "Come in."

Artagan hunches over a desk—a massive rolltop, each cubbyhole bulging with files and parchments—poring over a book. He doesn't look up as we enter. Instead, he puts his finger in the air, indicating he needs a moment. My attention roves the well-stocked bookshelves surrounding us, making the room seem more library than office. Calf-bound tomes sit alongside paperbacks and ancient scrolls, all crammed in well past the bursting point. The titles with metallic gilt etched on the spines are in French, Latin, Spanish, and languages I don't recognize. From the names I can read, they all have a common theme—folklore.

"Do you like my little collection?" Artagan says, walking around the desk toward us, a tumbler of Scotch held precariously in his hand.

"Impressive," I say.

He smiles. "There are no less than fifteen more boxes in storage. Some might say I have a problem."

I shrug. Artagan raises his glass and downs the liquor in one gulp. "We are on a schedule, but first things first." Abandoning the empty tumbler on a nearby side table, he returns to his desk and begins rummaging through its drawers. When his hand reemerges, a small antique pocket watch dangles from a dainty gold chain between his fingers. "A present. I hope it will help you remember the reason you do what you do," he says as he takes Leah's hand and sets the necklace in her palm.

A soft expression settles on Leah's lips, and she runs her fingers over the flowers etched on the front lid. "Daisies."

"Your favorite."

Her eyes move from the timepiece to meet Artagan's gaze. "How did you know?"

"Call it an educated guess." He says nothing more.

"Well, it's a beautiful pocket watch. Thank you."

"Ah, but sometimes things aren't what they appear. Open it." The inside reveals that the watch is a locket with a picture of Grady and Leah's mother on one side and a picture of me on the other. "Your family," Artagan says, "and the reason you carry on."

Moisture pools in Leah's eyes as she studies the photos.

With a jerk of her head, her eyes snap up, her forehead crinkling. "Where did you get this?"

"I pinched them out of your dorm a while back," Artagan says. "Don't fret. Those are just copies. I didn't cut up the originals."

"You went through my things?"

His voice dips into sarcasm. "Yes, your underwear drawer was thrilling. No worries, I saw nothing that wasn't out on display for all the world to see."

"That's not the point. You can't just march into someone's room—"

"My apologies," Artagan says, but in a way that suggests he'd do it again. "Now, press on the pin there, the one that appears to be the winding stem."

Leah mutters under her breath but does as she's asked. As her finger pushes down on the tiny pin, the back of the locket springs open, exposing a secret compartment. Inside, nestled in a pillow of navy velvet, is a small green pill I recognize at once to be hemlock.

I concentrate on my poker face, steering my focus away from the pill.

"It's a mixture of hemlock and salt," Artagan says. "The only thing that can kill us."

Comprehension streaks across Leah's face before she conceals her emotions behind a set of pursed lips.

"A few of us immortals carry the concoction on our person for protection. Despite Death's wish that we could be a big happy family, we're an untrusting bunch, sometimes for good reason—Vita, for example, and now perhaps her twin. For me, it's also a backup plan, in case I push Death too far. The chances you'll ever need it for that reason are slim to none. Look at me, over six hundred years old and still kicking in spite of my antics. It's best we keep it our secret. The other council members needn't know," he says. "Although I'm sure they'll suspect."

With a quick nod, she slips the chain over her head. The locket falls to her heart.

"Now, on to the reason for our meeting." Artagan clears his throat. "Death asked for a report on your progress. He took an interest in your mind-control abilities. Therefore, this afternoon, per his request, we will show off just how well you're doing."

Leah's mouth falls open, and she shuffles back a step or two, her hand cupping her locket. "So all the visions I've been having... he expects me to gather all those people at once? I'm not ready!"

"Yes, you are. I know it's a large job, but you will only need to focus on one person—the train operator."

Leah crosses her arms as if to form a barrier between herself and Artagan. "Great," she says, her voice loaded with sarcasm. "But what about shadow walking?"

"What about it?" Artagan asks, scrunching his brow.

"I've done it twice, once with Death and once with you, and both times I was just tagging along... and... and I'm not ready." Her voice grows urgent, the words piling up, one on top of another. "Besides, if he's only interested in seeing my mind-control abilities, why can't I do whatever I have to from here?"

I entwine our fingers, giving her hand a reassuring squeeze.

Artagan raises his hand to cut off my protest.

"Distance comes with disadvantages, at least in the beginning. So until you develop your skills, the closer you are to your target, the better. We can't risk any mistakes, not today. As for the shadow walking, we've talked about it. There are no tricks involved. All you have to do before stepping into the darkness is concentrate on the soul in your charge. Remember? After that, your instinct, for lack of a better word, will guide you. Like a compass that always points north, our compulsion always points us to the soul we must gather."

"And what about the way back? You said getting back is more difficult," Leah presses.

"I said it takes practice. And I'll be right by your side in case we end up in the drink." He chuckles. "Traveling to *any* place you wish is tricky. The sons and daughters of Death come by the skill naturally. We adoptees have to cultivate it. However, that level of shadow travel takes decades to master. It requires the ability to distinguish between the unique souls of a place and then focusing on their tenor."

I squint. "Soul of a place? Tenor?"

"How to explain?" Artagan sinks into a chair. He steeples his hands and presses his fingers to his mouth, thinking, and then his expression brightens. "It's similar to a good Scotch." He speaks with reverence, the way my father spoke of his Creator. "Much like Scotch absorbs some of its flavor from the barrel it's stored in, a place absorbs the impression of all the people who have lived there. In the words of Henry Wadsworth Longfellow, 'All houses wherein men have lived and died are haunted.' I assume you've heard this house's history."

Leah and I both nod.

"Tragedy imprints itself on even the inanimate." Artagan lets out a bitter chuckle. "People call places like this haunted, but that's not the case. A building with such a past as this house has an amplified tenor so strong that even mortals can pick up on it."

"So Jack is right." Leah's posture slumps. "The place isn't haunted. It's just seen a lot of action."

"Sorry to disappoint. For us, these places become beacons in the void. Although you might not travel without restrictions for the foreseeable future, soon enough, you'll hop from tainted location to tainted location like a stone skipping across a pond." Artagan pauses, leaning back into his chair. "After tonight, I'll block access to the main house, but you can still gain entry through the shadows of the grounds or the carriage house. I've smudged most of the rooms already, and once we've finished with this gathering, I'll smudge my office. But enough chitchat. We need to get down to business. So let's see if you've been paying attention. Who's on the agenda tonight?"

A grimace flickers across Leah's face. "There are so many," she mutters.

"I know that's how it appears. But there's only one you must control. The others' fates lie in the decisions of that one. Now concentrate. Who stands out from the clutter of souls in your mind?"

Leah's gaze falls to the floor while she thinks. After a moment, she says, "The train engineer."

"Any scenarios?"

Leah presses her lips tight together as if she's fighting thoughts in her head. "What if I'm wrong? What if this doesn't work?" She places her hand on her locket.

"No more stalling. It's become a habit. You're not wrong, and you know it. Trust yourself. Trust your gut," Artagan encourages.

After a moment, Leah's expression surrenders. "Her name is Lori Stapleton. She's an alcoholic. Been sober for years, but the temptation is still there. Her fiancé broke up with her yesterday. She bought a bottle of vodka this morning but then changed her mind and went to work, hoping it would take her mind off him and the alcohol. She has it with her, though. I made sure of it. It's hidden under the seat."

"And after that first nip, she won't be able to stop. Very good. Exactly what I would do. You'll need to remind her how much she misses her man. Tempt her into that first drink. Best to do that now, to give her time to become impaired."

Leah breathes deep and shivers a bit, her attention drifting to the floor. "Does vodka taste anything like wine? I had that once at a wedding."

A look of outrage springs to Artagan's features. "No! It certainly is not! Like wine? What's the world coming to?" He shakes his head. "Unfortunately, it's an oversight we'll have to remedy another time. You're stalling again."

Physically uncomfortable, Leah takes a calming breath and closes her eyes. Minutes drag before Leah opens her eyes again.

"Done?" Artagan asks.

"I think so," she says, not looking at him.

Artagan gestures to my leather jacket folded in my lap, his gaze glued on Leah. "I take it you've relented, and Jack will join us tonight?"

Drawing her mouth into a straight line, Leah bites at her lower lip and then nods.

Artagan turns. "Remember my rules?" he asks me.

"Keep my mouth shut, and no meddling," I recite, sounding very much like a schoolchild.

He nods once, seeming satisfied. "Let's go. And Jack, stay close, and follow us." Lacking any hesitation, he strides into the shadow on the far wall.

Leah follows. Beckoning to me over her left shoulder, she disappears.

I press my palms against the wall and run my hands over its solid surface. The mahogany paneling seems to disintegrate under my touch, and my hands sink into the shadow as if pushing through water. "Curious." I pull my hands away, and the wall solidifies. I wonder why I never did this before. It would have come in handy on quite a few occasions. I'm betting the answer is as simple as I didn't know I could. Besides, Artagan mentioned shadow walking involved faith. The spiritual gift has never been my strong suit. I recall Sally's words on the subject. *'Powerful stuff. Just a tad can move mountains.' Or walls, it would seem.* I smirk, staring at the solid surface.

Artagan's voice floods into my mind. *Any day, Jack. They say seeing is believing.*

I take a deep breath and step into the mist of the shadow. The darkness is sudden and complete, folding me in its penetrating chill, where I assume Leah and Artagan are waiting.

CHAPTER NINE

ONCE WHEN I WAS A child, my brother, Henry, tossed me into the shallows of Walker Pond when he found me asleep by the water's edge. I had skipped out on chores, leaving Henry to do them all himself, and I deserved what I got. I remember waking out of a peaceful sleep disoriented, not knowing which way was up, panic squeezing every ounce of oxygen from my lungs. Although lacking, it's the best description I can conjure of what I'm feeling now.

Groping through the murk, the world around me tilts and spins, messing with any sense of space or direction. The swirling motion causes my stomach to revolt, bile searing my throat. Unable to see through the unrelenting darkness, I rely on my hearing, but all is silent except for the sound of my heavy breathing echoing in my ears.

Something tugs at my sleeve, and I jerk away. The night I made my bargain with the council, I saw what lives in those shadows. That creature's red eyes are forever burned into my memory. My heart pounds, and my breathing speeds up. My eyes dart back and forth, but I see nothing except the blackness. A hand grabs me tight under the bicep, iron fingers digging into my flesh. Or are they claws? I contort, doing my best to twist out of the grip, but despite my struggle, the hand drags me forward. My field of vision bursts from a dark nothingness into a dimly lit void. Artagan and Leah stand in front of me.

"Faith, Jack. Find a wee bit now and again, would you?" Artagan grumbles.

"You could have helped him. Led him through," Leah snaps.

"I'm not the man's babysitter."

"Drop it, please. I'm fine," I say. "You need to focus on this job."

Her eyes are locked on mine. Leah's expression is one I recognize. She's concerned, and I wager after that spectacle, she's having second thoughts about letting me tag along. Who could blame her?

"Are you sure you're all right?" she breathes.

Embarrassed by my lack of faith, I nod, fixing my gaze on the scene in front of me.

Muted and lacking color, silhouettes and blurs of motion dance in front of us as if we're looking out fogged glass. As the murk recedes, it reveals an empty train station. A slanted overhang extends out to the edge of a stone-paved platform. Except for the occasional flooding pool of light cast by one of the suspended lamps, the boarding area lies in shadow. From our vantage point, we're emerging from a shadow along the station's rear wall.

I'm drenched in sweat and still a bit dizzy. The thought of fresh air beckons me. I step forward, but Artagan takes hold of my shoulder and shakes his head. Then, counting to two on his fingers, he points to the right. The slow rapping of high heels echoes down the long, paved platform. Through a thin veil of haze, I see two figures approach— an older gentleman supported by a petite younger woman. Although age and time mar the man's face, the similarities between him and his escort are plain—same broad-tipped nose and diamond-shaped chin. Father and daughter would be my guess.

As the two draw close, the man's foot catches on an uneven pavestone, sending him staggering toward us. It takes every ounce of restraint for me not to reach from the shadow and grab his arm as he stumbles into the wall. The daughter rushes to his side. Wrapping her arm around his waist, she props a shoulder under his armpit. Through it all, her expression remains unhampered. Either the girl's calm by nature, or she has done this before.

"I'm fine. Leave me be," he says, attempting to brush her away.

His daughter grumbles under her breath but complies.

The man sags against the wall, wheezing as he tries to catch his breath. Even though he shows no sign of detecting us, I hold still, not moving a muscle. At this close distance, it's clear he's not as old as I thought. Whatever he suffers from, his battle has been long and drawn out, leaving its unmistakable mark. The dark-violet circles under his hollow eyes emphasize the pasty-gray color of his skin. Deep depressions dent his cheeks, adding to his near-death appearance. As his strained expression turns imploring, the man shifts his gaze to the wall and stares straight at Artagan. Only an inch stands between them.

The muscle at the corner of Artagan's mouth twitches.

"We should've brought your wheelchair," the young woman says, drawing the man's attention away.

"Nonsense," he mutters then pushes away from the wall.

"Are you sure you're up to this, Dad?"

"Like I said, I'm fine. Besides, your aunt is expecting us," he protests. After some persistent urging, he sighs and takes his daughter's outstretched arm, and the two lumber down the long train platform, vanishing around the far corner.

Leah lets out a long breath. "Could he see us?" she asks.

"No, no matter what it seemed." Artagan fishes a small

pewter flask from his breast pocket, engraved with a coat of arms, a phase in Latin inscribed beneath the crest. It's been over a century since my last Latin lesson, but I'm able to translate the flourished script with some difficulty. *Truth, the daughter of time,* it reads.

After taking a quick nip, he glances back at Leah. "I know he doesn't appear to have long on this earth, but you'll find looks can be deceiving. Sometimes a man who seems to stand at death's door can live for years, while one who looks as healthy as a horse can drop dead without the slightest notice. Death likes to keep them guessing."

"But if you know he wants to die?" I ask, shifting my focus in the direction where the man disappeared.

"The bottom line is that mortals do not decide their death. Not how, not where, not when. And tonight is not that gentleman's night." Artagan's expression shifts from one of indifference to one with a distinct flavor of bitterness. *Unless you'd like to take care of him yourself?*

A cold prickle stirs at the base of my neck. I look away, shaking my head.

Artagan lets out an emotionless chuckle. "Didn't think so," he mutters. His smugness is infuriating.

I ignore him and walk down the platform toward Leah, who now stands a few paces away, studying an oversized subway map. Under a pane of plastic, colored lines branch out from the center in angular patterns.

"I thought there was a turn after Charles Station," she says, her finger running over a straight portion of the red line.

"Is it there or not?" Artagan asks, his foul mood from the previous event lingering.

Leah hesitates for a moment. "Yes, it's there. Right after the tunnel. I can see it here," she says, pointing to her temple. "According to the map, the next station is closed for renovation. I was thinking it's a pretty sharp turn, so if the conductor is speeding, that should work, don't you think?"

Artagan bobs his head, outwardly impressed. "With that curve, anything over forty will do the trick. And we can step into the shadows after Charles." Satisfied with the plan, he falls silent, sipping from his flask.

My eyes wander from Artagan to Leah. She's staring again, and from her taut expression, she's worrying. Probably about me. I feign a grin.

"You look better. You were green there for a bit. I should have warned you. Shadow walking is like riding the Tilt-A-Whirl at the fair."

"First off, stop worrying about me. I refuse to be a distraction. Second, the comparison wouldn't have helped. I've never ridden a Tilt-A-Whirl, and I don't think I ever will. Nothing about that experience was a selling point. Shadow, one. Me, zero." I wink, compelling the corners of my lips upward.

My tactic works, at least for the moment. Leah giggles. "That's nothing. You should see Grady after he rides the merry-go-round. Way greener than you. He still rides it every year and swears up and down he's not sick. You'd think—"

A train's whistle blows, cutting off Leah's words. Her face falls sober, looking uncomfortable once again.

Artagan pats her shoulder but otherwise ignores her nerves. "Your lead," he reminds her.

In the distance, a pinpoint of light spears through the darkness. Leah swallows hard. Her fingers wrap around her locket. Taking her free hand, I give it a gentle squeeze before letting go.

She leans her head against my shoulder and says, "I'm glad you're here."

"Where else would I be?" I kiss the top of her head.

The train slows in front of us, jerking before coming to a stop. I trail Artagan and Leah, stepping into a car filled with unsuspecting passengers. My eyes dart from face to face. Almost a hundred at a quick estimate, and there are four other cars besides this one, each full. Against my better judgment, I lean to Artagan's ear. "Which ones?" I whisper.

He smiles without an ounce of genuineness and whirls his pointer finger in the air.

My heart migrates into my throat. "All of them?" I mouth.

Except one. A vagrant sound asleep in the last car.

My eyes shy away from the throng of unsuspecting faces—all laughing, carefree souls who will soon be no more to this earth than a loved one's memory. A weightiness settles in the back of my throat, and I wish I'd taken Artagan up on his offer of a few swigs of liquid courage. Dragging my sweaty palms up and down my pant legs, I steel my emotions and look up, my gaze searching for Leah. She and Artagan have moved toward the engineer booth, only the back of their heads visible through the crowd. Weaving my way through the people, I follow.

As the train picks up speed, it lurches, jolting me sideways. I stagger and knock into an elderly lady. Beads scatter as her necklace hits the floor and roll into the dark corners of the car, most certain never to be seen again. An ornate silver crucifix lies at my feet.

A rosary. Of all the stupid... And at a time like this.

I bend and pick up the small cross off the dirty floor. From the intricate craftsmanship and the worn edges, the rosary is an antique. And by the lady's dismayed expression, it's probably a family heirloom. After brushing off the sand and grime on my sleeve, I hold out the pendant to the lady. "My apologies," I say.

Wrinkles stretch along the woman's age-worn cheeks as she smiles at me. Then without a word, she reaches out, but instead of taking her crucifix, she grabs my arm and yanks me to her. She's remarkably strong for a woman her age. The friendliness vanishes from her face, and she mouths, "I know why you're here." Her vigorous pale-gray eyes flick toward Leah and Artagan and then back to me.

The hairs on the back of my neck stand erect, and polite or not, I stare.

"Right now, you're wondering how I know so much?" Her dark smirk widens. "And what threat I might be to your plan."

A flush of adrenaline surges through my body. My eyes narrow, and the muscles in my jaw tense.

The woman releases my wrist. Settling back into her seat, she taps the cushion next to her, inviting me to sit. "I'm sure your friends can do without you for a little while. Gladys, by the way."

With her petite stature and puff of pure-white hair, it's hard to see this woman as threatening. Nevertheless, I know all too well never to judge a book by its cover. Although she might be nothing more than off her trolley, it's a risk I'm unwilling to chance. Who knows what havoc she could cause. Leah needs this gathering to go well. Death is watching. Therefore, I sit.

"I'm Jack," I say, resting my elbows on my knees. "So why are you here?"

Gladys smiles, seemingly delighted I'm playing along. "Because I decided today was the day. And unlike most, I can control my own destiny." She leans over and yanks an oversized patchwork bag out from under the seat. Riffling through its contents, she mumbles to herself. Her hand reemerges with a tin box—its sides dented and a scene of Santa and his reindeer flaking along the corners. She opens the lid and pushes the container toward me. "Gingersnap?"

"No, thank you." *God only knows what she put in them.*

"Suit yourself," she says, peering into the tin. "I'll admit they are better with tea, but no time for that, is there?"

Without taking a cookie for herself, she snaps the lid shut and stuffs it back into her bag.

"I haven't been on a train since I was a child, not since the Great Crash of '39. Do you remember it?"

I stare at her, shaking my head.

With no urging, Gladys continues. "I was one of five to survive. A miracle, they called me. My name was in all the papers. Losing both my mother and father at such an impressionable age—I was but thirteen—I didn't see my escape from death as such. Now, looking back, that's what it was. A miracle. Because of it, I've lived a remarkable life. Short by some standards, but long enough for me. We can't all be Endless, now, can we?"

My throat goes as dry as parchment, but I keep my face casual as if we are talking about the weather or some other mundane topic.

Gladys smooths out the skirt of her navy polka-dot dress with her palms. I see the struggle in her almond-shaped eyes—faith combating doubt. She tilts her chin up. "I want you to know I'm not scared. As I said, *I* chose to be here. On the other hand, I am anxious about the process, but I suppose that's only natural." She looks to me for confirmation. When she finds none, her firm expression wavers.

When she speaks again, the somber tone is gone, replaced by a jovial jaunt. "Oh, the things I've done. I was an opera singer back in the day. At twenty-nine, I sang with Edmund Chipp at the Royal Panopticon. It was quite an honor. The Queen herself came to hear us. Not bad for a girl from Cheapside. And I've traveled. Oh, have I traveled. I've sat on the banks of the Ganges, seen the Great Pyramids in all their glory—before the earthquake took their beauty—gleaming white in the high afternoon sun. I've witnessed the Northern Lights from the summit of Mount McKinley. Oh, what a sight. Yes, I've had a beautiful, adventurous life," she says, looking out the window.

My mind grapples with her words. I try to remember when the pyramids lost their luster. It was well before my time, that's for sure. But Edmund Chipp is a name I recognize. When I was a boy, my mother had made an uncharacteristic trip to London to hear him play. That would make Gladys close to my age. But I look twenty, and with her white hair and wrinkled skin, we appear generations apart.

Gladys goes on, a quizzical eye resting on me. "You've struggled. Lost love once. I can see it in your eyes."

I almost jump when she grabs me by the wrist. She twists my hand around, so the palm faces up. Then with a gentle touch like a goose-down feather, she traces each crease from my wrist to the base of my fingers, studying the crooked, gridded pattern as if they were telling her a story. "And you have more struggles to come." My stomach dips, and I pull my hand away, but I can't deny the truth in her words.

Gladys looks down, her long, graying lashes veiling her eyes. "Never mind this foolish old woman and her ramblings. I'm sure I don't know what I'm talking about half the time." When her gaze returns to mine, a reassuring smile flickers across her lips. "Always remember, 'It is not in the stars to hold our destiny but in ourselves.' I like to think I gave him that line, but I'm sure he wouldn't have agreed."

"Gave whom? William Shakespeare?" I ask as if the words hold no meaning.

"Yes, from *Julius Caesar*. William told me the Lord Chamberlain's Men did a wonderful job with its portrayal. Never saw the play myself. Back then, London was never a place I enjoyed."

I stare at her, still debating whether or not she's mad.

A robotic voice crackles from the speaker overhead. "Next stop Charles Station," it announces.

Time to go. Artagan's voice breaks into my thoughts.

Gladys's crooked knuckles turn white as she grips the crucifix, and she shrinks into her seat. Although questions still clutter my mind, the time for any inquisition is gone.

"Thank you for spending your time with me. It was a pleasure to meet you." Her voice comes out in a hush.

Now, Jack!

I nod to both of them and rise to my feet, but Gladys's bleak expression gives me pause. The lights flicker. Someone screams. Conflicted, I glance into the darkness— the way of my escape—but my feet don't move. When the lights return, Artagan and Leah have vanished.

As Charles Station flies by in a streak of colors, Gladys grasps my wrist, her viselike grip cutting off circulation to my hand. Panicked, people murmur to each other. Some of the passengers, anticipating what's coming, place their heads between their legs. Others shout. Others pray.

The train tips. A deafening sound of grating metal joins the choir of screams, and then all goes black. The last thing I remember is the sickening feeling of falling sideways before losing consciousness.

CHAPTER TEN

I WAKE TO A SHRILL RINGING in my ears.

My brain is slow to think. An acrid smoke pervades the air, suffocating what little oxygen I have in my lungs. So many parts hurt, it's useless to take inventory. I am lying on my back. Something hard and rutted presses into the base of my spine, warping my body into an uncomfortable position. Limbs cold as ice, and a coppery taste fresh in my mouth, I concentrate, trying to piece together what happened.

Moments whirl through my head—the crescendo of screams; the sound of grinding metal, unnerving like nails on a chalkboard; the frightened look on Gladys's pale face as the end drew near—all accompanied by a rambling welter of emotions.

I haul in a deep breath and cry out in pain as fire erupts in my abdomen. Gritting my teeth, trying to keep my breathing even, I force my eyes open.

Face to face with a bent sheet of metal, the full weight of my situation hits home in a rush of shock and annoyance. *Dammit!* Sandwiched between mangled steel and rubble, I find myself entombed in the wreckage. It's dark but not pitch-black. Dim light filters into the confined space, washing the colors from everything and casting ragged shadows along the walls of debris. Light, no matter how muted, suggests a possible escape from my makeshift tomb. I assume Artagan will come back for me, but after everything—getting lost in that dark vortex then refusing to leave the train when ordered—I doubt he'll be in any great hurry. Knowing him, despite the fact Leah's probably frantic right about now, he'll wait until the last second, just before the rescuers arrive, to make me sweat and teach me a lesson.

I rotate my head, stretching my neck to survey the dark reaches of the confined chamber, searching for the source of the light. The movement sends another jolt of white-hot agony through me, making me scream. Unable to see my body past the fragments of train and tunnel, I snake my hands through the tight space in front of my chest. I prod my fingertips down the cotton fabric toward my stomach, where the bulk of the pain originates. A warm stickiness has seeped through the thin layer of T-shirt. My fingers hit a piece of warped rebar jutting out of my abdomen.

Dammit, and dammit again!

I run a hand along the rough metal, but with no room to maneuver, I won't be able to pull it free even if I try. Setting my teeth to prepare myself for whatever pain is to come, I pat down my pockets in search of my jackknife. Even though I'm counting on Artagan's return, I'm not willing to gamble on it, not when there's an option of freeing myself. If a rescue crew finds my wounds healed around the rod still protruding from my belly, they will dub me a freak, or more dangerous, a miracle. Gladys's fateful words roll through my head. *My name was in all the papers.*

Nowadays, with the Internet, a story of such a miraculous survival—accompanied by pictures—would go viral, and then there'd be nowhere to hide. I shudder. Lucky for me, the rod's placement suggests there are no ribs involved, only flesh and muscle. My flimsy little knife would be a useless savior against bone.

By the time I dig the knife out of my pocket, I'm damp with perspiration, and my heart is pounding like a hammer in my chest. I place the collar of my jacket in my mouth and count to three. Then, sinking my teeth into the soft leather, I jab the tip of the blade into my flesh. At some point during the process, I must pass out because a murmur of voices rouses me back to consciousness. I shrink away from the noise. I hold my breath and listen, but all I hear is the sound of my accelerating breath echoing back at me.

"Found him," a deep, unfamiliar voice booms from somewhere overhead. Panic ricochets within me.

Artagan, where the hell are you?

Energized by fear, I paw at the surrounding shadows, now wishing to find an escape into the swirling void—the lesser of two evils—but as expected, my hands find solid stone and steel. Another noise. I freeze. There's a metallic moan of shifting wreckage above my head. The hair on my arms and legs stands on end, and I cringe. If only I could camouflage myself and disappear into the colors of grime like a chameleon.

Camouflage, huh? I think.

Not the best plan, but with the rescuers on my threshold, it will have to do.

Hands caked in blood and filth, I squeeze them past the debris up to my face. I swipe the crimson mud along my forehead in an attempt to hide the sickle-shaped birthmark above my left eye—my only distinguishing mark. Then, after dipping my fingers in the wound once more, I rub the blood across my face. Gravel rains down. I close my eyes. Stony grains tickle my cheeks and collect in the grooves around my nose and the hollows of my eyes. My only hope now is, in the confusion of a rescue effort, I'll find a moment to slip away.

A rush of air hits my face, but I keep my eyes closed tight. Two massive hands grab me by the shoulders, jerking me off the steel rod in one fell swoop. I scream, my eyes popping open, and I stare into the amused face of Otmar.

He towers over me, resembling the gods of Nordic myth, ones he probably inspired into being, brawny and severe. His hair, tied back with a leather cord, shows off the black flames of the fire tattoo twisting up his neck and disappearing beneath a well-trimmed beard. His amethyst-flecked eyes sparkle as his smile widens. "You were supposed to get off the train, dumbass."

He releases me. With my muscles quivering under the strain of standing, it's a fight to stay upright. I prop myself against a crumbled chunk of a cement piling. As I lean there, I look out across the mass of wreckage to avoid the smirks of my entertained onlooker and the throbbing in my gut.

A sixty-ton train going fifty miles per hour and plowing straight into a concrete wall has redesigned the closed subway station into a scene resembling a war zone. Clouds of smoke pour from piles of distorted steel and concrete boulders. The impact eviscerated the car we were in, tearing the metal away as if it were no more than tinfoil, contorting the frame into a deformed skeleton. The other train cars are stacked behind it like forgotten toy blocks. Bodies litter the rubble. No less horrific than this sight is the utter silence. It reminds me of France during the First World War right after an air raid.

The crunch of gravel jerks my attention away. Otmar glances over his shoulder. I cannot see anything past the Nordic's massive form, but lacking the will to move, I stay where I am.

A chuckle rumbles under Otmar's breath. "You're in for it now," he says then moves aside.

Artagan speeds toward us. From his flushed, mottled

skin and the engorged vein pulsing in his forehead, calling him angry would be an understatement. I straighten, pushing away from my support, but keep one hand on the rough cement for balance. Eyes fixed on mine, Artagan stares, unblinking.

"Sorry. I missed my stop." My voice is raspy. I choose not to make eye contact. Artagan will already assume I'm lying. I might as well not give him further evidence.

"Sorry? Mmph."

I glance over Artagan's shoulder to find what fury lies in wait in Leah's emerald-green irises. But Leah's not there. She's not anywhere.

My gaze jerks back to Artagan. "Where's Leah?"

Artagan glares at me from under a weighted brow. "She's home. I couldn't allow her to see all this, now could I? Not yet, anyway." Every one of Artagan's words brims with agitation, reverberating off the remnants of the tunnel walls.

Otmar steps forward, draping an arm across Artagan's shoulder. "You see, there's a delicate balance for these things," he says mockingly. "Especially when dealing with a former Ignorant. If not prepared properly, they might snap and wipe out a whole village the first chance they get." He nods toward Artagan, pointing with his chin. "Although in my opinion, he's too soft on the girl. Probably due to guilt."

Artagan removes the Viking's muscular arm with a shrug but says nothing. Instead, he chooses to examine me, eyes squinting in speculation, his expression never losing the enraged scowl. After grumbling a few curses, he holds his hand out to Otmar. "Your shirt."

Otmar's bushy eyebrows knit together in a deep frown. He glances at his faded *Return of the Jedi* T-shirt. The collar frayed, the graphic of Luke standing at the ready, lightsaber in hand, peeling around the edges are both telltale signs the shirt's a favorite. Then, bringing his arm across his chest, he says, "No."

"He can't very well heal correctly with his entrails hanging out, now can he? I need to strap him up to hold him together," Artagan says, smoothing back a spill of straight hair that has fallen into his face.

"Agreed. But use your own shirt."

Artagan gives Otmar a hard stare. "It's Versace."

There's a slight flicker across Otmar's lips much too weak to be a smile. "I don't give a rat's ass if it's made by Odin himself. I'm not giving you my shirt. Take one of theirs." He gestures to the scattering of bodies. "It's not like any of them need 'em."

My throat tightens at the thought of desecrating the ill-fated passengers further. Otmar's right—they don't *need* them, nor will any of them object to the despoiling. However, haven't they been through enough?

From the pang of reluctance in his eyes, some part of Artagan feels the same. After letting out a sigh of resignation, he removes his blazer in a quick, fluid movement and lays it folded on the rubble next to me, all the while giving me the evil eye. Artagan undoes the pearl-blue buttons then slips off his shirt. A long, delicate chain hangs around his neck, adorned with a small ring—far too small to be his own—that gleams gold in the flickering fluorescent light.

"Tear it into strips for me, would you?" he asks, tossing the shirt to Otmar, and his glare returns to me. "Damn good shirt." His tone is low and controlled. "You're replacing it."

I nod once.

Artagan shrugs the jacket back on, fastening the top button before he begins the arduous task of putting Humpty Dumpty back together again.

I choose not to watch while Artagan reassembles me and then ties strips of blue cotton tight around my midsection to secure my innards in place. He's a little rougher than necessary, I wager. The simplest movement releases rounds of fire searing new paths on their way through my gut. My knees buckle, and my body sways, forcing Otmar to step to my side and hold me vertical, his tree trunk of an arm tucked under my armpit for support. Artagan delivers a scathing lecture while he works, most of which I miss because of the sizable pain in my stomach and Otmar's chuckles in my ear. I try to escape the pain and humiliation by focusing my attention elsewhere, letting my eyes drift along my surroundings.

Whether from blood loss or the constant pain, an intense weariness washes over me. I feel removed as though I am watching the scene from a great distance. Under the weight of the lethargic fog, I'm able to stop thinking about the gruesome sights and see only shapes and colors until my eyes encounter an oversize patchwork bag sticking out of the rubble. My breathing hitches. When Artagan draws away to examine his handiwork, I bolt.

I find Gladys over a dip of wreckage. Her dress is wet, blood soaking through the navy-blue fabric and coloring the once-white polka dots red. One of her legs is twisted, bent in a way not quite natural. Skin and muscle are stripped back so I can see the white of bone. Her eyes are open, frozen in perpetual fear, and her thin, weathered hand still clutches the crucifix. I press two fingers to the hollow of her throat, searching for a pulse, but from the looks of her, Gladys is dead.

"You knew her?" Otmar asks from behind me.

"No, but I stayed on the train because of her." I add hastily, "She was frightened. Just before Charles Station, she caught hold of me and wouldn't let go. I suppose I could have made a frightened elderly lady release me, but under the circumstances, that seemed a bit heartless. Besides, my mother taught me never to leave a lady in distress." I pull my gaze away and look up.

Artagan's expression hovers between anger and puzzlement. The fine vertical lines between his brows deepen. When he speaks, it's clear anger has won out. "All this was because of a woman? This woman?" He points at Gladys's body. The speculation in his voice is thick.

I nod, lips pressed together.

"Give the kid a break. It's not as if we've never done something stupid for a woman," Otmar says.

Artagan purses his lips, inhales through his nose, and then kneels by Gladys's side next to me. His mouth softens, relaxing into a thin, grim line before he bows his head. After a moment of frozen reverence, he removes the pewter flask from his pocket and dabs alcohol on his thumb. He says a few more words in Latin then makes the sign of the cross first on her forehead, followed by the palms of her hands.

Artagan stands, brushing off the knees of his trousers. "The anointing may not be church sanctified—they'd never give this sacrament to one already dead. I'm sure they'd also frown on the use of spirits, but it's my ritual."

A moment later, the sirens come. With Artagan on my left and Otmar on my right, each lifts me by an arm and ushers me toward a nearby shadow. I close my eyes to escape the blur of motion I know will soon spiral about me. I'm not sure I can hold back the vomit a second time, and I'm sure retching on my liberators might be too much for their teetering patience.

Once the sensation of whirling stops, I open my eyes to find the inviting orange light of Artagan's office. Along with the safety of anonymity and the relief of being out of the shadows, the tingling warmth of healing greets me. I relax, never as happy by its miraculous arrival as I am now.

Otmar yawns, not bothering to cover his mouth. "I better get moving. That wasn't my last job tonight. What is it about full moons?"

"I'll be smudging off the rest of the house after you leave," Artagan reminds him.

Otmar mutters something in a language I don't recognize then leaves through the shadows.

"What did he say?" I ask.

"Loosely translated, he thinks I'm a moron," he says in a dismissive tone. He walks to the liquor cabinet and pours two drinks. After handing me one, he sinks into the cushions of one of the high-backed armchairs. Watching me over the glass, he says, "Now, would you like to tell me what the flaming hell that was all about?" His expression has changed, no longer angry, but his eyes hold a definite edge of warning.

I take a sizable swallow and let the smooth burn of Scotch chase away any misgivings before I start.

"That woman," I say, rolling the glass between my palms, "knew who we were, why we were on the train. At first, I thought she might be a threat. That's the reason I stayed with her. Maybe I should have dismissed her outlandish ramblings as those of a madwoman."

"But..." He gives a short, dry laugh. "There has to be a but."

"*But* Gladys knew things. She called me Endless."

Artagan's eyes narrow. "Gladys? There was no Gladys scheduled to be on the 107 tonight." A slight frown draws his eyebrows close together. "What else did she say?"

I tell him everything.

"None of this makes much sense," I say. "Edmund Thomas Chipp gave daily recitals at the Royal Panopticon. I know because my mother was a fan. The Panopticon was open two short years before it closed in 1856, reopening as the Alhambra Theatre. My mum talked of little else. Gladys said she sang there. At the age of twenty-nine, I think she said."

"And you believed her?"

"I did." I take another sip. "That makes Gladys fifteen

years my senior. However, from her appearance, she looked to be in her eighties, while I'm stuck at twenty." My voice ramps up as my brain struggles to see the feasibility in what I'm saying. "She also mentioned seeing the white gleam of the pyramids and helping Shakespeare write *Julius Caesar*."

I laugh. The story sounds ludicrous aloud, but I continue anyway. "I know the Great Pyramids used to be covered in polished white limestone, but I only learned it from books. I never witnessed it myself."

"Yes, that's right, but they had to remove many of the casting stones in the fourteenth century after an earthquake." He turns away so only the sharp lines of his profile are visible, tapping his pointer finger against his lips.

"Gladys's eyes were gray, not black like a Soulless," I continue. "So if not one of them and not an Endless, what was she? Another soul immortal with memories of her past? But that doesn't explain how she knew the fate of that train or how she knew who we were."

"Those are all excellent questions," he says. He looks me up and down and grimaces. "But ones that will have to wait. You best clean up unless you want Leah to see you looking like this. Your wounds have healed, but you still look like hell." He grins, all irritation forgotten. "One thing before you go. I want to offer you the use of my books. With Leah's training and all, I haven't had the time to make any progress on the reasons behind Leah's soul memories. I was thinking at least for the time being you could take the lion's share of the research. It will give you a way to feel useful when the other members are training Leah."

I nod.

"And while you're at it, you can research Gladys's peculiarities. It couldn't hurt to know more about her and her puzzling knowledge."

"So I'm still allowed on gatherings while you're in charge then?" I ask with a smidgeon of hope.

His face lapses into faint distraction. "Yes, as long as Leah hasn't changed her mind after your little stunt. To say she was upset is an understatement. Now, off with you before she sees you and you get yourself in more trouble than you already are."

Thanks be to God, I make it up to my bedroom without detection. I slowly remove my jacket. Although my body has healed, it's still tired and weak after being so battered. I hold the jacket up by the collar to give it the once-over. The blood will stain, but on the black leather, it won't show all that much. A slit of light draws my attention. With a curse, I push my fingers through a jagged gash. I hang the only true casualty of my rash decision over the curved arm of the settee and console myself with the fact that the hole is nothing duct tape won't fix.

Next, I empty my pockets—wallet, knife, cell phone, and last but not least, my father's pocket watch. I let my finger stroke the engraved lid before setting it on the nightstand next to the small pile of possessions. Then, stepping into the bathroom, I unwind the bandages and strip off my shirt and jeans, tossing the lot in a heap outside the door. They're torn to rags and covered with blood and filth, nothing worth salvaging.

In the hot shower, I tilt my head back and let the streams of water run through my crusted hair and down the length of my body, sending the evidence of my actions whirling down the drain. I emerge clean but not renewed. A heaviness remains in my limbs, and exhaustion is settling over me, dulling my senses—both probably aftereffects from the loss of blood. After wrapping myself in a towel, I open the door of the steam-filled room to the coolness of the bedroom to find Leah sitting cross-legged on my bed. Surprised, I stop mid-stride. Her gaze is not on me, but on the mound of ruined clothes on the floor.

"I can explain," I say, stepping out from the doorway into the full light of the room.

"I'm sure." Her eyes meet mine, straight on. A fierceness blazes in their depths. "I'm sure you're bursting with reasons why I shouldn't have worried, and why you needed to do whatever you did. You heal." She points to her temple. "I know that here, but that doesn't stop me from feeling scared and anxious when I know you're hurt."

Leah rises from the bed and walks toward me, her expression intense.

Water droplets drip from my hair onto the curve of my shoulders and roll down my chest and back, following the groove of my spine. Her eyes scan my body, searching for any trace of injury. Suddenly, I'm aware that, except for the terry-cloth towel slung around my hips, I am naked.

My gaze drops to the floor. I stand as still as stone as her soft, warm fingertips draw featherlight patterns first across the rigid muscles of my back then down the thin covering of dark hairs on my arm, not stopping their torturous march until they reach the planes of my chest.

She comes to a stop in front of me, her fingertip lingering at the tattoo that reads *Foi apporte la force* scripted in arched calligraphy over my heart. "You made me a promise, you know," she says, looking up at me.

It takes me a moment to assemble my thoughts. "I didn't stay on the train on purpose. Things just got out of control. I'm sorry you worried, but I was never in any danger, love. Artagan was there well before any rescuers came to dig me out."

"You were buried? In what? The wreckage?"

Crap, I planned to leave out that little detail. I give a half shrug.

If the look of outrage that flashes across Leah's face

could kill, she'd have dropped me right where I stand. She turns with a snap of her head and returns to the bed. She lifts my pocketknife off the nightstand. After opening the blade, she presses the sharpened edge to her forearm hard enough so the skin dents under the blade's pressure.

I lunge, almost losing my towel. Grabbing her by the wrist, I knock the knife to the floor. "What are you doing?"

"But I'd heal in an instant," Leah says. "So you still don't like the idea of me hurt or in pain. Why should I be any different?"

I suck in a large gulp of air to bring my emotions under control. As the burst of adrenaline slips away, the fatigue returns with a vengeance. "I'm sorry I made you worry."

"You already said that. Are you sure you're all right?"

"I'll be fine. I just need some sleep," I say, rubbing my forehead. "Can we discuss this more in the morning?"

After Leah returns to her room, I fall straight to sleep as soon as my head hits the pillow.

CHAPTER ELEVEN

I STARE AT A CEILING I can't see, counting sheep that don't exist. From sheer emotional exhaustion alone, I should have slept through the night. But close to two, my eyes sprang open, and I haven't been able to fall back to sleep since. I push up onto my elbow and punch my pillow into a more comfortable shape for the hundredth time. Flopping onto my back, I listen to the creaks and sighs of a familiar lullaby, soothing sounds that remind me of my childhood. Many a night as a boy, the song of my house—the wind whistling between the rafters, the moans as the foundation shifted, making itself more comfortable for a long winter's night—lulled me to sleep.

Every time I feel myself sinking into a much-needed slumber, visions of Gladys spring to life behind my eyelids. I may not have known her past our brief conversation or feel any personal grief for her death, but her passing still bothers me.

More struggles. Her words haunt me from the back of my mind. Was she a fortune-teller, a madwoman, or something else entirely?

I consider skulking down to Artagan's study and poring over his hoard of books, but in this leg of the research, none of his books will be of any use. I need to verify Gladys was telling me the truth, which means I need newspaper articles and records of some sort, not folklore. The library might have access to information I need, but there's a fly in the ointment. Portland Public Library closed hours ago.

I toss back the covers and stand, flexing my back to loosen the tension in my shoulders. A slight chill lifts the hair on the back of my neck and prickles my scalp. Unsure if nerves or the nip in the air is to blame, I retrieve the thick, downy quilt from the bed, wrapping it around me.

Light from the full moon brightens the room in monochromatic hues, softening all details with a blue reflecting gleam, rendering the lamp unnecessary. I plod toward the settee with some reluctance. With no librarian to bail me out this time when I botch things up, I fear I'm up shit creek.

I fumble through Leah's backpack, forgotten in my room after our afternoon of normalcy—an afternoon that feels like a lifetime ago and not just a few hours—to retrieve her laptop. With great care, I place the infernal device on the settee, hoping my gentleness might gain its help. Then, plopping down in front of it, I say a quick prayer to the technology gods just for good measure. But none of my efforts have any effect because when I flip open the lid, I am greeted by a request to enter a passcode.

I pull in a sharp hiss of air through my teeth. Rubbing my chin, I give the illuminated screen a long stare as if willing it to divulge its secrets. Birth dates, parents' names, favorite color, what might it be? I should be able to guess, but two lifetimes to choose from doubles all my choices. I begin with the obvious and hunt and peck my way through Leah's birth date. No luck, so I move on to Lydia's birthday. Still no good. After numerous attempts as safecracker followed by several Try Again messages, every button I click makes a god-awful buzzing noise. The words on the screen might as well be "Give up, loser."

Defeated, I climb back in bed.

Somewhere between dreamland and wakefulness, I hear the squeak of a door. I open my eyes to a narrow blade of orange light cutting through the blue dimness and catch a glimpse of a figure. Light shines through Leah's hair, encircling her shadowed face like a halo, before dark eclipses the room once more. I listen to the pattering of soft footfalls, then the mattress shifts under her weight and her body curls into me, the soft cotton of her T-shirt brushing my side.

"Leah?" I ask, more out of a lack of anything else to say.

"Were you expecting someone else?" I feel the curve of her grin against my bare shoulder.

I chuckle and rest my cheek on her silky hair, breathing in until the concerns about tonight's events are no more than a twinge in my mind. "I wasn't expecting you. It's a nice surprise."

"I couldn't sleep."

"Neither could I." I sigh into her hair. "I sleep better with you by my side." One corner of my mouth quirks upward.

Leah raises herself to look at me, her features lost in shadow. "You said staying on the train wasn't on purpose. I can't stop thinking about what kept you there."

I shift so I'm facing her. The weight of her gaze rests on my face. I can feel it, probing and intense. Self-conscious, I gulp in a breath. "I met a woman."

Although I cannot see her features, I imagine her eyes narrowing, making a small crease between her eyebrows.

"According to her, she was there by her own design because she knew."

"Knew what?"

"Everything, it seemed." I snort a short chuckle. "The woman claimed to know what we were, why you were there, what the train's future was. Her story was fascinating but completely unbelievable. At first, I thought she might be there to cause you problems. Hence, I sat with her. Then I wondered if she was sane. That's still up for debate, I suppose."

"What does your gut tell you?"

I force myself not to roll my eyes. "That she was telling the truth and had seen the things she claimed. But I don't know. From her appearance, she wasn't Endless, or Soulless, thank God."

"Could this woman be another soul immortal? With memories like I have?"

"Perhaps. Still, if everything she said was true, I'm not sure if that makes any sense. Although right now, from the little I know, it is my best guess. But it doesn't explain how she knew who we were."

"If she were, that would mean there have been at least three of us," she says more to herself.

"It would." Besides Leah and now possibly Gladys, there had been one other known soul immortal named Amun who also remembered past lives. Years earlier, he and Kemisi had fallen in love and married. From Artagan's story, they lived a long, happy life together until Amun's death. To Kemisi's surprise, when Amun's soul moved on to its next body, his memories of Kemisi went with him. Those recollections were so strong that he sought her out. Before Leah, the council believed Amun's retained memories were an abnormality. However, their story didn't have a happy ending. In the man's third life, all memories of Kemisi vanished, and he never returned.

"Did you Google her?" A glimmer of excitement brims in her words.

"Ah, well... about that," I grope, helpless, then rake my fingers through my matted hair in a nervous reflex.

Lost in enthusiasm, Leah doesn't seem to hear the tentative tone in my voice or see the guilty expression on my face, even after she turns on the light. She slips from the bed with all the eagerness of a child on Christmas but stops short when she sees her laptop sitting open. Her lips purse into a tight line—a sure sign of impending doom.

I avoid her gaze as I swing my legs off the bed and grab a shirt off the floor. "I tried Googling her after I remembered you left your laptop, er... but I hit a roadblock, um..." My words trail off, ending with a shrug.

Over on the settee, Leah stares at her computer screen. A flash of irritation passes over her face. My cheeks flare hot, and I find tugging on my shirt takes immense concentration.

"What did you do? It's frozen solid." Clear astonishment mounts in her voice.

I heave a sigh, hanging my head. "Did I break it then?"

"It's just locked up. Give me a minute. It needs to reboot." The reappearance of the casual tone in her answer suggests whatever I did is nothing but a minor nuisance and not a disaster. Her fingers drum against her sweatpants while she waits. After a minute or two, she returns to the bed with the computer, plopping cross-legged atop the coverlet next to me. "Okay, we're up and running."

I tilt my head in her direction. "Out of curiosity, what is the password?"

Her mouth twitches as if with the urge to make a comment, but she bites her lower lip instead. Then with a smile, she shakes her head. "No."

"That bad, huh?"

"No, but I think it would be better if you never touch my computer again."

"Fair enough."

She stifles a laugh. "So where do we start?"

"Well," I say, "her name was Gladys, no last name. She said she survived a train wreck in '39. Only five of them survived. She told me her name made it into all the papers, so that seems like a logical place to start."

"Agreed," she says as she types. "Where am I looking?"

"Britain. 1839. She mentioned being from Cheapside."

"1839? Not 1939?" she asks, frowning.

"That's right."

"Okay." Eyes fixed on the display, Leah's fingers tap a rhythmic beat along the keys. Her mouth, first screwed up in concentration, relaxes. "Okay, there was one, but not much information either, just a date, July 24, and a place. Whiston?"

"It's a small town in Northwest England. Then again, I'm sure it's grown into a city by now," I muse, but Leah doesn't hear me, too lost in the hunt.

"Here it is," she says, glancing up from the screen. "In a paper called the *Liverpool Mercury*. Let's see, it says there were seventy-five dead and only five survivors."

"That has to be it. It's got to be," I say, scooting closer and craning my neck to look over Leah's shoulder.

"Okay. Augustus Webber, of Liverpool, and Helen McMillian, of Oxford, Merrill and Betsy Hale, both of Whiston, all suffered injuries. A Gladys Anne Hathaway," Leah says, emphasizing the name, "of London, walked away without a scratch, and I quote, 'due to the providence of the Lord.'"

The confirmation of Gladys's story rouses another round of hope—hope that Gladys was more than a mere fortune-teller, hope that Gladys was indeed a soul immortal. Although with Gladys dead, I'm not sure how much help any of this research will be.

I realize Leah's still talking. "Her parents, Ezra and Agnes Hathaway, were both killed in the crash. She was thirteen. I can't imagine losing *both* parents so young."

"Nor can I. One was hard enough," I say. It's an experience Leah and I share. My father died when I was seven, and Leah's dad died when she was ten. I shake off the sadness and focus on the task. "How about Queen Victoria attending a concert given by Edmund Chipp at the Royal Panopticon in 1855? Can you find that in there?" I swish my hand at the computer, a strange waft of excitement slinking through me.

"Let's see." After a few quick keystrokes, she smiles. "Yup, here we go, in the *London Times*. "Edmund Thomas Chipp, Gladys Anne Hathaway Perform For Queen". Oh look, there's even a drawing."

In a black-and-white engraved image, a man sits at an impressive organ, its massive, tapered pipes lining the wall on either side of him. At his flank stands a woman dressed in a fancy gown, singing her heart out, with Queen Victoria sitting stoic in the front row. Although I'm sure it isn't accurate, the rendering showcases all the essential players, but the faces are small and the details vague.

"You said Gladys looked old. How old? Best guess," Leah says, her eyes focused on the screen.

"In her eighties."

"Okay, that means she was born in, what? The 1930s?"

I nod but say yes when I realize Leah isn't looking my way.

"So if Gladys was a soul immortal, then why didn't her name change from one life to the next? Mine did. I guess the last name could stay the same depending, but the first?"

"A family name, maybe? One that's been passed from one generation to the next. Must be."

Gladys's and my conversation thrusts into the forefront of my mind. The moment I thought Gladys truly was crazy—

"'It is not in the stars to hold our destiny but in ourselves.' I like to think I gave him that line, but I'm sure he wouldn't have agreed."

"Gave whom? William Shakespeare?"

I stare at the drawing, wheels turning. Then, glancing away from the image, I say, "This is a long shot, but I need you to find something else for me. A painting of William Shakespeare's wife, Anne Hathaway."

Leah narrows her eyes into slits, a little bewildered by my new path. Then as her eyes widen, she says, "You can't think—?"

"Just show me, please."

"All right." Leah puffs out her cheeks while she pursues my request. "I had to do a report on her portrait last year in art history. There's only one. Sir Nathaniel Curzon drew it years after Anne died, traced it from an Elizabethan portrait. It's the only surviving image. The original painting was destroyed or lost. Here it is." She turns the laptop so I can see the sketch.

I study the flowing lines of the woman's hair swept up under a rough illustration of a close-fitting cap. Quick, curved strokes represent the ruffled collar gathered tight around her throat. Both the cap and the ruffle are indicative of the sixteenth century. My attention wanders from her collar to a pair of bowed, thin lips and then up her defined Roman nose, settling on her almond-shaped eyes. Although Gladys's features were aged, the similarities are uncanny, if not identical.

"At the time I found it odd," Leah goes on, pulling me from my thoughts. "You'd think there would be more records of her existence, besides this"—she points at the display—"and a few remarks in legal documents. But I suppose she wasn't notable like her husband."

"Younger, but that's the woman I met today. I'd swear it."

"But." Leah pauses and her lips purse in thought. "You told me looking like Lydia was a fluke. What? Another fluke?"

I rub my hand across my chin. "I know it seems unlikely, but why not? And anyway, we should see this theory through to the end, see if it will be of any use to you and your status. Gladys mentioned controlling her destiny. Maybe you can, too."

"Free myself from the council, you mean. That's what

we're talking about, right?" Leah's voice is as placid as her face, but despite all her effort, I hear a hint of strain in it. She touches the locket Artagan gave her.

I can't deny that the thought hasn't crossed my mind. Hope stirs again, threading its way through the hesitations and the doubts to the forefront of my mind. "Well, yes, that would be the ultimate goal, wouldn't it? I'm not saying it's even possible. Artagan would like us to *believe* it's not."

Leah's expression remains skeptical.

"Look, even I know I'm grasping at straws here, but I'll never stop wishing or searching," I say.

"No, I guess not." Her gaze strays to the floor.

"Nor can I sit idly by if there's a possibility of setting you free. You can't ask that of me. It was you who asked me to follow my gut, to cling to hope. That's what I'm trying to do." I continue, "Artagan himself admits he doesn't understand everything when it comes to soul immortality, despite being one himself. From the brief time spent with the council in the catacombs, it was evident that the members don't have a complete understanding of this abnormality themselves." My throat tightens at the memory of my hours in the belly of that monastery, thinking I'd never see Leah again. I draw in a breath, not letting the feelings of remembered dread get a foothold, and go on. "And they have thousands of years of knowledge. Much more than Artagan. So who knows what you're capable of."

"But I'm not a soul immortal anymore. I'm immortal."

"True. But we don't know enough to assume anything." I settle back against my pillow and stretch out my legs in front of me. Eyes toward the ceiling, my fingers pluck at an eyebrow while I think. "We'll start with Kemisi. She'd be our best bet because of her relationship with Amun, and her friendship—I guess that's what you'd call it—with Artagan. He says he trusts her. That must be true since she'll be living here."

The corner of Leah's mouth curves upward, and she shakes her head. "I haven't even met Kemisi yet, and I know she and Artagan are friends," she says, closing the laptop. "He was telling me about her. He absolutely trusts her. And don't you see how his eyes light up every time he talks about her? I think he has a thing for her."

I shake my head in disagreement. "No."

"Why? Because of Amun?"

"It's just not a possibility."

Her animated expression drops. "Didn't you say Artagan found the man who once was Amun, living in the Midwest or somewhere like that?"

"Yes, in Duluth."

"Well, if nothing else, Kemisi and Artagan are close. I bet she's told him everything. Of course, if that's the case, that might mean Artagan's right, and this is a life sentence."

"I doubt she did. Not with their history."

Leah's eyes widen, brightening. "Artagan and Kemisi have *history*? I knew it. Spill!"

I raise my hands to slow the onslaught of questions I see brewing behind her eyes. "I don't know much, and I haven't overanalyzed it like I'm sure you're about to do. All Artagan said was the romance ended on less than amicable terms." I decide it's best to skip the part about Death giving Artagan his scar to avenge his daughter's honor. Although I have little doubt that Artagan deserved what he got, Leah's already worried enough about the possibility of Death's ability to eliminate immortals, namely me. No need to add fuel to the flame.

"Well, whatever happened, she must have forgiven him. Like you said, she's moving in."

"I couldn't tell you. I am no expert on the workings of the female mind. Even after a hundred and seventy years, you ladies are still a mystery."

Leah scowls, but there's a glint of humor in her eyes.

"Anyway, maybe we can find a tidbit hidden in Amun's story that no one deemed crucial. Something that will explain all this. Along with the use of Artagan's book collection, perhaps we can assemble enough pieces to make a clearer picture. It's a place to start, and who knows where that might take us."

"But I'm not a soul immortal anymore. Why does it matter?"

"We don't understand how any of this works. Because of that, we can't dismiss anything. We have to chase down every lead."

"Maybe." Her face grows preoccupied, a small frown puckering her brow. "You better be careful. What if Death finds out? Nothing stupid, remember?"

Triggered by the first glimmer of hope we've seen in weeks, I feel playful, buoyant even. I wrap my arms around Leah's waist. Then, in one fluid motion, I roll so I'm atop her, causing Leah to squeal. "I'll behave."

Leah looks up at me, a little breathless. "So, Mr. Hammond, what are you planning to do with me now?" One eyebrow quirks upward.

My cheeks grow warm, and I slide off her. I prop my head up on my elbow and leave my other hand resting across the concave dip of her abdomen. "Just don't lose faith, love. Not yet," I say, giving her a lopsided grin.

CHAPTER TWELVE

THE NEXT MORNING, NOT SURPRISINGLY, I wake alone. So as to abide by our compromise, after my playful shenanigans, Leah decided it would be best if she retired to her room for the rest of the night. Despite my secret wish for her to do otherwise, I agreed.

I roll my head on the pillow and open my eyes. The brightening dawn fills my room with a soft gray light. I lie quietly, hands folded behind my head, gazing out the window. A latticework of frost trims each pane, announcing winter's impending arrival. Wind whips off the water, rattling the window casings. Stripped bare of their fiery leaves, maple branches bend and sway, a stark, silhouetted entanglement against the overcast sky. My mind wanders. Is it possible that buried in the secrets of Gladys's life is some real promise? Or am I, like I told Leah, just clutching at straws, my wishful thinking in overdrive?

With Leah's burdens only becoming heavier, I cannot allow hope to slip through my fingers as I've done a million times before. True, my hope may be as frail and brittle as one of those fallen leaves. Still, I cling to it, not letting the storms of doubt strip it from me.

My cell phone vibrates on the nightstand. A look at the number tells me it's Grady.

"Hey," I say, my voice raspy from sleep.

"Finally, someone answers. It's about friggin' time," Grady says. The bitter note to his tone surprises me. Before I ask what's wrong, he continues. "Since Leah is avoiding my calls and emails like the plague, I figured I'd ask you why she's quitting school."

I feel a slight stiffening in my throat, and I swallow, attempting to remain composed. My thoughts flit about, seeking inspiration but finding none. "Well..." I say, floundering.

"Something's going on, dammit. Leah has wanted to be an artist since forever. I don't believe she'd up and quit for the lame excuse she gave Mom," he states, his words heated yet controlled. "Mom is convinced Leah's sick, that the doctors here in England missed something."

"I don't know what Leah told your mum—"

"Did you knock her up?"

My mouth falls open. Striving for nonchalance, I laugh. "No, nothing of the sort."

Crickets.

I can only imagine his expression—the cold glower of his steel-gray eyes creating a single deep crease between his thick eyebrows, his lips strained just a shade. I've seen that look before. He didn't believe me then, either.

I shift on the bed, uneasy. "I respect your sister too much to put her in that kind of position. Grady, I promise you, Leah isn't sick or pregnant. Beyond that, you'll need to talk to her."

"How'd I know you'd say that," he says, his tone hitting a balance between resentment and annoyance. His voice then grows cold, free of any emotion, as he continues. "Fine. Tell my sister to call Mom. She's upset that Leah missed Thanksgiving. I'll be home soon enough, since I've changed my plans. I'll be home for Christmas after all. She might avoid our mother, but she won't be able to avoid me for an entire month."

With a click, the phone goes dead.

I scrub a hand over my face. I know Grady to be an overprotective brother, a self-appointed role he assumed after their father's death. Leah often complains about it, but this time Grady has every reason to be concerned about his sister. We must come up with a better excuse for Leah dropping out of school than whatever story she dished up. If we don't, Grady will continue to press the matter, and we'll have no peace. I shrug on a shirt and yank on a pair of jeans. Then, raking my fingers through my hair for good measure, I head out the door.

As expected, I find Leah in her bedchamber. I lean against the doorframe of the bath and watch as she winds her flowing locks up into a messy bun. I decide the direct route's best and clear my throat.

Leah removes a bobby pin from between her teeth, stabbing it into the knot of hair, and smiles at me in the mirror. "Good morning."

"Morning. Your brother called." I sound shy, my voice low and wispy. "What excuse did you give your mum for leaving school? You never mentioned."

Leah turns to face me, her teeth clamped on her lower lip. She leans back against the sink, her eyes lingering on her feet. "The wedding."

I stare at her, a little confused.

With a deep breath, she looks me square in the eye. "I told her I was overwhelmed by the planning and all."

"But we haven't even set a date yet."

"I know, but my mom put me on the spot. I had a whole explanation thought up. But when she started grilling me, *poof*, it flew out the window, and I said the first thing that popped into my head. I told her that between the wedding and all my schoolwork, something had to give. Mom said we should hold off on getting married if it interfered with school, that we were both young, that we should try living together first." Leah smiles at this. "I told her you're old school, and we didn't want to wait. I doubt she bought my story completely because I was lying. But she pushed."

"No wonder Grady's upset. In the future, it might be a good idea to keep me in the loop, especially if you need me to continue a lie. Even a bad one." I sigh. "You're right. Your mum didn't buy your reason, so she made up her own. You need to call her. She believes you're sick again."

She flashes a quick glance toward the floor, a frown curling her mouth. "Does Grady think I'm sick too?"

"No, not exactly." The temperature rises in my face.

"What do you mean? What did Grady say to you?"

"Your brother has a theory of his own." I draw a deep breath through my nose. "He thinks you're pregnant."

"Did you give my brother a quick refresher about the birds and the bees and explain to him that we would have to have sex for that to be the case?" Her tone is sharp.

"I decided not to go into detail. I did tell him he was mistaken."

I'm not sure Leah hears me. Red-faced, her eyes glaze over. The muscles of her slender neck constrict. "And even if it were the case, he's one to talk! According to his last email, he's living with Charlotte now. I know they've known each other a few months, and he had a huge crush on her, but they've been dating, what? A minute and a half? If he thinks he gets to dictate how I live my life like he thought he could when he lived here, boy, is he going to be surprised."

"You are his little sister."

Leah casts me a glare that suggests she doesn't give a damn. "It's hypocritical. Wait until I get my hands on him. I wish he were here right now so I could beat his ass!"

"Well, it seems you got your wish."

"What do you mean?"

"There's been a change of plans," I say. "Grady's coming home for Christmas."

This news deflates Leah's anger. Her shoulders sag, and her gaze falls to the floor. "What am I going to tell him? And what am I going to tell my mom? I can't believe I made her think I'm sick all over again."

There's a long silence, and when Leah looks up, tears moisten her lashes.

I hold open my arms, and Leah steps into my embrace. Fibs and half truths flow into my mind with ease. I kiss her, and then I say, "Use Grady."

"Use him?" Her posture stiffens as she shifts in my arms.

"Yes," I say. "Unlike your mum, he knows what I am and enough of what happened in England. So tell him the truth."

Leah makes a face and tilts away.

"Not the whole truth," I say. "Elaborate on the parts he already knows. It's what I've done for years. Tell him my actions didn't just heal you but had the unexpected side effect of making you immortal—he can handle that much, I think—and because it's taking some adjustment, you're taking a semester or two off. It will get Grady off your back at least for the time being, and then he can help you deal with your mum. And maybe by the time we need to come up with a revised story, you'll be back in school." I wink.

Leah rolls her eyes but relaxes, most of the tension leaving her slender shoulders. "Not bad. I forget what a good liar you are because you're so bad at it with me."

As childish as it is, I fight the urge to stick out my tongue.

Leah steps back to the sink. "I've got to finish getting ready. If I hurry, we might have enough time to have breakfast together before I go to work. At Java," she adds, catching my wary expression.

Downstairs, I search the kitchen. I'm surprised to

find the cabinets and fridge stocked with many of Leah's favorites—Fruit Loops and Susy-Qs, even a pint of Lobster Mash in the freezer. Artagan has certainly done his homework. The thought gives me pause, forming a knot in my stomach. The words Artagan said the night Leah gathered Daniel Harris roll through my head. *Many details flowed in when you received the name for the gathering.* Once, Leah had been Artagan's assignment, but he saved her, for his benefit.

And mine.

I push the thought away and move on with the construction of breakfast. Since we don't have time for anything too elaborate—not that my cooking skills are anything to write home about beyond sausage and the occasional fried egg—I decide on Fruit Loops and then pop a couple of pieces of rye bread in the toaster. After making a pot of coffee, I set the table with fine bone china I find in the dining room cabinet and add candles for mood.

I step back, admiring my handiwork as the sound of her footsteps comes down the hall. I turn just as Leah hurries through the door.

"May I claim the pleasure of your company for breakfast, my lady?" I bow deeply at the waist, and then, like any gentleman worth his salt, I slide the chair out from the table, inviting her to sit.

"You're a goof," she says, stepping toward me. "But you're my goof. You always seem to know what I need. If I ever tell you otherwise, I'm lying." She smiles, slipping into her chair.

I pour the milk in her cereal bowl and take the seat across the table from her.

She surveys the spread. "Candles, too?"

"I thought you could use some romance."

Leah holds my gaze. Warmth flutters in the pit of my stomach, and I reach across the table to take her hand, my thumb stroking tiny circles on her palm.

Without warning, Otmar saunters into the kitchen. I frown and release Leah's hand as Otmar plops himself into the chair next to mine.

"Breakfast! Thanks," he says, snatching a piece of toast from my plate. I give him a long, level stare. He bites off a substantial mouthful, chewing it loudly, and regards me. "Well, you look better. You should have seen him the other night," he adds with a sidelong glance at Leah.

Nearly choking on my Fruit Loops, I catch his eye and shake my head a fraction of an inch. "Have you met Otmar?" I ask Leah, hoping to change the route of the conversation.

She nods, her eyes homed in on me.

"Yeah, Leah and I met. Right before I plucked your sorry ass out of the wreckage. Artagan's still grumbling about it. Is there coffee, too?" Otmar asks as he eyes my mug.

"Yes, in the pot," I say, cupping my hand over the rim.

"Ahhh." His gaze darts toward the counter as he brushes the crumbs from his beard.

"Speaking of Artagan, I need to talk to him," I say, my eyes avoiding Leah's now-penetrating stare.

Otmar tosses the rest of his—or more accurately, *my*—toast in his mouth, chewing it with great satisfaction. "He's off. Left an hour or two ago. He won't be back until tonight."

"Of course not," I mutter. The man seems to sense the precise moment I need to talk to him and disappears. "You wouldn't happen to know where?"

The corners of Otmar's mouth turn down, sinking beneath his beard. "Don't know. Don't care. He said it was personal, and I left it at that." His eyes flick to Leah. "Artagan will meet all of us at the cathedral, though. He wouldn't miss it."

"All? Do you mean I'm meeting the council tonight?" she asks, the color draining from her cheeks.

Nothing unexpected, I remind myself. I place my hand over Leah's and give it a gentle squeeze.

"Sorry, left that part out, didn't I? Yup, tonight's the night"—Otmar's smile broadens—"and it's my job to get you there on time. So be here at six sharp. Wear something decent. I don't want to miss out on any of the festivities," he says. The level of excitement in the man's voice is unnerving, especially taking into account what Artagan says Otmar thinks of as fun.

"Everyone will be there—Death, Thanatos, Muan, Domitilla, the protégés, the whole lot," Otmar adds as if that fact should be reassuring.

"Domitilla will be there?" My voice is cold and stiff. A distinct hollowness settles in my stomach. Fate has taken my newfound hope as a challenge and now enjoys testing its limits.

"She'll be there. Haven't heard otherwise."

Something feels lodged in my throat, and I swallow hard to clear it. I glance at Leah. Her anxious gaze has settled on me. "It's okay," I mouth, squeezing her hand once more.

"Nervous?" Otmar pipes in.

Leah's shoulders rise and fall.

"No need to be," he reassures her. "You're one of us now. And after your performance yesterday, you're all anyone can talk about today. Both of you are." He smirks at me.

"Great," I say and then force a laugh.

"And there's no reason you can't bring Jack if that's what's bothering you," Otmar goes on.

Her face lacking emotion, Leah shoves back her chair from the table, its legs grating against the tile. "I have to get to work," she says, pushing to her feet. "But I'll be back and ready by six."

Distracted, she walks away toward the door.

I follow her out into the foyer. "Leah?"

She ignores me, grappling with her coat.

"Hey." I catch her by the arm. "It will be okay."

Leah looks away but not in time to prevent me from seeing a shadow of fear drift across her face. She studies her nails and picks at splotches of blue paint wedged along the cuticles, indicating that at least she's still painting.

"She won't hurt you. I won't let her," I say, dropping my voice an octave.

She glances at me from under her long lashes. A faint twinge of confusion flashes across her face. "Who?"

"Domitilla, of course."

"You think that's what I'm worried about?"

"It would be natural if you were."

"Maybe." An expression of steadfast determination overtakes her features—the look a soldier might wear when readying for war. "But she's not my concern right now. You are."

"What? Don't worry about me. I'll be fine," I say.

"I won't let him do anything stupid," Otmar says, his sizable figure darkening the kitchen doorway. "I already promised Artagan I'd keep an eye on him. And I make the same promise to you."

"Thank you, but I'm capable of keeping an eye on myself," I say.

"Ha!" Leah looks me straight in the eye, raising her chin in challenge. "The last time you and Death were in the same room, you clocked him in the jaw."

"She has a point," Otmar chimes in, a broad grin splitting his face.

I ignore him, or at least I try to. "Like I said, I'll be fine."

Leah's posture has relaxed, but she's not looking at me. Her eyes are fixed on Otmar. "I feel much better knowing you'll keep an eye on him. Thank you." Leah grasps Otmar by the collar of his shirt. He bends at the waist as he lets

Leah tow his face toward hers. Then, rolling up onto her tiptoes, she gives him a quick peck on the cheek.

After Leah leaves, Otmar's attention dallies on the door for a moment. He rubs a large, square hand across his cheek and then breaks out in a deep, rich laugh, sending a rumble through his chest. "She's as fierce as any berserker." He blows air out between his lips in mild amusement. "And as persistent as one, too, I have a feeling."

I smirk. "You don't know the half of it. Now, about you keeping an eye on me."

"I have my marching orders. Best you get used to it. Remember, six sharp." He turns and lumbers away, the matter clearly settled in his mind.

CHAPTER THIRTEEN

TWINKLING CHRISTMAS LIGHTS DECORATE THE buildings and coil around the branches of the bare trees, shining in colorful splotches in the night. With Leah's hand tucked in the crook of my arm, we follow Otmar's broad back through the narrow streets, his long strides making it damn near impossible to keep up at a reasonable pace. The first snow of the season covers Portland in a thick white blanket. It muffles all sounds except for the crunch of our hurried footfalls.

Even with the church still blocks away, I feel Death's presence. My instincts buck and rear, but against every fiber of my being, I push forward, striving to keep up with Otmar's unrelenting pace.

Ever since I swung by Old Port Java to walk Leah home after work, she has kept her feelings under lock and key. Quiet and remote, her stone-faced facade secured in place, she will seem to the others a confident and determined girl. However, I know her well enough to see the mire of emotions hidden underneath the well-placed mask. The slight tightening at the corners of her mouth tells me she's stressed, scared even. The small vertical line between her eyebrows—that soft spot that always beckons me to kiss it—shows concern and hesitation. Despite my attentiveness, she doesn't look at me. Instead, she keeps her eyes committed to the path in front of her.

As we turn left onto High Street, the wind *whooshes*, sending a blinding billow of snow into our faces. Icy needles sting my cheeks. I duck my head and force my concentration on the uneven, snow-covered bricks beneath my feet.

"Almost there. The church is just ahead," Otmar calls over a shoulder.

Looming before us is a lofty tower, a mass of dark stone framed by moonlight. The imposing building lies in darkness. No signs of light shine from the countless stained-glass windows. Otmar leads us around to the south side of the church through a small walled graveyard to the cloister.

Otmar dips his head and walks under one of the low arches, disappearing into the darkness of the covered walkway. With some reluctance, Leah and I follow.

In the protection of the cloister, Otmar points at a shadow along the far wall. "We'll need to use the shadows from here. We don't want any prying eyes seeing us enter. Not that anyone is out on a night like this, but better safe than sorry. Ladies first."

Leah releases my arm and removes her fur-lined hood, the tip of her nose and cheeks pink from the cold. She takes two headlong steps, but at the shadow's threshold, she wavers. It's only a brief hesitation, but Otmar notices the pause.

"Let's not keep them waiting," he says.

"Just one question." She turns to face him. "Why didn't we step into a shadow back by the house? I know Artagan placed a barrier of sorts around it, but—"

"Hmph! Artagan's idea, not mine," Otmar says, his shoulders moving upward slightly, not quite a shrug. "He said it's supposed to help you feel normal, remind you you're still human. Normalcy in the face of chaos, or some such shit. But since Artagan's in charge of your training, I follow his instructions."

"Next time, how about we ignore him and take the shortcut. I won't tell, I promise. If I knew we weren't shadow walking here, I would have worn jeans, too, instead of this skirt. You are the one who said to dress nice," Leah adds, scrutinizing his casual choice of apparel—jeans and the collar of a faded T-shirt peeking past a beaten-to-hell brown biker jacket.

Otmar gives another grunt. "No, I said decent." He raises one sizable finger and wags it with the slow tempo of his words. "No holes, no tears, that's decent. You and Kemisi, geez. Like peas in a pod."

Leah darts a quick glance in my direction.

My definition of *decent* had been more in line with Otmar's, minus the T-shirt, but Leah had insisted I swap my jeans for a pair of slacks and add a tie. With her as tense as she was, I wasn't about to argue. I reach up to loosen the Winchester knot and unbutton my collar.

Otmar smiles, his teeth gleaming white in the beard. "She made you wear that, didn't she?" He chuckles, eyes focused on the navy tie. Not waiting for a response, he turns his attention back to Leah. "Artagan warned me about you. Enough stalling. Ready?"

Leah bites her lower lip and shakes her head before her face lapses back into remoteness. Then with a deep inhalation, she straightens her slouched shoulders and says, "Let's do this."

She seizes my hand. I squeeze back in reassurance, and with that, we step together into the shadow.

Inside, the only illumination comes from the streetlights shining in through the cobwebbed windows, sending elongated splotches of light along the high, vaulted ceiling. From a thick coat of dust and filth, it's clear the parishioners abandoned this building some time ago. Stale air dries out my mouth and replaces the moisture with the unpleasant taste of must. It is warmer here, though—a surprise I'm grateful for after the bitter cold outside.

I straighten my tie and turn to Leah. Occupied with stomping every ounce of snow off her calf-high boots, she takes a moment to realize I'm watching her. She gives me a weak smile and slips off her parka, pulling in a deep breath. She tugs at her sweater then brings a hand to her locket and pats it.

"Ready?" Otmar asks, sounding annoyed.

Leah sighs and nods.

We trail Otmar toward a set of double doors that leads to the inner sanctum. He stops short, his massive head still spangled with melting snow. One hand lingering on a handle of the door, his gaze passes over Leah and zeros in on me. He proceeds to repeat one of Artagan's lectures on etiquette. It's hard not to notice the recurrent theme—keeping my big mouth shut. Less heartfelt than one of Artagan's many homilies, the speech sounds rehearsed. All the while, I nod and hope, with no resistance on my part, his part will conclude more quickly.

An explosion of shouts and cheers erupts from behind the doors, causing Otmar to break off mid-sentence.

"*Swina bqllr!* They've started," he says, flinging open the door.

In the heart of the nave, an assembly of onlookers has convened in rowdy conversation. The hum of voices is like an electric current through the long and cavernous room. Another round of cheers erupts, and the crowd shifts, revealing a grisly scene. Kemisi sits mounted on the chest of a lankily built man, his white shirt smeared with blood. Her legs lock the man's arms to his side. She holds a bronze knife in each hand. Their thick, curved blades, plunged into the man's shoulders, pin him to the floor. Dark-red, almost burgundy, blood oozes from the wounds. The buzz of voices grows louder.

"Say it!" Kemisi shouts. Then with a smile, she twists the blades.

I watch as the helpless man's face contorts, and a whimper of pain escapes through his grimacing lips.

"You're all monsters," I hiss through my teeth then take a step forward, unsure of what I will do, only knowing I must do something, since I can't, in good conscience, stand by and watch while Kemisi tortures this man.

Otmar seizes me by the shoulder and breaks into a laugh when he sees my expression.

"It's not what you think," he whispers. "He agreed to this, believe it or not. When he did, I doubt he thought he'd get his ass whipped. Cocky bastard." His eyes return to the action. "He's not gonna die, no matter how much he might wish it right now. Serevo's immortal, just like the rest of us."

"Serevo?" My eyes snap back to Vita's chosen one, any sympathy I had for the man vanishing. Vita had given her council seat to Serevo with her dying breath, the seat that Leah now holds. Having it snatched away couldn't have sat well with him. I can't help worrying that Vita's vindictiveness runs through Serevo's veins, too, and if it does, I'm sure Leah will be his first target.

"Last chance," Kemisi says over the taunting exclamations of the crowd. "Say it now, or I'll gut you like a pig and restrain you until you've healed with your intestines hanging out. How long do you think it would take before you'd live that down?" She twists the blades again. Then, removing one in a quick motion, she presses the point into the base of his throat.

Serevo squirms. "Kemisi is the best."

"Louder," she says.

"Kemisi is the best!" he cries.

She smiles. "And?"

"I am but a lowly worm," he chokes out.

Shouts and hails follow. Kemisi jumps to her feet with

161

the nimbleness of a gazelle. She wipes the blades off on Serevo's shirt, her mouth quirking upward as she glances at him now sitting cross-legged on the floor, hunched over in pain.

"Took you long enough," she says.

Otmar grumbles something about Serevo still needing his mother's teat. Then, raising his voice above the chatter, he says, "Sir, if I may have a moment."

All faces turn in our direction, few of whom I recognize, with two notable absentees. Neither Artagan nor Domitilla is among them.

Dressed in a suit—black from head to toe—Death drifts forward, separating himself from the crowd with an unnerving grace. Thanatos and a small inky-haired man, whom I remember to be Akio, move with Death in perfect synchronicity.

Death comes to a stop in front of Leah. He takes her hands in his and kisses them both. Every ounce of me wants to step between them, but I stand firm, pressing my clenched hands into the sides of my legs to keep from breaking my promise.

"It is so good to see you, my dear Leah," Death says. "I've heard remarkable things about your training. I'm so pleased." His eyes glide past me, searching, and he cocks an eyebrow in Otmar's direction. "Where's Artagan?"

"He's running late. Met a redhead in Cadiz. Can't fault him for that, though, can we?" A giant-sized grin stretches across Otmar's face.

"Be sure he sees me when he arrives." From his tone, Death *can* fault Artagan for his absence and already does.

Otmar's smile vanishes, and he nods.

Death glances at me, his face freezing in cool reserve.

"Sir." I bend at the waist, hoping my expression doesn't give away any of the hatred I feel.

Death's keen eyes narrow, but then his expression

relaxes into a controlled calmness before his focus shifts back to Leah. "You've met Thanatos. And this is Akio."

The honey-skinned man slaps his hands to his sides and gives a rigid bow.

"Come. Let me introduce you to the others." Death offers his arm, and Leah steps forward to accept it.

Seeming to appear out of nowhere, Kemisi steps to Otmar's side as Death and Leah stroll away.

"Where is Artagan really?" Kemisi asks, brushing back the locks that curl damply around her face.

"No idea. I thought he'd be here by now," Otmar says low enough that no one else can hear. "He left this morning with only a word or two."

"Typical," Kemisi says. Her gaze slides to me. "It's good to see you again, Jack. *Ahlan wa sahlan.* Now you respond, *ahlan bīk.*"

"*Ahlan bīk.*" I bow my head.

Kemisi smiles and then eyes Otmar with renewed interest. She scans his choice of apparel with a grudging scowl. Then, tossing her ringlets, she walks away toward the nearest shadow.

Otmar chuckles. "What is it with women and ties?"

I cast him a quick, knowing smile, and then I turn to follow Leah, but I'm towed backward, Otmar's hand gripping my shoulder, stopping any progress.

"Let's observe from up there." Otmar gestures to a small bowed balcony situated high at the foot of a Rosetta stained-glass window.

I heave a sigh. "Do I have a choice?"

Otmar shakes his head. Then, taking me by the arm, he hustles me toward a spiral staircase tucked in the back corner.

"This is ridiculous," I say, pulling from his grip. "You've got to realize that, right?"

"And damn embarrassing, too, I imagine. But orders are orders. After you."

A string of obscenities flows through my head, but I only repeat two aloud. Then I straighten my shoulders, and with as much dignity as I can muster, I ascend the stairs, the whole time listening to Otmar's chuckles trailing behind me.

From my new perch, I watch as the guests assemble in small groups and engage in seamless conversation. The murmur of their voices blends into a soothing whirr. Muan and his brothers keep to themselves, for the most part, observing the others from the farthest side of the nave with an air of superiority and alertness.

"Besides the council members, who are all these people?" I ask.

"Many are descendants like you. That's Keiko over there. The perky brunette." Otmar points at a small girl in a pink kimono, giggling at something Leah said. "She's one of Akio's. And the tall, fair-haired man at her side belongs to Thanatos."

As Otmar introduces the cast of characters, my focus returns to Leah again and again. Death escorts her through the gauntlet of greeters. She holds her face in a perpetual smile, clearly overwhelmed. In passing, she glances up at me. I give her my best boyish grin and then push a thought into Leah's head. *See. I'm behaving.* This first attempt goes well, and the gesture has the desired effect. The strain in Leah's face eases, and she laughs. Weak and brief, but I'll take it.

In the far corner of an opposing balcony, movement draws my attention. I spot a figure lurking at the edge of a shadow. Domitilla steps forward out of the darkness and lounges against the railing. I study Domitilla out of the corner of my eye, her aqua irises glinting in the firelight. As she watches Leah, Domitilla appears serene, except for her hands. Those she clenches into tight little fists.

She senses my attention and turns to look at me, straightening her posture. Her eyes widen, and in them, I see the flicker of recognition, all suggestion of tranquility gone. Then, as quickly as I drew her interest, it falls away, settling on something on the far side of the room.

"There was a man in the village my last wife was from," Otmar says, beckoning my attention back. "Balder, his name was. He got a particular look whenever he saw my Freya. She was a beauty, with hair like fire, it was so red. Still, understanding can only go so far, and it didn't stop me from snapping that arsehole's neck," Otmar says curtly.

"What brought that up?"

"That's the same look that Balder got." He points with his chin to where Leah now stands with Muan.

Muan stares at her, his eyes shining. A slow smile builds across his face. Now and again, his tongue darts out to lick his lips as he moves closer, erasing the distance between them. The sight sounds numerous alarm bells. For what feels like the thousandth time this evening, my neck prickles. The sensation grows, pushing out the snarl forming in the back of my throat.

Artagan's voice comes out of the darkness behind me. "Your job was to keep the boy calm, not light him up like a stick of dynamite."

CHAPTER FOURTEEN

"Y OU'RE LATE," OTMAR SAYS. A broad smile lifts his high, flat cheeks.

"It couldn't be helped." Artagan glances in my direction, giving me a grudging smile. "Muan's curious. They all are. It's only natural."

Probably sensing he has become a feature attraction, the Soulless moves away and returns to his brothers' company.

"See," Artagan says, removing a box of cigarettes and holding it open for the taking. I decline, while Otmar takes two, keeping one and stuffing the other behind his ear. "What did I miss?"

"Just Kemisi whooping Serevo's ass and making him say uncle," Otmar says. "The exact phrase was 'Kemisi is the best. I am but a lowly worm.'"

Artagan laughs loud enough to bring several sets of eyes in our direction, including Kemisi's, her black leather pants and T-shirt now replaced by a low-cut cocktail dress in bright red.

"Attagirl," Artagan whispers.

"Death has been parading Leah around like a prized peacock ever since." There's an undeniable lack of humor in Otmar's voice.

"How are they accepting her?"

"Much as expected. You'll be happy to know Dom has kept her distance. Mosi, too. Oh, and dear old Dad wants to see you. He was wondering what kept you. I told him you were with a broad from Cadiz," Otmar says with a smirk.

"Cadiz, huh? Well, at least you have good taste."

"From the looks of him, Muan's been wondering where you were, too. His head's been on a swivel ever since we arrived. I imagine he's hoping to get another crack at you. He hasn't forgiven you for beating him. What is it now? Five? Or is it six times?"

"Seven," Artagan says, a slight smile visible on his lips. "But who's counting?"

"Not you." Otmar's white teeth gleam in the candlelight, and they exchange a long glance. One of Artagan's eyebrows flicks upward. Otmar nods. From their brief glances in my direction, the internal discussion is likely about me, a recap of my behavior. Behavior that should earn me a gold star and, hopefully, an early release from my babysitter.

I smile, waiting for word of my reprieve.

"Jack, stay with Otmar," Artagan says, heading toward the shadows.

"What? But I've been—"

"You heard me."

My glare tracks him into the darkness, but like the obedient little pointer my father had when I was a child, I stay put.

"He didn't always have that ramrod shoved up his ass." Otmar chuckles and leans forward onto the railing, which creaks in mad protest.

I glance at him, not sure I believe him.

"It's true. Artagan was a different man when he was with Olluna. She was a lovely woman, full of vim and vigor, and good for him."

"You knew Olluna?"

"Oh, aye. I went to their wedding. Beautiful ceremony. Free of all the pomp and circumstance because the village had no priest." Otmar cranes his neck to light his cigarette in the flame of the closest candle. He takes a long drag before continuing. "A woman, the midwife if I remember right, bound their hands, and Artagan and Olluna declared themselves married. Artagan called it a tethering of their hearts and souls. He was quite the romantic back then. They loved each other. That was evident. I half expected him to join her once the whole debacle with Vita was finished. But maybe he figured out what I've been telling him all along."

"And what would that be?"

"Valhalla's doors won't open for the likes of me. No heroic battles wait on my horizon. Who's there to fight? And no heaven either. I'm not repentant, even though I've broken every commandment, every law of human decency," he says with grim relish. "I think we all have. Haven't you?"

Not all of them, but he's right. I have broken my share. I grimace. "So we're damned then," I say, my voice barely loud enough to hear over the drone of conversation flowing up from the nave.

A long, throaty laugh rumbles through him, lighting up his eyes with humor. "Damned? Praise Odin, no! On Earth, we *are* the gods." He takes a puff on his cigarette and smiles. Wispy plumes of smoke drift from between his teeth.

I snort and then turn away before I say something that might get me into trouble.

Below us, Artagan strolls in Death's direction, addressing Akio and the tall, fair-haired man from Thanatos's family line before stepping into Death's audience. Artagan says a few words and holds out his hand in greeting then waits while Death stands staring and unmoving. After an extended pause, Death accepts the gesture, and the tension vanishes. The assembly shifts into a sociable mood once again.

A few moments later, a young woman dressed in moss green advances to Death's side.

"That's Rebekah," Otmar says. "Kemisi's protégé. Just as beautiful as her master."

Rebekah bends to Death's ear and speaks briefly before walking away. A bright smile curls Death's lips, and in a ringing shout, he announces, "Dinner is served."

I follow Otmar down the stairs and trail him through a small door at the front of the sanctuary where the last of the council members have just disappeared. Otmar ducks his head under the arch, and we step into a dimly lit room. The polished, dark wood-paneled walls gleam with flickering candlelight. In the center sits a table that would befit the richest king—place settings of gold, bowls brimming with food. It's a stark contrast to the rest of the building, so grimy and unattended.

By the time Otmar and I arrive, the other council members are all seated. I notice, with a sense of relief, that Domitilla is absent, Serevo joining us in her stead. Otmar leads me to the last empty chairs at the foot of the table, while Death sits at the head, Leah in the place of honor to his right. I catch her eye, giving her a smile before I take my seat.

A handful of servers, dressed all in gray, stand along the far wall. From their varying ages, at least half of them aren't Endless. One of them—a spry older lady with hair grayed to platinum—fills each stemmed glass with water. When she steps to my side, Otmar grins at her. "How old are you now, Sonya?" he asks.

A flash of panic shows on her face. "Eighty-nine, sir, but still going strong. I'm able to work rings around these youngsters." She smiles, not looking Otmar in the eye, and moves on to fill the next glass.

"Most of them are mortals," Otmar murmurs. "Servitude for immortality. Some will do anything for a chance to live a little longer, even wait on our sorry asses."

"But will Death honor the deal?"

"Oh, aye. As long as they keep up their end of the contract."

Otmar slaps a hunk of rare beef and a scoop of potato on each of our plates then gestures to my large goblet. After I hand it to him, he pours a generous portion of light, tawny liquid. I thank him and lift the cup to my lips. A sweet, delicate nectar flows over my tongue, followed by a tingling burn. It's like nothing I've ever tasted before.

"Mead," Otmar says. "Smooth, isn't it? I made it myself."

I nod, indulging in a rather long gulp.

"Careful, or the morning will find you under the table," he says.

I smile. Otmar underestimates my tolerance for alcohol. I take another large sip, this time closing my eyes, intoxicated by the mead's heady aroma.

As the night flows on, to my surprise, the council acts very much like a family with all the banter and relaxed conversation that goes with it. There's a camaraderie I hadn't expected. Even Artagan, the self-proclaimed black sheep, has his place. He leans back in his chair, laughing at something Kemisi has said, a glass of Scotch hanging surprisingly forgotten in his hand. Still, something in his demeanor feels forced, as if he's putting on a show.

Despite the amity, some fissures aren't so easy to hide. From the others' turned shoulders, Muan is more an intruder here than I am. Death is the only one at ease in the Soulless's presence. My gaze wanders back to Leah. She sits forward in her chair, listening to Kemisi. From her carefree demeanor, she appears unaware of the fractures revealing themselves around her. That, too, I deem a performance.

"Would you mind?" Lost in my thoughts, I missed what Thanatos said. I turn to find him staring from across the table. Thanatos must read the question in my eyes because he speaks again before I can ask him to repeat himself. "I find this whole phenomenon of soul immortals remembering past lives fascinating. I didn't have time to ask questions on our last two meetings. But now, would you mind?"

"Not at all," I say with complete sincerity, hoping my openness will lead to newfound knowledge about the soul immortal abnormality.

Thanatos seems delighted if a tad surprised. "Are there many parallels between them? Besides the memories."

I explain the handful of similarities between Leah and Lydia and then go into detail when telling him about their mountain of differences. Thanatos sits transfixed, nodding now and again at something I say. But throughout the conversation, I get the impression Thanatos's knowledge of the soul immortals is sparse at best, strengthening my assessment that Kemisi is our best shot within the council. Then again, I suppose it is just as likely Thanatos is holding information back, not wanting to share any family secrets with someone who is a stranger.

"So Leah looks exactly like her predecessor? Not just the eyes?" Thanatos asks then forks up a mouthful of potato.

I nod.

He chews slowly, regarding Leah. "That must have been unexpected, for lack of a better word."

I laugh. *That's an understatement.* "Yes, at first. But after the initial shock, it felt like the most natural thing in the world. Kind of like coming home after a long journey," I say, surprised by my frankness. Much like Leah, Thanatos has a way about him that makes me feel at ease—a fact of which I need to be both wary and vigilant.

From Thanatos's side, Mosi snorts, eyes still on his plate. Until this point, Mosi has been silent, more comfortable ignoring Leah's and my presence than acknowledging our existence. "You talk about this girl as if she's special, as if she's the cosmos itself. May I be the first to say, I don't see it."

"Mosi," Thanatos chides.

"It needs to be said." Mosi lifts his gaze from his plate to meet mine. "I suppose our expectations were high. Too high. She's a smart, determined young woman. I'll give you that, but she's also very ordinary." He glances to Serevo and then to Leah like he's comparing the two. Both seem unaware they've become the topic of conversation, eating their food and chatting with the surrounding guests.

"Very ordinary," Mosi repeats, a note of disapproval flitting across his face.

I stare at him, the muscles along my jaw going taut.

"According to Artagan, Leah is doing exceptionally well," Thanatos states.

"Yes. According to Artagan, I'm sure she is." Mosi's lips twitch with amusement when his gaze returns to me. "Take no offense, Jack. I only meant there is no sign of the notable traits you spoke of in the catacombs. No extraordinary merit that would cause the devotion you were willing to show. If Vita hadn't disrupted the bargain, it wouldn't have been an even exchange. Now the girl is just an Ignorant turned immortal."

And nothing that should have provoked Death to choose her over Serevo. I read the sentiment in his eyes. I focus my attention on my uneaten plate of beef and potato.

"Well, damn, Mosi. How on earth could the boy take offense to that?" Otmar leans his bulk back onto the arm of his chair. "Judging from his expression"—he gestures in my direction—"you should sleep with one eye open."

Thanatos flickers a reproachful glance at Otmar, and then he smiles at me. "What I think Mosi is trying to say in his candid way—"

"Pardon me, but I understood his meaning." My attention swings back to Mosi, who now grins under a veil of innocence. "I'd wager Death is more inclined to agree with my assessment of Leah than yours."

Mosi's posture stiffens, the cords in his neck going rigid. The indicators vanish as quickly as they appear, but both are telltale signs that Mosi doesn't agree with Death's decision of choosing Leah over Serevo. The wordless confirmation brings concerning questions to the forefront of my mind. Under the guise of acceptance, how many of the others feel the same way? Domitilla, for sure, but who else? And what if most of the members agree? Might that embolden Serevo to follow Vita's example, secretly killing a council member who gets in his way?

"Others may see Leah as ordinary," I say, "but to me..." I want to quote E. E. Cummings—"You are my sun, my moon, and all my stars." Leah is my everything. But I refrain. "Some things *are* worth dying for."

"And therein lies your problem," Akio interjects, animosity and recrimination coating his voice. He sets his glass down on the table. "You still think as a mortal and not as the demigod you are. Maybe not as powerful as us, but you're a deity nonetheless."

Stunned by the rapid shift of the conversation, I choke back a laugh. "I'm no deity, and neither are any of you."

A look of strong repugnance overtakes Akio's face, and he continues. "What is a god if not a being with supernatural powers, believed in and worshiped, idealized and followed?"

I laugh at that, uneasy, but the mead pushes me forward, making me bold. "You are believed in because mortals see evidence of what you're capable of daily, on the news, in the empty spaces in their lives that once held loved ones, but—" A foot presses down hard on my own.

"Enough, man, you've made your point," Otmar whispers.

I glance around at the guests to find most of their eyes on me. A deep murmur of discontent grows among them. At the other end of the table, Leah looks dazed, as if someone has just stabbed her in the stomach. Next to her, Kemisi gives Artagan a quick yet meaningful look. Artagan is preoccupied, but his eyes clear, and he shakes his head a fraction of an inch, seeming to find great interest in his tumbler.

"No, let him continue. How else will we change his mind?" Death says, waving away the interruption.

"I was just going to say you're feared, not worshiped," I say in a level voice, trying to keep my emotions in check.

Mosi gives a short grunt. "And what's that to us? Mortals are no more to us than rats on a sinking ship, not worth a second thought."

My lips curl, and I feel the last pretense of civility slipping from my face. It's only for a moment, but the reaction doesn't go unnoticed. Satisfied, Mosi rests back in his chair, smug and silent.

"You're the same as Artagan, and Brennus before him," Akio says, his voice remote as if the conversation barely interests him. "Death honors us by endowing us with his powers and the freedom from worrying about insignificant things such as an afterlife. Like any gift, one has to accept it. You are no more than a boy trying to prove his father wrong," he says then looks away. Discussion concluded.

Death clears his throat, commanding attention. All eyes fall away from me as they shift in Death's direction, except for Leah's. Her gaze stays planted on mine.

I turn my attention to Death.

He relaxes on his elbows and stares down the table at me. "Unlike Mosi and the others, I understand why you find what we do offensive. You lived a long time in the dark, unaware of what you are."

Death's eyes dart to Artagan for a brief moment before resting back on me. "Like I told you back in Leah's dorm room, I truly believe we're the ones who teach mortals life is worth living. Whether I find them in the safety of their bed or bleeding out on a lonely street corner, what does it matter? For them, meeting me, meeting any of us, is inevitable, for they are mortals. I've found it's how they lived their lives that makes the difference in how they accept me. Us." He sweeps his hand out, gesturing to his children. "Did they squander or embrace the time I granted them? And that is in no one's control but their own."

"Ed Growley didn't squander his life," I say. "Nor was he ready to die."

"I remember him. He was a rarity. How do you think most mortals would treat life if there were no end?" Death goes on, his voice flat and emotionless. "I'll tell you. They'd become lazy and complacent, more than they already are. Honestly, I believe your disdain for who we are has less to do with us and more to do with self-loathing." *The night you took Hake's soul was the night you embraced what you are.* Death's voice gushes into my thoughts like a free-flowing stream. *Guilt is powerful. Without it, you could be fated for much greater things, immortal scion of Brennus.*

"You sound just like him," I grumble. "Hake, too, could spin lies into golden words, making them sound like truth until the bottom fell out and you realized every word he uttered was for his own gain."

Death stares at me then smiles. "Something to think about."

My mind reeling from the heated discussion, I reach for my drink but find my goblet missing. Artagan stands beside me, downing its remains.

"Obviously, the boy can't hold his liquor," he says,

holding up the empty goblet. "It seems he's not as much like me as you all thought."

There's a burst of laughter, which sends a flood of heat across my cheeks. However, the diversion dissipates the tension, and the mood relaxes into one of joviality once again.

Artagan faces Soulless. "Muan, ready for that rematch? If that's all right with you, of course." He bobs his head in Death's direction.

Death's face folds up into a wide grin. "Yes, yes. Let the games begin."

CHAPTER FIFTEEN

BACK IN THE NAVE, WHILE Artagan and Otmar linger in the shadows, whispering strategy, Leah and I watch as the assembly mingles along the fringes. They mill about in high spirits, excited about whatever's coming. During my time in the dank catacombs, I remember talk of the games. And from the memory of blood smeared on both Otmar's and Mosi's faces, I imagine these games fall more in line with the Roman definition of entertainment than the modern, far-less-lethal version.

"And don't forget that right hook of his," Otmar reminds Artagan as they step toward us.

Artagan says nothing, only nods, his eyes fixed on Muan.

Across the room, the towering man brandishes a broad sword-shaped piece of wood, slicing and jabbing at an imaginary foe. At first glance, the weapon, adorned with feathers and a painted geometric design, looks like nothing more than a child's plaything. After further inspection, however, I notice razor-sharp pieces of metal embedded in the sides of the shank. It's clearly no toy.

"You fight with weapons?" Leah says, not bothering to hide her astonishment. "Real ones?"

Otmar snorts, lowering his bushy eyebrows. "Of course they're real. What would you have us use?"

"Nerf guns, maybe? Like normal people. You guys are insane," she says.

"Certifiable," Artagan says. He releases the tails of his gray-and-white pinstriped shirt and undoes the buttons, revealing once again the golden band on a silver chain dangling around his neck.

Artagan sheds his shirt and tosses it to Otmar. Then he turns to Leah. "Would you mind?" He lifts the chain over his head and lowers the ring into the well of Leah's open palm, letting the chain coil around the ring like a snake. "For safekeeping," he adds, closing her fingers around it, then he walks away.

Leah lifts the ring, shifting it back and forth. In the center of a cloverleaf sits a small, clear faceted diamond. Two rows of black lettering run around the delicate golden band. "I wonder what language this is," she murmurs, running a fingertip over the engraved letters.

Neither French nor Latin, my best guess would be Gaelic, but it would be just that, a guess. "Not sure."

Otmar leans in between us. "It was his mother's. The only thing he has left of his family. He almost never takes it off."

Leah gazes at the ornate script for another moment and then slips the chain over her head. The ring clinks as it rests next to her locket.

Artagan strolls to the front of the room. A young boy joins him, carrying a scythe. The long, curved blade flashes silver in the light as the boy passes the weapon over. Artagan says something to him, ruffling his hair, and smiles. As his grip tightens on the handle, Artagan glares across the expanse of the nave in Muan's direction. A dark smile curls Artagan's lips. My eyes widen as I see the tale of the night he killed a whole village to avenge Olluna's death come to life in front of me.

"Can't be," I whisper.

"Told you the story, did he?" Otmar asks, surveying me with a gleaming eye.

"Yes," I say, my mouth going dry. I clear my throat. "So is it?" I look back to the long-handled farm tool-turned-weapon.

"One and the same," Otmar confirms. "Now shush, Izel's about to begin," he says, gesturing to the bulky Soulless walking out from one of the darker corners, his wide mouth and bulging black eyes making him resemble a demonic frog.

Izel steps to the center of the room, stretching out his arms. The people fall silent. "Ah Puch to the Mayans and Malsumis to the Abenaki, Muan is known by many names and feared among men..."

There's a low, ominous groan from the crowd.

As Izel continues, undeterred, the dissenting murmurs swell. At first, I don't understand the reaction. Akio had chastised me for not seeing them as deities. Then I remember who Ah Puch was to the Mayans—their god of death. With this simple analogy, Izel has placed Muan and Death on the same playing field. From the frosty expressions on all their faces, a faux pas none of the children would ever make.

"And so, it is with great honor I present to you my brother, Muan." Izel ends his speech with a nod of his head in Death's direction. I catch a glimpse of Death over the rows of gawking heads. He stands unmoving. His mood appears neither amused nor angered, but the silence that follows is deafening.

Izel stares, white lipped, his vexed gaze glaring back at the unreceptive crowd, while Muan appears unbothered by the lack of enthusiasm. Now at the rear of the nave, he paces in silence like a caged lion, his deadpan eyes zeroed in on his rival.

"I'm up." Otmar flashes a smile before turning to the crowd. "Today I find myself blessed." His deep voice booms through the cavernous space. "For I have the pleasure—no, the honor to present to you the immortal scion of Brennus himself. This successor, one that many of you deemed unworthy of such a grand title, has lived up to our father's aspirations, proving himself again and again. In Germany, he saved a damsel, a descendant, mind you, from the trials and tortures of witchcraft. Then this once-lowly Ignorant amazed me when he wiped a city off the coast of Greece, sending the entire island to meet Hel with a single thought."

Leah's eyes flash away before turning to me. "An island off Greece? Is he saying Artagan destroyed Atlantis?"

"None of it's true," says a voice beside me, and I spin to find Kemisi standing at my shoulder, eyes fixed on the Viking. "And it's not like we don't know each other. But they don't care," she goes on, motioning toward the enthusiastic crowd. "It's good theater."

"So without further ado"—Otmar grins—"I give to you the one, the only, Artagan."

The room bursts into cheers and ovations. Whatever else he is, Otmar has a definite talent for theatrics, reminding me of one of the snake oil salesmen who wandered through Lidcombe on occasion, pushing their magical tonics.

Artagan steps forward and gives a dramatic bow, making it clear Otmar isn't the only showman on stage tonight. I notice many of the women—descendants and servers alike who are fully appreciative of Artagan's physique—whisper and murmur words of admiration. It appears Artagan isn't only popular among the mortal ladies, but the immortal ones as well. Their attraction doesn't go unnoticed. His eyes smolder as he meets the gaze of one of his admirers, and he gives her a quick nod of his head.

"Laying it on a little thick, don't you think?" Kemisi snaps at Otmar upon his return, a scowl marring her features.

He turns to her and grins in response, seeming quite proud of himself.

Kemisi mutters something and spins on her heels.

"What's up her ass?" Otmar grumbles, watching her walk away.

I say nothing, merely shrugging, unable to resist the anticipation of what's coming next.

"Thank you, Otmar, for that spirited introduction." Thanatos chuckles, taking center stage. He motions for the competitors to join him. Eyes fixed on one another, Muan and Artagan stride forward.

"The first to disarm their opponent or make them concede wins," Thanatos instructs, the amusement lingering in his voice. He raises a hand over his head. Then, bringing it down with a sharp motion, he shouts, "Begin!"

Sword outstretched, Muan charges, almost taking down Thanatos with his exuberance. Artagan dodges aside, evading the strike. He meets the second with the handle of his scythe.

Powerfully framed with a barreled chest and tree trunks for arms, Muan is a force to be reckoned with, but the battle is by no means one sided. Artagan might be wiry, but he's firmly muscled and agile on his feet. With a swing of his blade, he slices the fabric of Muan's shirt along the stomach, sending a wisp of dust drifting from the torn material. A roar of applause meets Artagan's success. But with no sign of blood, I'm left wondering if Artagan's blade missed the flesh behind the flimsy layer.

Muan lunges. Air explodes from Artagan as the hilt of the sword strikes him in the ribs. The crowd lets out a unified gasp. Artagan stumbles but only for an instant. Finding his footing, he whips around to face his opponent. He drops into a fighter's crouch, the blade held up at the ready. Muan matches Artagan's stance, his black gaze set on the point of Artagan's blade.

A prickling chill leaks down my spine as the battle carries on, and I'm pulled deeper into the action. Unable to drag my eyes away, I catch myself yelling out suggestions and insults from time to time.

Muan swings and misses, but his next strike finds flesh. Artagan staggers sideways. Blood streams down his arm, pouring from a deep, ragged laceration across his shoulder. Muan seizes the moment and strikes again. Using the wooden side of his sword, he hits Artagan behind the knees, dropping him to the ground.

"*Hrafnasueltir!* Quit sitting on your ass and get in there!" Otmar shouts.

Artagan ignores the Viking's commentary. His perceptive gaze stays glued on his opponent as he springs to his feet. Muan, seeing he has lost the advantage, backs away. Artagan charges. Then, veering off course at the last possible second, he leaps into the closest shadow. The crowd grows quiet. Muan's eyes flit around the room, his expression holding staunchly to its bland, impenetrable facade.

Then steel hums, and the long, curved blade whips out of a shadow at Muan's rear, striking him across the back. Muan screams out and arches forward. Artagan materializes out of the dark, swinging the blade again and again. Swirling puffs of smoke and ash accompany each slash Artagan lands.

I stare in dumbfounded disbelief. "What the...?"

"Strange, isn't it? They have no pulse. No blood in their veins," Otmar says. "Whatever dark magic keeps them alive is locked deep inside them, well protected."

The match comes to an abrupt end. Muan is on his knees, his shirt nothing but a shredded rag. With one hand, Artagan holds the blade of his scythe to Muan's jugular, and with the other, he clasps Muan's wooden sword high over his head, flaunting it.

The crowd bursts into cheers.

Otmar glances over at Mosi. With a bored look on his face, Otmar holds out his hand. Mosi grimaces and smacks a hundred-dollar bill into the outstretched palm.

"And..." Otmar smirks down at him. "The hand's feeling a little light."

Mosi glares back with a mixture of contempt and resentment before grumbling a few choice words. He fishes another hundred from his wallet and slaps it on top of the first. "That's it. That's all I got."

Hindered by handshakes and smacks on the back, when Artagan steps in front of us, a broad smile splits his face in two. Otmar gives him a congratulatory thump on the injured shoulder. Artagan laughs, wincing, and then the two make a quick exodus back to the dining hall in search of more mead.

"You enjoyed it, didn't you?" Leah gestures toward the center ring, where a small crew now cleans up the remnants of the fight, washing away the blood.

"Maybe a bit too much. Didn't you? Even a little?"

Leah's face holds a tinge of outrage. "No, not at all."

It takes me a second to realize she's teasing. She laughs at my rapidly changing expression and grabs my hand as a new pair of competitors prepare for the next match.

As the games continue, Akio shows off his mastery of the sword, winning handily against Mosi, and one of the Soulless brothers knocks himself unconscious after Otmar goads the brother into trying his hand at a different weapon—a flail.

Once festivities wind down, Artagan and Otmar stay behind, swapping old war stories with Thanatos, while Kemisi, Leah, and I return home. Tired, the ladies soon retire to their rooms. And I head for the coach house, too wired to sleep. The parts to repair Leah's old VW bug arrived weeks ago. However, between work and Leah's training, I haven't had time to fix it.

The coach house is chilly from steady drafts leaking

past cracks around the sills and through the gaping space under the doors. Rubbing my arms to warm them, I give Bessy a pining glance. My motorcycle sits along the far wall, covered by a tarp, waiting for spring. Along the opposite wall, stacks of wooden crates and a hodgepodge of forgotten items clutter the edge—several ladder-back chairs, at least two bed frames, and a sofa, its stuffing breaking through the frayed upholstery.

Utilizing one of the abandoned crates, I lay out the tools and parts I'll need to complete the job, and then, using another as a stool, I reexamine the fan belt. I've just removed the pulley nut when a voice speaks from behind me.

"So?"

I jump, nearly whacking my head on the deck lid. "What is it about you and sneaking up on people?"

Artagan leans against the rear fender, smirking. "Always so jumpy. I was just wondering how you thought it went tonight."

I grimace. "In my defense, Mosi's an asshole."

He chuckles. "No argument here. An elitist prick, through and through."

"And he doesn't like that Death chose Leah over Serevo, that's for damn certain," I say, peering back at the motor.

"I wouldn't be surprised, but what makes you think so?"

After wiping my greasy hands off on my jeans, I tell him about Mosi's and my heated exchange.

"Well, at least you didn't clock him in the jaw," he says, rubbing his stubbly chin.

"Believe me, I wanted to," I say then decide to ask the question that's been gnawing at me ever since I learned the council was on its way. "So now that the gang's all here, what does that mean for Leah's training? I know the others will be helping out, but does that mean it's out of your hands? Will Death be taking over now?"

"No, dear old Dad won't be staying. I'm still in charge. I've already asked Thanatos to take over in the mind-control department. It only makes sense. He is the master of the hocus-pocus crap." He smiles. "I'm sure I'll be receiving requests from the others soon enough."

"I assume Muan will still be involved?"

"I haven't heard otherwise."

Uneasiness tightens my throat. Something embedded in those coal-black eyes tells me he's capable of anything. I purse my lips and nod.

"Don't worry. I would never leave Leah alone with him," he assures me. "I'll insist on accompanying all of them. You have my word." With that, he stands.

I shove my anxiety down and cling to the only security afforded me—his promise. "Where are you off to?"

"I'm meeting up with Otmar at a place called The Thirsty Pig. He says it's ladies' night. Hopefully, brunette ladies' night." He grins, showing off his pearly whites. "Would you care to join us? We could make it a guys' night out. Otmar's buying."

I shake my head, snorting. "Thanks for the invite, but I think I'll pass. You do know there's more to life than whiskey and women, right?"

Artagan's lips press into a flat line, and he gives me a long, glassy stare. "Blasphemy—that's what that is. Besides, I don't think I'll take advice from a man who moved heaven and earth to be with a beautiful woman who's upstairs alone in her bed. And where is he? Here, working on a piece-of-shit car that looks like it would be better suited for the junkyard. That's not what I call living."

Warmth flushes my cheeks. "And jumping from bed to bed is?"

"I believe it's safe to say I have the majority on my side. So yes."

"Yeah, well, I guess I'm old school. It's the way my

mother raised me." I pause, inserting a screwdriver into one of the slots of the alternator pulley to hold it stationary. "Someday, you'll realize women are more than just a place to rest your John Thomas. Now hand me that 21-mm wrench."

"Rest?" Artagan laughs and then shakes his head. "Maybe that's your problem. Don't know what to do when you get your hands on a woman."

He pauses a moment to scrutinize me. I keep my gaze on the car's engine and don't say a word.

"Nah, you put on a good act, but that's all it is. You can't be a virgin. After a hundred-odd years, come on. More to the point, I know the details of your dealings with Hake and can guess the rest. He put you up in one of his brothels. The one on Granby Street. Even a priest wouldn't have come out of that den of iniquity unscathed."

The heat spreads from my cheeks, flooding my entire body. I hear my heartbeat drumming in my ears. "None of that is any of your business. The wrench," I demand, holding out my free hand.

"Methinks he doth protest too much. Have I hit a nerve?" With that, Artagan slips out through a shadow. "Enjoy your celibacy," he calls back, his words ringing in my head with a taunting air.

Damn him! Bloody bastard! I think, glowering at the shadow.

If I'm honest with myself, I don't know what happened during my stay in the brothel. Hake put all his best fighters up in one of his three houses with the freedom to enjoy whatever taste of London we desired. "Whatever keeps my boys happy," he said. I remember little if any of my time there. I was too strung out on opiates to recollect even the smallest detail, but I can guess, although I hope otherwise. I murmur a curse or two and return my concentration to the engine.

The job, by mechanic standards, is easy and doesn't

take long enough to divert my mind from the nuggets of truth in Artagan's words. Back inside the house, tempted by thoughts of Leah, I veer away from the staircase and find myself in Artagan's study. With him out gallivanting, I decide to take him up on his offer and peruse his vast collection of books, hoping to find answers about Leah's soul memories or Gladys's confusing past. I stand in the middle of the room, my gaze shifting from bookshelf to bookshelf, wondering where to start. I pile my arms with books, mostly on obscure folklore, and carry the books to the desk. My pulse quickens as I look over the imposing stack. Are the answers about Leah in there somewhere?

By a little past midnight, I've found nothing I deem useful. On the other hand, I've learned more than I ever needed to know about creatures like the huldra of Scandinavia and the succubus, tracing back to medieval legend. Much like sirens, both sound like men's justifications for boorish or adulterous behavior. "Sorry, honey. The succubus made me do it." It's not long before the tiny print begins to blur, so I throw in the towel and head to bed.

Once in my room, I undress and crawl under the covers. Moonlight streams through the windows, casting the room in silver light. As soon as my head hits the pillow, my mind becomes a hive of activity. I lie, eyes wide open, staring at the ceiling. I grab my iPod and scroll through my playlist. Flipping by The Black Keys, Muse, and John Lee Hooker, I move on to the classics. First, I listen to Beethoven and then Chopin, but not even his Nocturne in E minor can lull me to sleep.

Just before a quarter to six, I give up and get dressed, thankful that this is my weekend off. With Leah's car fixed, perhaps she and I can escape all this craziness for a while and head out of the city. She may not want to visit her mother, but we could head west, spend the day in the White Mountains. Those plans come to a screeching halt when I find a note slid under my door that reads *Gone to train. Be back around noon. Love, L.*

I groan and shove the now-crumpled slip of paper deep into my jeans pocket.

I'm up before the sun. A blanket of silence covers the house. I turn on the lights as I go, thinking a hot pot of coffee might put me in a better mood. At the end of the hallway, a light gleams from the kitchen. A rich aroma of spices envelops the hall, bidding me to discover its source. However, what greets me stops me in my tracks.

Kemisi sways in front of the stove, spatula in her hand, wearing nothing but a man's dress shirt—identical to the shirt Artagan was wearing last night.

Before being noticed, I back from the door and retreat down the hall, fuming. What is he thinking? With Artagan's laissez-faire attitude about women, I see nothing but carnage in the not-so-distant future. This time, Death might not be satisfied with a single scar across the cheek. It would have been far better for Artagan's well-being if he'd brought home any other brunette from ladies' night than the scene I just stumbled into. Shaking my head in disbelief, I whirl around the corner and bump into Artagan. His bare chest is further proof that my conclusion is correct.

I jab an accusatory finger at him. "What the hell did you do?"

"Good morning to you, too." He beams.

"You ass! You're going to hurt that woman all over again. What are you trying to do? Get a matching scar?" I stare at him, exasperated.

"Haven't you heard? Women like scars." Artagan chuckles. His jovial mood only irritates me further. "You're worried about me. That's sweet, touching even, but don't be. First off, Kemisi picked me up. And second, this morning she made it perfectly clear she doesn't want this to become anything serious. Strictly friends. With benefits, I suppose." Glancing toward the kitchen, he rubs the back of his neck, a strained expression rigid on his face.

"And you"—my brow furrows—"Mr. Manwhore, have a problem with that. Huh?"

Artagan purses his lips. "Manwhore? The word's a bit uncharacteristic for you, don't you think? Too modern."

I scowl. "I picked it up from Leah. She used it the other day to describe one of the regulars at the coffee shop. She says he has a new girl on his arm every other day. The term fits you perfectly."

He glares at me, and then his expression softens into one of resignation. "I swear if that woman came with an instruction manual, it would be easily several thousand pages, written in some obscure language like Sentinelese," he grumbles, maintaining a low voice, so only I can hear. "Kemisi's always been a bit maddening."

"And yet?" I fight a smile. "Leah's right. You do have a thing for her."

He tilts his chin down, pinching his lips together. "No, I don't."

"You sure?" My smile grows wider. "Maybe the leopard can change his spots."

"In the words of a boy who's now looking to get his face pummeled, none of that is any of your business." He turns and stalks toward the kitchen.

Some sense of morbid curiosity beckons me to follow.

When I enter the room, Artagan stands in the middle of the kitchen, drumming his fingers against his slacks as if he's trying to decide whether it would be prudent to greet Kemisi good morning. With a deep intake of breath, he takes a tentative step toward her.

Feeling like an intruder, I find a seat at the table and force my attention away, my foot tapping absentmindedly.

Following a moment of awkward silence, Kemisi places

a stack of steaming pita bread in the center of the table. "*Ahlan wa sahlan*, Jack."

"*Ahlan bĭk*," I respond. "Did I pronounce that correctly?"

"Flawlessly." Kemisi smiles. "I'm making *ful medames*, if you want to wake Leah. It's an Egyptian delicacy, not to mention one of my favorite breakfast foods." She returns to the counter to retrieve another bowl.

"Careful. She's *vegan*," Artagan mouths, rolling his eyes, as he takes the seat across the table from me.

Artagan leans back in his chair and props an ankle on his knee, jiggling his foot. A nervous tic, I assume. Now and again, he peers in Kemisi's direction.

It's as if I've stepped through the looking glass into some alternate dimension. Artagan's always suave and collected, especially around the opposite sex. I've never seen him in such a flustered state. Kemisi, on the other hand, appears oblivious to Artagan's condition, enthralled by her culinary creation, and that seems to frustrate Artagan further.

Methinks he doth protest too much. I push my thoughts into Artagan's mind, parroting his words from the night before. *Leah was right. You do have it bad.*

Belt up! Or I swear… The rest of his words are incoherent.

I suppress a laugh. I have to admit this morning is turning out much more enjoyable than I thought it would when I found Leah's note. Wait until I tell her. Snatching a pita from the plate, I glance in Kemisi's direction. "Thanks for the offer. I'm sure Leah would love it," I say, tearing the bread in two. "But she's training this morning."

Artagan's head flinches back, his eyes narrowing. "No, she's not. Thanatos requested time with her tonight. Other than that, her schedule is free."

"But she left me this." I fish the crumpled paper from my pocket and pass it to him, a knot forming in my gut.

Kemisi leans over Artagan's shoulder to glance at the

note. "There's only one who would be that disrespectful." She snorts in disgust. "Black-eyed devil."

I feel the blood rushing to my face as I realize what she's suggesting. "Wait, are you saying Leah's with Muan? Alone? But surely Death wouldn't allow him to hurt her, right?"

"Unfortunately, Death doesn't control Muan as much as he wishes he could," Kemisi says. "Muan and his brothers are capable of just about anything."

I'm on my feet now, and Artagan rises to meet me. He stands still a moment, calculating, then turns to Kemisi with a decision. "I'll get dressed. You call Otmar. The two of you can check out their usual haunts. We need to find her. Now!"

CHAPTER SIXTEEN

"**I**'LL MAKE THAT PERVERSION OF a man suffer!" My voice, flat before, is suddenly animated, filled with fury.

"And I'll help you," Artagan says, a bit of acidity in his own tone. He ducks under the lintel as he steps into the coach house. "But first we need to figure out where the bastard took her. Kemisi's correct. Muan *is* the only one who would disrespect the rules like this. It probably has something to do with last night. Maybe I should have let him win."

I pause by the door and glance around, deeming nothing out of the ordinary. "It's not your fault. It's that bloody bastard's. Obviously, Muan didn't bring her to this place, so why are we here?"

Artagan comes to a stop in front of a stack of crates, and his attention shifts away as he gropes through one. "The problem is Leah's thoughts are a tangled mess," he continues. "I'm having difficulty deciphering them. That's why I sent Kemisi and Otmar scouting, but it will do us no good to run off half-cocked before we know where he took her."

Artagan's hands emerge from a box, gripping two sheathed dirks. He holds out one of the knives. "Here."

"What good are these going to do? The man doesn't

bleed," I say, taking the sheath and fastening its belt around my waist.

Artagan does the same with his blade. "It will only slow him down, but that might be all we need."

"What if he... hurts her? Before we can..." Heat burns behind my eyes. I clench my fists so tightly my fingernails cut into my palm. Icy tendrils spread from the base of my neck and shoot tingling coils down my spine, sending prickles up along the crown of my head.

"Quiet. Let me listen." He looks away, closing his eyes.

Full of nervous energy, I pace, two fingers flicking against the hilt of my blade. Despite the frosty air, my palms are damp with sweat. As the panic takes a more substantial hold, the moisture spreads, breaking out across the back of my neck, and droplets of perspiration slither their way down my back between my shoulder blades.

After what feels like an eternity, Artagan says, "Good girl." His eyes open, and he turns. "They're still in the city. The Dogfish Bar and Lounge."

"Dogfish? I know the place! It's not far. Just over on Fore Street," I add, making a move for the door.

Artagan steps to block my path. "I'll need you to concentrate on the bar. On its tenor, remember?" Not waiting for an answer, he snatches me by the arm and hurls us toward a shadow.

I clear my mind of the cluttered emotions and do my best to visualize the seedy little hole-in-the-wall, focusing on remembering the exact clichéd stale-beer smell that permeated its walls.

The cobblestone street where we surface is dark and raw, the closely packed properties letting little of the rising sunshine into the cramped space. Our breaths puffing out in white vapors, I glance around, getting my bearings. It only takes a moment for me to realize my poor shadow-navigational skills have dumped us out a couple of blocks off course.

"This way," I call, darting into a nearby passageway that cuts between two of the buildings.

We reemerge on a narrow backstreet, flanked on either side by the rear of the buildings. Lines of rusted fire escapes coil up the brick walls like iron snakes. The Dogfish is easy to spot. It has a large mural of a shark with a Labrador's head painted over the bar's rear entrance. Except for a light in a second-story window, the rest of the building lies in darkness. A muffled scream breaks through the bleak morning air, resonating between the brick-layered walls. Grabbing me by the arm, Artagan speeds for a shadow.

As the black whirling emptiness dissolves, dumping us into the dimly lit void, Artagan draws the dirk from his belt with a flourish. I take a firm grip on my own blade and follow suit. Artagan places a finger to his lips then gestures to wait. The fog evaporates, revealing a scene through the thin shroud.

Leah crouches over an unmoving form sprawled on the floor. She holds a little gold letter opener tightly in her shaking hand, aiming the blade straight at Muan, who stands about three feet in front of her. Two of his brothers, their faces painted blue with black streaks across their eyes and mouths, flank him. Even through the bands of color, the man to Muan's right is recognizable as Izel, his bulging eyes a dead giveaway. The other man is a bit shorter than his brother, but with his thick biceps and barreled chest, he's by no means sparse.

Muan dips his hand into a terra-cotta bowl and then smears a thick layer of blood across his neck and face. After handing the bowl off to the shorter one, Muan smiles, the white gleam of his teeth showing in stark contrast with the black-red staining his skin. At this, the three begin to chant.

The crumpled body at Leah's feet stirs, rolling to its side, and reveals a man battered beyond recognition. His mouth moves as if he's trying to speak, but no sound more than bubbling rasps passes through his cracked lips. He goes limp, and then spasms jerk through his body with involuntary contractions. Removing a long-bladed knife from a sheath strapped to his thigh, Muan steps forward.

Artagan gestures for me to follow, and he strides toward the veil. But instead of passing through as before, he rebounds. He attempts again but to no avail. A sudden alarm bursts into Artagan's eyes, sending terror ripping through my chest. He presses his palms on the invisible barrier and runs his hands along it. I join him, the smooth, firm surface cold under my flushed palms. It's soon apparent the shadow has solidified around us, entombing us in its bowels.

"They've locked us in here somehow. Look for anything that appears out of place," Artagan says.

My eyes dart around the room. I hold my breath, praying we find what has blocked our entrance. A piece of pottery, sitting on a table at the far end of the room, catches my attention. The three-footed, bulbous jar—painted in brilliant brown, red, ivory, and black—seems out of place among the movie-related memorabilia cluttering the apartment. The head of an open-mouthed jaguar adorns the lid. I squint. A thin ribbon of faint purple smoke flows from the big cat's mouth.

"There," I say, pointing.

Artagan moves to my side and peers at the decorative jar. Accompanied by a quick bob of his head, his lips waver with the speed of a conversation—the silent rhythm impossible to decipher.

I look to Leah. Her expression brightens. She nods her head a fraction of an inch, taking a deep breath. Then with a burst of energy, she bolts in the direction of the jar.

Muan moves to block her path.

Leah swings the letter opener at him, aiming for his chest, but misses. Muan laughs. His meaty hand juts out. Leah ducks, but he catches her by the sleeve. With a hand full of fabric, Muan pulls Leah to him. She yelps, pulling away, but he jerks her closer.

Frantic, I thrust hard against the barrier, pushing to no avail. I'm forced to watch as Muan seizes Leah by the hair and bends her head backward with force. He then places the blade of his knife to her throat, nicking her skin. A single drop of crimson rolls down her exposed neck. Before the wound can heal, Muan leans in, and with a flick of his tongue, he licks it.

I feel as if I'm going mad. The prickle running the length of my spine spreads. From the tips of my fingers to the soles of my feet, my entire body turns cold like someone dipped me in ice water. I wind my hands into tight fists and accost the invisible barrier, striking it again and again, but only succeed in bloodying my knuckles.

Muan glances in the direction of our shadowy prison. He licks his lips as he pulls Leah closer still, pressing her against his chest. Shockingly, she curls into his embrace, but then, with a flash of gold, she sinks the letter opener deep into his thigh.

His black eyes widening, Muan clutches at his leg, and he stumbles back. I stare dumbfounded as blood as red as mine soaks through the fabric of his pants and around his fingers. No smoke. No ash. Only crimson.

I expect Izel and the other brother to assist Muan, but instead, they glide back, stunned, putting distance between themselves and their brother. Fear claims Muan's features. Favoring his good leg, he follows his brothers' lead, backing away from Leah.

Emboldened, Leah steps forward, blade lifted, readying for another strike.

The shorter brother mutters a measured chant low enough so only the rhythm, not the words, can be heard.

His hand delves into a leather pouch dangling from his belt. With a lightning-fast movement, he brings a clenched hand to his mouth and blows a red powder into Leah's face, blinding her. Izel slips the jar into a leather sack. After he pulls the bag's drawstrings tight, sealing off the purple smoke, the three Soulless disappear into a shadow.

Freed from our imprisonment, Artagan and I rush into the room. The thick smell of salt and iron is overwhelming, blended with a fetid odor of earth and incense. Leah stands as still as a statue, her clothes splattered with drying blood. Half her hair hangs across her shoulder, pulled from the lackadaisical bun during the attack. Her body trembles, and her crimson-smeared hand still clasps the letter opener in an iron grip.

I sheathe my blade and step toward her. "Leah?" I say almost in a whisper. "They're gone. You're safe now."

She gives no response. Her eyes are blank as if she doesn't hear me. So I repeat myself. Again, I receive no response. At that moment, I fear the savagery she witnessed has stained her far deeper than her skin and clothes.

I take another step. This time, I outstretch my arms. "Love, it's me. Jack."

Her gaze shoots in my direction, crazed and unfocused. Her grip tightens on the handle of the opener. "Get away from me! Or I'll cut you again!" she screams, swinging the blade.

"Hold her," Artagan commands, snatching a water bottle from a side table by the couch.

Seizing Leah, I restrain her arms, pinning them to her side. "What's wrong with her?"

"Just hold her!"

She fights, gnashing her teeth as if she's mad, but I keep her still, not letting her move as Artagan pours the entire contents of the water bottle over her powder-coated face. Then, restraining her swirling head with one hand, he uses the other to wipe the residue from her eyes, nose, and mouth. She sputters and coughs. Artagan takes a stride back and motions for me to let her go.

As Leah wrenches away, I see recognition glint in the murky depths of her eyes. She blinks several times, a flurry of emotions in her expression. She releases the letter opener, the blade giving a muted thump as it hits the thick carpet. "Jack! I-I," she stammers between breaths coming out in ragged bursts.

A sense of relief ripples through me, and I wrap an arm around her. "I'm here," I breathe into her ear.

"Why did you go with them? Do you realize what they could have done to you?" Artagan shouts, baring his teeth.

"Enough," I say to him, my body tensing. I want answers, too, but this isn't the time or place.

Leah's attention slips to Artagan. "You called me, told me to meet you here."

"I did not," Artagan protests.

Leah shakes her head, making her freed locks fly. "I know it wasn't you now, but it sounded like you. When I got here, and I found Muan and his brothers, I knew it was a trap. But by then it was too late. They said they needed *my* blood. When the man tried to protect me, they tortured him for it," she says, looking at the crumpled figure. "They told him they were going to remove his heart. I couldn't let them. Why would anyone want to do that?"

"Because they are an abomination," I say, my voice a little uneven, and I stroke her hair.

"The man kept begging for God to help him." Her hushed words come out slow with no inflection. "They just laughed and said no god could help him now. Nor would he want him to when they were done."

"So when *He* didn't show up," Artagan says, picking the letter opener up off the floor, "you decided to fill his shoes."

I shoot Artagan a stern glare.

Leah draws away from me just enough so she can see him. "I couldn't let them hurt him anymore."

His gaze drops back to the unmoving, bloodied figure. He sighs. "No, I suppose you couldn't."

Leah grows quiet, drifting into her own private thoughts.

My eyes settle on the bloody opener Artagan placed strategically in the man's stiffening hand. "Is there any way this can be traced back to her?" I ask.

"Although flesh and bone, we're much like phantoms. We don't leave traceable fingerprints, or hair or skin samples. There'll be no evidence we were ever here," Artagan says. He walks to a desk and rummages through the drawers, tossing the contents across the floor. "With a few well-placed clues, the police will search for a robber-turned-killer they'll never find."

Artagan steps back to survey his work. Then, removing the flask from the pocket of his blazer, he kneels at the man's side and mutters under his breath, finishing his ritual by drawing the sign of the cross on the man's forehead and palms.

"Well, at least he's at peace now," Artagan says, standing. He stares down at the man's bruised and swollen body. His face is streaked with yellow powder, the pain he felt in death plain in his expression. "No need for such brutality, ever. Poor bastard."

"He had a name. He was Eric Gammon," Leah says. The strength in her voice comes as a surprise to both Artagan and me.

"They all do, lassie." Artagan offers her the flask. "For your nerves."

Leah accepts it. She sniffs and draws back, wrinkling her nose.

"There's a bar downstairs. I'm sure I can find something less strong and more fitting for a lady."

Leah glares at Artagan over the rim. She straightens her shoulders and, before I can stop her, tosses back the flask, taking a rather large gulp. Her hand flies to her throat as she splutters scotch and then coughs until I feel obligated to thump her on the back.

"I'm okay," she says, red faced, waving my hand away.

"Burned, didn't it? Have another go. But this time, don't guzzle it like some common drunkard."

"I'm good. I think I'll stick to wine." She glances at Artagan, her manner turning sheepish, and she hands him back the flask. "Thank you, though. Sorry I snapped."

"Not to worry. You've had an eventful morning. I suppose I owe you an apology as well, accusing you of going with those appalling creatures willingly," Artagan says calmly, but there's a definite edge in his tone—concerned and hesitant, fearful even. He scans the shadows and then relaxes, continuing. "I'm proud of you. You stood up to them. But until we understand all that went on here, we need to keep what occurred to ourselves." He pauses. "Not even Kemisi and Otmar can know that you made Muan bleed."

Her brows crease over uneasy eyes. "So that did happen? I'm having a hard time determining what was real. It's like I remember everything through a fog."

"That was because of the powder Izel blew in your face. The disorientation will pass. From your reaction, it had some potent hallucinogenic properties. And yes, you most certainly did make Muan bleed. But why? That's the million-dollar question. So until we know, tell no one."

"But what about Muan? Don't you think he'll tell the others?" I ask.

"No. He'd do anything in his power to hide weakness. Even among his brothers. I doubt any of them, besides Izel and Pacal, will ever know." He looks to the shadows and then to Leah again. "We should get you back to the house so you can clean yourself up."

Once home, Leah showers. When she reemerges from the bathroom, she settles next to me on her bed. She lets her finger trace the zigzag pattern of the puffy quilt, lost to her own train of thought. I sprawl next to her, propping my head on my elbow. Past the placid gaze, I see a storm brewing in her eyes, and I use these quiet moments to dissect what might be going on in that beautiful head of hers.

"Jack?" Leah finally asks, her eyes riveted on the quilt. "If the Soulless are so secretive like Artagan said, why did they involve me in some ancient ritual right out of the Temple of Doom?"

"Artagan believes they took you because he humiliated Muan last night."

"Hmm." She purses her lips and looks at me. "I don't. It seemed much more than that. They talked about blood being powerful because of the magic residing in it." She swallows hard. "Do you really believe I can live this kind of life and not turn into a monster? Like Vita was? Truth, please. Not just what you know I want to hear."

"You are nothing like her," I say with all confidence.

Her gaze drifts and fixes out the window, staying there for a minute before returning. "That day when Artagan told us what Vita and Domitilla changed into, and that it could happen to me, I think I convinced myself that you were right, that none of their evil was part of me."

Anxiety sprouts in my chest. "And now?"

"I don't know," Leah says. "I've never liked causing anyone or anything physical pain. As a kid, my mom said I was the president of the insect catch-and-release program." Her lips turn into a weak grin. "Even spiders, the big hairy ones, were safe under my watch. At school, while other girls screamed or tried to whack them with their sneakers, I'd catch them and find them a new home in the woods around the playground.

"Before that first gathering, Artagan warned me about the euphoria that comes with taking a life, and that I needed to fight against it. I've felt ashamed and guilty, even angry, but never euphoric. Not once, not even after the train crash when all those people lost their lives because of what I did." She hunches her shoulders and averts her gaze.

"Never?" The muscle at the corner of my mouth twitches upward. "Why didn't you tell me?"

"I didn't tell Artagan, either. I didn't want you two to worry."

"Worry? That's the best news I've ever heard." I break into a smile.

"Don't get too excited. This morning, when I cut Muan, I didn't even notice the blood. All I saw was the pain in his face. The realization that I had caused it gave me such a buzz. No, more than that, I wanted to go further. If there were a way, I would have killed him right then, because I wanted to see him writhe and suffer. I wanted him dead."

As the revelation leaves her lips, Leah turns pallid. I capture her by the chin, and she turns her face toward me. "When he touched you like he did, I wanted to break through that barrier and rip him to shreds. Even now, in the back of my mind, I'm playing with ways I could kill him. If taking his life was a possibility, God would have to have mercy on him because I wouldn't."

A snarl of bloodlust breaks through my lips. Embarrassed, I look away. Taking a deep breath, I feel a confession brewing on the tip of my tongue and wonder what Leah's reaction will be to this next admission. "I killed a man. His name was Richard Hake. He was a wicked man who preyed on the weak and exploited them for money. He threatened to expose me because he knew I was different. So I killed him. I'd like to think it was to protect all those lives he was destroying, but I know better. I did it to protect my secret." After a moment's pause, I ask, "Do you think I'm evil?"

"Of course not! How could you ask that?"

I let out the faintest sigh of relief. "Well then, if I'm not evil, then neither are you. You'd just seen Muan torture a man to death. Even the pope would have gotten a thrill out of seeing that piece of rubbish squirm." My mouth twists into a sneer. "When you gripped that blade and stood your ground, you did it to protect Eric Gammon from any more suffering. That was brave and kind. Vita wouldn't have done that. She would have rejoiced in that man's pain. You're not the monster here. The Soulless are. And if anything, this morning proves how far from Vita you truly are."

My reassurance seems to comfort her, and our conversation proceeds jerkily without further mention of the Soulless, Vita, or tainted blood.

As soon as Leah is resting, I disentangle myself from her embrace. She mumbles softly, but then her breath resumes the even tempo of deep sleep. I kiss her on the brow and then steal from the room to find Artagan. With over six hundred years of knowledge, he has to have at least an inkling of what's going on, no matter what he said back in Gammon's apartment.

CHAPTER SEVENTEEN

THROUGH THE CRACKED DOOR OF **Artagan's** study, the murmur of a one-sided conversation floats out into the hall. I consider leaving and returning later, but his next words stop me in my tracks.

"Please listen. The girl has abilities, and not ones I've seen before."

I edge closer, being careful of any squeaking floorboards, and lean against the wall to listen.

"You know I'd share the source of this information," Artagan says. A long silence hangs in the air before he speaks again. "Dammit! Listen! Whatever I might be, I'm not one of them." He puffs out a sharp exhalation and adds resentfully, "Well, if you'd agree to meet every once in a while, maybe you would."

Following another pause, he goes on, his voice growing more animated with each syllable. "I hoped you'd be able to tell me more than that... Yes, I understand. But I'm not the enemy here, Tobias."

Tobias? Who the hell is Tobias? Artagan made his instructions clear. *Tell no one.* My jaw clenches, but I force the mixture of anger and unease down. I need to listen.

He chuckles, an edge of irritation ringing clear in his tone. "Yes, I'm sure she'd disagree. How is your mother?...

Yes, yes. I understand. Hear me out. This girl, Leah—there's something different about her. Do you know what would cause a Soulless to bleed?... That's exactly what I'm implying... Tobias? Are you there?" A flurry of expletives follows, and then the room falls quiet.

I push the door open with my foot. Artagan sits, shoulders slumped as he rests his elbows on his knees, a tumbler teetering in his grasp. With papers spread out across his desk and books scattered about the floor, it looks like a tornado hit the room.

"You said not to tell a soul," I say, my tone controlled. "Who's Tobias? What does he know about Leah?"

Artagan ignores me, not even having the courtesy to acknowledge my presence. The odor of alcohol wafts from him in a plume.

"Are you even listening?" I say. "Or are you too drunk to give a damn?"

"I don't think I've ever been shitfaced in my life." He glances up from his drink, unconcerned at my tone. "And there's nothing wrong with my hearing, whatever my moral shortcomings may be," he says and downs the rest of the liquor. He stares at me for another passing moment, a critical glint in his eyes. The air of hostility between us intensifies.

I inhale, steadying my nerves. "I trust you. I swear I do. But you promised no secrets."

"No, I implied no secrets. And I suppose having doubts is your way of showing your faith in me?"

"That's not—look. If you won't tell me, you have to tell Leah. Whatever this is, it's clearly about her. She has the right to know."

"I'd rather you didn't tell her about this conversation at all."

"Why not? What are you hiding? And don't say nothing because that's clearly not the case."

"Enough." He raises his hand. "I don't have time for

this." Then, setting his tumbler down in the middle of the flurry of papers, he pushes up from his seat, and with a steady gait, he moves past me. I reach out to grab him, catching the sleeve of his jacket. The material slips through my fingers, and I'm left gripping nothing but air. At the door, he pauses long enough to glance at me over his shoulder. "Don't do anything foolish while I'm gone."

"Gone? Where the hell—?" The door shuts with a resounding thud, cutting off my question and leaving me alone in his study. A glutton for punishment, I chase after him, but as I should have expected, I don't find him. I return to his office and explore the clutter of papers, but I see nothing that suggests where he went or who Tobias is.

The next day, the storm in Leah's eyes has returned. We sit in silence at the kitchen table. Leah stares at her plate of scrambled eggs, pushing the fluffy lumps around with her fork. Ever since she woke, her expression has remained haunted, trepidation lurking under the surface. *Still processing* is all she's told me. In a way, this response has eased my mind. If she had gotten up this morning without a care in the world, that would have been far more worrisome. Fear and edginess are natural reactions to everything that happened to her yesterday.

While eating a bowl of Cap'n Crunch, I'm distracted now and again by Otmar as he digs his way through the contents of the refrigerator. I watch as he removes each container. After examining each one, he opens the lid and sniffs. Every time, he scrunches his nose and, with a curse, thrusts it back into the fridge.

"Here you are," Kemisi says, appearing in the doorway. Her face glows, but something about the smile looks fake, almost forced. "I want to go over a few things with you after breakfast."

Leah peers up as Kemisi slips into the chair by her side before turning her attention back to her eggs.

"Don't worry," Kemisi adds. "It will be fun. Artagan suggested I teach you *my* specialty."

"He's back, then," I say.

Kemisi offers me an apologetic smile. "No, Artagan texted me."

"What do you mean? Where is he?" Leah asks, her eyes snapping up from her untouched plate.

Kemisi's smile turns serious, her amber gaze unsettled. "In typical Artagan fashion, he left that part out," she says. "And if experience holds true, I don't expect him back anytime soon. He put me in charge of your training until his return."

Leah glances from Kemisi to me, her eyes wide with surprise. "Did you know?"

I nod but then feel the need to clarify. "He mentioned late last night he was leaving, but that's all. I hoped he'd be back this morning. But it seems—" I frown.

Leah's animated eyes turn dark with thought as they drift away from me, resting sightlessly out a window at the far end of the kitchen. I touch her arm. She gives me a brief, distracted glance and tries to smile.

"One more thing," Kemisi says. "I hope you understand, Jack, but I can't allow you to accompany Leah on any more gatherings."

I answer her with a quick bob of my head.

"Why not?" Leah's voice spikes with agitation. "It's not Jack's fault Artagan took off."

"It's nothing personal. But he is Artagan's descendant, not mine, and I don't break the rules for anyone."

"Don't break the rules, huh?" Otmar chimes in, setting a Tupperware container of leftovers on the table and slumping into a chair next to me. "So Death knows Artagan skipped town and you're covering for him?"

"Hush. You're just pissed because he didn't ask you to take charge," Kemisi says.

Otmar grumbles something under his breath.

Kemisi smirks. Clearing her throat, she continues. "Like I was saying, today will be fun. I'm going to teach you to fight. Artagan believes a knife would be the best weapon for you. And I agree."

Leah pulls and twists at a strand of hair, her eyes falling away again.

"Don't worry," Kemisi reassures her. "After a few lessons, you'll know how to defend yourself. Just in case."

"Isn't there anything Death can do?" I say.

Otmar snorts. "To control Muan? No. The Soulless have always been out of his control. Whether Death likes to admit that or not is another story."

With the picture of Leah clutched in Muan's arms still fresh in my mind, I tighten the grip on my spoon. "I'll tell you what. If that black-eyed demon wants to get to her again, he'll have to go through me."

Kemisi's expression pinched, she stares at me. "When Muan comes calling next time—which he will—he'll wait until she's alone again. If nothing else, he is a creature of habit."

I sigh. "I only meant—"

"Besides," Kemisi continues, cutting me off, "the knight-in-shining-armor sentiment is sweet, but damn boring if you're the damsel. Sometimes the woman wants to be in on the action, likes doing some of the saving herself. Am I right, Leah?"

Leah nods in affirmation, a smile playing around the edges of her lips.

Otmar leans close. "See what I've been dealing with all these years?" The brawny Viking's grin widens, indicating that he's joking, but that doesn't stop Kemisi from scowling at him. Unconcerned, his attention returns to the plastic container on the table, and he pokes at the contents with his fork. "What is this?"

"Brussels sprouts and tofu stir-fry," Kemisi says.

Otmar puckers his mouth up as if he just tasted a lemon. "Better suited for a cow. A man needs red meat."

"First off, it wasn't for you. That was my lunch," Kemisi says. "And second, if you don't like what I cook, get off your lazy ass and use the damn stove."

Otmar shrugs and shoves a large forkful into his mouth, chewing it noisily.

"Eat up. You'll need your strength." Kemisi smiles, and her attention darts back and forth between Otmar and me. "I'm in need of two assistants."

"She means training dummies," Otmar says, scooping up another mouthful.

After breakfast, Kemisi has Otmar and me move the black lacquered coffee table from the center of the front parlor, and the lesson begins.

"Knives are light, easy to control. Because of your size, once trained, you should be quick," Kemisi says. The golden blade of her dagger gleams as she removes it from a leather sheath concealed by a flowing blouse. She balances the hilt on her finger, just an inch from the blade. "The balancing point. This is where you want to grip your knife. That way it will fit relaxed in your hand. We'll focus on the underhand thrust," she instructs as she demonstrates. "An overhand strike is perfect as long as your opponent is smaller. But since most of your rivals will be closer to Otmar's size, you'll only want to use it after you've taken them to the ground."

Leah stares up at the Viking's considerable height, comparing their size difference. She glances at Kemisi with a quizzical frown. "You can take *him* to the ground?"

Kemisi reaches up and grabs Otmar by the shoulder. With a pendulum swing of her leg, she kicks him along the calf, knocking him off balance. His back hits the floor, pushing air from his lungs in a sudden burst.

"Size doesn't matter as much as technique," she says with a smile. "Gravity always wins."

As Otmar heaves himself to his feet, Kemisi commands him to remove his shirt. Without objection, Otmar does as he's told, pulling his T-shirt over his head and tossing it onto the sofa. Then, folding his arms behind his back, he waits for further instructions. However, once Kemisi turns her back to him, engrossed in explaining the finer points of hand-to-hand combat with a blade, Otmar begins posing like a prizefighter, flexing his muscles and twitching his brawny pecs independently of each other. Leah purses her lips, hiding her amusement, while I attempt rather unsuccessfully to keep my attention on Kemisi.

Otmar grins upon seeing our reactions but exchanges the smile for an expression of bland detachment as Kemisi's glare turns in his direction.

"I can see your reflection, you know." She gestures to the bay window across the room. "Now, quit fooling around. I need you to be serious for thirty seconds."

Otmar bobs his head in agreement, even if it is a bit grudgingly.

Satisfied, Kemisi continues. "There are a few sweet spots I want you to aim for. Here." She points the tip of her blade at the center of Otmar's chest, nicking the skin just under the breastbone. A single red drop trickles from the cut before it heals. "Drive your blade straight up as hard as you can to hit the heart, but the lungs are good, too." She then makes Otmar spin around, and she points to the spot below his ribcage to the left of the spine. "Into the abdominal aorta. Or here, from either side of the spine"—she drops the blade to his lower back—"you can stab upward into the kidneys. All these spots will send a man to his knees, immortal or not. It will give you time to seize his weapon. Or give you time to escape."

Then, to demonstrate, Kemisi jabs the blade into Otmar's lower back with a forcible thrust, sinking the knife up to its hilt into the muscular flesh right of the spine.

Otmar drops like a stone, letting out a loud, lengthy groan as he falls.

"See?" Kemisi yanks out the crimson-covered blade. Then, crouching in front of him, she says with a smile, "That's for eating my lunch."

With Kemisi's retribution exacted, we spend the rest of the morning teaching Leah how to fight. Kemisi works with her on hand-to-hand techniques, while Otmar and I take turns being the training dummies.

The following afternoon features a similar training session. This routine continues as days become a week, then two, and Leah's time becomes less and less her own. When she isn't working on her mind control with Thanatos, she's with Kemisi, working on one fighting technique or another. On these days, I serve as a training dummy. I watch with relief as Leah consistently improves. At this rate, Leah will be able to protect herself against the Soulless in no time. However, I fear not enough training in the world can guard Leah against the dread of Christmas break and the arrival of her brother.

CHAPTER EIGHTEEN

L EAH STARES AT HER PURPLE-POLISHED nails, picking at the cuticles in silence as we wait on a bench in baggage claim. Close to nine, Portland Jetport is quiet, caught in a lull of the wax and wane of traffic. Every now and again, Leah takes a quick peek first at the clock on her phone then at the arrival-and-departure monitor, her leg bouncing more frantically with each passing second.

"With everything you've been through, you can handle Grady," I say, placing a hand on her bobbing knee.

"Tell that to my flip-flopping stomach." She steals a sideward glance at the monitor once again.

A small chuckle rumbles through my chest. "He's your brother, which means he loves you, and he misses you."

"You're right. I'm sure everything will be fine," she says, rolling her eyes.

Craning my neck to see past the luggage carousels, I peer at the row of automatic doors that leads to the parking garage as a mother with two children in tow walks in. "I expected your mum to be here by now."

"Oh, she's not coming, thank God. I think one interrogator is all I can take." Leah blows a puff of air through her lips and looks at her feet. "She texted me. She got a bunch of last-minute orders. A lot of vases and bowls, by the sounds of it. She said they'd keep her busy until Christmas."

"Well, then, no reason to be nervous," I say, reaching out and tucking a loose strand of hair behind her ear. "Grady's a piece of cake. Just stick with the story. Besides, didn't he say he was bringing Charlotte in his last email? He won't be able to give you a hard time with her around."

"I hadn't thought of that. But I can't stop hearing my mom telling me lies are complicated, and the truth is easier because you have nothing to remember."

"You're telling the truth. Mostly," I add, smiling at her worried expression. "You're just leaving out some of the details. Besides, you've done this before, with the dreams of me."

"That was different. That was personal."

"And this isn't?"

Leah mumbles something and looks back to the monitor.

"Remember, we're staying at my apartment while Grady's here. Since your brother knows Olluna and the Golden Butterfly by heart, it's best we don't mention the story's lead character, at least by name."

She bites her lower lip and glances at me.

"Don't tell me," I say. "You already mentioned Artagan, didn't you?"

Leah blushes. "I might have added we were living with him at Westward Mansion. You said you'd told Sally Artagan was your uncle, so I figured it wasn't a big deal."

I run a hand through my hair.

"Before you freak, I told Grady his name was Art. Arty, actually. Are you sure I didn't tell you any of this? I could have sworn I did."

"No, you didn't. I assure you I would have remembered the name Uncle Arty." I laugh once without humor. "Although I'd love to see his face when he hears you renamed him, maybe it's a good thing he's not around."

I exhale, ignoring the pang of irritation in the pit of my stomach that sprouts to life every time I think of Artagan's untimely departure. Nearly three weeks have passed, and none of us has heard a word from him.

"I'm afraid you've made this more complicated than it needed to be, though," I continue with a sigh. "Grady already knows about the immortal world. And now you've exposed Artagan."

"Grady won't tell anyone," she says, overemphasizing the last word. "Besides, you saw all those servers at the dinner. Obviously, some mortals know about us."

"But it wasn't your secret to tell. It was Artagan's. I'll let Kemisi and Otmar know we might have a visitor."

"First off, I didn't actually tell Grady Artagan is immortal."

"Your brother's not a fool. If Arty"—I smile—"is my uncle, it's implied. Secondly?"

"You don't need to tell Otmar and Kemisi. Grady's heard the stories of Westward Mansion, and he won't set a toe inside the place. Haunted houses have always freaked him out. He'll be heading to Mom's in the morning, anyway."

"Are you sure? I assumed Grady would stay around here, close to you."

A rumble of voices draws my attention from Leah's taut expression. Luggage in tow, a group of passengers meanders toward us from the direction of the gates. I catch sight of Grady's shaggy blond head bobbing over the throng. I stand and hold out my hand. "It's showtime."

"Lee-lee!" Grady sweeps her off her feet into a bear hug. After a beat, he releases her and steps back, his lips turned up into an all-encompassing smile. "Boy, did I miss you!"

"I missed you, too." Leah looks over Grady's shoulder. "Where's Charlotte? You said she was coming."

"She was," he says, "but family calls. Her mom fell a couple of days ago while hanging some Christmas lights.

She broke her leg in three places. They say she'll be all right, but she has a long recovery ahead. Charlotte decided to go home and help out over the break."

"Glad her mom's okay." Leah gnaws on her lip and looks at the floor.

"Don't worry. Charlotte will visit this summer. You and Mom will have plenty of time to make sure she's good enough for your big brother."

"It's the other way around," she says, straight faced. "I'm still trying to figure out what she sees in you."

"Ha-ha," he says, ruffling her hair.

A buzzer blares, and the carousel to our left groans and squeals as it revolves. A tense unease falls between the siblings while we wait for Grady's luggage.

"Do you need a ride in the morning? Or are we driving you to your mom's tonight?" I say to break the silence.

"No, you can drop me off at the Holiday Village over on Spring." Grady smirks, mischief flickering in his steel-gray eyes. I stare at him, and he ignores me, yanking a black suitcase off the carousel. "I'll probably visit Mom over the weekend, but other than that I'm staying in Portland until Christmas Eve, then I'll head to Mom's and spend a week with her before I go back to York. Surprise!"

Leah stiffens. "I don't need you keeping an eye on me," she says in a disgruntled tone.

"It's not all about you. I want to catch up with some of my buddies."

Leah glares at him suspiciously.

"Besides," he goes on, "I still have lesson plans to go over for my new class, The Culture of Medieval Times. Exciting stuff. Just my luck, the academic board approved the class a week ago, so if I stay with Mom, we both know what will happen," he says, pulling up his collar around his chin as we head out the doors to the parking garage.

She nods. "She'll have you cleaning the barn, delivering orders, and doing every odd-job she can think of."

"Which would leave me no time to put the finishing touches on any of my lessons."

"You don't have to stay in a hotel," I chime in. "I kept the lease on my apartment. It's not much, but I can guarantee no bedbugs, at least. You're welcome to it."

"Are you serious? That would be awesome! Thanks, I owe you one." Grady smiles and gives me a thump on the back.

During the drive, Grady prattles on about his students and Charlotte, only needing the slightest nudge from me to keep the conversation moving. However, once we cross the threshold into the apartment, Grady's mood changes, shifting into a serious tone. The siblings' eyes lock as if in a private conversation. Unfortunately for Leah, she looks away first, emboldening her brother.

"Jack, I need a minute alone with my sister. We have some things to sort out."

I exchange a quick glance with Leah. Her expression flashes with a momentary stab of panic, then struggling to compose herself, she gives me a reluctant nod.

"You sure?" I say. Stubbornness is a major component in both their characters. This little exchange is bound to turn into a contest of wills, a competition between two immovable objects.

She nods again, this time with more confidence.

"All right, I'll make the bed and see if I can scrounge up some clean towels."

Once in the bedroom, I sit on the corner of the bed, lifting a forgotten glass from the nightstand. I need something in my hands. I shift the glass from palm to palm, my feet tapping with nervous energy. From here, all I can do is hope Grady isn't heaping a new pile of guilt onto Leah's already-full plate.

I stand and begin to pace, too anxious to stay to put. The walls in the apartment are paper thin, and as their mumblings turn into a lively debate, I find I'm able to hear the complete conversation, not just a word or phrase here or there. I feel like an interloper, but I listen just the same.

"Between missing Thanksgiving and quitting school, Mom's still worried about you. When you avoid her like that, it makes things hard on her," Grady says.

"I had to work on Thanksgiving. I told her that."

"Sure you did, because Old Port Java is a hotspot for holiday dining. I know they were closed. I called Rachel."

"You did what?" Her voice bubbles over with exasperation.

"She told me you'd been missing a lot of work lately."

"A lot? Try five days in the past six weeks," Leah says, her tone rough with stress.

"For you, that's a lot, and you know it."

"Back off. I've been busy."

"With planning a wedding, right?" He snorts. "I'm disappointed. I thought I taught you to lie better than that. You had to know Mom would see straight through it. In high school, she watched you juggle being president of the art club, the drama club, not to mention that part-time job at Ames. And you still graduated with honors."

"That's because I got the math tutor."

"No, that's because you worked your ass off. So why in the world you thought Mom would buy that feeble excuse, I have no idea."

"She pushed, okay?" Leah says, her voice devoid of any real emotion. "It was the first thing that popped into my head, so I went with it. Since we're rehashing things, though, I have a bone to pick with you, too."

"Oh no, here we go," he observes, sarcasm saturating his voice.

Grady's tone irritates me, but I fight the urge to barge into the living room.

"You had no right to call Jack and ask him if he got me pregnant," Leah says.

Grady laughs with a notable lack of humor. "He told you that?"

"Of course he did."

"Okay. I overreacted."

"You think?"

I hear a rustle of fabric as someone stands and begins to pace the room. From the weighty footfalls, it's Grady. "Look, I'm worried about you. Mom's worried about you. As I told Jack, she was convinced you were sick again. And when you refused to return any of my calls—"

"You flipped out," Leah says. "And you know why I didn't return your calls? I knew what you'd say. You'd do what you've always done—tell me what I should do. Tell me I'm silly. At some point, I have to make my own decisions without your input, and that time is now. Ever since Dad died—"

"I have opinions because I care," he says. "If you'd called me, told me what was going on, *really* going on, I would have tried to help. But all I knew, because you wouldn't talk to me, was that you were giving up a dream you've had forever."

"Just because you're five years older doesn't mean you get to boss me around. Everyone is telling me what I can and can't do. I'm sick of it!"

"And what am I supposed to do if I see you doing something stupid?" Grady fires back.

"Shut up. Let me make a mistake without your endless commentary. Besides, I haven't given up my painting, just school. For the time being."

I hear him sigh, and I imagine his anger deflating like a balloon. "I can see how that might be pretty annoying. Remind me to tell you about Charlotte's mom. It seems I can't do anything right in her eyes." A hush hangs in the air before his gaze returns to his sister. "So immortality isn't as easy as it is in all those fairy tales, huh?"

"It's hard to explain."

"Nothing worthwhile is ever easy."

"Did you seriously just use a Mom line?"

"Yeah, I guess I did." Grady laughs. "I still can't get over you two staying at Westward House. How do you sleep? With everything that supposedly happened, the place must have bad juju."

"We see a ghost about every night," Leah says with the utmost seriousness.

There's a long silence, and then she breaks into laughter. "I'm kidding. Geez. Has Charlotte figured out what a wimp you are?"

"Wimp or not, you won't get me near that place. Just walking by it used to give me the creeps." He pauses. "Don't worry about Mom. I'll take care of it. I'll tell her something, like you're working on an exhibition for a London gallery or somewhere exotic. But it's not a sure thing, so you don't want anyone to know."

Leah snorts and then lets out a long sigh. "I hate lying to her."

"Well, unless you plan on telling her the truth, it's our only option. Besides, someday your work will be in exhibitions all over the world. We're just putting the cart before the horse by a year or two."

I can tell from their tone the storm has passed. Returning the glass to the dresser, I head for the living room. I lean against the doorframe, peering back and forth between their faces. "Safe to come in?"

Leah smiles but stays silent, only bobbing her head.

As I walk to her side, Grady jabs me playfully in the arm. I grin, my hand flashing out to cuff him across the head.

Laughing, he looks to his sister. "So is this doofus treating you right?"

"I couldn't make it without him," she says, slipping her hand into mine.

"Good. Wouldn't want to beat his ass," Grady says.

I give him a look, one that dares him to try.

He laughs again, and then his joking demeanor turns earnest. "When you've gotten a handle on everything else, Lee-lee, you need to go back to school."

"You're doing it again."

"I am, aren't I? This is going to take some practice. Let's try it again." Grady pushes up his sleeves like he's preparing to do manual labor. "Once you have everything under control, are you planning to go back to school?"

Leah tries not to smile but fails. "Yes, I promise." She looks up at me. "Jack's uncle said he might be able to get me into the École des Beaux-Arts. How cool would that be?" Her voice sparks with laughter. All the weight of the previous conversation has lifted from her face.

"Right, Uncle Arty. Immortality runs in the family," Grady says.

I shrug.

"Lucky bastard. All I got is high blood pressure and the promise of hereditary baldness." He pushes his mop of shaggy hair out of his face. "But the École des Beaux-Arts. Wow. That was always your dream school." He smiles at Leah. "This uncle must have connections, not to mention money. I suppose when time's on your side, you have plenty of opportunities to invest. I can't imagine the stories he could tell."

Grady casts a discouraged eye in my direction. Apparently, he hasn't forgiven me for my lack of information. Back in York, after I told Grady I was immortal, born in 1841, as a history teacher he was full of questions, asking me about every detail from the Crimean War to the Irish famine. Shamefully, I had to admit that I'd been less than observant throughout the years.

"When do I get to meet him?" Grady eyes a loose thread hanging from his sleeve as if he doesn't care much about my answer.

For the first time since Artagan took off, I'm glad he's

not here. "I'm afraid you won't," I say. "His job calls him away a lot, and I fear he won't return until after Christmas. Maybe longer. He's an antiquities dealer in France," I add, making a mental note that should Artagan return before Grady goes back to England, I must tell him about his new profession and nickname. I fight a chuckle at the thought of his expression.

"Another time, then." Grady brings his hand to his mouth to smother a yawn.

"That's our cue," Leah says. "We'll let you settle in. You must be exhausted from the flight."

"Nah." Grady shakes his head. "Let's get takeout. I've been craving the Lotus Blossom for weeks. Just one bite of Mr. Chang's egg rolls, and I can die a happy man."

Over boxes of General Tso's chicken and sweet-and-sour pork, and two large orders of egg rolls, we immerse ourselves in catching up with each other's lives. Leah shares what she can, telling Grady all about her ever-growing list of museums she plans to visit. Grady chats about his life in England, my favorite story being the first time Charlotte talked him into playing cricket.

"Cricket's a tougher game than I gave it credit for," Grady says. "I learned the hard way about the necessity of quality protective gear. That's for sure. Unless I want to sing soprano for the rest of my life."

I laugh.

"I would have paid money to see that," Leah says.

"I'm sure Charlotte has a video she'd love to share." His attention drifts for a moment. "She's perfect for me, Lee-lee. She laughs at all my jokes, even the awful puns. Weird, I know."

"Brave woman." I grin.

"Or foolish. I'm not sure which. I think I'm rubbing off on her, though. She told me this one on the way to the airport. Why did Karl Marx dislike Earl Grey tea?" Grady says, chuckling.

Leah rolls her eyes. "Oh, glory. God help me."

"Come on, just humor me."

"Fine. Why?" I hear the defeat in Leah's voice.

"Because all proper-tea is theft."

Leah and I groan in unison.

Grady ignores the reaction. "How about this one? A Roman walks into a bar and asks for a martinus—"

"No more. That was my one for the day. You better treat Charlotte right," Leah says. "I'm pretty sure she's the only woman on the planet that can bear your brand of humor."

"You're right. It takes a special woman to handle all this," he says, displaying himself as if he's a prize to be won.

I laugh and shake my head. "Yeah, too much class and sophistication there."

"That's what I'm saying," Grady says.

By the time we break open the fortune cookies, the conversation has come full circle, with Grady chattering on about his first love once again—history.

"That reminds me. I need your expertise," Leah says to Grady, stacking the dirty plates. The corners of her mouth twitch as she fights a smile. "Back in college, you wrote a thesis on name trends, didn't you?"

"It was a little more involved than that." He seems genuinely offended. "I charted the history of given names in Britain, and how their fall from popularity reflected social cues. Like, for example, any name connected with Catholicism became wildly unpopular after Henry the Eighth separated the Church of England from the pope's authority. Why?"

"I'm searching for a Victorian name beginning with F." She gives me a sheepish glance and heads for the kitchen. Grady grabs the glasses and follows.

I stifle a groan. I should have seen this coming.

"That's a bit vague. I'm sure Jack would be a better resource than I am," Grady says, glancing at me as I enter the room, but then goes on. "Let's see. Florence or Felicity. They were both popular back then."

"No, I need a boy's name." Leah flashes me a wicked grin as she turns on the faucet, filling the sink with sudsy water.

I grab a dish towel, feigning disinterest.

"Fredrick—" Grady stops short, casting a suspicious eye first to Leah and then to me. As he jumps to conclusions, his face turns as red as a beet, big-brother mode galloping into overdrive. "You said you weren't—"

"Pregnant?" she says, offering him a bemused smile. "No, I didn't. I said it was none of your business."

"Shit! I was right. You are expecting!" He spins to face me, his hand doubling into a fist.

Leah bounds in front of me, arms spread wide. "Oh my god! What are you going to do? Hit him?"

"Damn straight if he knocked up my baby sister." He glowers at me over her shoulder.

"Grow up, please," Leah says. "What are you? Twelve? It's just a stupid misunderstanding. I'm one hundred percent not pregnant. The reason I want to know about Victorian names is because I'm trying to figure out Jack's middle name, and he won't tell me."

"Oh." Grady chuckles with nervous undertones. He then clears his throat, looking in my direction. "Sorry, man. No hard feelings?"

I laugh once at his shamefaced expression. "No blood, no foul. Besides, I would have done the same thing if I were in your shoes."

"Great. I have two adolescents on my hands. Now that's all cleared up, back to my question. Names beginning with F, please," Leah says, face beaming. Grady's eyes flash to mine.

I give a noncommittal shrug and force a grin.

"No way," he says. "I'm not helping you. Remember Jimmy Lowe."

"Oh, him," Leah says with a roll of her eyes. "He deserved what he got."

"When you found out his middle name was Carol, you were ruthless."

"I was eleven."

"Ruth-less," he says, overemphasizing the syllables.

"He called me tinsel-teeth for months. I was already self-conscious about my braces. He made it ten times worse."

"No, he called you that for a week before I told him to knock it off." Grady regards me with a sympathetic look. "Don't worry. I got your back. She won't get any information out of me. Band of brothers and all." He raises a fist.

Leah's eyebrows scrunch together, annoyed. "Band of brothers? Oh, please. Two seconds ago you were ready to rip him a new one."

Grady opens his mouth to say something, something argumentative from his expression, but he stops himself, takes a quick breath, and begins again. "So how's all the wedding planning going?"

"We haven't even started, not really," Leah says a little apprehensively, pulling the plug out of the sink.

"The adjusting and all?" That suspicious gleam returns to Grady's eyes.

Leah nods. "I need to find a dress. Then there's the guest list and the invitations, not to mention the date. I was talking with Rachel yesterday. She said when her sister got married, most churches book a year in advance."

"A year!" I swallow hard.

"Don't panic," Leah says. "After the holidays, I was thinking of asking Mom if we could get married under the trees in her backyard. Granted, they aren't elms, but still kinda fitting for us. Don't you think? I know it's not a church, but think about it," she goes on, not waiting for my answer. Her hand gestures become more pronounced as her excitement builds. "We could hang paper lanterns in the branches, ropes of lilacs and daisies lining the aisle. It would be beautiful. I bet Mom will let us have the reception in the barn. Plenty of room for dancing."

Warmth ignites in my chest, and visions of Leah walking down the aisle of some country church—like one you'd find in the Cotswolds—dressed in white satin and French lace fill my mind. She'll be such a beautiful bride. *My bride,* I think, smiling at her.

"I see you haven't been thinking about this at all," I say.

"Just a little." Leah bumps my arm with her shoulder.

"So when is this dream wedding taking place?" Grady asks.

"June, maybe. How about the fifteenth?" She glances at me and then to Grady. "You will be on summer break, right? Can you be back by then?"

"With bells on," Grady says. "And since I won't be around to help out with any of the planning, let's go wedding dress shopping tomorrow."

Leah stares.

Grady raises his hands, confused. "What?"

"You're kidding," she says. "Do you remember the last time you went dress shopping with me? For prom? Mom forced you against both our wills. It was six hours of hell and complaining. The whole time, I thought about strangling you with a clothes hanger. Why would you want to put either of us through that again?"

"Because you're my baby sister and tormenting you is my job." Grady grabs a hold of Leah with one hand and musses her hair with the other, laughing at her annoyed expression when he releases her.

Grady's presence brings a bit of normalcy back into our lives. To my relief, Leah and I become expert jugglers, able to keep the world of family and the world of the reapers from colliding. During the day, Grady drowns himself in research, and with his innate fear of haunted places, he has no desire to tour the mansion. So when Leah isn't training, we spend our evenings at my old apartment, eating takeout and watching football or old movies with Grady. But with Christmas on the horizon and Leah's mother insisting we spend the holidays with family, I hope our juggling abilities are strong enough and Leah doesn't crack under the added pressure.

CHAPTER NINETEEN

"I HAVE NO IDEA WHAT TO give your sister for Christmas," I confess, stuffing Grady's newly purchased book, *The Social Milieu of the Middle Ages*, in a plastic bag.

Grady clears his throat, the corner of his mouth lifting upward. "You realize Christmas is a little over a week away?"

"I do realize that. Thank you," I grumble, scowling at him. "You're one to talk. Wasn't it you who showed up the day of his sister's birthday, looking for a rare, out-of-print book? If I remember right, I saved your ass."

"Might have been. Sounds like me." He laughs. It echoes in the empty shop, ringing among the bookshelves. A cough chases his amusement away, and he covers his mouth with the inside of his elbow until the fit subsides. "You could always buy her a book," he suggests after excusing himself. "She loves Austen. *Pride and Prejudice*, maybe."

Mr. Darcy. I roll my eyes.

"Or not." Grady chuckles. "Oh, that's right. My sister mentioned once you aren't a member of the Darcy fan club."

"I thought of a book. Maybe not that particular book. If

there was one she really wanted, that would be the perfect choice. But she hasn't given me any hints, and I want whatever I get her to be special."

"Well, you'll never beat mine. Warm, cozy, the forever hug. The Snuggie. Best gift ever. I got Charlotte one, and she loves it. But be warned," he says with a bit of forbidding in his tone. "As memorable as the perfect gift can be, the wrong one can be equally as devastating. I know someone who gave their girlfriend an ironing board. I guess she had mentioned she needed one a few times. Poor Tyler thought it was a hint. It wasn't. That was their one and only Christmas. But no pressure."

"You're an ass."

"Tell me something I don't know." Grady's smile grows at my dubious expression, and then he glances at his watch. "Now that I've caused enough trauma here, I'd better get back to the grind. We're still on for tonight, right? The Patriots are on at seven," he reminds me, snatching the bag off the counter.

I grimace. "Er, Leah didn't call you?" This morning Leah informed me she and Kemisi would be going out tonight. She gave me no details, but I glimpsed something in her eyes that told me it wasn't a night with the girls. For about a half a second, I consider telling Grady neither of us can make it. Deep down, I'm still hoping that Kemisi will relent and allow me to go with them. However, I know that possibility is as likely as Artagan giving up Scotch. And since the thought of another night alone sounds less than inviting, I change my mind.

"The coffee shop Christmas party is tonight," I lie. "Rachel didn't tell Leah about it until yesterday. So it looks like it's just you and me. I'm out of work around six. I thought I'd pick up pizzas from Portland Pie."

Grady answers with a nod, coughing again until I feel obligated to grab him a bottled water from the back.

"You okay?" I ask.

"Yeah, just a stupid tickle. Got up with it this morning," he mutters and takes another sip.

As soon as Grady is out the door, I text Leah, telling her about my little white lie just in case her brother stops by Old Port Java. I ask her to let me know when she's finished, and I'll come back to the house. Although Leah seems to handle each gathering more stoically, she remains haunted for hours when she returns as if, at least for a while, a piece of herself lingers behind with the victim.

Just as I pull on my jacket, readying to depart for the day, I receive a text from Grady informing me that his stupid little tickle has evolved into a full-blown case of the flu, leaving my evening gallingly free and clear.

The glow of the streetlights gleams in through the windows, throwing long, distorted shadows across the paneled walls. The grandfather clock strikes two, its hollow gongs echoing up the dark expanse of the hallway from the foyer below, but Leah still isn't back yet. Somehow, the mansion feels bigger, lonelier without her here. However, with Artagan MIA and Kemisi's steadfast opposition to bending the rules to allow me to tag along, evenings alone are a situation I'd best get used to.

My stomach growls again, reminding me why I ventured out of bed at this godforsaken hour. I dash down the stairs and head for the kitchen.

Ransacking the refrigerator, I paw my way through containers of leftovers and jars of condiments. Shoved near the back, tucked away on the bottom shelf, I find promise in the form of mashed potatoes, and then discover a jar of onion gravy in the door. When I unearth sausages hidden in the meat tray under Kemisi's packages of tofu, I practically cheer aloud.

The sizzling and popping of the sausages frying in the

pan fills the silence. The aromas of cooking meat and spices push my hunger into overdrive. With a plate of bangers and mash in one hand and a beer in the other, I flip on the light switch with my elbow and walk into the dining room.

Settled at the long table, I'm about to take my first bite when I hear a noise—the faint sound of voices too muffled to make out. Because of the ladies' absence and Otmar's departure to Madrid, I should have the whole place to myself.

I turn my head, trying to gauge the direction of the voices, but hear nothing except the faint tick-tock of the clock in the foyer. I chalk the noises up to my haunted imagination combined with the creaks and squeaks of an old house and return to my meal.

A wail brings me to my feet.

Long and loud, Leah's cry banishes any notion I'd been hallucinating. My body hot with flooding adrenaline, I speed my way toward the keening, heading for the hallway at the rear of the dining room. I map out the corridor in my head—the number of doors, how the passage veers left, ending at Artagan's office, abandoned for weeks—and step into the narrow hall.

The blackness slows my gait, but I decide against turning on any lights. Not knowing what I'm walking into, I want the element of surprise in my arsenal if needed. Feeling my way, I move as swiftly as I can, listening at each door and then checking the room before moving on to the next. Everything is silent, and I wonder if I chose the wrong direction. I consider retreating and searching another part of the house, but something in my gut tells me to keep moving forward.

Around the corner, the first hint of light comes into view. At the far end of the hall, Artagan's office door stands ajar, casting a block of light on the adjacent wall.

I hear the sounds of hushed sobbing. Placing each step with silent caution, I inch toward the opening.

"There, there." I freeze. It's Artagan, his voice weakened from some emotion. "We'll get you through this somehow. I promise."

Silence follows. I wait, my back pressed against the wall, listening.

"Get me through it! No! I won't!" Leah's words explode from the room. The desperation in her tone propels me into the office just as she rushes at Artagan. Screaming, Leah pounds on his broad chest with tiny fists, the sound of the blows thudding against his ribs. Artagan does nothing to stop the assault. Balled hands restrained at his side, his face is hard, but his eyes project a sad softness. He stands stoically, allowing Leah to strike him again and again.

Still struggling to make sense of the scene I've stumbled into, I grab Leah around the waist, swinging her thrashing body away from him. Her red, puffy eyes are wild, mirroring those of a cornered animal. My attention snaps to Artagan. "You've been gone for weeks. Disappeared with no explanation. What did you do?"

He ignores me, his focus glued to Leah. "You have no choice," he says.

"No!" She clings to me as if I'm a life raft in a vast, dark ocean. My grip tightens, and I hold her close.

He steps closer, bending his head so he and Leah are eye to eye. His expression is unreadable. "You know what will happen if you don't. Is that what you want?"

"Of course not," Leah says. "Help me save him. Please."

"I cannot." He draws in a deep breath and straightens.

"Can't or won't?" Leah asks.

Artagan gives her a long, assessing look. "I'm here to assist, but in the end, this gathering is your responsibility, lassie."

"Don't call me that!" she shrieks.

231

Artagan glances away for a moment then nods. "I understand you're angry. This is an unfair burden to carry, but the consequences will be dire if you refuse," he says, the emphasis on each syllable cold and mechanical.

"I don't care about myself if it means sacrificing him," Leah says, and her rigid posture slackens. "You helped Jack save me. Please help me. I'm begging you." Her voice breaks.

"You were different—a soul immortal—something your brother is not," he says, clinching the argument. "There is nothing any of us can do to save him."

I feel breathless, as though someone has punched me hard in the gut. But somehow with great effort, I keep my breathing steady. "You can't mean Death expects Leah to gather her brother."

"I do, and he does," Artagan confirms.

I tighten my arms around Leah and pull in a long breath to regain my crumbling composure.

"Then what was any of this for!" Leah wrenches away, her hand clawing at her necklace. "Death... he said... if I behaved, played by the rules, he wouldn't touch my family. He would allow them to die of old age."

"Death seldom makes deals he gains nothing from," Artagan says.

"Y-You said the same thing! Gave me this damned necklace to remind me! But that was all bullshit too, wasn't it?" The delicate chain snaps as she rips the locket from her neck. She throws it, barely missing Artagan's head. The necklace hits the opposite wall and clatters to the floor.

Artagan stares at her. His expression teeters between defeat and remorse. He closes his eyes, dragging in a deep breath through his nose. When they open again, the defeat has vanished, leaving only a note of regret. "I am sorry," he says. Then, unlatching the door, Artagan steps out into the darkened corridor and closes it behind him.

I stand, still in shock, cradling Leah's trembling body in my arms.

"Liar! Liar!" she screams at the door before her words splinter into uncontrollable sobs.

"Shhh, love," I say, stroking her hair. Her legs give out. With her secure in my arms, I guide her to the floor. Waves of helplessness and anger crash over me. I want so much to make her a vow to find an escape from this darkest night, pledge to save Grady. Instead, I do the only thing I can. I hold her and mourn along with her, her frail body shaking against me.

I'm unsure how much time has passed when the door creaks, and I glance up. Kemisi slips into the room, a steaming mug cupped in her hands.

"Leah, this will help calm you, help you sleep. Artagan sent it," she adds, kneeling in front of us.

I take the cup from her and press the rim to Leah's lips. Without opening her eyes, Leah turns her head away. "Please, just a sip, love," I breathe into her ear.

Leah opens her eyes at my voice. She struggles to sit upright and then accepts the mug. Her hand trembles, and I wrap my fingers around hers to help navigate the cup to her mouth. She drinks about half the contents before her eyes close again, and she sags against my chest.

Kemisi collects the mug and stands. I glance up at her, my brows scrunching together in a deep frown. "Can I ask you something?" I say.

"That depends on what you want to know."

"I'm pretty sure I know the answer already." Somehow I manage to keep my voice steady. "If Leah refuses to gather her brother, she'll be forced to face Shadow Death, am I right?"

"I'm afraid so," she says, an apprehensive thread woven into her gentle tone.

I nod mechanically. "Where's Artagan?"

"His bedroom, I believe," Kemisi replies then leaves the room.

I gather Leah up in my arms, her head lolling against my shoulder, and carry her upstairs to her bedroom. I lie next to her on the bed, listening to the even tempo of her breathing. Only when I'm sure Leah won't wake anytime soon do I slip out the door and into the silent hallway.

A strip of light gleaming from beneath Artagan's bedroom door suggests Kemisi was right, and he's there. I knock. When I get no answer, I try the knob, and it opens.

The room is smaller than Leah's and mine, and far less furnished—a single bed and a matching dresser in the far corner, a writing desk surrounded by stacks of books covering the floor and most of the available flat surfaces. Artagan leans at the desk, chin in his hands, staring at one of his books. His only company is a half-empty bottle of Scotch.

I step into the room, closing the door behind me. The smell of burnt sage—pungent and sweet—stings my nose and eyes. I watch Artagan for a long moment. He looks as weary as I feel. Shoulders slumped, he sits motionless, engrossed in the pages.

"Leah can't take her brother. You know that, right?" I say. Unexpectedly, my tone is authoritative, and my voice collected.

Artagan startles. Apparently, he hadn't heard me come in. He turns his head to look at me, but he says nothing, so I continue. "I thought Death didn't allow council members to gather their own family, after Morrighan and all."

"So did I. But it's an unwritten rule, and Death is a ball-breaker." His eyes drift in thought. There's a depth of uncertainty hidden under the confident façade. It's a look I've never seen on his face before. "I suspect Domitilla is involved," he goes on, rambling as though speaking more to himself than to me. "She's been complaining I wasn't aptly punished for what happened to Vita. Perhaps Death finally listened to her. But still, there must be more. Maybe with more time—"

"Taking Grady punishes Leah, not you."

One eyebrow rises. "Only Leah? Widen your scope."

I frown, my eyes narrowing.

"I have to admit it's a brilliant plan. Domitilla believes Leah will never take her brother, and her refusal will send her to Shadow Death. In desolation, Dom assumes you'll gobble down the hemlock concoction without a second thought. I cannot fault her logic. And with another heir snatched away, only I will be left. And Domitilla will be but one step away from Vita's ultimate plan."

"The line of Brennus demolished. Clever bitch." I sink onto the corner of his bed. Artagan offers his bottle, and I accept it, almost with reverence. I take a long swill, feeling the warmth trickle down the back of my throat, and then another before handing the bottle back.

"Justice for Vita. Check. Revenge on me. Check. Two birds, one stone." Artagan takes another swig. "This whole time, we've been so focused on Muan and his brothers that she was able to slip through the cracks. I'd always assumed Vita was both the brawn and brains of the little duo. I was wrong. I hate being wrong."

Artagan looks down at the floor, one hand clenched around the neck of the bottle, tight enough to leave his knuckles white. "Still, the question remains—why has Death gone along with this in the first place? What did Domitilla offer him? He must be gaining something substantial, not just Domitilla's happiness, to risk this level of dissent among his children. I'd love to find out. It might be useful, but I probably never will."

"So she's won," I sigh.

"Not quite yet. Since we don't know Domitilla's scheme, it's a gamble for Leah to take her brother. She might be playing right into Domitilla's hands. That being said, I do have the makings of a plan of my own. Not as foolproof as I'd like, but it is something."

I open my mouth to reply but then close it.

Artagan raises a thick eyebrow, inviting me to continue.

"What made you change your mind? You told Leah she had no choice." I take a deep breath, the sickly-sweet smell stinging my nose again. "Ah, the sage."

He nods. "Since I wasn't sure if my office had been smudged over the last few weeks, I had to play the dutiful son. Understand, even if this plan succeeds and Death lets this cup pass from Leah, it won't change the fact that another council member will gather her brother. When Death decrees it's a mortal's time, no one can amend that decision. If Grady were immortal, even a touch, we'd have something to work with." His attention drops back to the book. "My sympathies. I know he's your friend."

"Yes, and a good man." I swallow the lump forming in my throat. "What's the plan?"

"I'll tell you, but your only job is Leah. That's it. It's your turn to keep *her* from doing anything stupid, while I try to pull magic out of my arse."

The internal debate between defiance and agreement must show on my face because he leans forward, pointing his index finger straight at me. "I'm serious. If this is to work, you must stay out of it. I need to play on the dissent arising in the council. They'd never trust you. Otmar and Kemisi have agreed to help. The members are nervous and on edge. They don't know what Leah will decide, and they'll fear this could turn out the way things did with Morrighan."

"Could she? Could Leah become the next Morrighan or Vita's clone by gathering her brother?"

"It's a valid concern, and we can use this to our advantage. If we can stoke the fire and make it grow, maybe Death will be forced to change his mind and give the assignment to another."

"And what if it doesn't work?" I ask, my voice scarcely audible.

I see the wheels turning behind his calculating eyes, making the horizontal line along his forehead deepen. "That will depend on what you're willing to do. You and Leah, that is," he says, rising from his chair and fastening the top button of his blazer. "But no need to think about that now. Let me see what I can do first. All right?"

I nod and rub my hands across my face, hoping the action might wipe away my weariness with it. When I look up, Artagan has vanished out the door. I grab his Scotch and take a large mouthful. Then, pushing myself to my feet, I steel my nerves before I return to Leah.

The soft, steady sound of her gentle breathing fills the room. I crawl into bed next to her. I must nod off because I am jolted awake by Leah thrashing, as if she's trying to run.

It's early morning. A faint pink glow shines on Leah's face, which is glossy with sweat. Tears roll down her cheeks from under her closed lids. She breathes heavily, with gasping sounds. I grab her by her shoulders, holding her steady. "Leah. Leah, wake up."

Her eyes pop open at my voice, her face darkened by haunting images. She attempts to catch her breath as if she has been running for miles.

"Bad dreams?" I smooth the wet hair back from her face.

Leah jerks her head away, turning to stare out the window. "I don't want to talk about it."

"All right," I say. "I'll see about more tea, to help you—"

"For God's sake, Jack, will you stop trying to fix things? There's no fixing this," she snaps.

I flinch. I open my mouth several times to say something, but each time, I snap it shut, realizing I have no idea what to say. The silence grows awkward, and the mere inches between us feel like miles. At a loss, I swing my legs off the edge of the bed. Propping my elbows on my legs, I lean forward and focus on my hands as they hang between my knees.

"Jack." I look back to find Leah sitting up, studying me. A brief grimace of discomfit crosses her face before she speaks again. "I'm sorry. My thoughts and emotions are a jumbled mess right now. The tea won't help. What I need is time to think."

I nod, moving in to hold her again.

"Alone," she adds, looking away.

I sit a moment in a sort of trance, gazing down at the striped grain of the floor. Then with a bob of my head, I leave and go to the solitude of my room.

The morning sky brightens then thickens with a gray haze. I sit on my bed, staring out the window. Leah's right. Nothing I can say will take away the pain of the impending loss of her brother. No comforting deeds will strip the burden off her shoulders of what Death expects of her.

I exhale, trying to relax the tense muscles in my shoulders and neck, and hold tight to the sliver of hope that Artagan may be successful.

CHAPTER TWENTY

OVER THE NEXT FEW DAYS, I see little of Artagan. I grow impatient for a tidbit of news about how his plan is proceeding because Leah grows more distant with each passing hour, folding further into herself. I wish she would open up and let me comfort her, but it's as though she has driven a wedge between herself and the entire world, and with every relentless swing of the pendulum, the chasm expands.

I strive not to take her increasing remoteness personally and concentrate my energy on what little I can do, mainly scouring Artagan's book collection for the smallest morsel, anything, that might help. But every time Leah recoils from my touch or asks me to leave her alone, that goal becomes more challenging. No matter how I feel about my culpability in this situation, deep down, I know Leah will never blame me. Still, something buried in those green irises scares me.

With Grady still sick, I haven't had to face him and pretend all is well, a circumstance I'm selfishly grateful for. I'm not sure I'm capable of that kind of deception. Nausea rolls through me, expanding into a consuming ache, at the thought of my friend.

I shake off the remorse, not allowing myself to dwell

on Grady's doomed future, and continue up the stairs, carrying a tray of food to Leah's room—a plate of scrambled eggs and buttered toast and a cup of herbal tea. It's become my morning ritual over the last few days.

Halfway up the stairs, Kemisi meets me. "How's Leah?"

"More remote," I say, choosing to leave out the detail that today she has trouble even looking at me.

She purses her lips and bobs her head. "I'm not one to question my father's decisions, but this—it's cruel. I could have never taken Amun. And before now, there was always an unsaid reassurance I'd never have to. We might be Death's children, but we're human, too. And that part of us isn't made for gathering the ones we love," she says, peering into the shadows. "I've talked to Father, asked him to reconsider, and explained to him the mistake he's repeating. I don't know if I changed his mind, but I wanted you to know I tried."

Hands full, I give her a courteous bow of my head. "Thank you. I'm sure that wasn't easy."

Kemisi smiles and then turns to continue down the staircase, her mess of curls bouncing as she goes. Although I find no real hope in her words, I'm grateful she attempted to change the tide of what's coming.

I nudge the bedroom door open with my foot. The room is just as dim as I left it, but to my surprise, Leah has moved. No longer curled in her bed, she sits in a chair by the window, a blanket wrapped around her shoulders. However, the room still emanates the same aura I've grown accustomed to in recent days. Anguish and anger drip from the ceiling and ooze from the walls.

"You're up," I say, placing the tray on the small table next to her. "I know you told me you weren't hungry, but you should eat something."

Staring out the window, Leah appears not to hear me. Then she stirs and seems to come out of her listlessness. I decide this is a good thing, no matter what the alternative is. Maybe she'll talk, let out all those pent-up emotions. I move to put a hand on her back, but she pulls away from my touch.

"I've made a decision," she says. Rising to her feet, she lets the blanket drop from her shoulders onto the seat of the chair and walks to the window. Outside, the sky is overcast. A storm is brewing on the horizon. I step toward her, but she waves me away again, pressing her forehead against the cold pane of the window. She closes her eyes tight, as though she's attempting to seal herself off from the outside world.

"Please, love, you can't keep shutting me out," I say, the nervousness raising my voice an octave.

When Leah opens her eyes, a new fire resides there. She straightens her shoulders, and she faces me with nothing but distance in her expression. Outwardly, she's composed, but I can see the quickening heartbeat pulsing in the hollow of her throat. She takes in a deep breath before she speaks. "I've decided I'm going to take Grady."

"What?"

"I have to," she says.

My jaw tenses, but I keep my voice calm, although I want to scream. "I think we should wait. See if Artagan can find a way. If not, well, then we'll cross that bridge when we come to it."

"Do you think I'm stupid?" she fires back so fast it startles me.

I shake my head back and forth, bewildered. "Of course not."

"Artagan isn't out there trying to save my brother. He's trying to find a way to pass the job to someone else, to keep *his* family safe. To keep *you* from doing something reckless. It's always been about you. Grady will die no matter what. Since I can't save him, the least I can do for my brother is to make sure his death is painless. Can you imagine what his last hours will be like if Death relents

241

and hands his passing to, let's say, Domitilla, or worse, Muan? I've seen what the Soulless can do. I can't let Grady's final hours be like that."

I step forward, but she shifts away, reclaiming the distance.

"Or maybe I'm just tired of fighting," she says.

I choke down the lump forming in my throat and try reason again. "But how can taking your brother be an option? Remember what Artagan said it did to Morrighan? We'll find another way."

"That, right there." She jabs her finger in the air. "Telling me what to do. That stops today."

"I'm not trying to tell you what to do. I'm just scared that taking your brother could destroy the very essence of who you are. Grady wouldn't want you to give up every part of yourself for him. I know he wouldn't."

I draw a quick breath in through my nostrils and glance at the floor. "This is all my fault. I know you don't like hearing me say that. Don't be mad. It's just..." I look up to find Leah staring at me, her face calm.

"I'm not mad," she says. A faint smile shadows her mouth, reminding me of Vita's sinister grin. I resist the urge to step backward. "I agree with you. It is your fault. It's because of you I'm a member of the council in the first place."

Stunned, I lick my drying lips, trying to find the words.

"I want you to leave." She points at the door.

"Leah, please don't push me away. I'm sorry. You have to know I never meant for any of this to happen."

"Oh, I believe you. But it doesn't matter because I can't forgive you. I wouldn't let myself even if I could. Grady will never be married, never have kids. He'll never—" Leah's voice falters, cutting off her words. She wraps her arms around herself and looks away, eyes brimming with moisture.

The muscles in my chest clench so tight I have trouble drawing in a full breath, and I reach out to her.

"Don't touch me!" she shouts, cringing with revulsion. She catches her lower lip between her teeth as though to bite back tears.

Unwilling to let Leah shove me away again, I step forward, and to my relief, she doesn't move away. She stays as still as a stone while my fingers travel down the back of her arm, and then I catch her hand tight within mine. We stand connected for a long moment before she wrenches her hand free.

"I feel nothing," she says, almost with a smile. The suppressed hatred in her voice strikes me low in my stomach.

"I don't believe you," I say, searching her face for a glimmer of the girl who loves me.

"I almost forgot." She slips my grandmother's ring off her finger and holds it out.

"Please don't do this."

She ignores my plea and pushes the ring toward me.

"I don't want it," I say through my teeth, looking down at the gold band tucked in the well of her hand. "It belongs to you."

Leah reaches out and seizes my wrist.

I wince, her touch sending a familiar electrifying heat racing through me.

She presses the promise ring into my palm, the circular edge pushing hard into the flesh. Without a word, she closes my fingers shut around the ring, and with a "goodbye," she turns her back to me.

I stand numb, repeating her words in my head, trying to rearrange them into a different meaning. But each time, I come up with the same conclusion. Leah doesn't want me. My vision blurs, and I blink, a flood of emotion threatening to drown me. My feet seem cemented in place.

Leah spins around, jolting me backward. Her intense

expression splinters, leaving a sea of emotion in its wake. "Damn it, Jack! Do I have to spell it out for you?" She takes a step, placing herself in front of me. "I wish I'd never dreamt of you. I wish you'd never come here. I would cut you out of every facet of my life and every memory if I could because loving you has come with too big a sacrifice."

Eyes filled with resentment, she stares at me, jabbing her finger toward the door. "Now leave! I never want to see you again," she says, putting every speck of hatred into each syllable. I catch a glimpse of everything I've cost her—her freedom, art school, a relationship with her mother, and now, her brother's life. The look stops any argument I can wage because I know every time Leah looks at me, she'll only ever see her brother and the future she lost.

I stumble out into the hall and make it the short distance to my room, my mind spinning around the central fact that Leah doesn't want me. I slip the gold band onto my left pinky and stare at the five rectangular-cut emeralds—each the exact color of Leah's eyes. I remember the night I slipped the ring onto Leah's delicate finger and she promised to be my wife. At that moment, I had thought the worst was behind us. How wrong I had been.

I pull back my arm, and in a fury of grief and pain, I slam my fist hard against the dark walnut armoire. Assaulting the defenseless wood, I ignore the stinging throbs in my hand. Blood seeps from my battered knuckles. My knees buckle, and I slump to the floor. I cover my face with my hands, and tears slide hot between my fingers. I feel rather than hear a mangled sound rising in my throat, shredding me from the inside out as it mounts. Behind my closed lids, memories replay with earth-shattering clarity—Leah's angry eyes sparking with a green flame, and her voice, emotionless and sharp, echoing in my ears.

She doesn't love you, the voices repeat in my head.

"Leave me alone. Please," I whisper to nobody, trembling.

Lydia's death left scars. Not physical ones, but ones

every bit as permanent. Leah had swooped into my life, and her presence alone had snatched me from the darkness of my mind. Now with her departure, she has thrust me back, deeper into the bottomless void than I've ever been. If only I could tear her out of my heart as completely as she ripped me from hers.

Despair claws at me. I let it pull me under, and retreat into some remote place in my mind, where there is nothing but me and a hollow disconnect. I have no idea how long I sit there on the cold floor, my back to the wall. Leaving is the only half-intelligible thought my mind produces.

I'll drive so bloody far away she'll never cross my mind again.

My internal voice laughs at me for even entertaining such a notion.

I ignore it and hoist myself to my feet. I close my eyes to get my balance but quickly open them again before any memories can assault me. Lumbering like the old man I am, I make my way to the closet. In a trance, I fumble my way through the contents of my duffel, searching for my old friend. When I feel the smooth, worn cylinder of wood and fluff of feathers of the dart under my fingers, I let the breath I had been holding escape through my lips.

With a sense of somber ceremony, I spread the yellowed map along the wall and then push a thumbtack into each curled corner as I have done a thousand times before. I run my fingers over the pin-size holes that mar its frail paper surface, letting the tips skim over the hole that had brought me here, a mere half-inch off the Maine coast. The sensation thrusts thoughts of Leah into the forefront of my mind, and against my will, memories begin their somber roll.

I remember a similar bone-deep need from a century ago. The longing for a future I thought I'd never have again and the depression that followed. However, that was child's play compared to this hell, because Lydia didn't leave me of her own volition. Death stole her from me. But Leah... Leah did.

Following one deep, shaky breath, I kiss the dart. My hands tremble so much I almost drop it twice. I stop mid-throw. Words of long ago, almost forgotten, spin into my mind. "It's our choices that make us men," my brother had told me. By then he was Captain Henry Hammond. He spent the night at home before being shipped off to war. I remember staying up into the wee hours of the morning as Henry spilled his words of wisdom for his eager-to-please little brother. How I idolized him.

I let my arm fall limp at my side. *Can I leave, knowing Leah is still in harm's way? Is that the kind of man I am?*

"Damned if I will," I say, slamming the dart on the nightstand, half-mad, fully determined. I've loved Leah with every ounce of my soul, with a profound and undying passion. I still do. I promised to keep her safe. As long as I have breath left in my body, I will. Besides, where I need to go isn't on any map.

I hang my head, my brain working behind an expressionless face. If Artagan is right, and Leah receiving her brother's assignment is Domitilla's plan for revenge, she probably planned for two scenarios. Either Leah agrees to take Grady, or she doesn't. Although Domitilla probably planned that Leah wouldn't take her brother, I have to assume that Dom strategized and prepared for both options. If that's the case, taking either path might very well lead to the same end. But what if I toss a wrench in the plan and give Dom something she doesn't expect? What if I tell Grady the truth?

I hear the rush of blood pounding in my ears as awareness of where these thoughts are leading dawns. Out of pure desperation, I ponder the idea. I know what Grady will do if he finds out what his little sister is facing. He'll go to any lengths to keep her safe, just as I will—a fact that was proven the night I went to the Concilium

Animarum to give my life for Leah's. Grady offered to go with me without a second thought. I saw the glint of determination in his eyes. He was ready to put everything he had on the line to save his sister. And I know Grady would willingly take his own life to save her now.

As the details fall into place, fear, horror, grief, and guilt all wash over me in consecutive swells. I shove the emotions back, slamming them behind an imaginary door, and I slip my phone out of my pocket. I need to know if Artagan thinks this idea has any merit. I'm surprised when my cell vibrates in my hand. A quick glance at the screen tells me it's the very man I need to speak to.

"I was just going to ring you. Have you had any success?" I ask, skipping the formalities. My stomach knots with anticipation as I wait for an answer, hoping to God that Artagan says yes.

"When the hell were one of you going to tell me that Leah is refusing to take her brother?"

"What are you talking about? I just left her. Le—" I have a hard time saying her name aloud. I steel my emotions before I continue. "Leah is saying yes."

"Domitilla called a meeting. She told Death that Leah refused, and Dom asked to take the assignment herself. Death is considering her proposal, Jack. I need you to go to her brother and protect him until I sort this thing out. No one can gather him but Leah unless I tell you otherwise. Understand? Bring him to the house. I'll meet you there as soon as I can."

I feel sick to my stomach. "What if Grady *accidentally* found out what was going on and took his own life? Would that be breaking any rules?"

"Interesting idea, but for it to work without complications, she'd have to tell her brother herself."

"Is anyone going to ask Leah? Or are they just going to take Domitilla's word?"

"I don't know. Something underhanded is going on,

that's for sure... Shit! Leah's here. I have to go. Get yourself to Grady's now." Artagan says, his voice hushed but firm.

After Artagan hangs up, I snatch my leather jacket off the settee. As I dash for the door, I pat the right pocket where I stash my plastic bag of hemlock mixture for safekeeping. It's there, waiting for me when I'm ready for it.

CHAPTER TWENTY-ONE

A S I PUSH OUT THROUGH the back door, an arctic blast of air and an ever-thickening layer of white greet me. In the dying light of day, with the tenor of my apartment set in my mind and the memory of its dank, dusty smell in my nostrils, I step into a shadow cast by one of the overhanging walls of the mansion.

With luck, I reemerge from the shadow into the long, deserted hallway outside my old apartment. The only noise I hear comes from the beat of rap music thudding from the neighboring flat.

I step to the door and pat along the top lip of the frame for the spare key. After wiping the grime off on my jeans, I slip the key into the lock, and the door opens with a click.

All the apartment lights are on, but it's quiet—eerily so. Memories of Leah seem to permeate the very walls. I call out, but again I get no answer. In the living room, my eyes scan a menagerie of history books, all on the Battle of Hastings, scattered across the coffee table. Grady's laptop sits open, humming, waiting for the next keystroke. A cell phone sits next to it. His coat is gone but not his car keys. A dull thud sounds through the apartment like a heavy object being knocked over, followed by a moan. Both noises come from the bedroom.

The room reeks of fear and vomit. In the far corner, half-hidden by the bed, is Grady, slumped on the floor against the wall, head resting in between his knees. I pause only long enough to check the darkened corners. Then, crossing the room, I lay my hand on his shoulder.

He cowers, trying to move away.

"It's Jack," I say, crouching in front of him.

Grady looks up at me. A sheen of sweat drenches his hair and the collar of his shirt. He stares at me a moment with an unfocused gaze. Then his expression tightens as if he's questioning what is real and what is illusion.

Then he clenches his teeth, his body goes rigid, and he lets out a groan. I draw back, puzzled by his condition. At first glance, I see no marks, no reason for this level of discomfort. I lean closer to examine him further and see thin streaks of a faint yellow powder across his face. Most of it has been washed away by sweat, but the remainder clings in the grooves around his nose and mouth. I recognize the substance immediately.

The Soulless. My pulse picks up speed. I glance around, taking a quick assessment of the shadows once more. Seeing nothing abnormal, I turn back to Grady. "Let's get you out of here."

Grady hisses with exertion as I hoist him to his feet. He falters and weaves then leans against me to keep himself upright, slowly regaining his faculties. I watch as his mouth tries to form words, but nothing more than a faint wheeze passes his parched, cracked lips. He licks them a few times before attempting once more, but then his gaze flashes away for an instant. He grips my arm, hauling me closer. "Run," he says, his voice no more than a coarse exhalation.

"An audience!" a melodic voice sings from behind me. I freeze. I don't need to see her face to know who the voice's owner is. Domitilla strolls out from one of the darkened corners, Muan and his brother Pacal trailing at her heels.

I could easily take Domitilla or possibly either of the brothers alone, but not all three at once.

As if on command, Muan steps in behind Grady, pulling him backward. Pacal pauses, standing smug and silent behind me. All the while, Domitilla ambles around the room, admiring her long red fingernails.

"What are you doing here, Domitilla?" I ask curtly, deciding to play dumb. Hopefully, it will buy me some time until Artagan discovers we're not at the house and comes looking for us.

She stops and faces me. "Oh, just looking for a bit of fun. The boys were keeping Grady entertained while I was tying up some loose ends." She rotates the full force of her gaze to Grady. "I suppose I should apologize before we begin. I'm sure your sister would have had a much gentler method than me. Don't you agree, Jack? In his sleep, or something instantaneous, a car crash perhaps."

Grady's brow furrows and focuses his attention on me.

I look away, attempting to ignore him, and focus on Domitilla. "I hope it's worth the price. I imagine the punishment for taking another's job is pretty steep."

"Haven't you heard?" A cold smile expands across Domitilla's face, reminding me of her sister. "Leah said no."

I give a slight shake of my head. "You're lying."

"Why would I?" Her hand now hovers above Grady's shoulder, only centimeters away.

Outnumbered and outgunned, I fear my chances of saving Grady from a painful death are growing slim. Time is running out. However, maybe there's still an opportunity to save Leah from the fate of Shadow Death.

"Well, then," I say, keeping my voice devoid of any sentiment that might betray me, "maybe we can make a deal."

She drops her hand and glides closer, her eyes glinting with curiosity. "Go on."

"One of the last in the line of Brennus in place of a girl Mosi himself called ordinary, no more than an Ignorant turned immortal. I know you agree."

"A life for a life." Domitilla snickers. "I think we've been here before." Her expression hardens, and she continues. "I'm not rash like my sister was. She was always far too impulsive, hence she usually left the scheming to me. If Vita had told me of her plan to switch the hemlock mixture with belladonna to summon the Shadow of Death, I would have told her no, and none of us would be here right now. You'd be dead. So would Leah"—she shrugs—"her soul waiting in line to carry on with her next meaningless existence."

Grady growls something incoherent. I hush him and turn my attention back to Domitilla.

"Well, everything will be set right soon enough." She waves a graceful hand, dismissing the matter, and she targets her concentration on Grady. "Shall we get on with it?"

"I know how this has to end. I know Leah must die," I say, locking all sentiment behind an emotionless mask.

All fall silent. I'm sure Grady's eyes are on me now, but I resist the urge to glance in his direction, keeping my gaze fixed on Domitilla, who has stopped short. Her attention returns, one eyebrow arching. I've caught her by surprise.

Good.

"Death must have his pound of flesh for disobedience," I continue. "It's the destination I want to negotiate."

I half expect Domitilla to laugh me off, but she doesn't. Instead, she cocks her head, so I continue. "What I'm suggesting is a reversal of Vita's plan. Give Leah hemlock tea instead of belladonna. If you agree, my fate is yours."

"And if I'm caught?"

"Pin the blame on me. I won't deny it. I'll even write a letter of confession, if you want," I say. "We both know

Leah had nothing to do with what happened to your sister. So let's leave her out of it. Vita's plan was to send me to Shadow Death. Me, not Leah. You and I could give Vita her dying wish. Perhaps I've committed no immortal crimes yet, but I'm sure your conscience wouldn't have an issue with pointing me in the right direction. After Leah has taken the hemlock, I'll do whatever you ask."

Her expression spirals into a mocking grimace. "Anything?"

I nod once, feeling a constriction in the pit of my stomach.

Domitilla glides forward, so only inches stand between us. "Hmm, so many possibilities," she says, playing with the button of my shirt. "Including tainting the *noble* line of Brennus with my bloodline. What a tempting prospect. Why haven't I ever thought of this before?" Her cold gaze rakes over me, traveling with a brazen appreciation from the crown of my head to the toes of my scuffed sneakers.

I stand still, concealing all repugnance.

"Maybe I should make you prove it," she says, brushing the back of her hand along my cheek. Taking hold of me by the collar, she yanks me toward her and presses her mouth to mine. My hands ball into fists at my sides. I feel her annoyance when her lips discover my passive resistance. She kisses me long and hard, biting my lower lip hard enough to draw blood before taking a stride back.

I lift my chin in an attempt to look unfazed, but inside, nausea rolls in waves.

"Colder than a witch's tit." She laughs. "You'd think you'd be better at convincing me with so much on the line."

I hesitate, but only long enough to disconnect my mind from my body. Then, giving permission to my lips, I kiss her with as much passion as I can fake.

"So tempting," Domitilla says, stepping away. "Pity it's not worth the risk. Although I would have loved to see

Artagan's face when he realized what I had set in motion. But Father is not as forgiving of my transgressions as you think. On that note, I suppose we should get on with it." Her icy glare returns to Grady. "This will hurt. Quite a bit, I'm afraid. Blame it on your loving sister." She stalks toward him, and Grady shrinks back. However, with Muan at his stern, he has nowhere to go.

I lunge, wanting to do something—anything—but Pacal's hands catch me by the forearms, and he holds me in place. "Don't touch him, you bitch," I spit.

Domitilla grins at me over her shoulder and raises her long, delicate hand. In a swirl of motion, the tips of her fingers alight on Grady's chest. With that gentle touch, all strength leaves his body. He staggers sideward as if he might faint. Eyes springing wide, a hiss erupts from him—the sound of shock and strangled breathing—and he drops like a stone. While his fingers claw at his throat, as if he's attempting to loosen some unseen grip, his body thrashes with sudden spasms. One violent lurch brings his face into view. Pain twists his mouth.

With a laugh, Pacal releases me, and the three vanish into the shadows.

I scramble to Grady and drop to my knees. After hoisting his head into my lap, I smooth the mop of hair from his face. His eyes are closed, but his lips move. I catch bits and pieces of disjointed words.

"I'm here, Grady," I say. Then, taking his hand, I begin to recite the Lord's Prayer.

Just as the last words leave my lips, another round of spasms hits Grady. His body contorts, muscles jerking involuntarily. I grip his shoulders and try to hold his thrashing body still, but my efforts do no good against his violent struggles. The pain-filled lines of his face ease as a laborious wheeze passes his lips.

In a pool of sweat and piss, Grady lies motionless. Peeling back his collar, I feel frantically for a pulse.

Nothing. My whole body begins to quiver. Through misting eyes, I stare in dazed horror at the body of my friend, knowing I'll never be able to save Leah now. Her fate was sealed with her brother's final gasp.

"So for the first time in her vile existence, Dom was telling the truth. She told me in the shadows I was too late." Artagan's voice comes from behind me, making me jump, but I cannot pull my eyes from Grady's pale face. Moving as silently as a shadow, he steps next to me. "We have to go."

My dampened eyes flick to him. "Leah? Where is she?"

Artagan's gaze falls away, his chin lowering to his chest, but not before I see his lips compress with regret.

My vision goes black around the edges. I close my eyes tight. "She's gone, then. Punished," I choke out.

With a trembling hand, I reach for my hemlock.

CHAPTER TWENTY-TWO

"N OT SO FAST, ROMEO," ARTAGAN says, gripping my forearm. "Leah's not dead. Not yet, anyway."

I wrench myself free. "Where is she?"

He glares into the shadows. "I'll tell you. But first, let's go back to my office and have a drink."

"I don't want a bloody drink!"

I do have a plan. His voice flows into my head. *However, I need to know one thing. Whatever has happened between you two, are you still willing to die for Leah?*

I'm on my feet.

"That's what I figured," he says, smiling grimly.

Before we leave, I retrieve a patchwork quilt from the bed to cover Grady's body. As he did with Gladys, Artagan begins his ritual, dabbing alcohol from the pewter flask onto his fingers. I stare down at my friend's lifeless face, vaguely aware of Artagan's movements around us.

Memories lap at the shores of my mind, threatening to crash over me once again. I push the thoughts away to keep my mind blank. For me to be any help to Artagan and his plan, my numbness must remain. Eventually, the detachment will shrivel away, leaving me to the wolves of my memories, but I'm determined to hang on to it as long as I can.

Artagan places a hand on my shoulder, jolting me out

of my trance. "There's nothing more we can do for him. We need to go." *While we can still save Leah.*

I nod, pulling myself from my stupor, and I follow Artagan into the shadows.

Back in the privacy of his office, I toss my leather jacket over the back of the armchair and turn to face him. "Now, tell me where Leah is and what this plan of yours entails."

Artagan doesn't reply. Instead, he moves to the liquor cabinet, where he sets out two tumblers. After pouring an ample serving of Scotch in each glass, he holds one out for me, his expression altering into a slight frown.

I accept his offering. God knows I need it.

"Leah is being held at the cathedral, awaiting punishment. She refused."

"But Leah made it very clear. She was planning to take her brother."

"It was obvious, at least to me, that Leah wanted to say yes. But some outside force was controlling her words."

My expression stiffens. "Domitilla."

"I suspect so. Or her henchman, Serevo."

I tighten my grip on the glass and take a long swig, draining it.

Artagan refills my tumbler and leans back, half sitting on the desk, his eyes fixed on me with mild speculation. I remain stone faced, staring straight at him. Thankfully, after a moment of silence, Artagan continues.

"Leah's execution is set for tomorrow morning at dawn. Thus, before the sun rises, someone must smuggle her hemlock. It's Leah's only escape route now. You see that, right?" he says. The tentative tone in his voice is palpable.

"I do." I'm a little surprised by how calm my voice sounds. Any natural responses are strangely detached, such that I feel nothing. Death was the very thing I risked body and soul to save Leah from, but now dying is the only avenue to her salvation. *Ironic.* "I'd hoped it wouldn't come to this. However, with Grady dead, I agree with you, it's the only viable option. I even tried to make a similar deal with Domitilla today."

Artagan snorts. "I can imagine how that went."

"Desperate times." I manage a small laugh. "What do I need to do? Leah's being guarded, I assume."

"Yes, by Otmar. He's never broken protocol for me before—a little white lie here and there, but nothing more. So I was a bit surprised when he agreed to help."

"How about Kemisi? Is she going to help, too?"

"She doesn't know what we're up to. You'll have to forgive me, but I'd rather not put her in harm's way in case this all goes to shit." Artagan takes a drink from his glass. "As you might expect, Leah's cell has been smudged. But that works to our advantage because once you're inside, the two of you will have complete privacy."

My eyes snap to his, and I shake my head. "I can't do that. As you said yourself, things have changed between her and me. She won't want to see me. I'll help any way I can—life, limb, and blood—but you will have to take the hemlock to her yourself." Not wanting to dwell on the subject, I ask, "Where are they keeping her?"

"The lower level. At the far end of the eastern corridor. Unfortunately, there's no real reason for anyone besides Otmar to be down there tonight, which is a double-edged sword. The passageways are peppered with corners and alcoves. If someone had the inclination to keep tabs on people's comings and goings, there are lots of places to hide."

Artagan pauses, taking his time to study me. His forehead wrinkles, a thin vertical line running between his brows. Then, sliding the gold-and-onyx ring off his pinky, he holds it out. "Here. There are two pills inside. One for her and one for you."

"I said I can't." I want my voice to be cold, controlled, but it quivers at the end.

Artagan's mouth twitches at the corner as a flicker of sympathy mixed with a gleam of humor forces its way past his seeming indifference. "I heard what you said. I just didn't think you meant it. Things aren't always how they appear." He slides the ring back onto his finger and fishes an envelope out of his pocket.

"This might change your mind," he says, swaying it slowly and deliberately between his forefinger and his thumb, and he gives me a sidelong glance. "It's addressed to you."

I glance at the window, not wanting him to see the heartache I'm sure has sprung to life across my face. I strive to hide the pain and say, "I've heard enough of her words today. Just tell me what you need me to do, and let's get on with it."

"Aren't you even a little curious?" he asks, still waving the letter in front of me. His lips produce a small, conspiratorial smile.

"God help me." I snatch at the envelope, making a low sound of exasperation in my throat. When I find the top flap already sliced open, my gaze darts back to his, heat flushing my cheeks. "You read it?"

Artagan shrugs in answer, rubbing at the coarse stubble that has sprouted along his jaw. His face reveals only a mild interest, but his eyes glint with mischief. Then he gives a short laugh. "Are you going to read it or just glare at me the whole evening?"

I remove the folded letter. My pulse rate quickens as I stare at Leah's wobbly handwriting and the dots of smudged ink caused by tears. Then, taking in a long, labored breath, I begin to read.

After reading the first word, my name, I stop. A nervous energy buzzes through my body, but I stifle it, and my hands start to shake. Trying to settle my nerves, I swallow hard and begin again.

Jack,

I'm sorry for everything I said. It nearly killed

me. Please believe I had no choice. It was the only way I could think of to keep you safe.

I had a vision. It wasn't clear, just flashes, but from them, I knew Death would end up torturing and at best killing you for trying to protect me. Maybe it's selfish, but I refused to let you suffer like that for me. I remembered what Artagan said about Death not being able to see the Endless. I knew I needed to get you as far away from here, away from me as I could. And I knew there was only one way you would leave. You had to believe I blamed you, hated you. You'd have never left me otherwise. But every word was a lie.

A lie. All lies. A warmth blooms in my chest, and I continue.

I hope you can forgive me. I love you, Jack Hammond, more than anything or anyone in this world. I don't blame you for any of it. When you ran to the council to offer yourself in my place, there was no way you could have foreseen this. You had one goal, and that was to keep me safe. How could I ever blame you for that? I'll repeat it because you're too stubborn to believe me the first time. None of this is your fault!

I have to go before I lose my nerve. We'll be together again someday. Call it a gut feeling. I love you!

Forever,
Leah

My fingertips glide over her words as the promise within them engulfs me, burning away the numbness and doubts. The feeling of hope glows beneath my ribs, and despite the array of uncertainties that lie ahead, my face breaks into a broad smile. I look at Artagan, and he pushes to a standing position.

"Ready?" He holds his poison ring out again.

I nod, accepting the ring and sliding it onto my finger.

"I can take you as far as the entrance to the corridor. After that, you're on your own. I almost forgot to ask, you have your hemlock on you, right?"

"Yes, of course," I say, still dazed. I slip the plastic bag from the pocket of my jacket and offer it to Artagan.

"No, no. Keep it. It's not for me. Otmar is stepping out on a limb for us. We'll repay him with plausible deniability. He'll search you and find your little stash. When the council finds out you and Leah are dead"—sadness touches Artagan's eyes for a brief second—"Death will question Otmar. That little package will help him prove he did his job. And I, being the slippery little son of a bitch that I am, must have pulled one over on him."

"But what about you?"

"Nah, nothing for you to worry about. I'll be fine."

In the burrows of St. Joseph, Artagan is alert, checking around each stone corner and alcove as we go. Flickering pools of light from the wall sconces are the only sources of illumination. The corridors, lined with thick wooden doors, smell of dank earth. My heart beats in a jerky rhythm as I follow Artagan's lead.

"Leah is being held right down that hall, at the far end," Artagan says in a low, level voice as he peers around the latest corner. "Remember you have until daybreak. Be gone by then."

I glance down the corridor. The knowledge that Leah is so close surges through me like a rush of adrenaline. I feel a new thump of excitement merge with nerves in the pit of my stomach as the longing grows. "Before I go," I whisper, "something is going on between Dom and the Soulless. They're working together."

Artagan's brow furrows. "They hate one another. Always have."

"Well, it looks like they've found common ground. Take care of yourself. Watch your back."

Without warning, Artagan grabs me and pulls me into an embrace—quick and fierce—and then he's gone, disappearing into the gloom. I stand stunned, realizing this will be the last time I'll ever see him. I wish I had thought to thank him for everything he has done. Pushing the remorse away, I turn back toward the passageway that leads to Leah.

CHAPTER TWENTY-THREE

A T THE FAR END OF the corridor, I find Otmar, as promised. His hair tied back with a thin leather cord, he leans against the granite block wall, playing his iPod, humming to himself. He glances up. His expression, half-obscured by his beard, turns grave and sympathetic.

"There you are. Artagan mentioned you might stop by," he says, pushing from the wall. "I was out all night in Bangladesh, and now I pulled guard duty. Thanatos and Akio didn't even have jobs today, but no, call in the Viking. Leah's what, five-four?" He yawns, scratching his whiskers, but his eyes are alert and dart from corner to corner. Then he winks. "All right, hands up. Let's get on with it."

I raise my arms in the air over my head, and he pats me down. With dramatic flair, he snags the plastic bag from my jacket pocket. Holding it high, he thrusts his nose within inches of my face. "Thought you were gonna pull one over on me, did you?"

"I had to try," I say, letting my shoulders slump, playing along with the charade.

A small grin sprouts within the grove of whiskers. "I suppose you did," Otmar says, stuffing the bag into the back pocket of his jeans. *I'll knock twice should a problem arise and you need to hurry things along.*

He gropes through his pockets. His hand soon reappears, a small wrought-iron key held between his steady fingers.

"May I borrow your cord?" I ask, pointing to his ponytail.

His eyes narrow, a tad suspicious.

"Unless you know a good priest?" I add.

A smile of understanding spreads across his face, teeth shining in the light of the sconces. He sobers as he pulls the leather twine loose, letting his thick mane fall free around his shoulders, and hands it over.

With a nod of thanks, I shove the cord into my pocket.

Otmar pushes the key into the lock. The massive door—close to three inches thick—squeaks on its hinges as it swings wide. A pungent scent of sage wafts from the room. Without a word or even a gesture of goodbye, Otmar grabs me by the arm and thrusts me inside. The door thuds closed behind me, and I hear the tumblers click into place.

The room is narrow and sparsely furnished with only a single chair set by a small hearth. The dancing light from the fire dyes the chamber a soft light gold in the flickering glow. Leah sits on a bed of blankets laid out on the floor by the hearth. Curled into herself, she hides her face, but her hands, laced together and covering her knees, are tightly clenched. Waves of relief and anxiety wash over me simultaneously, and I stand in silence by the door.

"I already gave you my answer," Leah says in a cold, resolute voice, but she doesn't look in my direction. Stray wisps of hair hang in her tear-stained face, and she wipes them back. After a moment, she peers toward the door and then stares without speaking. A tremor runs down her throat, but still she says nothing.

"I got your letter," I say, stepping forward.

Eyes widening, she scrambles to her feet. "You shouldn't be here. Get out!"

Both hands outstretched, Leah bolts toward me and slams into me with all of her weight, all one hundred fifteen pounds of her. She tries to push me toward the door, but I make no effort to move.

"Did you hear me?" she says. "You have to leave!"

I seize her by the wrists. "I'm not going anywhere."

Still struggling, her eyes lock with mine. I see longing there, and a suggestion of nervousness that matches my own, but no hint of anger or reproach. Both have vanished.

"Listen," I say with fierce determination, giving her a little shake. "There's nowhere else for me to be. Our fates are intertwined. Always have been, always will be." I lean down and press my lips to the top of her head, breathing in the tart sweetness, a scent I was sure I'd never smell again.

"You shouldn't be here," she says again, but her voice is unsteady, all fight gone. This time, she doesn't attempt to pull away. Instead, she clings to me, her body trembling. "But I'm so glad you are. Grady's dead." She speaks into the folds of my shirt.

The anguish in her voice makes my chest constrict. "I know, love. I'm so sorry."

"How do you know? Were you there? Was it painless?" She looks up.

The memory of Grady's pained face pushes into my mind. I'm unable to meet her gaze, but my silence speaks the truth when my mouth cannot.

"My brother deserved much more. Oh God, Grady. Who was it? Who gathered my brother? I want to know."

A fresh wave of helplessness washes over me, and I tighten my arms around her. "Domitilla," I say softly.

"Oh God! I wanted to say yes... I tried to. Why couldn't I just say yes?" Her words break into convulsing sobs. Her legs buckle, and we sink together to the floor. I hold Leah against me while her grief slowly drains, her tears soaking through the fabric of my shirt. Once her sobs diminish into muffled sniffles, I shift my weight to retrieve my handkerchief from my pocket and hand it to her.

Leah dabs her eyes and cheeks. "You still shouldn't have come."

"I'm right where I belong."

"No matter what it costs you?" Leah shakes her head. Her strained lips quiver upward into nearly a smile, and then the words flow out of her like a cascade of water over a broken dam.

"You've sacrificed far more than me," I tell her. "You never see yourself as others see you, you know. As I see you. You don't think of yourself as brave and selfless, but you are. The courage you showed in the face of such tragedy is staggering."

Tears well afresh in her eyes. "A lot of good that did. Domitilla—"

"Grady's at peace now. Focus on that."

She nods, sniffling, and wipes at her nose. "I'm not the only one who doesn't see myself clearly. I used that against you. Fed your insecurities. When I saw you believed me, saw the hurt in your eyes, I wanted to die right there." She lowers her head.

I brush back the tangled curtain of hair and bend my head to peer at her face. "We're together now. I am a little surprised you haven't asked me about my plan yet, though."

Her face jerks up. "Plan?"

"You must have known I wouldn't come to you without a trick or two up my sleeve."

Reclining on the blankets, I tell Leah about what Artagan and I discussed. She doesn't speak, letting me talk freely, only nodding from time to time. Her face is a controlled mask, making her emotions hard to read. When I finish, I flip up the black onyx on Artagan's ring, exposing two small green pills. "One for you, and one for me."

With Leah's eyes fixed on the pills, I stay quiet and glance away, not wanting to increase her discomfort while she processes it all.

"Jack," she says a moment later. There is a sense of urgency in her voice, and I peer at her. She smiles at me, her eyes bright, filled with some emotion. "Kiss me."

I do as she asks, pressing my lips gently against hers.

"No, dammit! Kiss me!" she commands, jerking me to her.

Her lips crush against mine with a thinly disguised hunger, her teeth grazing my lower lip. I growl, pulling her tighter against me. I trail feverish kisses down her neck. Her hands delve under my shirt and run along the planes of my stomach. Despite the heat her touch causes, I tremble as if a chill wind caresses my skin. Her fingers drift along the waistband of my jeans, and she whispers into my ear, "Make love to me."

Body craving for her touch, I pull away.

"No," she says, the defeat in her voice palpable.

I gaze into Leah's pleading face. My thumb traces the outline of her mouth. Her lips feel like velvet. "I want you. I want you so much I can hardly breathe. Marry me first. Right here and now."

Her expression turns first confused then saddened. "I'll always regret that we didn't just elope to Vegas or meet up at City Hall one afternoon. The frills don't seem all that important anymore." She glances at our only company, a dust-covered statue of St. Joseph, his eyes raised to heaven. "But here? How?"

"Is that a yes?" I smirk, giving her a sidelong glance.

"Of course it's a yes."

"Again, you underestimate me." I stand, holding out my hands to her, palms up, in an invitation for her to join me. Leah slips her hands into mine. Her fingers are cold and quivering. I help her to her feet.

"First things first," I say, sliding my grandmother's ring

off my pinky. Leah extends her left hand, and I return the promise to its rightful place. Then, digging the thin strip of leather out of my pocket, I dangle it in the air.

She stares with a skeptical eye first at the swaying cord and then at me.

I tell her the story of Artagan's wedding, how with no priest, Artagan and Olluna found a way.

"I know there are no paper lanterns or aisle upon aisle trimmed with flowers, but under the circumstances, God will have to be our priest tonight."

Leah entwines her fingers with mine. I bring her hand to my lips and kiss it. Then, pressing our wrists together, my hand grips Leah's forearm, and she does the same.

"Hold this, please," I say, offering her one end of the cord.

Perspiration blooms across my palms, causing the cord to slip from my grip twice as I wrap it around our wrists. I swallow hard before speaking. "I, Jack Hammond, tether my heart and soul with yours. Before God, I take you, Leah Nicole Winters, to be my wife, because, for me, your love has made all the difference. What we share is rare. It survived separation and the passage of time. I love you, Green Eyes." My voice may not shake, but my fingers do as together we tie the loose ends into a knot, binding our wrists.

Leah looks up, tears beading on her lashes. "I take you to be my husband, before God and the whole universe. I know most people are never lucky enough to find what we have. You're right. Our love is rare. And strong. So strong, it will survive death once again. I know without a shadow of a doubt I will love you forever."

Moisture pools in my own eyes. "Forever," I vow, because *till death* could never be long enough. No matter where I end up—Heaven or Hell, or some gray space in between—one constant will remain unchanged. As in life and carried forth in death, Leah will be in my heart, woven into the very fabric of my soul.

My free hand cups her cheek, and with a gentle touch, she places her fingers over mine. "You may kiss your bride," she says, a seductive lilt in her voice.

I fumble with the knot. It feels like an eternity before the looped cord releases its hold. All the while, butterflies take flight, fluttering in multitudes against the walls of my stomach. I lean in. Leah's eyes close, and her mouth parts, welcoming mine.

After a moment, Leah is the one to step away. She glances at the blankets, and then meeting my eyes directly, she says, "Now what," an undeniable lilt in her voice.

A shiver of mingled fear and anticipation shoots through me as I unbutton first the cuffs of my sleeves and then the top three buttons at the throat, only breaking my gaze from hers when I yank the shirt over my head. Leah studies me and then steps closer. She kisses my chest and tugs at the waistband of my jeans. With a firm jerk, they fall to the floor.

I run my thumb along the silkiness of Leah's cheek. Then, cupping her face in my palm, I kiss her. When our lips touch this time, all my nerves vanish, leaving only expectancy and desire behind. I attempt to be careful—God knows I try—but our lips move together with a feral need. My hands slide down her back and fist in the loose fabric of her blouse. I draw the length of her body hard against mine. Tremors of desire shoot through me as an electric charge explodes between us, and I begin to flounder at the small, dainty buttons of her blouse. The progress is torturously slow.

"Dammit," I mutter under my breath, pulling away to scowl at the infernal fasteners.

Leah lets out a small giggle and takes pity on me. Her delicate hands are nimble, and I watch, swallowing hard, as each button undone exposes more lace and flesh. I bend and scoop Leah up in my arms and carry her to the makeshift bed.

Clothes scattered around us, we lie together naked in the cocoon of blankets. I run my fingertips over the rose-petal softness of her skin, memorizing the gentle curves of her body, every touch savored and treasured because these moments will almost certainly have to last me an eternity.

"You're so beautiful," I say, my voice hoarse.

Leah bends upward, her mouth searching for mine. I draw back, not wanting to rush, kissing her first on the cheek and then at the corner of her mouth. I brush my lips along her jaw and down the curves of her body to the hollow dip of her stomach. Leah lets out little gasps as I place a kiss on each breast.

"I love you," I say. Then I move, covering her body with my own.

Afterward, I lounge in the blankets, listening to Leah's labored breathing as it slows to quiet breaths. She rolls onto her side, laying her head in the hollow of my shoulder, and runs her fingertips in small circular patterns through the sprinkling of springy hair along my chest. I close my eyes, enjoying the sensation.

"Are you afraid?" she asks, breaking me out of my trance. "Of dying?"

I turn my face toward her, kissing her on the soft spot in between her eyebrows. "I've been afraid of many things over the years," I say, tightening my arm around her.

"Somehow it's hard to imagine you being scared of anything."

"Ah, well, I don't know about that." I don't mention my greatest fear—the fear of losing her—knowing it will only cause her pain after the hours we've both been through.

She hasn't forgiven herself for the heartache she caused me, necessary or not. I see it in her eyes. "Discovery, mainly, I guess. Then there was the fear of what kind of immortal I was. And if I'm honest, I'm not too fond of pigs either."

Leah laughs. "Pigs? But they're so cute, with curly pink tails."

"Trust me. They're more sinister than they appear. One charged me when I was a boy. I haven't forgiven them since." I smile before growing serious again. "Compared to those things, dying with the one I love seems to pale in comparison. So no, I'm not."

Strangely enough, even with all the misgivings about where I'll end up, this is the truth. A steadfast relief has settled over me, much like the tranquility that comes to a convicted man waiting his turn for the gallows. It seems once the fight drains away, all that's left is finding peace and making amends with the things in your past. God may not be able to overlook my transgression, but I have asked him for absolution, anyway. *The first step to redemption,* my father always said. Although it's probably too little, too late for divine forgiveness, surprisingly, at this moment, I find I have forgiven myself. Maybe that will have to do.

Trying not to disturb Leah's position, her head still resting in the dip of my shoulder, I stretch for my jeans strewn by my head and dig my watch from the depths of the pocket. I unlatch the golden lid, the decorative design glinting in the dim firelight. It's a little after three in the morning. I watch as the second hand speeds its way toward the twelve and snap the lid shut. The metaphor "time is a thief" has never felt truer than tonight.

"Is it time?" Leah asks.

"No, not yet. We have a bit left." I touch her hair, smoothing it out of her eyes.

"Before paradise," she adds, a smile fading from her face as she glances up.

I nod in feigned agreement.

It grows chilly in our small prison cell as the fire dwindles. I squat before the hearth, adding another log and stoking the embers until the fire blazes again. Returning to bed, I find Leah's gaze trained on my handkerchief, her index finger lingering over the hand-stitched initials.

I crawl back into the pool of warmth, and Leah curls into me. My muscles relax as the chill in my limbs thaws. I take a long breath. "Fitzwilliam. My Christian name is John Fitzwilliam." I pronounce the name formally, each syllable distinct and slow. "Although no one ever called me John. Only Jack."

Leah pulls away, craning her neck so she can see my face. "But you hate Darcy."

"Hate is a little excessive," I say.

With a petulant set to her mouth, Leah stares up at me.

I puff out my cheeks. "Fine. However, my mother didn't name me after him, thanks be to God. My maternal grandfather was Fitzwilliam Algar Abbott."

"Algar?" Leah makes a small sound in her throat. "It could have been worse, then. Your mother could have named you that."

Unable to disagree, I let out a chuckle. "I never met my grandfather. I would have liked to, but he died well before I was born. My mother spoke fondly of him, though, saying what a kind-hearted, gentle father he was."

"We can meet him today then. Him and your mother." She looks back to the handkerchief. "You should be proud to be his namesake."

"Yes, I suppose I should."

She shifts against my chest so she can see my face without craning her neck. "What's your beef with Darcy? I've always wondered."

"I know it's silly, holding a grudge against a fictional character." I let out a short laugh. "But I knew a man very much like Darcy. You would have sworn he was Austen's inspiration if there hadn't been so many years separating the two. His name was Grandville Philips. You might recognize the name."

"Wait. Wasn't that the guy Sir Robert wanted Lydia to dump you for?"

"Yes. Philips was Lydia's cousin."

"Ewww." Leah wrinkles her nose as if she has just smelled something foul.

"It was standard practice at the time," I assure her. "And Philips was considered a most advantageous match. A lot more favorable than a marriage to the late vicar's son."

"That doesn't make it any less disgusting."

I shrug. "The college I attended was Philips's alma mater. He had graduated a few years earlier, but the rumors of his rude, self-important reputation still lingered. I met him in person once, at a party in London. From what I could tell from our brief encounter, the rumors were valid. He had all Darcy's worst traits tied up in a tidy little package. Although in the public's eyes, his money trumped any personality flaws. I didn't know Sir Robert planned to marry Lydia off to him until after her death, or I would have whisked her off to Scotland."

"But unlike Grandville Philips, Darcy changed."

I give a contemptuous snort. "Maybe, but that's something people outside fiction seldom do."

She meets my slanting gaze with a long, level look. "You've changed."

"That's because of you." I give her a quick kiss on the tip of her nose.

Over the next hour, our conversation drifts from one subject to another, neither one of us willing to admit that our time on earth is growing short.

"What if I wasn't running late that morning?" Leah

asks, staring at the ceiling. "What do you think would have happened?"

"Which morning was that? You running late doesn't exactly narrow things down," I tease.

"Ha-ha. You're funny. The morning we first met. You ran into me and shoved me into a puddle. Remember? Very ungallant, by the way."

"Ah, that morning." I grin.

"You were so shy, barely able to look at me. Let alone speak." She laughs.

"I wonder why," I say, reaching to stroke her hair.

"Then later, when I caught you peeking in the windows at Old Port Java, I knew it was only a matter of time before you'd wander in and introduce yourself."

I freeze. "You saw me?"

"Of course I did. You're kinda hard to miss, Jack," she says then kisses the top of my shoulder. "I rushed out of the coffee shop once, you know. To find you. But you were gone. So I waited and waited."

"I was playing hard to get."

"No, you weren't. You were just being you," she says.

I laugh, charmed by her honesty.

"And when you worked up the nerve to kiss me, it was on the hand."

"I wanted you to know my intentions were honorable," I interject.

"Well, honorable or not, that kiss made my arm tingle all the way down to my toes. And none of my thoughts were very respectable either." She lays her fingers on my bare chest and runs her feather-light touch back and forth in a path from breastbone to abdomen. "That was the moment I knew."

"Knew what?" I ask, my voice a little shaky.

"That I was right." She smiles at me. "That even though it made no sense at all, my dreams were of real events, and somehow we *had* known each other all those years ago."

I grip her about the waist, rolling us so I end up on top. I stare hungrily into her eyes. "Yes, I do."

"Do what?" she asks, a little breathless.

"I believe we would have found each other. Eventually. Even if I didn't run into you on that dreary morning. Even if I didn't move to Portland. Despite my Doubting Thomas ways, I can't deny we were always meant to be together."

I press my mouth to hers. Our lips slide together, untamed and eager. Her fingers grip my hair, trying to draw me closer, as my tongue skims the curve of her bottom lip. She groans, holding me tighter, and we make love once more, the finality of it all offering an edge to the passion.

An hour before dawn, we dress. The anxiety has vanished, leaving behind only an air of inevitability. I come up behind her and wrap my arms around her waist. "Are you ready for a new adventure, Mrs. Hammond?" I murmur into the golden cloud of her hair. I keep the sadness out of my voice, remembering above all else, Leah will soon be safe from harm.

Leah turns and pats at the perpetual cowlick that spikes up on the crown of my head, trying to tame it. From the way the corner of her mouth lifts in a reluctant smile, she has little success. I press my lips to hers, and then unwillingly, I release her. Flipping open the ring, I dump the pills into my palm. With a mixture of angst and resolution, I hold them out to her, but she doesn't move. Her eyes are vacant as if she's staring at some distant place.

"Leah," I say, shaking her shoulder with my free hand.

Leah's eyes, now alert, fix on mine. Without warning,

she slaps at my hand, causing the pills to drop to the floor. Before even a word can fly from my mouth, her heel crashes down, crushing the pills into powder, which she then brushes away with the toe of her sneaker.

"What did you do?" I yell.

Two quick raps break through the hush of the room. My heart leaps. Panic-ridden, I reach for my concoction of hemlock before remembering Otmar confiscated it. The thick door opens, its hinges squeaking in complaint, and I look straight into the amused face of Domitilla.

I thrust myself in front of Leah, holding up my forearm as a shield. A shiver coils at the base of my neck and runs like icy pins and needles down my back. A low growl rumbles deep within me.

"I was wondering if you'd be here," Domitilla says, her tone filled with malice and humor. Her attention roves around the room. "A love nest. How quaint."

I tense, glaring at her.

"That's right, you're a gentleman. You'd never kiss and tell." She winks. The corners of her mouth inch upward until it breaks into a sinister smile.

As Domitilla circles us, I keep her at my front and Leah to my back. Leah's voice echoes in my head, but her words muddle together, a flurry of urgent sounds. I keep my focus on Domitilla's slow advance. Her eyes are watchful, looking for any signs of weakness. Our only hope now is that I can subdue her and retrieve my bag from Otmar, or find Artagan.

Domitilla glances toward the door, but I hear no sound—a diversion tactic. Her ploy gives me the small window of opportunity I was praying for. I lunge and smack into her with the full force of my weight. She yelps in pain and surprise. I thrust my forearm into her throat and slam her hard against the wall. "That's for Grady," I hiss into her ear so only she can hear. She struggles, trying to break my hold, but I only push harder, staring straight into her eyes, now darkened with shock.

A sharp pain across the back of my head brings me to my knees. Someone drags me backward, and Leah screams.

Head throbbing, I look up into the eyes of my subduer, which burn red from their shadowy orbits. Death hovers above me. A sharp prickle of alarm runs up my spine. I twist to free myself from his grip, but there's no escape. With no more exertion than it would take to swat away a fly, Death lifts me and hurls me across the narrow room. I hit the far wall and fall with a heavy thud to the flagstone.

Small, bright flashes zigzag through my vision. I stagger to my feet, bracing my shoulder against the rock wall to keep my balance, readying myself to defend. Out of the corner of my eye, I see Leah, held in Domitilla's clutches. Past the buzzing in my ears, I can hear Leah begging for me.

Death stalks toward me in silence.

Listen to me! I think, praying my words are invading Leah's thoughts. *There's a plastic bag of hemlock in the back pocket of Otmar's jeans. Get it any way you can!*

With a flick of Death's hand, I sail across the room and slam against the wall with a crushing blow, causing the air to explode from my lungs. Moaning, I roll to my side, and against my will, blackness closes in.

CHAPTER TWENTY-FOUR

I SURFACE OUT OF A DISORIENTING darkness. Every inch of my body throbs with each beat of my heart, and fatigue encumbers my senses. All I want to do is sleep, but I force my lids open. At first, the world blurs around me. I blink and then blink again. The surroundings come back into focus bit by bit. For a moment, I'm confused when all I find is the dull gray of a vaulted ceiling. As my thoughts begin to clear, the memories flood in with perfect clarity.

Leah.

I jerk upward in a sudden panic. The room tilts and spins, and once again I'm lying flat on my back on the cold floor, but not before seeing what I already feared. I am alone in the narrow, shadowed room that first served as Leah's cell then as our bridal chamber.

I grit my teeth and make a fumbling effort to stand. The smallest exertion feels colossal. Another wave of dizziness comes over me, making me sway, but I manage to stay upright. Regardless of the chill shrouding the room—the once-blazing hearth has dwindled into a handful of glowing coals—beads of perspiration soak my face and drench my back.

How long have I been out?

I pause at the door, gripping the frame to steady

myself. Then with a deep breath, I make my way down the hallway, back the way I came. After every few paces, I have no choice but to sag against the wall to catch my breath. A swell of fear rises in my veins because I know if I find Leah in front of the council, all that will be left for me to do is watch the Shadow of Death tear all I love apart. But I keep moving, because no matter what the future holds, I cannot let her face it alone.

All the while, I grapple for a strategy, trying to assemble a half-decent plan to keep her out of the grip of Shadow Death. The only thought my foggy mind produces hinges on my ability to repossess the hemlock hidden away in Otmar's pocket. If Leah hasn't been able to retrieve it, then I must. Somehow.

Everything will be all right, Jack, a voice breaks through the anxiety, soft and rhythmic like a melody. Even though I know it's only my subconscious, I latch on to the sound, letting illusion give me the strength to move forward. Despite the gravity of the situation looming ahead, that voice—her voice—helps me hold on to a shred of hope. Maybe small and frail, but hope nonetheless. Still, one memory stalks me. The image of Leah smashing the tiny capsules beneath her heel replays in my mind.

Why did she do it?

I shove the question from my mind and push on. At the end of the corridor, the wall rounds into a curve. Stairs. If my calculations are correct, this particular set should lead me to the far corner of the vestibule.

The spiral stairwell ascends in dizzying flights. Between the diminished light and my throbbing head, I find it difficult to approximate the distance from one stair to the next. I stumble numerous times.

When I finally emerge out of the gloom, I stand stunned, staring at the sunshine pouring through the windows and casting the narthex in a golden glow. As the glowing embers in the fireplace indicated, I've been out long than a few minutes or even an hour. Though still morning, it's well past dawn—the time Artagan said the council scheduled Leah's punishment. A cold desperation spreads through my veins. I clench my hands into tight knots as emotion hits, leaving me winded and weak. My vision telescopes until all I see is a pinpoint of light in the darkness.

Then Leah's voice pierces through my grief. At first, I believe it's only an illusion. But when I hear it again, I know it's real. The voice is not the fanciful one my imagination conjures up, but one full of stress and worry. I turn and face the set of double doors that leads to the nave.

One door sits ajar. So as not to be seen, I keep to the shadows, pushing the door open a bit more to peer in. At the center of the expansive room, Leah stands, eyes staring down at her feet as she sways in place. Members of the council and their descendants cluster in groups of two and three about the room, leaving a wide berth between themselves and Leah. Artagan waits by her side, his back to me. While I can't see his face, I sense the tension rolling off him even from this distance. Before them all, Death stands with Thanatos, their heads drawn together in deep conversation.

From the murky threshold, I scan the room, looking for Otmar. Easily six foot seven and burly, he's not hard to spot towering over the crowd, leaning against a column at the far side of the nave. His eyes grim and cheeks drained of color, he's unable to look in Leah's direction. All are good signs that maybe I can sway him to help once more.

"Would you care to join us?" Death's voice rises over the murmur of the assembly, capturing my focus. I move deeper into the shadow of the archway, a knot forming in my stomach. My eyes return to Death. I relax when I find his attention fixed on the opposite side of the room, well away from my little hiding spot. Then his gaze shifts, focusing his attention on the doorway in which I stand. He swishes one finger in the air, and the shadow cloaking my whereabouts dissolves, leaving me exposed in a beam of light.

All faces turn in my direction.

"I said, join us," Death repeats, his voice only a soft exhalation—part irritated but mostly amused.

I pray for enough strength to make it through and shove the door open wide, the need for evasiveness gone. I feel as though I'm on the edge of some precipice. I take in a long, steady breath, releasing it to ease my nerves, and step into the room. Leah and I exchange a long glance, and I look away.

"Pardon the interruption." I try to keep my voice formal, but I hear the steeliness in my tone.

A faint murmur of voices follows my progress as I make my way around the small bands of immortals toward Leah. Lips curl into mocking smiles and eyebrows lower into scowls as I go by. Clearly, the story of my botched attempt to save Leah has made its way to the masses. I walk past them, my eyes focused straight ahead.

At Leah's side, I slip my hand into hers. I risk a brief look in Artagan's direction. He doesn't acknowledge my arrival. I'm pleasantly surprised to see Otmar has moved to Artagan's right. A bit of luck, then.

I concentrate, aiming my thoughts toward Artagan. *Otmar has my hemlock in his back pocket. If you—*

Too late. It takes every ounce of my strength not to look at him. Artagan must sense this because he adds, *Death has it now.*

As the last flimsy thread of hope snaps, something deep inside me breaks. I hold tight to the warm hand in mine. Although I know there's nothing I can do to save its possessor—all options have been depleted—that won't stop me from protecting Leah. *Not until the last breath leaves my body,* I promise myself. Because anything less would go against my nature.

Death's attention moves from council member to

council member, and then as he speaks, his eyes land on the beauty by my side. "Leah Winters, immortal scion of Vita, you have been found guilty of our highest crime, the refusal of gathering an assignment."

Leah looks as if she wants to reply but reconsiders. Shoulders slumping, she looks away.

"From this day forward, you will live out the remainder of your eternal existence far from all you love in Shadow Death. As I said, I wish this had turned out differently," he says, sounding a touch too sympathetic. "Step forward and receive your punishment."

A growl bubbles from my throat. I swing Leah behind me and, in doing so, seal my fate.

"Jack, no," Leah murmurs.

"Shhh," I say so only she can hear. My gaze stays fixed on Death as I cast the only card I have left. "The trial was a sham. Leah was under mind control. She intended to carry out her duties. And if you or your children believe otherwise, you are being fooled."

A stirring reaction rises from the crowd.

Death's eyes are cold with amusement. "Leah refused. We all heard it. It's only natural the girl regrets that decision now and wishes for a different outcome, but the trial was valid," he says, and silence falls over the assembly.

Death snaps his fingers, summoning Akio to step toward me. I turn to face him, keeping Leah behind me. His sparse structure doesn't fool me. I've seen his speed and agility in the games, and Otmar has told me stories. According to one of the tales, Akio sailed with the Minamoto clan into battle to gather the six-year-old Emperor Antoku. Akio's cunning, ruthless tactics took the young emperor's life and, in the process, won a decisive victory for the Minamoto that put an end to a five-year war. Otmar claims the blade strapped to Akio's waist is a sacred sword said to be lost at sea that same day. He brought it back, presenting it to Death. So touched was he, Death insisted Akio keep it as a show of his loyalty.

Akio doesn't advance but hangs back, a purposeful expression thinning his lips.

A cutting pain across my shoulders answers my defiance, and an unseen force shoves me flat to the floor, pinning me down. Akio walks around me. Then, taking Leah by the elbow, he steers her toward Death. Leah resists, but Akio tightens his grip on her arm, making her wince, and forces her forward.

I feel something robust and seething surge inside me, past the pain, past the unseen force, compelling me up. "Take your hands off my wife, you bloody bastard," I say, rage chafing my voice raw.

A buzz of whispers builds around us. Over Akio's shoulder, I see Death. One brow raised, his eyes zero in on me, alight with a new emotion. What? Disbelief? Humor? I'm not sure which description fits. He barks a sharp order for silence. Then in a blink, he disappears. I catch a flicker of movement a little too late. Before I can react, he reappears from a swirl of shadow at my side.

Death seizes me by the wrist. Pushing his thumb against the outer part of my hand, he jams it between the thin bones. Pain spikes. It feels as if the bones might shatter from the pressure of his grip. I try to pull away but only doom myself further. In one fluid motion, Death flips my wrist and drives my hand down toward my inner arm. With my limb trapped in place, I can't move without intense pain.

"As I told Artagan not that long ago, all I want is what's best for all of you. Going behind my back and plotting against my decisions is futile. Even the greatest civilizations have fallen when the people have forgotten their loyalties and not adhered to the laws. We can learn from them. As your father and head, I love you and care for you. And I will not allow this kind of treachery to destroy us, which means from this day forward any of my children or their descendants discovered working against me will face the consequences." Death strolls around the room while he speaks, towing me with him. Every movement sends a bolt of pain up my arm and straight through the top of my head. Dizzy, I keep my eyes fixed on the floor as I shuffle, bent forward at his side.

Death forces me to my knees. "Jack, here, was planning Leah's escape. Even after all of you found her guilty. Now, let him serve as a reminder."

"No!" Leah shouts.

I control the fear rising within me. "Don't look, love. Close your eyes," I say firmly. I cannot see Leah's face, but I imagine the air of uncomprehending horror that must overwhelm it now. *And above all else remember I love—*

With a quick twist of my arm, Death halts all thoughts and drives my teeth together. I hear Leah shriek my name. A bolt of agony sears through my arm as the muscles and ligaments are stretched to their limit, bringing me to the edge of fainting.

A cold sweat breaks out across my forehead as my body bends and contorts to his will. Then he brings my arm hard across his knee. There's a sickening snap, and a scream barrels up my throat. I clench my teeth tight to restrain it, but the attempt does no good, and the bloodcurdling sound breaks from my lips. Death releases me. I collapse to the floor in a quivering heap.

Warm wetness soaks the thin cotton fabric of my sleeve. My arm is bent at an odd angle, and I see a glimpse of the white shard of bone jutting through torn flesh past the rip in my sleeve. I cradle my deformed arm tightly against my chest and scoot away, fighting through nausea and dizziness, not allowing myself to lose consciousness. Blood seeps from the wound in warm crimson streams, soaking into the layer of dust that covers the floor. I feel myself growing weaker by the minute.

Death turns his head away with an air of grim satisfaction. "Keep an eye on him, Pacal. I want him to witness this."

Pacal seizes me by the shoulders and yanks me to my feet. Pain ripples through me in successive waves, and I wobble. His bronze arm darts around my neck.

"Bring the cup," Death commands.

Out of the shadows, a thin young woman from Leah's welcoming dinner appears, her dress exchanged for a flowing cloak. Held high, level with her eyes, she carries the golden chalice—an object that still haunts my dreams. It glitters in the sunlight, dancing across the relief-carved skeletons encircling the rim.

Six shrouded figures follow her, marching in line formation out of the darkness. They approach with pageantry, the hems of their long black cloaks swishing across the uneven floorboards in lapping waves. The dull thud of feet thrums in a rhythmic beat, like an executioner's drum, relentless and cruel. As the final figure passes—a boy, his face still rounded by youth—I catch a flash of silver, a chance ray of sun glinting along the blade of a bone-handled dagger laid across his outstretched palms.

The thin woman glides to a stop in front of Death. In the wake of a theatrical bow, she places the cup in Death's outspread hands and then takes her place with the other black-cloaked figures who have banded together at the foot of the apse's stairs. The boy waits by Death's side, a detached expression on his innocent face, the knife still resting in his open hands.

"Would the accuser come forward," Death says. A thick layer of formality coats his voice. Domitilla slides out from the crowd, satisfaction twisting her lips into a smile.

Thanatos takes the knife from the boy. Domitilla rolls up the sleeve of her blouse and holds her arm out over the lip of the cup. Thanatos grips her wrist, and then, following a quick flick of the blade across Domitilla's ivory skin, three drops of blood drip from the wound into the steaming liquid before the cut knits back together.

After a ceremonial bow, both Thanatos and Domitilla return to their places, and Death signals Akio to bring Leah forward. The nave is quiet, charged with electricity like the moments before a storm. Even the shadows themselves seem to have breath and movement.

"Just a sip will do," Death says, offering Leah the cup.

"No!" Aided by a burst of adrenaline, I grab onto Pacal's arm with the hand of my uninjured arm. Catching him off guard, I'm able to pull down and create some space. Then, reeling my head backward, I strike my captor solidly in the nose. His grip loosens, but he doesn't release me.

Pacal's hot, sulfur-laden breath growls at my ear, followed by a fist delivering a crushing blow to my left side. Pain ripples through me in successive waves, and my knees buckle.

"No more! Get him out of here," Death hisses through clenched teeth. "I'll decide what to do with him when we're finished."

In desperation, my gaze darts to Leah as Pacal hauls me away toward the shadows between the columns. The world around me compresses until I see nothing but Leah's face, the scene around us fading away. And for a fleeting moment, there's only Leah and me.

I love you, her voice whispers in my head.

I love you, too.

"And I'm sorry." *I should have never smashed those pills. I believed... It doesn't matter now. I was wrong.* Her voice shatters into a sob, breaking the spell and thrusting us back into the here and now.

"Wherever *he* sends you, I will find you!" I shout as Pacal drags me from the room.

Once in the seclusion of the shadow, Pacal presses the thumb of his free hand deep into my wound. Dizziness crashes over me, and he clamps his hand over my mouth to stifle the scream.

"No more trouble out of you," he growls. "I don't want to miss the show."

The pain waxes and wanes, and an acute numbness spreads, starting in my toes and fingertips and extending into my arms and legs. My thoughts become fuzzy, as though I'm watching everything from a distance behind a curtain. Any moment I'll wake up from this dream, with Leah curled by my side. Seconds pass like hours, but everything remains the same, reality barring my escape from this nightmare.

Through the thin veil of the shadow, all I can do is watch. Eyes full of tears, Leah stares at the spot where Pacal and I disappeared as if she's desperate to see me one last time. Her fraught expression turns resigned, and she turns back to Death.

Leah grips the ornate cup with both hands, and pressing the gilded rim to her lips, she drinks. Death retrieves the chalice and steps back to wait. At first, Leah shows no reaction. She turns to say something to Artagan but stops. I'd thought she was pale already. Now all traces of color drain from her cheeks, leaving her face dead white. She falls to the floor, body convulsing and mouth frothing.

As Leah's fit subsides, a screech reverberates through the nave, shaking the walls and rumbling beneath my feet. My stomach contracts in terror as a shadowy mass rises like a mountain of black mist. I quell a shudder, my heart rate picking up speed as memories of my dealings with this beast flow in. The creature's vaporous tendrils roll out along the floor. The black-cloaked group begins a soft chant, and the candles dim. As the creature curls back in on itself, it takes on a more humanoid form. Two vermilion orbs emerge from its shadowed depths, materializing into a set of eyes full of a dark intelligence.

Leah cries out, attempting to crawl backward, but

she makes limited progress before the creature lunges. Clutching Leah by the ankle, it soars high into the air. Black vapors whirling, the shadow beast tosses Leah repeatedly, but each time, unlike with Vita, none of Leah's precious flesh and bone tears away. As it grows frustrated, the creature spins faster, taking Leah with it. Each unproductive toss is accompanied by an earsplitting wail, rising in pitch, like that of a terrified child. The shadowy being drops Leah in a crumpled pile on the floor, and in a torrent of wind and vapor, it disappears through a nearby shadow, letting out a final bloodcurdling screech as it flies away.

Confused mutterings build out of the wake of silence. I stare at Leah's unmoving form. An unbalanced array of emotions—shock, fear, distrust, and even hope—shoots through me in less than a second. I lunge forward, but I'm held back by Pacal's firm hold.

A wheezy gasp erupts behind me, making the tiny hairs on the back of my neck bristle. The grip loosens from around my neck. Pacal's large frame reels at my side, clinging to my shoulder to steady himself. His black eyes are as round as saucers. I watch in disbelief as the irises turn from vacant pits to a lively, rich mocha brown. As he arches in pain, blood mixed with saliva foams from his mouth in a gurgled burst as a crimson-covered blade spears through his upper abdomen.

CHAPTER TWENTY-FIVE

PACAL LIES SPRAWLED AT MY feet, his vacant brown eyes staring, boring straight into mine. The blood leaking through his T-shirt just beneath the sternum confirms I'm not hallucinating. Pacal, one of the unkillable Soulless, is dead. I turn to find my liberator. However, whoever it was has vanished, denying me even a glimpse. I force my attention away from the gruesome scene and stare through the veil of shadow toward the nave.

The room's tenor has changed. I sense it even through the thin barrier. Gone are the ceremony and the feelings of spirited anticipation, leaving concern and confusion in their wake. In the middle of the room, Death and the council members huddle together in an intense discussion, not noticing me. The Soulless are notably absent, including Muan.

Leah stands, leaning on Artagan for support, flanked by Serevo and Thanatos's protégé. The circles under Leah's eyes have grown darker in color. Her lips pressed tight, every now and again her glance flickers away from the group toward the spot where I disappeared and now stand hidden from view. Even in the face of the perilous unknown, she's worried about me.

Teeth clenched in fierce determination, I hobble out of

the shadow, my broken arm folded across my chest. My feet feel like weights. The smallest step takes immense effort, making me sweat freely.

Leah's gaze turns in my direction. Upon seeing me, she breaks free of Artagan's support and rushes to my side before either Serevo or Thanatos can react. Her gaze fixes on my mangled arm, a welter of emotions wrestling for mastery of her features. From the look of her eyebrows knitting together into an unmistakable scowl, worry wins out.

With my uninjured arm, I pull Leah to my side and say, "It's nothing. I'll be fine." Even I can hear the lie in my words. I've never taken this long to heal.

Leah's frown deepens, but before she can speak, Death's voice floods the room.

"You are full of surprises, Jack. I'll give you that. It's not often I'm taken unaware. I've underestimated you."

All eyes now glued on Leah's and my reunion, Death steps away from his children and glances toward the shadows at the rear wall where Pacal and I disappeared moments ago. "No coward either, it seems. Although you're a fool for returning."

I smile, baring my teeth, but I force myself to keep my commentary private.

In silence, Death advances. Akio follows behind him, drawing his sword as he matches Death's slow, steady stride.

"This has nothing to do with him," Leah blurts out. Although her voice is shrill from fear, she makes a move to step forward. I grab hold of her, and in a burst of utter desperation, I swing her behind me to take up a defensive stance in front of her. But in a moment, Leah is at my side again, her hand grasping mine.

"Together," she says, and I nod.

Death comes to an abrupt stop, several paces still lying between us.

"Scared? I can hear the speed of your pulse from here," he says, eyes locked on me. His amiable grin widens into a contortion of pearly teeth, full of contempt. A growl rips through his chest, causing his children to flinch or step back. Then I watch in disbelief as Death bursts into a pillar of black flame. The heat scorches the floor and sends blistering hot air into our faces. An odor that was only hinted at before—earth and sulfur and decay—overtakes the room. It smells as if the hollows of Tartarus itself have opened before us.

A dark outline of a figure—tall and cadaverously thin—rises through the flames, first doubling then tripling in height. As the master of the underworld steps forward, the cinders of Death's ordinary facade fall away, shrouding his shoulders and cascading to the ground, becoming a veiled robe.

Paler than a skull, Death's skin is translucent—so sheer I can see working muscles and black veins underneath. The long robe seems to shimmer with his movements, fleeting glimpses of distorted, tortured faces appearing in the flowing fabric. It's almost as though I hear moans and muffled wails of the damned emitting from it.

He stares at me, and somehow I stare back. His eyes flare like the tips of red-hot pokers, and in them, I see my end. Pain isn't enough any longer. My death is the only thing that will squelch his anger now. I'm sure of it.

Apparently coming to the same conclusion, Artagan thrusts himself forward. Kemisi jumps into his path, and with the force of one of Otmar's legendary berserkers, she pushes Artagan back. Otmar catches him by the arms to restrain him.

I tighten my grip around Leah's hand, still secure in mine. Her fingers have grown icy cold. I plant a thought into her mind. *When Death strikes, it will be at me. I want you to run. Don't look back. Just run.*

I give a quick glance over my shoulder to make sure my words have sunk in.

Leah stares up at me, her eyes full of doubt and tears.

"Paradise, remember," I whisper, squeezing her hand.

Pulling in a deep breath, she nods, and I shift my attention back to Death, satisfied that at least some hope remains.

Death holds out a skeletal hand. With a quick bow, Akio relinquishes the sword to his father. Thin lips curled back in irritation, Death readies the sword to strike.

I steel my nerves.

A deafening crackle echoes through the expanse as if a bolt of electricity splintered the air right over our heads. Three figures materialize in front of Leah and me, blocking Death's approach.

Hooded, each holds in their grasp a long, golden rapier. I stare dumbfounded when I realize Death and the council members are all standing immobilized, petrified in mid-movement. Their shadowed faces are frozen in shock and anger, all except for Artagan's. A triumphant smile—expansive and smug—lies frozen upon his lips.

I hover protectively at Leah's side. One newcomer, the largest of the three, swings his head and peers at us around the rim of his hood, revealing a Grecian profile and a pair of striking eyes. Their color takes me aback—a radiant, glistening silver.

As my momentary fascination crumbles away, I make use of the sudden change in the situation. My grip tightens on Leah's hand, and I spin around to find an escape through the closest shadow but instead find myself looking down into another set of eyes—sharp, youthful, and full of concern.

"Sally? What the...? Where did you...? How?" My focus settles on a rapier she clutches in her pudgy hand. Every detail of the sword matches the ones belonging to the strangers, from the intricate, sweeping pattern of the handle to the long, thin blade, with one notable exception—blood coats the blade. My wide eyes return to her face. "It was you."

"Sally! Let's go!" the silver-eyed man says, the authority in his voice unmistakable. "I can't hold him much longer."

"No time for explanations now, dear," Sally says, wiping the blade on her skirt and slipping the rapier into a sheath strapped about her waist. Then she vanishes from my side, only to reappear behind Leah and me. As she lays her hands on our shoulders, I have just enough time to glimpse Death breaking free of his petrified state before the scene flashes from sight.

It's as though I'm falling upward, like gravity no longer has a hold over us. The ground beneath me has disappeared, a howling wind rushing past my ears. Around us, colors churn. I feel Leah at my side, then we speed upward and then jolt sideward. Without warning, my feet slam into the ground. My knees buckle, and my back strikes the floor with a forcible smack. A wave of white-hot pain shoots up my arm. I clamp my teeth into the soft tissue of my cheek to suppress the scream that barrels up my throat. A small room with faded floral wallpaper rotates dizzily overhead. I close my eyes and drift.

A voice breaks through the lethargic haze. "Help me get him into the chair."

No, I think groggily, and then I feel hands lifting me. The pain following the movement jolts me back to the surface. My eyes snap open, and I find myself sitting in a straight-backed chair in a small parlor filled with overstuffed furniture and doilies galore. A fire crackles behind me, its heat warming my back.

A petite woman with short-cropped blond hair that sticks out in every direction kneels beside me, grasping my arm. I attempt to pull away.

"You need to hold still. Nadya is only trying to help," Sally says, taking a step into my view.

"Leah? Where is she?" I force out past my cracked lips, trying to glance around the room.

"I'm here." Leah slides to my side and takes hold of my hand with both hers. "Now, let them help you."

Too tired to speak, I bob my head.

Nadya cuts the fabric of my sleeve up past my elbow with a pair of scissors. Then she peels back the bloody sheath and examines the wound first with her eyes and then with her fingertips. I focus my attention away from the injury and try to concentrate on Nadya's face. Her features are well defined and angular. The smooth ivory skin of her forehead wrinkles every now and again as her fingers explore, assessing the damage. I suck in my breath whenever she touches a particularly tender spot. Each time, she apologizes before moving on with her assessment.

After placing my arm across my lap, Nadya's eyes slide to mine, their gray-green depths full of sympathy. "I can heal your arm," she says with the utmost certainty. "But I'll have to set the bone first. Because of the extent of your injury, there might be some long-term damage and loss of function. You will have a scar, a fairly substantial one, I'm afraid."

"Someone told me once women like scars, even find them sexy. Hopefully, he wasn't lying." My mouth twitches as a flicker of amusement forces its way through the pain. I glance at Leah. Her expression is serious, and she doesn't seem to find my attempt at wit the least bit funny.

Nadya snorts. "Well, at least Death didn't damage your sense of humor," she says and then glances at Sally. "We'll need towels and hot water. Whiskey, too. Or laudanum, if you have it. Please tell Alasdair I'll need his help."

Sally presses her lips tightly together but then nods and slips with haste from the room. She returns a moment later with towels slung over her arm and two bottles in hand—a tall one filled with deep-amber liquid and a tiny cobalt-blue one.

A wiry, slightly effeminate youth carrying a basin of steaming water follows her. The light dusting of freckles across the boy's cheeks and the bridge of his nose make him look young—fourteen maybe—but he carries himself with the confidence of someone much older. Behind him, the silver-eyed man ambles in. Although not much taller than me, he's more sturdily built. With the hood of his sweatshirt now removed, I can see his face, not just the peculiar eyes. I'll admit I'm surprised to find the rest of his features so ordinary—a long, straight nose, square jaw, and perpetual grimace on a pair of thin lips, evident by the deep frown lines, all topped with a full head of wavy black hair.

To Sally's dismay, I refuse the opiates. I reach out and grab hold of the long neck of the whiskey bottle. The bottle feels heavy, as if it weighs hundreds of pounds. Despite my shaky grip, I'm able to lift the smooth lip to my mouth. I take several gulps and then cough and gag, but drain the bottle of its contents nonetheless. Soon my vision grows a little blurry around the edges, and my thought patterns sway off course now and again. Still, the liquor does little to numb the acute pain in my arm.

"Alasdair, you take him around the shoulders and hold him tight," Nadya instructs and then looks away from the boy to the silver-eyed man. "I'll need you to pull on the arm to draw the protruding bone back through the skin."

My stomach rolls with unease, and I find it difficult to swallow.

Alasdair smiles at me as he pushes back a mop of red hair from his eyes. He slips a piece of leather into my mouth. "Bite down. Hard."

I nod in thanks and understanding.

Following Nadya's instructions, Alasdair steps behind my chair and seizes me by the shoulders, his fingers digging into rigid muscle. As the silver-eyed man's hands wrap around my wrist, I squeeze my eyes shut and set my teeth into the supple hide, preparing for the worst. Nothing could have readied me for the utter agony. A scream breaks through my dry lips, and I fear I may retch. The taste of bile mixed with alcohol sours my mouth. The hands release me, and I slump back in the chair, my arm dropping to my side. My breathing comes in labored bursts.

The lilt of Leah's voice hovering by my ear tells me it's almost over. I nod once but keep my eyes closed.

A pair of small hands cups my forearm, pushing and probing. As the sharp pain mellows into a throbbing ache, a scorching heat devours my arm. Just as fast as the sensation arrived, it flashes away. At first, the absence of pain is all I comprehend. I open my eyes and peer at my forearm in wonder. I flex the muscles. A renewed strength pounds its way through my veins, as good as new. The only evidence that remains of the injury is a scar snaking in a jagged pattern up my outer forearm—similar to the one that adorns Artagan's cheek.

"Amazing," I say.

Sally smiles. "Nadya is quite a talented healer. She was a nurse during the Revolutionary War, requested by George Washington himself. And this is Tobias," she says, patting the silver-eyed man on the shoulder the way a proud mother would. "We couldn't have saved you without him. No one but him could have held Death back."

Tobias?

Although not an uncommon name—I've known a couple in my time—the coincidence is too much to overlook. I peer in Tobias's direction to find him staring at me. An expression full of contempt crosses his face, and I break eye contact, returning my attention to Sally.

Noticing Tobias's and my silent exchange, Sally goes

on. "We're lucky he agreed to help. We couldn't have done it without him."

"Thank you for this." I gesture to my arm. "And for helping Leah and me escape. I'm in your debt." I bow my head.

"Don't thank me," Tobias says. The hairs on the back of my neck bristle at his curt tone. "I didn't do it for you. Sally and Nadya forced my hand." He turns to Leah. "She's Endless, one of *his*. Death won't be happy we took her. We have no idea what he'll—"

"She's one of us, too," Nadya interrupts, her voice rising, exasperated. She seizes Tobias's hand, preventing him from turning away. "We couldn't just leave her there."

"But we should have," he says.

"Tobias!" Sally says in a stern tone.

Not pausing to argue further, Tobias wrenches his arm free and walks away. Nadya purses her lips into a hard line and follows Tobias from the room.

"Don't worry about him," Alasdair says with a dismissive wave. "Nadya will make him see. She always does." He smiles and trails the path of his companions.

"Alasdair's right," Sally says. "Tobias just believes he's protecting us. He doesn't know you like I do. I suppose it doesn't help that his father was Endless. As you can imagine, it makes matters more complicated."

"*Was* Endless?" Leah asks.

"Tobias said he died a long time ago. It must wear on a man to hate what he came from. He's worried that, since you're a council member, you'll lead Death to us."

Leah's expression turns earnest. "I would never."

"I know, dear," Sally says, "but Tobias's prejudices run deep, instilled in him by his mother. It clouds his thinking. However, this is my house, and I decide who stays and who goes. And you're staying." She gives a quick jerk of her head, the matter settled. "You both must have a lot of questions. Only natural."

"So many I'm not sure I know where to start," Leah says.

I lean forward, resting my elbows on my knees. "Where are we? That seems to be a good enough place to begin as any."

"You're safe. But I think it's best if that's all I tell you for now, because of the others," Sally says with a quick glance at the empty door.

"Back there in the shadows, you killed Pacal, the Soulless," I say.

"Every creature of legend has a fatal weakness. For the Soulless, it's us. We call it accelerated metamorphosis. Basically, with just a touch, we can move them through time, back to the moment before their soul was lost. Once they're mortal again, the rest is just killing. A stab to the heart or lungs or a slash to the throat finishes them off fairly quickly."

"So you're immortals?" Leah asks.

"We are, but on our own terms," Sally says. "However, Death knows how to take our lives. That's if he can find us, and with our skill set, that's easier said than done."

Lips parting, Leah leans forward. "What are you?"

Sally fights back a chuckle, looking again at the door. Then, with a committed set to her jaw, her gaze returns to us.

My stomach gives an embarrassingly loud growl, bringing a grin back to Sally's lips.

"How about I get us something to eat? And a clean shirt," Sally adds, scowling at mine. "Then we'll start at the beginning. My beginning."

Waiting for Sally to return, Leah sits on the sofa while I pace, filled with nervous energy. Too many unanswered questions fill my mind. As I pass by the fireplace, the gold ring forgotten on my finger gleams in the firelight, distracting me from my thoughts. I gaze down at Artagan's poison ring and begin to twist it around my finger, wondering how much of a hand he had in this rescue and what his connection to Tobias might be.

"I'm sure he's okay," Leah says. "He's a crafty dude. Besides, Otmar and Kemisi will keep him out of any real trouble."

As long as Death doesn't figure out he was behind this. "You're probably right, but I can't help wondering when I'll see him again. I have a few questions only he can answer."

Leah cocks her head, clearly not buying my reason.

I sigh. "And yes, despite his deceitfulness and his philandering behavior, I've gotten used to having him around." I smile and then grow serious again. "Did you see Artagan's face? That smug grin he gets when he knows he's right. He knew about Tobias, maybe even Sally and the rest of them, too. Whatever they are, Artagan knew they could help us. It looks like I owe him again."

"We both do."

I stand in front of the fireplace, staring into the flickering flame. Artagan shrouds my thoughts. I let my eyes wander over a menagerie of photographs lining the mantel. A black-and-white picture in a dark-walnut frame catches my eye, distracting me from my current train of thought.

"Leah, look at this." I point at the photo.

Two women, each dressed in a drop-waist dress, stand arm in arm in front of a Studebaker Special Six. The lady on the left is Sally, her salt-and-pepper hair twisted up and disappearing under a bell-contoured hat. She hasn't aged a day. But it's Sally's companion who commands my attention. Although she appears to be younger than the time I met her—mid-thirties at most—with her small, distinct Roman nose and almond-shaped eyes, I recognize her at once.

"It's Gladys," I say, so low I'm not sure Leah hears me.

Leah steps to my side and studies the photo. Her eyes widen as she looks at me. "Is that who I think it is?"

"Yes, it's me," Sally says from behind us, taking us both by surprise.

A copper-skinned girl carrying a tea set follows Sally. The girl barely acknowledges our presence as she sets the teapot and three matching cups on an oval table by the sofa before disappearing back into the kitchen.

"That's Itzel. Never mind her. She's a shy one," Sally says as she places a platter full of finger sandwiches next to the tea set. Smiling, she then hands me a plaid shirt that was hanging over her shoulder, and her eyes glance toward the photograph. "The picture was taken in the spring of 1922. That era had the loveliest hats. The woman by my side is Gladys. She was like a daughter. I bought her that car for her birthday. She was turning ninety-two."

"Ninety-two?" I cast a fleeting look at the photo.

"Yes. Gladys was like you." Sally's gaze rests on Leah. "She started out as a soul immortal too. My dear friend lived many lives before she transformed into a Timeless. But I'm getting ahead of myself. Sit, eat, and I'll tell you my story."

CHAPTER TWENTY-SIX

MY RUINED SHIRT EXCHANGED FOR a new one, I settle next to Leah on the sofa, balancing a plate stacked with egg-salad sandwiches on my lap. A teacup in hand, Sally sits in an overstuffed chair by the fireplace. She clears her throat and begins.

"I was born Sarah Prudence Marbury in August 1648."

I jerk my head back and glance at Leah. She stares at Sally, her mouth agape. "1648! That would make you, what?" Leah begins to count on her fingers, her eyes growing wider. "Almost 370 years old. Two hundred years older than Jack."

"It would." Sally smiles, amused. "Back then, I seemed like any other girl. I'm one of seven children. My father, a baker, moved the family to the Massachusetts Bay Colony, and we settled in Boston. In 1666, a smallpox epidemic ravaged the area. I, along with my two younger sisters, contracted the disease. Abigail and Constance both died, while I, who seemed to be the sickest of the three, survived. A sovereign act of God, they called it.

"A year after my miraculous recovery, I married Isaiah Barrowe, a farmer from Salem Village. Unaccustomed to farm life, I struggled. A patient husband and kind teacher, Isaiah taught me many things. One day while I was helping him deliver a breeched foal, the mare kicked me in the temple. Again, I had a brush with death, and again, I survived. It wasn't long afterward I had visions and dreams of future events. Just snippets here and there. While some of them never came true, some did. The future is tricky. One can't always rely on what one *sees*, because what's to come is so easily influenced. A million tiny decisions can alter it from one path to another.

"I never told a soul about my ability, not even Isaiah. Witchcraft was an accepted reality in seventeenth-century New England, punishable by death. Puritans believed in the invisible world of witches and specters as much as they believed in the rocks and rivers." She chuckles, shaking her head.

I take the opportunity to peer at Leah. Her expression of bewilderment has vanished, leaving a mixture of wonder and captivation in its place. I feel much the same. If this story is any indication, Sally has certainly lived an extraordinary life.

"I was able to keep my new gift well concealed," Sally goes on, "and life went on as normal. Isaiah and I had five children and lived happily together until his death in 1689. After that, tranquility ceased. I found myself involved in some bitter land disputes with the Putnam family and drew their anger again when I opposed the hiring of a Reverend Samuel Pariss. So when the accusations of witchcraft started running rampant, I can't say I was surprised when Putnam's maidservant, Mercy Lewis, pointed an accusatory finger my way." Sally pauses, her expression turning inward as she runs a forefinger up her cup to wipe away a dribble of spilled tea.

"Like my friend Giles Corey, I refused to play their games. To prove my guilt, they bound my hands and feet, attached me to a boulder, and tossed me into Wilkins Pond. Whether because of damaged ropes or loose knots or fate alone, I floated to the surface. Little did I know at the time, I had just survived my third brush with death and had been turned Timeless. I felt nothing remarkable with the transformation.

"With proof that I was an instrument of Satan"—she rolls her eyes—"they took me to the gallows. Imagine everyone's surprise, including mine, when after two attempts, I didn't die. It's a good thing they didn't attempt to drown me again, or they would have been successful, since after we become Timeless, our third brush with death is the only way my kind can die. Afraid of my wrath, they released me and returned all my property. The elders went as far as to expunge my name from all the records in hopes I wouldn't curse them. But little did any of us know I'm much more than a witch. So much more."

Sally grins over the rim of her teacup, and her face transforms. She's sixty, then twenty, then fifteen, and then ninety. My eyes widen, and so does Sally's smile. "I'm a descendant of Time through her daughter Clotho, one of the Moirai."

My eyebrows dart up, remembering Artagan's history lesson.

"The Fates. Those are Death's daughters," Leah says, beating me to the punch.

"Yes. Centuries ago, it seems Death and Time were a bit of an item. Time claims Death tried to steal their children from her. Of course, I lived long enough to know there are two sides to every story. Whatever happened between them, she hates him for it, going as far as passing her hatred on to her children. Not just to the Fates, but to Tobias too. I'm getting off track again. We have all the time in the world to gossip about our family drama." She chuckles, looking at Leah.

"Our family? So you're saying, what? I'm Timeless?" Leah shifts uncomfortably in her seat.

Sally smiles.

"Along with being Endless," I say.

"Well, she's not really Endless, now, is she? Not naturally, at least. Death turned her into one." Sally's attention turns back to Leah. "From what I understand, genetic mutations are rare in both the Endless and the Timeless family lines, showing up randomly through our lineage. Tobias says for one to have a chance to become Endless, both the mother and the father have to carry the Endless gene, while a soul immortal inherits their mutation from one parent."

"Yes, that's right," I say, remembering Artagan explaining it almost identically.

"Things are much the same for the Timeless. Except for us, there is no chance for any abnormality if only one parent carries the gene, unless"—she sticks a pudgy finger in the air—"the other parent is a carrier of the Endless gene. When that happens, as long as the soul immortal survives their three brushes with death like any Timeless must do, they become Timeless as well."

"So what you're saying is because she lived through cancer, a car accident, and escaped Shadow Death, Leah's Timeless?"

Sally confirms with a bob of her head.

"And if I had succeeded in saving her from either the accident or punishment, she wouldn't be?"

"Well, there's no telling. The future is mystery most of the time."

"Huh," I say, rubbing my stubbled chin. "Remind me not to question your gut feelings again."

Leah tilts her head and smirks in my direction.

"It's the Fates—Clotho, Lachesis, and Atropos—that decide," Sally says. "They all have to agree to save just one of us. That's a miracle in itself because from what I hear, they do little besides argue among themselves, like most sisters do, I suppose. Nadya says that's why there are so few of us." Sally chuckles.

"Is it common? A soul-immortal-slash-Timeless?"

"No. It's rare but not unheard of. That being said, you are the first one *I've* ever met that was an Endless—natural or otherwise—who was transformed into a Timeless. And I'm over three hundred and fifty years old."

Leah rubs her arm, her attention drifting away.

Upon seeing her discomfort, Sally continues. "Then again, I can only speak for Clotho's line. We don't have much contact with the others. No real need." An eager smile spreads across her lips. "There's no telling what talents you'll have, though. It's all very exciting."

"Like a science experiment," Leah grumbles.

"I suppose." Sally's smile has faded, but it still lurks at the corners of her mouth and in the creases around her eyes. "Gladys remembered every life she ever lived. All five of them. Is it the same for you?"

Leah bobs her head, then she and I exchange a meaningful glance. The question of Leah's dreams of me and her memories of her past life as Lydia Ashford answered at last.

"In the church, did the shadow creature refuse to judge me because the Fates stepped in on my behalf?"

"Oh, yes, that. That horrid creature *couldn't* judge you, dear, because it can't harm an innocent soul. Or in your case, two." Sally nods at Leah's stomach.

Shock freezes on my face. Then my gaze slides to Leah's abdomen, where her hand now presses against the hollow curve. I swallow hard, relaxing a little, torn between exaltation and panic.

"Are you saying I'm pregnant?" Leah whispers. "But we only... it was just... how can you be sure?"

"My friend Gladys was a talented seer, and she was never wrong, not once," Sally says as her gaze wanders to the mantel. "Many of us have the gift, but only a few can make that claim. I've been wrong countless times. Before her death, she told me you were coming. She didn't know when or why. She just knew. A gut feeling, she called it. She also told me that when you arrived you would be pregnant with twins, and I should do everything in my power to keep them safe. It would seem congratulations are in order," Sally says, the amusement steadfast in her voice.

Correctly deeming Leah and I need a moment to ourselves after such news, Sally shows us upstairs to our room. The chamber is large as bedrooms go, with faded striped wallpaper and regal furnishings. At the far end, the sun shines in through a bay window with gossamer curtains that float like white clouds down to the floor. A marble-tiled fireplace similar to the one in the parlor holds the remains of a slow-flickering flame.

After stoking the fire, Sally pauses at the door. "I must ask you not to shadow walk while you're with us. The shadows are Death's realm, and he'll have a much easier time finding you if you enter them. You'd lead him straight to us."

"We won't. I promise. Neither Leah nor I will do anything to jeopardize any of you," I say.

Sally exits with a nod, a little smirk still curving her weathered lips. As soon as the door latches, Leah collapses backward onto the bed, followed by a twang of objecting springs. I sink down next to her.

A father. I rake my fingers through my hair. *Bloody hell.*

The next several minutes proceed in stunned silence, my mind occupied by two distinct but opposing paths of thought—a list of my qualifications for fatherhood, or lack thereof, on one path, and a sense of unfathomable joy on the other.

"Are you happy?" Leah asks, breaking through the quiet. Her tone is a little tentative, and she gives me a shadow of one of her usual smiles. "I get this is unexpected and all, but I guess I thought you always wanted kids." She looks away.

I lie down and roll to face her, sliding an arm around her waist so we're close together. "Of course I'm happy. Shocked, and I'll admit, a bit nervous, but the woman I love with all my heart is making me a father. How could I not be happy? Ecstatic, even? For so long, I never believed I'd have a family of my own. And now..." My mouth breaks into a smile. "But how are you feeling?"

"Honestly, right now, I'm wondering what the Fates were thinking. I know nothing about babies. I've never even babysat," she says, her strained voice hushed. "And twins!"

"Well, love, we're even then because neither do I. I guess we'll just have to figure it out together."

Leah seems satisfied with my response, at least for the time being. She curls into my side. Her breathing soon fades into the unvarying cadence of slumber. Despite everything that has happened, in this instant, I feel at peace. I close my eyes and drift off into slumber.

When I wake, I'm alone in our bed.

Wrapped in a blanket, Leah stands on the other side of the room, gazing out the bay window into the moonlit night. Admiring her shape in the makeshift toga, I rise and cross the short expanse. I step in behind her and wrap my arms around her, pressing my lips to the top of her head. We stand locked together, swaying slightly.

Out the window, the crystals of newly fallen snow sparkle in the full moon's mellow glow. Across a dark body of water, lights glitter in starry clusters from the shore. It feels like we're in a different world, one free of death and monsters.

"What are you thinking about?" I ask, my voice only a whisper.

"My mom," she says, not hiding the echo of sadness.

She leans her head back against my chest. "I'm not sure I can stay here if it will put her in danger. I have to find a way to keep you all safe." Her hand falls to her stomach.

I draw in a tense breath and weigh my words carefully. "Love—"

"Let me finish. I dreamt of my mom. It was a glimpse into the future. I'm sure it was. From what I could decipher, she's safe, at least for now, and in time she'll be happy again. I know Sally said visions don't always come true, but my heart tells me this one will. Tomorrow, I'll talk to Sally about writing my mom. I understand it's not safe to visit her, but maybe a letter would be okay. I don't have any idea what I'm going to say yet, but I can't have her worrying about me. Not with Grady—" She stops, pulling in a shuddering breath, and I tighten my embrace. "It helps to know I'll see her again someday and that she'll meet her grandchildren."

I move a hand to Leah's stomach, placing my palm over her hand. Somewhere deep down, I wonder what changes these two tiny miracles will bring with them. What if they're mortals? That would mean more goodbyes. Unease sparks in my chest, but I push it away, not willing to think about that possibility now. Granting myself a moment of happiness doesn't seem like too much to allow after everything Leah and I have been through.

A warm hand rests over my fingers with a feathery lightness. Leah turns in my arms, her eyes holding mine. "Like I've said a thousand times, it's all going to be all right. I just know it." She speaks with assurance.

I smile down at her and kiss her between her brows. Hope surges, warming my heart like the sun. I know what is past is gone. Ahead of us lies the great unknown, and a future full of promise.

EPILOGUE

ARTAGAN

"**W**HERE IS JACK?" DEATH'S TONE is serene, almost relaxing. Almost.

I heave myself up onto my elbows from the damp, grimy floor but find myself startlingly weak, my arms buckling under my weight. I try again, this time succeeding. My hair is in my eyes, pasted to my face with sweat and blood. I shake my head, managing to free it. I glare up at him, his real appearance concealed once more in a human form.

"Piss off!" I say.

Death casts a condemnatory glance over my battered and naked body before crouching in front of me. In the deepest chamber of the church, with the light of a dwindling fire at his back, his face is shadowed so only the shine of his eyes shows in the dim light. He lets out a sigh, and when he speaks again, his voice is hushed. "I wish it hadn't come to this, you know. I have shown you nothing but patience, but today that stops. A father can only give his son so much leeway. You will tell me what I need to know, one way or another."

With a curt bob of his head, he stands and begins

pacing. The whole time, he watches me, his eyes vigilant for any signs of a change of heart. Then his mouth curls into a self-satisfied grin. I realize where the smug smile comes from when the urge to renounce autonomy and relinquish control crashes over me.

Muscles contract and rebel. The fibers of my willpower stretch and begin to unravel. Without warning, an explosion of blue luminescence ignites behind my lids, followed by images of what life could be like if I were an obedient *son*. A woman with similar features to Olluna beckons me. Each scene is a skewed perspective of happiness and love. An age-old pang stabs my gut as Death plays with my feelings of resentment, inadequacy, and loneliness, making them harder to ignore.

As the pounding pressure dwindles, the illusion shifts. Olluna's double disappears, and Kemisi's image replaces hers. This new hallucination comes from my imagination since I doubt her father would conjure such a memory. I breathe deep and push the thought from my mind. Some desires must remain out of reach no matter how much I might wish otherwise.

I groan, letting myself drop to the floor again, and roll away from his gaze. "Quit the parlor tricks and get on with it."

"You thought, rather foolishly, that you were a step ahead of me, that you had discovered things about that girl I didn't already identify." I hear the anger building in Death's words. "I've known Leah was special for some time. Since the moment Thanatos told me about the canvases she painted of Jack. Why else would I have chosen her to be on my council? Because I believed your lies about Serevo?" He laughs.

"Soul immortals with a Timeless lineage are so rare," Death goes on. "Choosing Leah for the council left me in a bind. With my pledge to the council, I couldn't attempt to slaughter her without just cause, now could I? I knew

Leah's family was the key. She loved them, so I believed she would never agree to take one of them. Her selflessness surprised me. When Domitilla came to me, claiming Leah refused to gather her brother, it seemed fate had forged a new avenue to my goal. It was clear to me the girl was being mind-controlled. She didn't want to refuse. You could see that in her eyes. But as I'm sure you're aware, many of my children *secretly* disagreed with my choice to place Leah on the council over Serevo. So I allowed a vote, knowing enough of them would overlook their concerns about Leah turning into another Morrighan and that they would choose to punish her. After that, it was out of my hands and up to fate. But my plan worked." He smiles. "I now have a Timeless on my council. Yes, there was a sacrifice, but it was well worth it."

"Says you." With a grunt, I push myself back up onto my elbow. "I suppose having a member on the council who can keep the Soulless in line would be useful." I'm a little surprised how calm and reasonable my voice sounds, not betraying the dread brewing within me. I know where our little game of Truth or Consequences is heading.

His expression remains composed, but a small muscle flexes along the side of his neck.

"Or is there more?" I ask. "Their demise, perhaps? The Timeless can kill a Soulless, or am I wrong? By making Leah Timeless, you've placed a target on Leah's back. The Soulless' main goal now will be to kill her. She's safer where she is."

"You don't think I thought of that? Leah's last brush with death wasn't with belladonna. Belladonna can't kill an Endless—it only marks them for punishment. The Shadow Creature is under my control. Nothing will touch her without my say-so. And any risk to her is far outweighed by the rewards. With a Timeless under my control, we can finally rid this world of the Soulless. My plan is finally attainable."

"But you didn't plan for everything, did you? You need my help since you didn't expect the Timeless would spring Leah from the lion's den. And even if they did, you knew Leah wouldn't leave with them as long as her beloved's fate was in the balance. You never thought they'd take Jack, too, did you?"

The thin line of his lips tightens, making the grooves around his mouth grow deeper. "But you did. Why?"

I grin.

"Be advised, today my patience is extremely low," he says with a note of warning in his tone. "Enough talking. Tell me where your descendant is, because we both know wherever Jack may be, Leah's not far away."

Snorting, I look past him to the fire.

"No, then?"

I swallow hard, forcing down the bitter taste that has risen at the back of my throat, and wait for my death. I'm a little surprised when, in my peripheral view, I see Death raise his hand. Palm up, he curls his fingers twice, beckoning to a shadow cast by an overhanging wall.

An audience. Fantastic.

Domitilla, probably. I assumed, when Leah refused, Death gave Dom permission to take Grady and fooled her into believing his plan was for Leah to spend an eternity in Shadow Death as retribution for Vita. Once Leah survived, he'd have to make amends. Maybe I'm the consolation prize.

It takes a moment or two, but following a flutter of black feathers, a shadowed figure creeps from the darkened corner. Too small for Domitilla, the newcomer's pale skin shimmers in the faint firelight, standing out in stark contrast to her jet-black hair, which hangs long and stringy over her shoulders. Every movement is graceful and calculating. As she arches into a crouch, her steely eyes flit about the room, as a wild animal's might when gauging its surroundings.

Something about this diminutive girl is unnerving, and the first thrill of true fear flows through me. Before now, I thought Death merely meant to kill me when he didn't get the answers he required. But with this stranger's arrival, I fear he might have more in store.

My adrenaline spikes, and I reach for my gold-and-onyx poison ring, only then remembering I gave it to Jack hours before. Like Icarus, it seems overconfidence will be my final undoing.

Still crouched at the far end of the room, the girl hums, dragging a single finger in circular patterns in the dirt. Once in a while, her gaze finds me, causing my unease to grow, but it isn't until Death speaks again that I understand the reason.

"Morrighan, my good girl," he coos. "Look what I have for you. A new plaything."

With a final glance around, Morrighan stands and slinks toward me. Squatting in front of me, she reaches out a small hand, her lips curling into an angelic smile. I cringe as she lays her fingertips on my head. I'm surprised to find her touch is as light as a feather and soothing. But suddenly, her gray eyes turn white, all color disappearing, and the innocent grin transforms into one full of malice.

My body stiffens, legs springing straight, and my hands clench into fists pinned to my sides as a surge of energy like thousands of tiny electric shocks floods through me. Against my will, I let out an unearthly moan. When the round of torture—severe and exquisite—comes to its end, bile overtakes my mouth, and I'm able to roll to my side before being ill.

"Just tell me what I need to know, Artagan, and this all will be over. You can go home," Death says. "All forgiven."

Eyes shut tight, I stay silent, lips bound by both stubbornness and loyalty to family. The next surge comes, even stronger and more ruthless than the first, when Morrighan touches me again.

"Artagan," a sweet voice says through the pain. "Look at me."

My mind is groggy, and I fight to open my eyes. Kemisi's face is inches from mine. I reach up hesitantly, fearing she's only in my imagination, and stroke a soft curl of her hair between my fingers.

"You shouldn't be here," I manage to push out.

"If you tell Death what he needs to know, we can be together," she says. "Please tell him where Jack is, and all this will stop."

The pain dwindles, allowing me to pull in a full breath. Deep down I wonder how Kemisi can ask this of me. I thought she knew me better. I know I must refuse her, but not yet. I want one more moment with her, just one more touch. Running my thumb along the curve of her cheek, I set the silky feeling to memory. The honey color of her skin has always reminded me of rowan wood, but in the dim light, it appears richer, darker. I fix my attention on her almond-shaped eyes, and the fantasy shatters. Their color isn't the lively caramel brown I know so well, but a deadpan gray.

"You're not her! Get away from me, you bitch!" I use my last ounce of strength to push the imposter away.

The angelic smile returns to her lips, and Kemisi's face transforms back into Morrighan's pallid one. She lets out a snarl as her upper lip curls, showing off a set of pointed teeth. Her hands jut out like claws and clamp around my throat. I cannot breathe, and my body thrashes with the demand for air. I grab at her hands, trying to pry them loose, but to no avail. As her grip tightens, my breathing grows shallow, and I go willingly into the dark.

ACKNOWLEDGMENTS

This novel could not have come into being without the help of some wonderful people:

To my husband, Craig, and my daughters, Elizabeth and Nicole. Your love and support means the world to me. Thank you for being my sounding boards. And to my dearest friend, Audrey, for her continuous encouragement throughout this journey.

To the Red Adept Publishing team for all your hard work and dedication. Special thanks to my editors, Sarah and Jen, whose input and guidance made this novel shine.

To Susan for helping me whip my manuscript into shape. And to my beta readers—Lea, Beth, and Sarah—for their advice and countless read throughs.

To Doshu Allan Viernes and Shihan Jennifer Viernes of the Greater Portland School of Jukado for all their help with self-defense. Your input was invaluable.

To Heather and Lorria for answering my strange and I'm sure sometimes disturbing medical questions. I'm so grateful for all your help.

And finally, to God, who makes all things possible.

ABOUT THE AUTHOR

Since childhood, Jen Printy has been writing. Whether stories about a fantasy world or everyday life in Maine, Jen loved losing herself in the worlds she created on paper. The arts in all forms have always been an important part of Jen's life, a love instilled in her by her father. When Jen isn't writing, she's sculpting as a freelance doll artist.

Jen lives with her husband, two daughters, and diva dog Cookie in southern Maine, where she loves spending time with friends and family, finding treasures along the seashore, or enjoying a Guinness at her favorite local pub.

www.ingramcontent.com/pod-product-compliance
Lightning Source LLC
Chambersburg PA
CBHW020251200626
46816CB00001BA/231